W9-AAG-801

CHOCOLATE STAR

CHOCOLATE STAR

SHEILA COPELAND

St. Martin's Press New York

 For information, address St. Martin's Press, 175 Fifth Avenue, New York, N.Y. 10010.

Design by Bryanna Millis

ISBN 0-312-15493-3

For my mother,
Georgia,
because you always said I could do this;
and in memory of my father,
John,
I know you're in heaven watching.

We are beautiful people, created in a spectrum of colors that range from double-double chocolate to golden vanilla to caramel and butterscotch cream—skin tones so beautiful that the most befitting descriptions would suggest various flavors of candy found in a fine box of chocolates . . .

—Sheila Copeland

Thank-Yous

First and foremost, to my Lord and Savior, Jesus Christ, in whom I live and move and have all my being, for bestowing me with the gift. Also, the Adams, the Bowens, Erma Byrd, Georgia Copeland, Sandy Coutsakis, Cocoa DeWalt, Rosiland Lee, Michele McCoy, Johnny Newman, Iola Noah, and Bill Whitten.

I love you all,
for shining so brightly in my life.

Special thanks to Paul C. Levine, Linda Smith, and Fame Renaissance and Jennifer Weis for helping *Chocolate Star* to shine even brighter.

I have loved you with an everlasting love.

—Jeremiah 31:3

By humility and the fear of the Lord are riches and honor and life . . .

—Proverbs 22:4

PRELUDE

THE HOUSE stood arrogantly at the top of Somera Road in the Bel Air Estates, proudly reflecting the opulence of its owners. It was the biggest and the best money could buy. Seven bedrooms and seven baths, a master suite with his-and-her bathrooms, not to mention every other kind of room imaginable, including a state-of-the-art recording studio and a screening room.

The estate's immaculate, sprawling grounds flaunted basketball and tennis courts, an exercise room with Nautilus equipment, and a black-rock pool that resembled a lush tropical lagoon with its cascading waterfalls and swim-up bar. The realtor had listed the estate as an entertainer's paradise—some might have called it Fantasy Island.

There was a choice of several cars—matching Mercedeses, Porsches, or the Range Rovers—a myriad of exquisite jewels, furs, Italian furnishings, priceless art, and more money than one could spend in a lifetime. Closets filled with designer and custom-made clothing, shoes, and accessories could serve as inventory for several clothing shops. But this was no paradise—because this house was not a home.

They were gone now—all of life's real pleasures. All that was left were things, lots and lots of beautiful things. But wasn't this the plan? Wasn't this the dream?

Wise men have always said to be careful what you ask for because you just might get it . . .

ONE

SYLK ROSS held the basketball firmly in his hands, perspiration dripping from his smooth chocolate skin, his black curly hair plastered to his head. He could feel every ridge and dot of the ball's surface. The sound of Nikes squeaking on the University of Pennsylvania's basketball court, the smell of acrid sweat, and the noise from screaming fans affected him like a drug.

He licked his lips and chomped on a piece of bubblegum. His chiseled Indian features were intense with concentration. At the three-point line, he focused on the basket and tossed up a pretty one. As the ball swished through the net, he felt a tingling sensation permeate all six feet and seven inches of his lean, muscular, two-hundred-pound body.

I love this game, he thought. He smiled as he slapped a high five with Ty Williams, the team's center, and ran up the court for the next layup. He could hear the cheerleaders chanting, "Sylk, Sylk, he's our man, if he can't do it nobody can."

Sylk wiped the perspiration from his brow with the back of his hand and took a quick glance at the scoreboard. He groaned at the sight of the visitors' six-point lead with less than thirty seconds on the clock. We have to win this one. I'm tired of losing games. If we don't start winning some games, no one will ever take us seriously and I won't make the NBA draft. Ty passed him the ball again and Sylk tossed in one of his sweet hook shots.

When he heard the buzzer signaling the end of the game, he sighed disgustedly. We lost another game, he thought, as he shook hands with several players from the opposing team. If I could have gotten the ball more, we would have won. As the team filed out in silence to the locker room, Sylk paused to pick up the basketball and shot it from midcourt. He watched it sail through the air, swish through the net, and bounce several times before it rolled under a bleacher.

"Sylk, Sylk, he's my man, if he can't do it nobody can," a single female voice sang.

Sylk knew who it was without even looking. Tatyana Shelby, the finest honey on the cheerleading squad. "Hey, Tatyana, what's up?" Sylk flashed beautiful even teeth in a dimpled smile that was as sweet as sugar. He picked up his water bottle and took several long drinks as he focused his attention on her.

Tatyana smiled back. "Great game."

"Thanks." She is so beautiful. Tatyana was tall, thin, and a beautiful cocoa brown. Her short cheerleader skirt made her long, shapely legs appear endless. She wore her hair cut short and straight, like the actress Halle Berry. She had a smile that could melt butter and brown eyes that sparkled with excitement.

"Want to catch a movie later?" she asked, still smiling. She bent down to gather up her pom-poms.

"Sorry, Tatyana, I've got some studying to do. Maybe some other time."

"Okay, pretty boy, you just let me know when." Tatyana winked.

Ty, who had been listening to the entire conversation, practically kicked the locker room door off its hinges. "The man is brain damaged at twenty years old," he exclaimed once they were inside. "Brain damaged. Sylk, you definitely have a problem, turning down a honey like that. Man, what's wrong with you? She's handin' it to you on a silver platter."

"Take it easy, Ty, you act like I killed somebody."

"You might as well, because passin' up a date with Tatyana Shelby is definitely a crime."

Sylk laughed as he reached into his locker and took out a tube of Calvin Klein shower gel and a bottle of Vidal Sassoon shampoo. "Ty, you know me and Rhonda are engaged."

"But a little on the side never hurt nobody." Ty, who resembled a bulldog in the face, was charming when it came to the ladies, but he could never pull a beauty like Tatyana. And if he did, it was only because he was a jock. He peeled off the U Penn jersey and shook his head in dismay. "Imagine havin' a honey like that just beggin' to give it away."

"I would never cheat on Rhonda. I love her. We're getting married as soon as I get out of here and into the NBA."

"Married?" The word rolled off Ty's lips like poison. "Man, once you get into the NBA you'll have women all over you and you want to get married?"

"Read my lips, Ty. We're getting married. I don't care about all the women. I just want to play basketball." Sylk threw a towel over his shoulder and sat on the bench.

"Yeah, I heard that. Play basketball. That's what we all want to do." Ty took a seat on the bench next to Sylk, who was deep in thought.

"But if we keep losing games like this, none of us will make it to the NBA."

"I know. I've been thinkin' about that, man." Ty glanced around the locker room and lowered his voice. "I've got a plan."

"A plan? What kind of plan?" The muscles in Sylk's strong jaw flexed as he focused on his teammate.

Ty shook his head. "I can't get into it now. We'll talk later at home."

"Cool." Sylk watched Ty head for the showers. I wonder how me and Ty Williams ever become roommates and best friends. We're as different as night and day. The only thing we really have in common is basketball.

Later that night Sylk sat across from Rhonda in the university's business library. The big old building with its countless books, old wooden tables, and cold linoleum floors was abnormally quiet for a Saturday evening. Unable to concentrate on his studies, he stared at the University of Pennsylvania seal on his notebook. In his third year at U Penn's business school, Sylk had maintained a 3.5 grade point average his first two years.

I wonder if I chose the right school, he thought as he sat staring into space. By the end of his junior year in high school, he had been recruited by every college with a major basketball program. The recruiters from the University of Michigan and Ohio State were always at my home games, he remembered sadly. He traced the gold-embossed U Penn seal with his finger. If I had gone to one of those schools I wouldn't be concerned with being noticed by the NBA. Everyone told me I was crazy for coming here. I was. But I have to have a business degree from the University of Pennsylvania so I can manage my own basketball career. Now, I'm always in the library studying or busting my butt at practice for a team that never wins. I might not even have a career. He flipped his statistics textbook closed, feeling extremely discouraged.

"Sean," Rhonda called softly. "Is something wrong?" Only his family and Rhonda called him Sean. Rhonda Simmons had been his girl since tenth grade. She was petite, sweet, extremely cute, and a journalism major at Temple University. She pushed her newswriting notes aside, giving him her full attention.

"No, babe, I was just thinking." He picked up his pencil and drummed lightly on his notebook.

"Thinking about what, Sean?" She reached for his hand.

"I was wondering if I made the right decision by coming here."

"Does this have something to do with the game you lost this evening?"

"Yeah, but not only today's game. We haven't had one good season yet. And no one has been picked for the draft since I've been here. I should have gone to another school," he complained.

"Another school?"

"Yeah. UCLA, Duke . . . a school that knows how to play basketball and win, anywhere but here." He opened his textbook and flipped it closed again.

"You know how to play basketball. You're one of the best players in the country."

"I know that and you know that, the problem is letting the NBA know it."

"Well, I believe you picked the right school, and when it's time the NBA will definitely know all about Sean Ross," she proclaimed without hesitation.

"And why would you believe that? I certainly haven't been in the news the last few years."

"Because we prayed."

Sean felt the tension that had been mounting inside of him slowly lessen. Deep in his heart, he knew Rhonda was right.

"Sean, we discussed all of this when you decided you wanted to come here. We prayed about it, and your father prayed, too, so everything is going to be just fine."

"You're right," he agreed, brightening. "You're absolutely right. I just didn't think things were going to be this hard."

"Nothing worth having comes easily."

"Yeah, I know, baby, I know." He let out a long sigh. "It's just that things have always been so easy for me."

"Your dad was very happy when you chose U Penn. That was a crazy time with all those recruiters offering you cars and money."

"I know." He smiled, feeling better. Rhonda always knew the right thing to say. "Remember the one who offered me a Porsche?"

"Yeah, I remember." Rhonda laughed. "Those recruiters were all crazy, trying to take my baby away from me." She gently stroked the back of his hand and smiled warmly into his eyes. "I'm so glad you stayed in Philadelphia. It's hard enough trying to see you with both of us in the same city. I would never get to see you if you had gone away to school."

Sean got up and came around the table so he could sit next to her. "I love you." He kissed her gently on the lips. "You always know how to make me feel better."

She ran her hand through his curly hair and gently caressed his face. "I love you, too, Sean. I always have and I always will."

Sean heard bells chiming in the towering steeple of the old Methodist church where his father was pastor as he pulled into the parking lot Sunday morning. This church had been a second home to him for as long as he could remember. He liked to get to church early, while it was still empty, so he could go into the sanctuary and spend time alone. He loved to run his hand along the cool smooth wood of the pews and sit there, quietly absorbing the peacefulness, basking in the strength and presence of God.

It feels so good to be here, he thought, thumbing through his Bible. He could feel the pressures of school and basketball lift almost immediately. He bowed his head for a moment of thanks, and then turned to the Book of Psalms in his Bible. As he flipped through the Bible, he smiled at the old-fashioned photographs that flooded his mind with wonderful memories. He remembered sitting in church with his grandmother, trying to imagine the stories depicted in the colored engravings in her old Bible. She would give him the Bible and a piece of peppermint candy every Sunday to keep him quiet during service. He remembered giving his heart to

Jesus when he was ten, solemnly promising to always obey God's Word.

"Sean." The sound of his name brought him back into the present. "I didn't know you were here, son."

"Hi, Daddy." He grinned and rose to his feet, anticipating the strong, firm hug his father always gave him. After embracing warmly, Sean followed his father into his office.

"Is everything okay, son?" his father inquired, searching his face. "You seemed a million miles away." He gathered his sermon notes into a neat pile next to his Bibles.

Sean could tell he had been studying in preparation for the morning service. He wanted to talk about the team and school but he knew there was no time now. "Yeah, Daddy, everything is fine. I was just thinking about Grandma."

"Grandma," the pastor repeated, smiling. "God bless her soul. Are you going to stay for dinner?"

"I don't think so. I don't have a lot of time and I need to talk to you about school, Daddy. Do you think Mommy would get mad if I just took a plate back with me?"

"She'd only be mad if you didn't. Your mother will be here any minute, so you can work that out with her yourself." He gave Sean another hug. "I'm glad you're here, son. I miss having you around."

"I miss you, too, Daddy." He felt himself getting a little choked up. "I'll see you later." He watched his father walk into his private study. I've got the best father in the world.

"There's my baby boy," he heard his mother exclaim as she entered her husband's office with a burst of energy. "I knew that was your car parked in my spot."

"Sorry, Mommy." He planted a kiss firmly on her cheek. "I thought you were already here with Daddy."

"Sean, you know your father is over here at the crack of dawn on Sunday mornings. I can barely get him to have breakfast because he's in such a big hurry to get here. Besides, I use the time to start my Sunday dinner. You will be staying, won't you?"

"Mommy, I can't. I've got to get back to school. I have an exam in the morning. Will you fix me a plate?"

"Sure, baby." She smiled as she caressed her son's cheek.

"Thanks, Mommy." Sean flashed his irresistible smile. "Fix enough for Ty, too."

But once he arrived at the house after church, he knew he would never make it back to school as planned. He smiled contentedly at the sight of his family's comfortable three-story house. It was a crisp, sunny fall day. He noticed the leaves on the large oak trees in the front yard had turned orange, gold, and yellow. The forest green house with white trim against an azure sky and the yard sprinkled with colorful leaves gave him a wonderful feeling.

The moment he entered the house he could smell Sunday dinner. Fried chicken, black-eyed peas, collard greens, and apple pie. Mommy must have known I was coming. She made all my favorite foods. He was in the kitchen sampling the fried chicken when his older identical twin brothers, Kyle and Kirk, came in.

The twins were not as tall as Sean, but they were just as handsome. They possessed the same chocolate skin and black curly hair, which all of the boys had inherited from their mother.

"Well, look who's in our kitchen," teased Kirk.

"Magic Johnson." Kyle laughed. "Can we have your autograph?"

"Sure." Sean laughed. "For a hundred dollars."

"Oh, no, Sean's gettin' the big head," continued Kyle.

"I see," Kirk agreed, trying to be serious. "I think we need to take him outside and show him who the real ball players are in the family."

Sean laughed heartily. His brothers would do just about anything to challenge him to a game now. It wasn't always like that. When they were kids, they never let him play until he started winning games for the opposition. Then they decided to choose him first for their own team. Wanting to impress his brothers, he would move so quickly across the court to score, no one had time to get into position and guard him. And if someone did, he would outmaneuver his opponent with dizzying footwork that had everyone's head spinning.

"I'll play you guys, but I'm getting Daddy so we can kick your behinds quickly and I can get back to school."

"Aw, man, you think you and Grandpa are going to whip us?" asked Kirk, who was married and had a baby girl.

"All day long! Daddy!" he yelled, summoning his father from the family room couch. "I need you to help me beat Kyle and Kirk in a game of basketball real fast."

"Sure," his father agreed quickly. Sean grinned at his handsome forty-five-year-old father. He was in excellent shape. It was easy to see where Sean had inherited his matinee idol looks and athletic build.

"Let's kill 'em, Daddy."

Sean and his father won three games in a row. Exhausted, the twins stretched out in the grass to catch their breath.

"Pitiful, just pitiful." Sean, pretending to be disgusted, shook his head and made a face at the twins.

"Yeah, serves you right." The boys' father laughed. "Calling me Grandpa."

"Now I hope you two remember who the real ball players are in the Ross family." Sean gulped down a bottle of Evian. "Daddy and I could spot you twenty points and we'd still win."

"Aw, man, see now you're trying to dog us out. We just wanted you to feel good since you been away at school and all, so I thought we'd go easy on you. We didn't want to hurt your feelings because you might not come back home, and then Mommy would get all mad at us," Kyle explained very logically.

"Right." Sean laughed. "You guys talk crazy."

"Would you like to play three more?" Kirk asked.

"No, I've got to get back to school. But since you want to go out like that, I'll bring Ty with me next time and you guys won't even score once."

"Name the time and place," Kirk yelled after him. "We'll be there."

After several slices of his mother's apple pie with vanilla Häagen-Dazs ice cream, Sean and his father retreated to his father's library for a talk. Sean thought the cozy room was the perfect place to glean his father's wisdom. The familiar classical music he heard playing in the background was soothing, but the good times were over. Now it was time to discuss the real issue at hand.

"Daddy, I think I chose the wrong school," he blurted out. "The team loses all the time and I'm afraid I won't be eligible for the NBA draft."

"Afraid Sean? God hasn't given you a spirit of fear." His father's gentle, firm words pierced Sean's heart. His words always did, especially when he quoted Scripture, which was exactly what he was doing now.

"But . . ." Sean started searching for an excuse.

"Didn't you and I sit here in this very room and pray about what school you should go to?" He gazed directly into Sean's eyes with a look that penetrated to the core of his son's soul.

"Yes, sir." Sean answered quietly, the muscles in his jaw flexing. He could hear the clock on his father's desk ticking away. It seemed to echo the pulse of his beating heart.

"Sean, the Lord placed you in the University of Pennsylvania for a reason. I was so proud when you decided on that school. Those recruiters made you a lot of tempting offers and you could have really lost your head. You used wisdom by thinking not only of your basketball career, but your education, too."

He got up from his desk and looked out the window. Sean knew his father was looking at his flower garden planted directly in front of the window. After several minutes, his father turned to face him.

"I'm very proud of you, Sean. You've done well in school, in basketball, and you've maintained your commitment to God. And you know the Lord has been with you all the way. Just remember one thing. No matter what the jersey says, you're on His team. If it's His will for you to play in the NBA, you'll get there, son, no matter what school you attend."

TWO

TOPAZ CAREFULLY poured steaming hot water into a Lenox china teacup over a tea bag of cinnamon apple tea and gently set the matching teapot on the antique dressing table. She was in her mother's room and she had to be careful. The combination of the aromatic tea and the scent of expensive perfume was intoxicating. She glanced around at the extravagant, oversized antiques that her mother had stuffed into the tiny bedroom while she spooned honey and lemon into her steeping tea. Topaz loved her mother's room, especially her dressing table.

Various shades of Lancôme and Clinique foundation, palettes of eye shadow and blush, kohl eyeliner pencils, and countless makeup brushes were haphazardly arranged on the table. A crystal tray held a collection of perfumes: Joy, Escada, Opium, Tiffany, Obsession, Poison, and Coco Chanel. A jewelry box overflowed with faux pearls, Chanel earrings, rhinestone necklaces, and numerous pieces of golden Napier jewelry. The drawers of the adjacent armoire were perfumed with sachets and filled with designer silk scarfs, cashmere sweaters, and silk lingerie.

I've got to win, Topaz thought for the hundredth time as she sat down at the dressing table clad in her favorite pink satin robe. I've just got to win. She took a few sips of the hot tea and began to warm up her voice by singing scales, watching herself sing as she brushed her thick tawny hair.

"Baby, oh, baby," she sang sexily and sweetly into the hair brush. With a slight toss of the head, she flipped her hair over one shoulder, smiled, batted her amber eyes, and laughed. "Thank you very much, thank you very much," she chanted breathlessly to a pretend audience. "I love you." She blew kisses at herself in the mirror and laughed again. She was always pretending to be some famous singer. She glanced at the Waterford crystal clock on the dressing table. "Oh, my! I've got to hurry."

She dabbed makeup on her flawless, creamy butterscotch complexion, remembering to do it the way her mother had shown her, and twisted her long, naturally curly hair into an elegant chignon. Now for that awful dress. She let out a long sigh as she carefully lifted the white silk peau de soie and organza gown from a pink satin hanger.

If I only didn't have to wear this silly dress. She drew her thick, bushy eyebrows together in a frown as she stepped into the gown. Why couldn't I wear something short, black, and sexy? She studied her appearance carefully in the full-length antique mirror. The gown clung gently to her long, lean figure that curved nicely in all the right places. I look like a little girl, she decided, still frowning at the dress, disappointed because there would be no short, black dress tonight. This was the night of her debutante ball, and all the girls were required to wear conservative white gowns.

"Honey, you look beautiful!" Topaz caught sight of her mother's reflection in the mirror. Lisa Black, a cinnamon-colored beauty, was in her mid thirties. She looked stunning in a black Chanel evening dress. Topaz watched her make last-minute touches to her makeup, admiring her mother's innate elegance, runway model looks, and the way she entered a room with such a captivating presence. Then Topaz took another unrewarding look at her own reflection in the mirror.

"Do I, Mother?" she asked uncertainly, turning to face her mother.

"Do you what?" Lisa replied, zeroing in on her daughter's makeup rather than her conversation.

"Do I really look beautiful?"

"Of course you do, baby. Now look at me." Topaz closed her eyes while her mother dusted her face lightly with translucent powder. The girl wished her mother would pay more attention to what she was saying than her makeup.

"There." Lisa took a step backward to admire her handiwork. "You look just like a queen."

"Oh, Mother, I just have to win the title. Keisha said some executives from a record company were coming. Maybe they'll like my voice and give me a record deal."

"You'll be crowned queen of the cotillion, the president of the record company will fall madly in love with you, sign you to a million-dollar record deal, then you'll become a big star and make lots of money so your poor mother can retire and live happily ever after," Lisa assured her. "Topaz, you can't lose: you are the prettiest girl in the entire chapter of Atlanta John-and-Jane."

Topaz smiled easily, relieved for the moment. She caught a whiff of her mother's favorite perfume, Escada, as her mother pressed a cheek to her forehead, which reminded Topaz to dab a few drops of the fragrance on her own wrists and behind her ears. She glanced in the mirror one last time and sighed again at the silky wisps of hair gently framing her face. Even my perfect hair isn't perfect tonight.

Her mother picked up a small, beautifully wrapped box and handed it to her. "What's this?" A smile found its way onto Topaz's face. She loved presents.

"Something for a queen."

Topaz ripped the package open to find a small white Chanel evening bag. "Oh, Mother! Thank you!" Topaz knew Chanel bags were very expensive, and though her mother's personal-image consulting business did well, this was definitely a luxury. "I'll be the only debutante at the cotillion with a real Chanel bag."

She posed in the mirror with the new bag, imagining the looks on the other girls' faces when they saw it. The sound of the doorbell summoned her back to the present. "That's Vaughn. See you later, Mother."

Topaz dashed downstairs to open the door for Vaughn, a real cutey and the most popular senior from her high school. She watched his face light up at the sight of her, and she smiled.

"Hello, Vaughn!" Her leggy five-foot-nine frame seemed to have a mind of its own whenever she came in contact with the opposite sex. Her voice seemed huskier, too. "Ready to go?" Gracefully, she ran a hand across her hair to the nape of her neck, smoothing it with the elegance of the Queen of Sheba. She felt her hips sway gently as she picked up her purse and wrap. Vaughn was still standing in the same place. She wanted to laugh as she stood there watching him try to remember his name.

"Hi, Topaz," he finally stuttered. "You look real nice."

"Thanks, Vaughn, you look nice, too." He did make a handsome escort in his rented black tuxedo, although he wasn't much of a conversationalist around her.

Topaz felt her adrenaline rise as they pulled into the parking lot of the Hyatt on Peachtree Street in downtown Atlanta. She glanced at herself in every mirror as Vaughn ushered her down the hotel corridor and into the small banquet room next to the Grand Ballroom where the debutantes were waiting for the cotillion to begin.

Every eye was on her when she entered the room with Vaughn. They made a striking pair. She noticed the girls casually eyeing her dress and Chanel bag. She had positioned the bag perfectly so it couldn't be missed. Maybe this dress isn't so bad after all, she decided, pleased with all the attention.

When she saw her friends Keisha and Debbie waving to her from across the room, she carefully removed her gloved arm from Vaughn's strong grip. She smiled politely at him and rushed to join the girls while Vaughn reluctantly joined the other escorts who were holding court in front of the punch bowl. "Girlfriend, you look fabulous!" offered Keisha as the girls touched cheeks. Keisha, a gorgeous, honey-brown girl with cropped black hair, was her sassy best friend.

"Thanks, Keisha!" Topaz was feeling much better about her debutante gown now. "Darling, you look smashing, too!"

"Did your mother loan you her Chanel bag?" Debbie interrupted. Topaz only tolerated Debbie because she was Keisha's cousin. I'm going to try extra hard to be nice to her tonight, Topaz reminded herself, as she looked in Debbie's direction to make eye contact.

"Mother bought me my own in honor of the big event." Topaz proudly displayed her bag. Topaz thought Debbie needed to do something about her skin because makeup did very little to help the girl's severe acne problem. And she wasn't nearly as pretty as Topaz or Keisha. "Mother said queens should always have Chanel bags."

Topaz ignored Debbie's look of disgust. Debbie's jealous, she concluded. I can't help it if my mother buys me pretty things and hers doesn't.

"Did you see what Kara is wearing?" Keisha asked, changing the subject. "And she thinks she's going to be the queen."

Topaz felt her stomach churn slightly. "Where is she?"

"Over by the punch bowl talking to Vaughn," replied Debbie.

Topaz gave her competition a once-over. Kara was wearing a Laura Ashley antique lace dress. Her long hair was curled Shirley Temple–style. She looks nice, Topaz thought, hating to admit it. She really looks cute.

Kara, not quite as tall as Topaz, was the color of toasted almonds, with midnight blue eyes. Topaz and Keisha often referred to them as evil eyes. Kara's father was a municipal court judge and her mother was one of the city's council members. Kara tucked her arm through Vaughn's and looked directly at Topaz.

"Girl, how come you're not over there with your man?" Debbie teased. "Vaughn is too fine."

"He's not my man. And if Kara wants him, she can have him. She'll need someone to console her when she sees me crowned queen tonight."

"I heard that." Keisha reached for Topaz's hand and gave her a very ladylike high five.

"Keisha, look at her," Topaz whispered. "Her dress is hideous. It looks like it came from the swap meet. And to think she has money. If I went around looking like that, my mother would disown me."

Topaz felt her stomach twist up in knots. Oh, God, what if I lose? What if I lose? I couldn't take it, I think I'd die. "I thought this thing was supposed to start by now," Topaz snapped, glancing at her wristwatch.

"You know black people," said Keisha, laughing, "never on time."

Topaz felt she'd explode if she had to sit still a minute longer. "Let's see if we can see what's going on in the ballroom."

She found a small space in the room divider where she could peek into the ballroom. She recognized a lot of the debutantes' parents, families, and friends, all dressed to kill. She could see they were wearing diamonds as big as rocks, gold necklaces and earrings she knew were real, and strands of genuine pearls. Minks and sables, silks and satin—every major designer was represented well. "They must have cleaned out every department store and boutique in the city of Atlanta," Topaz commented to Keisha, who had found another peephole.

"I know," Keisha readily agreed. "I heard Kara's mother even went to New York City for her clothes."

"You'd never know it." Topaz laughed wickedly. "Keisha, do you see anybody that looks like they're from a record company in the audience?"

"Look!" Keisha whispered loudly. "There's Germain Gradney. I wonder what he's doing here."

"Who's Germain Gradney?" Debbie, who had joined the girls, was looking for another peephole.

"Does he work for a record company?" Topaz inquired.

"Girl, please! See that fine brother over there with the Armani tux?" Keisha asked.

"I see him." Topaz had already noticed him. He was very handsome, extremely well dressed with a medium build and dark curly hair that accentuated his café au lait skin. Everything about him screamed money. "He's a junior in premed at Morehouse," Keisha explained. "Both of his parents are doctors and they're loaded. He used to date my sister, Angie. He has a lot of class. He really knows how to treat a girl. He always took her out to the best restaurants, the theater, concerts, the ballet, picked her up in a Mercedes, too. His parents drive those big expensive ones."

"Wow!" exclaimed Debbie. "Why did she break up with him?"

"I don't know what happened. She never told me, but I would have never let that brother go."

Topaz watched Germain take a seat not far from her mother. He sure sounds like someone I'd like to know. He's older, too, not like the guys from school who never have enough money for a nice date and can't hold a decent conversation. The sound of a spoon tapping on a glass interrupted her from her thoughts.

"Ladies, ladies, it's time to begin." Amelia Richards, president of this local chapter of John-and-Jane, owned the largest Cadillac dealership in the city. Topaz noticed that her silver-grey fox fur was exactly the same shade as her hair color. The room silenced at once. The girls knew she meant business.

Topaz felt Vaughn's hand slide gently into hers once they were in the hotel corridor. Instead of her usual feeling of repulsion, she gripped it tightly. "I'm glad you're here," she whispered loudly, trying to be heard over the sound of rustling petticoats as they lined up in the hall, waiting for the processional to begin. Vaughn smiled and squeezed her hand.

After the first two bars of music, Topaz swallowed hard and remembered to count as the right tips of twelve pairs of new white shoes stepped forward in unison. She heard oohs and aahs echo throughout the crowd as the young ladies entered the room. She knew everyone was watching them. They were as resplendent as twelve brides in virginal white. She held her head high and surveyed the room like a queen, ignoring the eyes that bored through her, praising and envying her mesmerizing beauty.

She caught her mother's eye and smiled in her direction. Then she looked directly at Germain, and when she thought she had his eye, she smiled again. Her heart was pounding so hard she knew everyone could see it beating through her dress. Topaz thought they'd never make it to the debutantes' reserved tables. Vaughn helped her with her chair.

Before she had time to catch her breath, she heard her name announced. Vaughn ushered her to the center of the stage where she made an elegant curtsy to the audience and to Mrs. Richards. She heard the room bellow with thunderous applause and felt her spirits rise with all the attention. She looked out into a sea of faces and on impulse decided to flash one of her most radiant smiles. By the time she was seated again, her stomach had stopped doing flip-flops and she felt quite composed.

Keisha led off in the talent show. She played Mozart's "Fantasia in D Minor" wonderfully. Debbie recited poetry and then Miss Kara took the stage, preparing to sing. Topaz stiffened in her seat, wondering what she was planning to perform.

Kara nodded at her pianist and smiled into the microphone. "Hi, I'm Kara Glenn." Then she began to sing a slightly off-key rendition of "People."

Topaz heard Keisha, who was sitting next to her, stifle a giggle while Kara continued singing. By the time she got to the end of the first line, Kara was so flat she sounded like she had fallen off the world. Topaz fought the urge to laugh even though the corners of her mouth were twitching. Tears were streaming out of Keisha's eyes and down her cheeks.

"You're ruining your makeup," Topaz whispered, dabbing

gently at the corner of her own eye with a tissue. She took out a mirrored compact to survey the damage.

"I don't care," Keisha cried, laughing. "Somebody should gong her."

Topaz pushed her compact across the table to her friend. "I gotta go. I'm next."

"Girlfriend, we already know who the queen is," Keisha whispered as Topaz walked away.

Sparse applause ushered Kara off the stage. When the room was silent again, Topaz took a deep breath and walked out onto the stage.

"Good evening." There was a soft huskiness in her voice. "I'm Topaz Black." She closed her eyes and bowed her head, anticipating the first strains of music. The accompaniment to "Saving All My Love for You" filled her ears and then her soul.

Topaz sang softly and clearly into the microphone. Her hips begin to sway gently and gracefully to the music while her right foot kept a steady beat that vibrated through her lithe body like a heartbeat. She felt currents of electricity sweep through her as her body and voice took over the song.

"Sing it, girl," someone yelled from the audience.

She snatched the mike from its stand with a vengeance and walked back and forth across the stage, connecting easily with the audience. People were on their feet, but Topaz hardly noticed. All she felt and heard was the music. She felt every word, emotion ripping her into tormenting pain. As she belted out the last words of the song, her strong, clear voice resonated clearly throughout the ballroom. The audience shrieked and screamed in delight.

Topaz stood frozen with her arms thrust over head, unable to move or breathe. "Thank you," she finally whispered into the mike. "Thank you very much." Applause followed her all the way to her seat. She wiped the perspiration from her face, unconcerned about her own makeup for once, feeling the rush of a newfound high. Keisha pressed her compact into her hand. For a lack of anything better to do, Topaz opened it and studied her reflection in the mirror.

"I ruined my makeup," she whispered to Keisha, not really caring.

"Girlfriend, you turned it out." Keisha beamed.

Topaz grinned happily as she brushed her perspiration-soaked face with fresh powder. I did it. I won.

With the talent exhibition over, Mrs. Richards was back on stage with a small diamond tiara sitting on a red velvet pillow. It was finally time to announce the winner.

With a pair of rhinestone bifocals perched elegantly on the tip of her nose, she began by announcing all sorts of awards, including those for academics, philanthropic contributions, and congeniality. Topaz felt her adrenaline surging. She drummed her freshly manicured nails on the banquet table in a nervous beat until she felt Keisha's cool steady fingers spread themselves over her restless hand.

"And now, the moment we've all been waiting for," Mrs. Richards continued excitedly. Topaz took a deep breath. "Our queen, Miss Kara Glenn."

THREE

GUNTHER KNEW what was in the letter without even opening it. The expensive linen stationery engraved with the Bridgeforth Academy crest immediately commanded his attention when it slid out from among the numerous bills and miscellaneous advertisements stuffed in the mailbox. He tossed the rest of the mail on the old metal desk in his father's unkempt office and rushed upstairs to his room to scrutinize the envelope further in privacy.

He placed the letter, still unopened, exactly in the center of his desk and sat down to contemplate every letter on the envelope. "Mr. Gunther Lawrence, Los Angeles, California" was neatly typed in the middle of the envelope. He felt a surge of pride well up inside him at the sight of his name. He sat there staring at the envelope for over an hour, wanting to savor this moment for as long as he could. He knew the information it contained would change his life forever.

I did it, he wanted to shout from the rooftops. I won a scholarship to a private boarding school in Deerfield, Massachusetts. Now I can finally get out of South Central L.A., away from all the gang banging, away from the sound of sirens, police helicopters, and gunshots outside my bedroom window every night, away from Dorsey High School, and away from this house.

Gunther glanced up at the large, wooden bookcases neatly lined with books in alphabetical order. Unlike his brothers' rooms with posters of rappers, singers, and basketball players, his room was filled with books, all types of books—autobiographies, history and travel books, and lots of thick novels. Other than an old, scarred wooden bureau, a bed, and his desk, Gunther's immaculate room seemed cold and bare, but to him it was paradise.

Finally, he slit open the envelope and read his letter of acceptance to Bridgeforth Academy. He read it over and over and over.

This is the best thing that ever happened to me, he realized, extremely pleased with himself.

"Gunther!" His oldest brother, Charles Jr., yelled from downstairs, interrupting his thoughts. "Get down here and clean up the kitchen before Pops gets home!"

"Okay," Gunther yelled through the door. "I'll be right there." He folded the letter and placed it back in its envelope and tucked it safely away in a desk drawer. He had chores to do and today was his turn to clean the kitchen.

As Gunther came into the kitchen, he saw his older brother, Marshall, on the service porch, doing the family's laundry. Charles Jr. was vacuuming the living room. The brothers had shared all of the household chores since their parents split up when Gunther was five.

Their parents had been partners in a joint business venture. Gunther's mother, Rita, with a degree in architectural design from Tuskegee, was the creative side of the Lawrence Design Group. Charles Sr., the contractor, would supply the construction crews for the company's projects. But when none of their clients seemed to appreciate, much less afford, Rita's fabulous creations, the business failed. Charles said Rita was too bourgeois and too flamboyant. Rita accused Charles of being small-minded with a ghetto mentality, so the partnership and the family were divided.

Now the boys lived in a large old house near Adams Boulevard in South Central with Charles, whose fledgling construction business was now a lucrative source of income for the family with several government contracts. Their two sisters lived with Rita in a very elegant townhouse in the San Fernando valley. Rita had become an extremely ambitious and successful designer for a development company in Century City that designed multimillion-dollar homes and office buildings.

Why couldn't I live with Rita, too? Gunther wondered constantly. He had never called her mother. I could go to a magnet school with honors' classes where the kids wouldn't pick on me for being smart and call me a nerd. Gunther, a straight-A student, had a protruding overbite and severe acne, but at fifteen years old he was almost six feet tall with a nice muscular body. But Rita felt boys needed a father more than a mother, despite Gunther's incessant requests to live with her and his sisters. Gunther frowned momentarily as he pushed away thoughts of his unhappy childhood. That's history now. I'm going to Bridgeforth.

I hope I make lots of friends at Bridgeforth, he thought as he neatly stacked and sorted the dishes. "Bridgeforth Academy!" he whispered to himself, grinning. He started to share the good news with his brothers, but then he decided against it.

They won't care. Charles Jr. would probably say something stupid like "Do they have fields of deer in Deerfield?" And then Marshall would say, "You're stupid for wanting to go to an all-boy school. Don't you like girls?"

Nope, I'm not telling them, Gunther decided, as he soaped and rinsed the breakfast dishes. I'll call Rita when I finish the kitchen. She'll be proud because she can tell all her friends I did something important, and maybe she'll even let me stay at her house when I come home on vacations. She might even give me a going-away party. Gunther smiled as he put away the clean dishes, thinking about the scholarship and the surprise party he hoped his mother would give for him. Now that his chores were done, he went into the family room to telephone his mother and flipped on the television. He could hear Charles Jr. and Marshall outside playing one-on-one. I can't wait to tell Rita, she'll be so happy. He whistled as he dialed his mother's number at work.

"Rita Lawrence," she answered, picking up her private line on the first ring.

"Hello, Rita, it's me, Gunther. I called to tell you—"

"What is it, Gunther?" she replied, cutting him off. "I'm in the middle of a big project."

She never has time for me, he reflected, trying to conceal the fresh stab of pain in his heart and in his voice before he spoke. "I won a scholarship to Bridgeforth Academy," he said flatly.

"That's nice, Gunther . . . Jim, can you hand me those plans over there?" He knew she was speaking to her assistant.

She doesn't even care, he realized. She cares more about those stupid old buildings than me. "The school's in Massachusetts, Rita. And I won a full scholarship."

"That's really great, Gunther. I have to go now. Tell your father I haven't received his check for the girls."

"Yes, Rita." Gunther was extremely upset by her lack of interest in his good news. The phone clicked and the dull sound of the dial tone filled his ear. He slowly hung up the phone and quickly brushed away a tear. "I'm not going to cry," he whispered angrily through gritted teeth. "I'm not going to cry." He squeezed his eyes closed, shriveling his face, trying to fight back the tears. He remembered the last time he had spoken to her, and the promise he had made to himself never to call her again after she flat out refused to let him come to her house to recuperate from the mumps.

"She just doesn't love me." He flipped the channels on the television. "She doesn't care about anything except her job and money." The tears won as they swelled out of his eyes and down his cheeks. "I guess I won't be having any surprise party," he muttered as he kicked the old, scuffed coffee table in front of him. "I hate her. And I hate this ugly house."

While his mother's three-bedroom townhouse was beautifully decorated, his father's only concern was that their house was clean and the refrigerator filled with food. Gunther glanced around the family room at the beat-up old couches and the 35-inch state-of-the-art Sony television set. He felt thoroughly disgusted as he flipped from channel to channel until he found an episode of one of his favorite shows, *The Brady Bunch*.

He sniffed and settled back on the sofa. He could still hear his brothers shooting hoops. He had watched *The Brady Bunch* for as long as he could remember. There wasn't a single episode that he hadn't already seen. As he watched Carol Brady and Alice happily prepare dinner for the family, he suddenly realized he was hungry. Pops didn't put anything out for dinner. That means he'll probably bring home somebody's nasty fried chicken. I wish we could go out for Chinese or Indian food.

Gunther watched the Brady family sit down to dinner. They were all laughing and having a good time. They have a pretty house, too. He switched channels again and found an episode of *Sanford and Son*. Look at Fred Sanford, living in that old raggedy house eating fried chicken and black-eyed peas. He's pathetic. Gunther switched back to *The Brady Bunch*. It was a different episode and the family was vacationing in Hawaii. I wish I had a family like that. Gunther sat staring at the television, deep in thought. I wonder what the guys at Bridgeforth will be like. Maybe they'll be like the kids on *The Brady Bunch*.

Mike, the regional director of the scholarship program, had

told all the applicants that boarding schools had very few black students and that tuition was very high, the same as college.

"What kind of people could afford to send their children to Bridgeforth?" he asked himself out loud. "Rich people," he concluded. "Rich white people. White people have everything," he rationalized, feeling somewhat jealous. "Black people don't have nothin'."

He watched the Brady family sit down to a luau. They were all dressed in Hawaiian costumes. It must cost a lot of money to take an entire family to Hawaii, Gunther reasoned. Rich people have all the fun. "I wish I was rich." He gave the coffee table another swift kick and glanced up at the television set at the happy Brady family.

"And I wish I was white . . ."

FOUR

SEAN LAUGHED as he watched Ty practically inhale the plate of fried chicken, black-eyed peas, and collard greens in a matter of seconds. "Your mom sure can cook, Sylk," Ty finally managed to say between mouthfuls of food.

"You should have come with me, Ty. I had a great time. After dinner we played basketball. Me and my daddy against my twin brothers. My brothers were talkin' all this stuff about how they were going to beat us. Man, we killed those guys." Sean smiled happily, remembering the game. "And after we whipped them three times, Kirk had the nerve to challenge you and me to a game."

Ty laughed as he took a large slice of hot apple pie out of the microwave and doused it with swirls of whipped cream. He licked his fingers and dug in. "Your family sounds real nice, man. I'll have to go home with you next time."

"Sure, Ty, you're welcome any time. I've got the best family in the world." Sean opened the refrigerator and shook his head at the sight of three cans of Heineken, a half-empty bottle of white zinfandel, and a carton of orange juice. My roommate the party animal. He poured himself a glass of juice, closed the refrigerator door, and took a seat at the dining room table with Ty. Sean glanced around the living area of their two-bedroom student apartment and sighed. He was starting to feel homesick. The apartment always seemed so bleak to him in comparison to his parents' comfortable home.

"Yo, Sylk." Ty leaped up from the table and tossed his empty plates into the kitchen sink. "I've got everything figured out."

"What you talkin' about, man?"

"The plan . . ."

"What plan?"

"The plan that's going to get us noticed so we can get out of here and into the NBA."

"Oh." Sean wasn't really interested but he pretended to be to appease his friend. "What did you come up with?"

"Well, it's like this. Coach always designs the layups to get everyone into the game. All we have to do is change things around so you and I control the ball. You're the point guard. Instead of passing the ball, you throw it in or just toss it to me. We could pull Mitch Matthews in on this, too, since he's the other guard," Ty continued. "And between the three of us, we could dominate the game."

"I don't think so, Ty." He could still hear his father's words of advice ever so clearly.

"You don't think so? Are you crazy? Do you want to end up like Jimmy Strictland, playing for a team in Europe?" Sean stared at the orange pulp clinging to the rim of his glass. "Come on, Sylk!" Ty was shouting. "You know Jimmy was good enough. He should be playing in the NBA. But nobody ever saw him play. Just like nobody ever sees us play."

Sean fingered the moisture that had collected on the outside of his glass. Ty would never understand him wanting to trust the Lord. I don't even understand it myself sometimes. But I know I've got to. Sean felt the muscles in his jawline grow taut.

"I can't do it, Ty. I'm sorry. But I've got to do this the right way. Things are going to be fine. You'll see. I've got some studying to do. Good night." He got up from the table and went into his bedroom in order to avoid any further conversation with Ty.

Several days later Sean suited up with the team in the locker room for their game against Indiana State. Sean was lacing up his Nikes when Ty came in with his gear. "Yo, man, I was starting to wonder if you were going to make it," he said smiling.

"Now you know I got to shoot them hoops." Ty was unusually cool as he put down his bag, pulled off his sweats, and hung them inside his locker. He was already wearing his uniform.

As the team warmed up by practicing free throws and jump shots, Sean felt his adrenaline start to flow. I love this game. He leaped through the air and slammed the ball through the hoop. Minutes later, he heard the buzzer, informing the players that the warm-up period was over. As the team took their places on the bench, the cheerleaders ran onto the floor to perform a quick routine. Sean watched the girls combine gymnastics with the latest street dances in a very entertaining number. Without realizing it, he found himself watching Tatyana.

"Go for it, Sylk," he heard Ty say. "You know, you can't keep your eyes off her."

Sean looked away quickly, feeling embarrassed because he knew Ty was right.

"And don't give me that stuff about Rhonda and being engaged."

"Okay, Ty, you got me." Sean laughed. "Tatyana's a beautiful lady. What can I say?"

"Ask her out on a date, man. What's your problem? Why don't you loosen up and live a little and stop being so square?"

The announcement of the starting lineup interrupted Ty from his tirade. But Sean still felt the sting of Ty's biting words as they entered the first quarter.

I'm tired of this crap. Ty's unsolicited comments had made him angry. I'm tired of people doggin' me. Without realizing it, he held onto the ball when he should have passed it and dunked three in a row. That was great, he thought, feeling a little better. For the rest of the game, he fought for every rebound and stole the ball every chance he could and scored. His aggressive playing seemed to extinguish his anger. By halftime, he noticed U Penn was ahead by more than twenty-five points.

"Man, if I knew makin' you mad would win us a game, I would have done it a lot sooner," joked Ty.

Sean drained his water bottle and stretched his legs. "The game's not over yet, Ty."

"That's true, but if you play the second half the way you played the first half, we'll definitely win."

"I sure hope so, man. I like winning."

Back on the court for the second half, Sean continued to score. With seconds left in the game, Indiana State called for time out. Sean glanced up at the scoreboard and saw that U Penn was still ahead by ten points. Tatyana led the girls in a quick cheer. As the team walked back onto the court, Sean heard the crowd chant "Sylk, Sylk, Sylk." He smiled and waved. It made him feel good to hear them call his name. He realized that this was the first time in three years he had played a decent game. Indiana sank its last

basket as the final buzzer sounded and U Penn won by eight points.

The students ran down on the court to congratulate the team. No one ever dreamed they'd beat Indiana State. Sean recognized very few of the people congratulating him, but they all knew his name. "Great game, Sylk," he heard over and over. Tatyana kissed him right on the lips.

"Congratulations, baby," she whispered in his ear. He gave her a gentle squeeze around the waist.

"Thanks, babe." He grinned.

Inside the locker room the team was carrying on like they had just won the playoffs.

"Now that's what I call basketball!" Ty gave Sean a high five.

The team's winning streak continued for the next seven games. On the night of the big game against Michigan State, Sean noticed all the local media setting up their equipment as he and Ty cut through the gymnasium on their way to the locker room.

"Look, man." Ty nudged him and pointed. "Even ESPN is here."

Sean's million-dollar smile lit up his handsome face. "Tyrone, my friend, we are now on our way to the big time."

"Sylk Ross?" A man wearing an ESPN blazer stepped in front of them.

"Yes?" Sean couldn't help wondering what the man wanted. He felt the muscles in his jawline flex as his heart began to race.

"I'm Chuck Zimmerman from ESPN," the man offered, shaking hands with Sean. "I've heard so much about you. It's a pleasure to finally meet you."

"Thank you." I wonder what he's heard about me.

"And you must be Ty Williams, U Penn's illustrious center," Zimmerman continued. He turned to shake Ty's hand. "You two are quite a combination."

"Thanks, Chuck," said Ty. "But you ain't seen nothin' yet."

Chuck laughed. "I understand you two are roommates and best friends."

"That's right." Ty grasped Sean firmly around the shoulders. "We're a winning combination."

"Great. We're here covering tonight's game and we'd also like to include a feature on the two of you. You know, school, family life, your goals, that kind of stuff."

"Oh, sure. That sounds great." Sean was so excited, he could barely keep still.

"Fine. You two get suited up so we can get some footage of you on the court."

"All right, Chuck." Ty grabbed Chuck's hand and shook it. "We'll be right back."

"Man, what team do you want to play on?" Ty asked Sean in the locker room.

"You know, Ty, I've never really thought about it. But it would be nice to warm up with Magic and Kareem."

"Yeah, I heard that, or with the Knicks or the Bulls. I like those Seventy-sixers, too."

"Face it, Ty," Sean said, laughing as they raced back to the gym, "we'd be glad to play for anyone in the NBA."

Back in the gym they started warming up. Sean dunked several balls before he tossed in his pretty hook shot. Ty, ever the clown, flew through the air and hung from the net.

"I see how you got the name Sylk," Chuck commented later. "We've got some great stuff. We'll do the live interview after the game."

By now the rest of the team was out on the floor. Sean smiled as he watched the stands quickly fill. Every home game was already sold out for the rest of the year. He still remembered the days when very few students came to the games. He saw his parents and Rhonda in their usual seats and waved. When the buzzer sounded, Sean could hardly keep still. As he took his seat on the bench, he saw the cheerleaders seated on the gym floor. "Hi, Tatyana." He flashed a brilliant smile. She blew him a kiss in return.

While the starting lineup for the opposition was announced, Ty nudged him and pointed out Dr. E slipping into a reserved seat. Dr. E at one of our games. Sean was ecstatic when he walked onto the court. But as the centers jumped for the ball, all thoughts except winning the game left Sean's mind. He held onto the ball or passed it to Ty. Sean dunked, tossed in sweet hook shots, and sank several beautiful three-pointers.

When the final buzzer sounded, Sean had scored twenty-nine points and U Penn had beaten Michigan State by five points. The gymnasium was in an uproar. Tatyana threw herself into Sean's arms.

"Party at our place," Ty announced to the team and the cheerleaders.

Chuck Zimmerman pulled Sean aside and turned him to face the camera. "I have Sylk Ross here with me, U Penn's dynamic point guard. Sylk just led his team to its eighth consecutive win, scoring a whopping twenty-nine points in tonight's game against Michigan State. Sylk, how does it feel to be on top?" Chuck stuck a microphone in front of him.

"It feels real good, Chuck, real good. This is my third year playing for U Penn and so far it's been the most exciting."

"So why the difference now?"

"Well, Chuck, I'd have to say we've all been playing a lot harder and a lot better. We've got a lot of great talent on this team, Ty Williams, Mitch Matthews. We got started a little late this season but we'll win the playoffs next year." Sean finished with a smile and wiped the perspiration from his brow.

"Is this something I can count on Sylk?" Chuck teased.

"Sure, Chuck, write it down. U Penn will sweep the playoffs next year."

"Remember, you heard it right here on ESPN." Chuck flashed a plastic Pepsodent smile into the camera until a cameraman informed him that he was no longer filming. "Okay, guys, let's see if we can get a few words from Dr. E."

"Great game, son. Your game has really improved." Sean's father joined him on the court.

"Thanks, Daddy."

"You guys beat Michigan State."

"We did, didn't we." Sean smiled. "Hi, Mommy, hi, Rhonda." He kissed them both on the cheek. "Let me go shower and change. I smell like a skunk."

"But you're my baby skunk." His mother grabbed him and hugged him.

"Son, we're going on home. See you tomorrow?"

"Of course, Daddy, there's no place I'd rather be than in the house of the Lord."

His father grinned and kissed him. "Sean, you really bless my heart."

"Daddy." Sean was blushing. "The guys will really think I'm strange if they see you kissing me." He protested, but he really didn't mind. "Bye, Mommy." He kissed his mother again and strolled across the gym with Rhonda.

"Man, where you been?" Ty asked as soon as he entered the locker room.

"Talking to Chuck Zimmerman and my family."

"You know we havin' the victory party."

"Ty, I've got to take a shower." He grabbed his plastic case of toiletries. "I'll be right back."

Sean felt his body relax in the hot, steamy shower. He leaned against the wall, allowing the water to penetrate his body. So much has happened. The interview with ESPN, the team's new winning streak, me scoring twenty-nine points in the game. I actually scored twenty-nine points. He smiled. And Dr. E came to our game. Dr. E . . . Dr. E. What's wrong with me? I didn't even talk to him. Sean quickly turned off the water, wrapped a towel around his waist, and hurried back into the locker room. He saw the guys standing around talking, probably about some specific play or the party.

He was reaching into his locker for the Mitchum when he heard a voice behind him say, "Well it's about time you came out of there."

Sean turned around to find Dr. E standing behind him. "Dr. E, I'm so sorry," Sean sputtered. "I was just on my way to see if I could find you."

"Man, you ain't got nothin' to be apologizing for. You just played a serious game of basketball."

Sean relaxed and smiled. "Thank you. And it's a pleasure to meet you." He was very humble as he extended his hand. "You're one of the great ones."

"Thanks." Dr. E smiled. He was easy to talk to and Sean liked him immediately. "And you and my man Ty here are definitely on your way to greatness, too."

Chuck Zimmerman pushed open the locker room door. "Dr. E, you're still here, wonderful. I wanted to get some footage of you and Sylk."

"Sure, Chuck. Whatever you like." Dr. E turned to whisper in Sean's ear. "Sylk, get dressed unless you want to give the women a thrill. Otherwise, these guys will shoot you nude if you let them."

"Thanks, man," Sean whispered to Dr. E. "Chuck, I'll be right back."

When Sean returned from dressing, the cameras were set up. Rhonda was in the locker room talking to Ty.

"Here's the man of the hour." Chuck flashed a plastic smile. "Dr. E, let's get a shot of you congratulating Sylk after the big game. You guys can start whenever you're ready."

Dr. E nodded and turned to face Sean. "Sylk Ross, you're one of the finest young players I've seen in a long time, and you've got yourself a wonderful career ahead of you."

"Thank you." Sean was sincere and appreciative of the superstar's generous remarks. "It's been a real honor meeting you, and I can't wait to get you out on the court." Sean heard his teammates and the camera crew break out into laughter.

"That sounded like a challenge to me." Dr. E laughed. "You come up to the house for a little one-on-one and I'll show you how to play some real basketball, young man."

"You name the place and time." Sean flashed a handsome smile. "I'll be there."

"That's a wrap," Chuck informed them. "Gentlemen, it's been my pleasure, good night."

"I've got to go, too. But I was serious about you coming up to the house. You too, Ty." Dr. E wrote out his number and handed it to Sean. "You're welcome anytime."

"Thanks, Dr. E," Sean called out as he left the locker room. "We'll be there."

Back at Sean and Ty's apartment, Tatyana and the girls were waiting with sodas, beer, wine, and bags of munchies. "Someone said there was a victory party?" Tatyana gave Sean a coy look.

"There's definitely a party if you're here, pretty lady." Ty relieved Tatyana of the bags of refreshments she was holding. Sean took the remaining bags from the other girls and the group filed into the apartment.

Tatyana found the music and put on "Don't You Want Me?" She danced alone in the middle of the floor, singing every word, looking directly at Sean. The rest of the team had arrived, but no one made an effort to dance with her. She was so good, they all preferred watching her. Ty quickly set out drinks and munchies and joined her on the floor. But it was more than obvious that Tatyana's dance was for Sean. She sang to him the entire time, completely ignoring Ty and Rhonda. Sean was so embarrassed.

"Who's that girl, Sean?" Rhonda demanded.

"That's Tatyana, our head cheerleader."

"Well, she certainly has a thing for you." Rhonda's tone was cool. She opened the refrigerator to get a soda and gasped at the sight of all the beer and wine. "Sean, did you see all this alcohol?"

"Yeah, I saw it," he replied nonchalantly. "It's a party and they want to drink."

"But that alcohol is in your refrigerator."

"It's Ty's refrigerator, too, Rhonda. And I can't stop him from buying alcohol or drinking it."

"Well, you certainly don't have to live here with him." Sean could tell by her tone that she was irritated. She watched the group dance in the living room.

"I'm not moving, Rhonda. Ty's my friend. I like living here."

"Sean, I can't see how you can consider these people your friends or how you could like living here. You know your father would never approve of this. What's wrong with you?"

"No, the question is what's wrong with you, Rhonda?" She was making him angry. He hated the way she brought his father into the conversation every time he did something she didn't approve of.

"Nothing," she mumbled.

"Would you like to dance?"

"No."

"Rhonda, is this about Tatyana?" She said nothing, avoiding his glance. She's about to cry, he realized. "Come on." He was gentle with her when he removed the can of Coke from her hand and lead her into his bedroom. "Let's go in here where we can talk."

But once they were inside she still wouldn't look at him. "I'm not in love with her, Rhonda. I'm in love with you."

"But she flirted with you like that with me right there. Doesn't she know you have a fiancee?" Now her tears flowed in a steady stream. Sean found a tissue and gently wiped them.

"Baby, girls are always going to flirt with me, but it doesn't mean I want them. I chose you."

"But she's so pretty. Do you mean you never thought about her once?" She searched his eyes.

"Sure, she's pretty, and yes, I've looked at her. I'm a man, Rhonda. But that's where it ends. You're the only girl for me." He pulled her close and held her tightly. "I love you, silly girl."

"I love you, too," he heard her whisper between her sobs.

Sean held her tighter. He could hear the team partying out in the living room to "Stop to Love." They sounded like they were having so much fun. This is the team's first victory party and I should be out there. I got them that victory, he pouted, unhappy because he wasn't celebrating with his teammates. Well I'm gonna party anyway.

He glanced at Rhonda who had pulled her shoes off and curled up under a blanket. I can't leave her. That wouldn't be right. He sighed and flipped on the television. He felt Rhonda take his hand and he closed his eyes. I'm tired, he suddenly realized, and I still have to take her home. He kept his eyes closed while he listened to the sportscaster relay the highlights of the day's major games. He snapped on the VCR just in time to record footage of himself tossing in a gorgeous three-pointer.

It was a great day, he reflected. He lay there recapping his own day once the news was finished. Dr. E said I was one of the finest players he'd seen in a long time, and I did my first interview with ESPN. "It's really happening," he whispered. "I'm actually on my way to the big time . . . the NBA."

FIVE

TOPAZ FELT herself grow numb as the room thundered with applause. It's a mistake. She gasped and fought the urge to hyperventilate. It's a horrible, awful mistake. She stared up at the magnificent crystal chandelier suspended over the ballroom and mindlessly counted the individual crystal teardrops, waiting to hear Mrs. Richards apologize for her apparent error. But when Topaz heard Kara's squeals of delight, she knew the contest was over. Kara had really won.

Topaz's heart sank as she watched Kara mount the stairs and prance across the stage to Mrs. Richards. That was supposed to be me, she told herself, making a valiant effort to hold back the tears.

"She only won because her parents bought the entire souvenir book." Keisha flipped through the program book. "And they probably paid for that stupid silver fur coat Amelia's wearing along with her matching silver hair."

Topaz tried to force a smile as she glanced at the countless pages with photos of Kara, letters to Kara, poems to Kara . . . Kara, Kara, Kara. So this is what the entire thing came down to, she suddenly realized: money. She felt the tears slide down her cheeks, one by one, and then in a steady stream. I never had a chance. And it doesn't even matter that I sang my heart out.

She sniffed and wiped her eyes with the back of her hand, fumbling through her bag for a tissue. Topaz had worked hard selling ads for the competition. Her mother had even helped, but they just hadn't sold enough. And Keisha was probably right. Kara's parents were loaded. Their money and connections had garnered their daughter the title of queen.

Topaz reluctantly got to her feet with the rest of the audience and watched as Mrs. Richards placed the rhinestone tiara on top of Kara's picture-perfect Shirley Temple curls.

"There'll be no living with her now," Keisha whispered. She looked at Topaz's tear-streaked face, handed her a handkerchief from her own bag, and gave her friend a hug. "I know it hurts, girl, but you've got to fix your makeup. You'll definitely be part of Miss Thing's court and when you go up there, you walk across that stage like Miss America. You can't let her think she won."

"You're right, Keisha." Topaz sniffed, opened her bag, and found a tube of lipstick and her mirrored compact. I don't have on a stitch of makeup. Mother would kill me if she saw my face like this. She quickly brushed translucent powder over her face and reapplied the pink lipstick. She gave herself a once-over in the mirror and snapped the compact closed. There, that's better.

"You really were the best," offered Vaughn. "You sang circles around her and she wishes she was as beautiful as you."

"Thanks, Vaughn." Topaz was kind for once. She knew he was only trying to make her feel better.

Back on stage, Mrs. Richards was reading more names. "And these are the ladies of the court."

Topaz heard the girls shriek and shrill as they jumped to their feet and dashed up the stairs to the stage. I didn't even make the court. She fought the urge to cry again. Topaz turned around to glance at her mother when she heard Mrs. Richards call out her name. She had just about lost all hope of being on the court.

She felt her sunken spirit begin to soar when she heard all of the applause especially for her. Topaz stood gracefully, ran her small, thin fingers elegantly over her hair, and mounted the stage with the poise and confidence of Miss America. When she reached Mrs. Richards, she faced the audience, curtsied, and flashed a dazzling smile.

I should have been queen, she reasoned sadly. Not part of the queen's court. I was the best, but I lost just because I don't have money. It isn't fair, she wanted to shout. It just isn't fair. Topaz forced a smile when she saw her mother at the foot of the stage taking pictures. Cameras flashed continuously as each girl was presented with flowers. Now that the queen and her court were officially presented, the ceremony was over.

"All that fuss and it's over already." Lisa brushed a small clump of powder from her daughter's face.

"Mother, please!" Topaz yelled, stepping out of her mother's reach. "Would you leave my face alone for once?"

"Darling, please, lower your voice." Lisa smiled at several ladies who were passing by. "People are watching."

"I don't care who's watching," Topaz replied, stamping her foot. "Mother, I lost and all you seem to care about is how my makeup looks."

"I'm sorry you lost, sweetheart, but you sang beautifully. Are those record company executives here?"

"I don't know, Mother," she almost screamed in exasperation. "I haven't seen anybody. Can we go home now?"

"Go home? Darling, no. There's a lovely party planned. We should go mingle." Lisa pushed Topaz towards the banquet room. "There are all sorts of people here."

"Fine. You stay and mingle. I'm going home. I have to get my purse from Keisha." She stormed off through the crowded ballroom in search of Keisha, tossing her bouquet of flowers on a table where it landed among crystal goblets half-filled with ice water. She saw Kara still on the stage taking pictures and looked away quickly. The pain she felt was too fresh.

"Topaz, Topaz Black," she heard someone say directly behind her.

"What?" she snapped, whipping around to find herself looking straight into Germain Gradney's smiling hazel eyes.

"I think you dropped these." His voice was kind and his words gentle. He extended her discarded bouquet of flowers.

He is too fine. She felt her knees weaken and a pulling sensation in her stomach sent shivers throughout her body. "I didn't drop them." She was unable to control the smile that had taken over her full pouty lips. "I threw them away."

"Here." Germain handed her the flowers. "You might want them later."

"Thank you." She took the bouquet of flowers and fingered the petals, waiting to see what he would say next.

She's the most beautiful girl I've ever seen. Germain was completely at a loss for words. Topaz's beautiful amber eyes were slightly red, and he knew she'd been crying, probably because she hadn't been crowned queen. He wanted to hold her, to just stand there looking at her forever.

Her statuesque figure curved perfectly in all the right places. I'd love to see those long legs of hers. And that hair . . . He fought the urge to remove her hair clip so he could run his hands through the thick locks of blond hair and watch it fall around her face. He could feel himself begin to desire her. Talk about love at first sight. I've got to say something or else she'll think I'm an idiot.

"You're the most beautiful girl I've ever seen," Germain finally said. "And you don't need a contest to let anyone know you're a queen."

"Thank you." She blushed. I can't believe I'm blushing. No one has ever made me feel like this before.

"Would you like to go into the banquet room and get something to eat?"

"Yes, but not until you tell me your name." Topaz gazed up at him through lowered lashes. I can't let him know I already know his name.

Germain was embarrassed. This girl has caused me to lose all my wits. I can't believe I didn't tell her my name. "Germain, Germain Gradney," he told her, relieved that he was still able to speak. "Come on, let's go."

She felt him touch her gently around the waist as he led her into the banquet room. The mere touch of his hand made her tingle from head to toe. Just wait until Keisha sees me with Germain.

In the adjoining room the hotel staff was serving a fabulous buffet dinner—oysters on the half shell, shrimp cocktail, a side of rare beef, cornish game hens stuffed with wild rice, new potatoes, lightly steamed asparagus tips, various pasta and fruit salads, tossed salad, fresh baked rolls, and raspberry sorbet. The room buzzed with conversation. Waiters rushed back and forth with pitchers of ice water, iced tea, and mixed drinks.

"I'll get dinner," Germain offered. "Why don't you find us some seats?"

"Okay." Topaz was in seventh heaven. "I have to find my friend Keisha. She has my purse."

"Keisha Nichols?"

"Yes . . ." Topaz scoped the room. "There she is!" Keisha was seated at a table with her parents and Debbie.

"I know Keisha's family well. Maybe we can sit with them. I'll be over as soon as I get the food."

Topaz practically ran over to the table. "Keisha!" She knelt down beside her so they could talk privately.

"Hey, girl. I was looking for you. Where've you been?" She looked at Topaz's smiling face. "Wait, you didn't kick Miss Thing's behind and take her tiara?"

"No." Topaz laughed. "Guess who I met?"

"Who?" Keisha smiled, sensing Topaz's excitement. "Somebody from a record company?"

"No, I met Germain Gradney. He's in line getting our dinner."

"Our dinner?" Keisha raised an eyebrow of interest.

"Yes, our dinner." Topaz flashed a triumphant grin.

"You're kidding? Really?"

"Yes! Girl, he is too fine. I like him . . . a lot."

"Oooh, girl," Keisha squealed. "I told you he was nice." The girls squealed together and grinned.

"Wait, he's coming." Keisha whispered. "Debbie, move over and let Topaz sit there." Debbie obeyed her orders and Topaz slid into the seat next to Keisha just as Germain walked up with dinner.

"Topaz, I didn't know what to get you so I brought a little bit of everything." He handed her a dinner plate. "Good evening, Dr. and Mrs. Nichols. Hi, Keisha." Debbie politely moved over another seat and Germain sat down next to Topaz.

"Good evening, Germain," said Dr. Nichols. "How've you been?"

"Just fine, sir." He looked at Topaz. "Is everything okay?"

"Yes, Germain, everything's fine. Thank you." She smiled. Topaz wasn't a bit hungry, but she didn't want to hurt Germain's feelings, so she forced herself to eat one of the fresh jumbo prawns on her plate.

"How's the premed program coming along, Germain?" Dr. Nichols inquired.

"Just fine, sir. I'm going to apply to medical school at Johns Hopkins University." Topaz felt Keisha's knee sharply nudge hers. She looked up from her plate to see Keisha give her an I-told-you-so look.

"Excellent, Germain, excellent. I have several friends on staff there so let me know if you need a recommendation."

"I will, Dr. Nichols, and thank you."

"Polite, too," whispered Keisha. "Lisa would love him."

Topaz bit her tongue to keep from laughing. Mother would love him. Mother . . . she suddenly remembered. Where is she?

She glanced around the room and found Lisa engrossed in conversation with an extremely handsome man. Leave it to Mother to attract the attention of the best-looking man in the room. But I did well myself tonight, she thought, glancing at Germain.

She saw Kara seated with her parents and a cousin who was her escort for the evening. "The queen couldn't even get a date," she whispered to Keisha, referring to Kara's cousin. Keisha's reply was a wicked grin.

"Are your parents here?" Germain wanted to know.

"My mother's here. Would you like to meet her?"

"Sure." He stood to assist Topaz with her chair. "Where is she?" Topaz took Germain's hand and led him across the room.

"Mother." She interrupted the conversation with the handsome stranger and stood in between the man and her mother. "I'd like you to meet a new friend. This is Germain Gradney. Germain, my mother, Lisa Black."

"I can't believe you're her mother." Germain was surprised because Lisa was so young. She was only sixteen when Topaz was born. "You look like you should be her sister."

"Thank you, Germain." Lisa flashed a dazzling smile identical to Topaz's. "I'm very pleased to meet you. You wouldn't be related to Dr. Michelle Gradney, would you?"

"She's only my mother."

"That's right, Germain. I know you. Your mother is one of my clients. She talks about you all the time. You're attending Morehouse. You're going to be a doctor, too." Lisa was extremely impressed.

"That's right. I intend to specialize in cosmetic surgery." It was obvious that Germain was proud of his career goals.

"Good for you, Germain. And do tell your mother I said hello." Lisa introduced the handsome stranger. He was also a doctor. It figures. Topaz looked the man up and down. Mother wouldn't be interested if he didn't have money.

"Where's your father?" Germain inquired.

"I don't know. I've never met him. He and my mother never married because his family said my mother wasn't good enough for him. He's some big attorney in Boston."

"I'm sorry." Some of the sparkle faded from Germain's twinkling eyes.

"Oh, don't worry about it. He can't help it if he's a jerk."

Topaz focused her attention on the back wall and pretended she didn't care.

"He certainly is a jerk. Missing out on the opportunity to be part of his beautiful daughter's life."

An uncontrollable smile found its way onto Topaz's lips again. He always knows the right thing to say.

She could hear the first few bars of "Sweet Love" playing softly in the background. Now that everyone had eaten, it was time to dance. The first song was exclusively for the debutantes. Germain ushered Topaz onto the floor. Holding her gently by the waist, he moved her gracefully around the dance floor.

He's taller than me, too, she observed, resting her head on his shoulder. Anita Baker's sultry vocals and the scent of Germain's Tiffany fragrance made a heady combination. Topaz sighed contentedly and held Germain a little tighter. I could stay in his arms forever. She felt like she was dreaming. I hope this song never ends.

"Topaz," Germain whispered softly. His breath was warm on her ear.

"Yes?" She lifted her head from his shoulder and gazed up into his eyes.

"What are you doing after the cotillion? Even better, what are you doing for the rest of your life?" He smiled into her amber eyes.

She felt light-headed and that wonderful, tingly, pulling sensation was back in her stomach. "I don't know, Mr. Gradney. What did you have in mind?"

SIX

NEW ENGLAND was a refreshing change from Southern California. The air was so fresh and crisp. Gunther loved Bridgeforth's beautiful campus with its sprawling green lawns and hills speckled with red, orange, and yellow leaves. He waded through the leaves on the sidewalk on his way to the dormitory. Gunther had just left his guidance counselor's office where he had chosen classes for the first semester of his junior year: trigonometry, film history, twentieth-century American literature, French II, human physiology, and racquetball.

He snapped off "Smooth Operator," slipped off the headphones of his Sony Walkman, and paused to look at the clock in the chapel tower, which had just began to chime, announcing the noon hour. The campus's Gothic architecture seemed formidable, yet it silently exuded power. Gunther felt his stomach growl with hunger and he remembered it was time for lunch, so he ran the rest of the way to the dormitory, sprinting up the stairs to the room he shared with Pete Wingate and Doug Sanders.

He smiled at the sight of the neat, sunny room with beds, desks, and bureaus in triplicate. He had fallen in love with the room the moment he saw it. There was a large bay window that looked out on the lake and Massachusetts's majestic purple mountains.

No one was allowed to hang pictures or posters on the walls; however, each of the guys had a large cork bulletin board to decorate. Pete's showcased an eclectic grouping of beautiful women, beautiful cars, and gorgeous, remote, tropical vacation spots. Doug's was covered with photos of his favorite rock'n'roll bands.

Gunther hadn't made any decisions about what to hang on his, but he had thumbtacked a snapshot of him with his brothers and his father in the center of the board. He stared at the photograph, wondering why he had even placed it there. It's not like I miss them or anything. He had literally counted the days until he left for school. Gunther pulled the photo off the bulletin board and tossed it in his desk drawer. He didn't want any reminders of his family or home.

He dropped his bookbag filled with brand new books for his classes onto his bed and headed for the dining room. He wanted to pore over the textbooks now, but he had promised to meet Pete and Doug for lunch.

From the steam table Gunther selected chicken noodle soup, two grilled-cheese sandwiches, fresh tossed salad from the salad bar, and apple turnovers from the dessert table. He searched the dining room for his roommates and found them at a table near the back of the room.

"Hey, guys." He placed his tray on the table and slid into the seat across from Doug, a redhead with green eyes and a healthy sprinkling of freckles, and next to Pete, a good-looking tawny blond with the requisite blue eyes. "What's happening?"

"Lunch." Pete greeted him over his daily copy of the *Wall Street Journal*, which he seemed to be devouring with apparent pleasure.

"Lunch?" Gunther took an oversized bite from one of his sandwiches. "You call that lunch? Man, what is that stuff?" He frowned at the mixture of cottage cheese and pineapple in front of Pete.

"Yeah, Pete," agreed Doug. "That stuff is gross."

"Why, this is cottage cheese, a completely healthy and nutritious meal, mostly protein with very little fat." He ate a large mouthful of the concoction to prove his point.

"But does it taste good?" Gunther was still frowning. "That's all I want to know."

"Nope, not really, dude," Pete confessed. "You get used to it. But let me tell you this, like milk, it does a body good." Gunther and Doug chuckled and shook their heads. Pete's sense of humor could be a bit dry at times.

"Anything worth mentioning in the stocks today?" Doug asked.

"It's really dry, Doug. The Dow Jones is down. But there's a really nice piece in here on my dad's bank." Pete folded the paper in half and handed it to Doug. "So many banks have started to close, but ours hasn't had any problems."

"That's because your dad gets all of his rich friends to put their money in your bank." Doug laughed as he quickly skimmed the article and passed it to Gunther.

"That's not true." Pete ate another large spoonful of cottage cheese. Gunther said nothing. He just stared at the newspaper and then his roommates in total amazement.

"Oh, come on, Pete, the Bank of Manhattan? That bank doesn't allow you to open a checking account with less than a million dollars."

"No way." Pete laughed. "That's just a rumor."

"Your father owns a bank?" Gunther was finally able to speak.

"He's a major shareholder," corrected Pete. "Along with my uncles and my grandfather. My great-great-grandfather started the bank almost a hundred years ago. Everyone in the family has shares, too. When I finish college I'm going to work with my dad in investments."

Job security in your own bank. How nice, thought Gunther.

"So you're going to major in finance?" asked Doug.

"Yeah, dude." Pete picked up the sports section from the *New York Times* and continued reading. "And I'll probably go to Harvard because my dad, uncles, and grandfather all went there."

"I know all about family tradition. My dad and my grandfather attended Bridgeforth and Yale," offered Doug. "So I'll get my B.A. in economics from Yale and then get my J.D. from Georgetown University."

Gunther brushed the crumbs from his apple turnover into a neat pile on the crisp linen tablecloth. He was starting to feel uncomfortable because he couldn't join in. I can't believe these guys already know what college they're going to and what they plan to major in. I haven't even thought about college yet or what I want to do.

"Isn't your dad a senator for Massachusetts?" Pete asked Doug.

"Yeah. That's another thing that runs in the family. Politics. I've spent most of my life in Washington."

"It must be exciting," said Pete, "socializing with Ron and

Nancy. They've been to several of my father's annual Christmas parties. We made sizable contributions to his presidential campaigns."

"Ron and Nancy?" Gunther uttered in complete shock. "Are you talking about Ronald Reagan, the President?"

"In the flesh." Pete acted as though there was nothing unusual about the President being in his home. "What does your family do, Gunther?" He fixed his cobalt blue eyes on him.

Gunther felt his heart lodge itself in his throat as his blood pressure escalated twenty points. What do I tell them? The truth will never do. "Development," he finally heard himself say. "My father owns a real-estate development company in Southern California and my mother is a designer. She designs million-dollar office buildings and she's also done several homes for famous celebrities." He sighed with relief after he responded. My father in real estate development. That wasn't a total lie. He almost laughed out loud, pleased with his cleverness.

"That sounds really cool." Doug pushed his tray aside and fingered the salt shaker. "California is a great place for real-estate development. Who are some of the celebrities your mother designed homes for?"

"Let's see . . ." Gunther mused, stalling for time. "She did a house for the owner of some major studio . . . She does so many of them, I can't keep up."

"Was it Lew Wasserman?" Pete offered. "He's CEO of MCA and a real good friend of the family."

Darn. This white boy and his family know everybody. "No, it wasn't him. I think it was Berry Gordy. Yeah, that's who it was," Gunther lied.

"Cool," said Doug. "He's a really nice man. I've met him before at one of the inaugurations. Do you know Kidd Maxx?"

"No, I haven't had the pleasure yet, but my mom did a house for one of his brothers." Gunther continued his fantastic story. It'll be just my luck that Kidd Maxx provided the entertainment for one of those stupid Christmas parties.

"Well, I'd love to sit here and continue discussing who's who in Hollywood and Washington but I've got a polo game." Pete picked up his tray of dirty dishes and headed towards the kitchen.

"That's right," said Doug. "I almost forgot about that. I signed up, too. Would you like to play, Gunther?"

"I've never played." Gunther felt totally out of place.

"Do you ride?" asked Pete.

Ride what? Gunther wanted to shout. "I . . . I'm not sure what you're talking about," he confessed, feeling quite foolish now.

"Horses, dude, horses." Doug laughed.

"No. No, I don't."

"No problem, you can take up horseback riding here. Then once you learn to ride, I'll teach you how to play polo," Pete offered with a warm smile.

"Okay." Gunther was relieved that his roommates hadn't decided to kick him to the curb. "I'll catch you dudes later."

He watched his roommates walk away. They were both wearing Levis with pastel-colored oxford shirts, blazers, and Top-Siders. He sat at the dining room table a little longer and studied several other students who were dressed in the same type of clothing. Although uniforms weren't required at the academy, this seemed to be the standard in preppie attire.

Gunther studied his own clothing once he was back at the dorm. He usually wore denim jeans with a T-shirt or sweatshirt and a pair of Nikes. This will never do, he realized. My clothes are totally wrong. He grabbed his checkbook and one of his mystery best-sellers but cast it aside for Pete's discarded copy of the *Wall Street Journal*. He glanced at the stack of magazines and newspapers on Pete and Doug's desks. There was a copy of the *New York Times*, which had already been read, and current issues of *Newsweek* and *U.S. News and World Report*. He picked up the *Newsweek* and tucked it under his arm along with the *Wall Street Journal* and made a mental note to go to the library to read those very magazines every week. "Pete and Doug aren't going to make me feel stupid."

In town, he perused the racks of several clothing stores before purchasing several pairs of Levis 501s, pink, blue, and white oxford shirts, a pair of deck shoes, and black and blue blazers. His father had given him money in case of an emergency. His new image certainly qualified. Gunther smiled at his reflection in the dressing room mirror at the Gap. "Hey, dude, what's happening?" he asked his mirrored reflection, mimicking Pete's aloof speech. "Want to take in a game of polo?

"Hey . . ." He was astonished by how well he had imitated

Pete. Wouldn't it be great if I really talked that way? Right then and there, he knew he had to affect a New York accent. It would be just the thing to complete his new eastern preppie image.

Gunther decided to wear his new clothes back to school. He sat on the bus reading Pete's *Wall Street Journal* and feeling really important. I must look important, because people are staring at me. Let them stare. He was pleased with all the attention. Because I am important. I know important people. One of these days, Pete and Doug, who just happen to be my friends, will be the movers and shakers in the worlds of high finance and politics, and I'm definitely going to be there, too.

Bridgeforth had a very small black student population. One day, as Gunther was on his way to the dorms with Pete, Kwame Robinson, one of three blacks in the senior class, walked up to them.

"Yo, brotha, what's happenin'?" Kwame was friendly despite Gunther's deadpan face. He took Gunther's hand and gave him the customary black handshake. "I'm Kwame Robinson. You're Gunther Lawrence, right?"

"Yeah, dude, what's happening?" Gunther eyed Kwame's red, black, and green beret with contempt. "Pete and I were on our way to play a game of pool."

"How you doin', Pete?" Kwame asked politely.

"Hi, Kwame." Pete smiled. "How've you been?"

"Good, man. Real good. Gunther, could I talk with you a minute, my brotha?"

Brother? I'm not your brother, Gunther thought, becoming annoyed, especially since he had called him that in front of Pete.

"Look, Gunther. Just meet me in the lounge when you're done. Meanwhile, I'll warm up on the table so I can beat you, quickly and easily." Pete flashed a dazzling wicked smile at Gunther as he walked away.

"Okay, dude, I'll see you in a few." Gunther watched Pete walk out of hearing distance before he spoke. "Yeah, dude, so what did you want to talk to me about?" he asked rudely.

"We have a Black Student Alliance and I wanted to invite you to come out and be a part of it, man. We have weekly meetings. Some of the brothas are real good cooks, so sometimes we get together and prepare a soul food dinner or go to parties given by

Black Student Alliances at other schools. We also put on programs during Black History Month and we raise money for various community organizations. But most important, we just want to support you in case you're having challenges with classes, teachers, or adjusting to the school."

"Well, dude, everything is just fine with me, so I see no need for me to join your little club. School's great and I love it here. I'm not into soul food. To be perfectly honest, I hate it. And I didn't come all the way to Massachusetts from South Central L.A. to hang out with the brothers. Isn't this supposed to be a better chance?" Gunther finished sarcastically.

"It's brothers like you that always forget where you come from." Kwame was furious. "You just get yourself through the door and then you close it. Brotha, I really feel sorry for you. You think those guys are your friends? Just wait till those white boys kick your black behind to the curb, then you'll see. Later, brother." He didn't even wait for Gunther to reply before he hurriedly walked away.

"Soul food dinner," Gunther grumbled under his breath, walking towards the student lounge. "How dare he insult me like that!" I can see them sucking on a bunch of chicken bones now. From that day forward, Gunther avoided every black student on campus.

Junior year passed by with a breeze. Before Gunther knew it, he was on his way back to Los Angeles for the summer. Gunther wore his favorite Levis and Top-Siders for the plane ride back to the West Coast. When his father met him at the airport, they were very formal with each other, shaking hands as though they were merely business acquaintances.

Gunther could think of very little to say in the car on the way home, so he read his *Wall Street Journal*. He glanced at his father out of the corner of his eye. I hope he notices how important I am now. And he was actually looking forward to seeing his brothers. Maybe they'll see I've changed and treat me differently.

"Hey, man," Charles Jr. called as he walked in the door. "How've you been?"

"Great, dude. How's everything with you?" Gunther looked around the empty house with its shabby furnishings and immediately wished for his room with the bay window at Bridgeforth. I bet Pete and Doug have beautiful homes. He resented that both boys had fabulous vacation plans for the summer. How come white people have to have everything?

"What's happening, Marshall?"

"Nothin' man." Marshall was cool with his younger brother.

"Man, where'd you get them funny lookin' shoes?" Charles Jr. laughed.

"Yeah, dude," said Marshall, mocking Gunther. "How come you talk so funny?"

Gunther wanted to turn and run out the door but there was nowhere to go. He was home for the summer. He looked at his brothers with disgust as they rolled on the floor laughing. They hadn't changed one bit, and they were making fun of him as usual.

"You dudes are really showing your ignorance because all rich boys talk and dress this way," Gunther calmly told them when their laughter subsided.

"Man, you're as phony as a three-dollar bill." Charles Jr. laughed.

"Yeah," agreed Marshall. "And you ain't hardly rich."

"I will be one day," he retorted, promising himself more than his brothers. "I'll be a multi-millionaire. You'll see."

SEVEN

SEAN DROPPED the heavy box of books on the floor, fell across the naked mattress on his bed, and sighed with relief. "That's the last of those."

It was late September and Philadelphia was sweltering. He picked up a huge glass of ice water from the floor and emptied it in a series of gulps while he watched Kyle and Kirk enter the bedroom carrying his suitcases and clothing on hangers.

"Oh, excuse me, Magic Johnson. Is there anything else you'd like me to do?" Kyle deposited two large suitcases in the middle of the floor. "Perhaps you'd like some more water?" Kyle stood at attention waiting for his brother's response.

"Sure, man. There's a couple of bottles of Evian chilling in the freezer."

"And where would you like me to put your designer wardrobe, Magic?" Kirk asked, playing the role of the humble servant.

"Just hang it in the closet, Kirk." Sean laughed.

"Man, you know he really thinks he's a star." Kyle tossed Kirk a bottle of water. "Lounging around here and drinking Evian water while we do all the work."

"Lounging around? Those books were heavy." Sean jumped up from the bed. "Those clothes you guys brought up were lightweight compared to all those boxes of books that I carried up here." He watched his brothers guzzle down the Evian. "And you could at least offer me some of my own water."

Kirk retrieved another bottle from the kitchen and tossed it to Sean. "Nice place, man."

"Thanks." Sean gave the apartment an admiring glance. "I like it, too. Coach picked it out and leased all the furniture after me and Ty told him we needed something off campus so we could have our privacy."

"That one ninety E is real sweet, too," said Kyle. "How did you manage that one?"

"Ty and I had a long talk with Coach over the summer. We put U Penn on the map last year, so we thought we deserved a little something extra for all our hard work. Do you know how much publicity this school received last year? And I won't even mention the fact that all of our games are already sold out for this year." Sean unlocked a suitcase and began tossing underwear and socks into dresser drawers.

"Look, man, you don't have to convince us." Kyle collected the empty water bottles. "I'm glad to see things happening for you. Just make sure that's you talking and not Ty."

"What's that supposed to mean?" Sean paused from unpacking to look at his brother, the muscles in his strong jawline flexing. "I worked my behind off last year. We even made it to the Final Four. You know Mitch Matthews was drafted by the Celtics. That's because I got ESPN in here and I got the team noticed." He continued to toss clothing in the bureau.

"No one's disputing your accomplishments, Sean," said Kirk, getting into the conversation. "Kyle's just telling you to be careful."

"Be careful of what?" Sean demanded.

"This," said Kyle, gesturing wildly. "A penthouse apartment with a panoramic view of the city, exercise room, indoor pool, and shopping mall. A Mercedes with SYLK on the license plates. Hanging out at Dr. E's house and at the 76ers' games . . . clubbing."

"So what's wrong with all that stuff?" Sean asked innocently. He stared at his brother waiting for his response. "I'm just having a good time."

"A good time," Ty repeated. He entered the room with a suitcase in each hand and a smile plastered across his bulldoggish face. "Sounds like a plan to me. Yo, G, what up?"

"Hey, Terrible Ty, you got it. Welcome back." Sean jumped up from the bed and greeted Ty warmly with a hug.

"Double K, what's happenin'?" Ty shook hands with the twins. "You guys ready to help me move my things in next?"

"Nope, I don't think so." Kirk's tone and demeanor were cool. "I promised my wife I'd do the grocery shopping. I'm going to pick up some steaks and chops while I'm at the supermarket and barbecue tonight. Why don't you and Rhonda join us, Sean?"

Sean felt his brothers' eyes searching his face for a response. "Barbecue sounds great, Kirk, but I'm going to have to pass. I'm taking Ty to dinner. We've got a lot of catching up to do." He bent down and tossed his sweats into a drawer to avert his brother's glance.

"Sounds like a plan to me," Ty agreed. "Yo, Sylk, why don't we have our own barbecue? A little housewarming party so we can christen this slammin' apartment."

"Yeah." Sean was excited. "Except we need to get some refreshments. There's nothing in the fridge but Evian."

"Don't worry about a thing." Ty gathered up his suitcases and disappeared into his own master bedroom suite. "Just leave everything to me."

"You guys want to hang out a while longer?" Sean asked his brothers. "You could call Karla and have her bring Kyrie over here."

"Naw, money." Kirk was already in the living room, opening the front door. "We've got to roll."

"Let us know if you need anything," Kyle offered.

"Thanks, guys." Sean watched his brothers walk down the hall towards the elevator. "Thanks for everything." I hope Kirk isn't upset about the barbecue, but those guys don't like Ty for some reason. And it wouldn't have been right for me to leave Ty alone his first night back.

Sean returned to his room and made up the bed with brand new, emerald green Fieldcrest sheets and a matching fluffy down comforter. He hung the coordinating towels in his bathroom and smiled at his comfortable bedroom suite. "It's on." Rhonda had purchased the linens from Strawbridges for him. "Rhonda," he mumbled. "I have to invite her to the party." He picked up the phone and quickly dialed her number, only to reach her answering machine. I wonder where she is. Disappointed, he hung up the phone. Maybe she went out to dinner with some of her girlfriends.

He heard the doorbell as he put away the last suitcase. Moments later, Ty stuck his head in the room. "Time to rock 'n' roll."

"I'm right behind you." Sean followed Ty into the living room where he saw Tatyana and Danielle, another U Penn cheerleader, in the kitchen taking steaks, chicken, potatoes, and salad ingredients out of plastic grocery bags.

"Hey, pretty boy, what's been happening?" Tatyana smiled at Sean as she lifted a cake with fresh strawberries and whipped cream out of the bag. She seemed more beautiful than ever. Sean could tell her hair had been freshly cut and her gorgeous cocoa skin had taken on a reddish hue from the summer sun. He could make out the silhouette of her perfectly toned legs and firm derriere under a crimson-and-black chiffon cover-up. *She's wearing Opium and it's driving me crazy. She is too fine.*

"Hi, Tatyana," he finally spoke, cool and easily. "Hi, Danielle."

"I thought we'd have a nice little private party for four." Ty opened one of several bottles of champagne the girls had purchased.

I've never tasted alcohol before. Sean felt his heart skip a beat as he watched Ty pour the sparkling liquid into four champagne flutes.

"The girls bought the crystal for us as a housewarming present." Ty handed Sean a glass. "How 'bout a toast?"

Sean swallowed hard, trying to dislodge the thick lump that had formed in his throat.

"Naw, man, you got it."

"Cool." Ty raised his glass and grinned. "To my homeboy and partner, Sylk. May our senior year be only the beginning of what's to come. May the dynamic duo break every record there is to break, sweep the NCAA playoffs and sign NBA contracts for megabucks. To this def apartment and to the two finest honeys in Philly. Peace." Glasses tinkled as the four young people gently touched the flutes in a toast. Sean stared at the pale gold liquid for several minutes.

"Go on, Sylk, drink up," Ty urged.

Sean took a tiny sip of champagne. It tasted sweet, yet it was very sour, almost bitter. *I don't like it.* But he knew Ty was watching him so he quickly drank the rest. *I'm not in the mood for Ty's snide remarks tonight.* He placed the glass on the counter. Seconds later he felt lightheaded.

"Wow," Sean exclaimed, taking a seat at the bar in the kitchen.

"You need another glass," Ty insisted, refilling his glass quickly. Sean stared at the fresh glass of champagne until he heard Tatyana close the oven door.

"Okay, guys. How about a swim while those potatoes bake?" Tatyana took a seat next to Sean at the bar.

He felt himself yearn for the touch of her hands on his body. It must be the alcohol, he surmised, downing a second glass. "Yeah, let's go for a swim." Sean grinned at Tatyana and jumped off the barstool. "I'll get my trunks."

"I'm with that. Last one in is a rotten egg," Ty yelled, racing to his room. Sean snickered all the way to his suite. He was starting to enjoy the champagne and their little party.

They all drank more champagne and swam in the pool while Ty grilled the steaks and chicken. After dinner, the group adjourned to the Jacuzzi with another bottle of champagne. Sean felt wonderfully intoxicated from the superb dinner, glasses of champagne, the Indian summer night, and Tatyana's fragrant perfume. The swirling, therapeutic jets of the Jacuzzi relaxed him completely.

Danielle, a cinnamon honey with a long flowing weave, was sitting in Ty's lap and they were kissing. Sean looked away as he felt Tatyana's legs wrap around his. But he knew he was in heaven when she ran her finger gently down the tip of his nose, delicately around his lips and across the muscles in his jawline. Moments later, he felt her mouth over his and as their tongues intertwined, he automatically reached for her breasts.

"We're going upstairs." Ty helped Danielle climb out of the Jacuzzi. The sound of his voice summoned Sean out of paradise.

"Good night, you guys," Danielle called out, looking at Tatyana. Sean watched them walk towards the elevator, arm in arm. Everyone knew what would come next.

"Shall we go, too?" Tatyana whispered in his ear.

"Naw," he replied quickly. "Let's go for another swim." Sean dove smoothly into the water, swimming underneath for half the length of the pool. Its coolness was refreshing after the hot Jacuzzi.

What I am doing? he asked himself, remembering his promise to the Lord to remain a virgin until he married. He heard Tatyana dive in and swim in his direction. She swam up to him in the shallow end of the pool, wrapped her legs around his firm chocolate body, and began kissing him again. He could barely push her away.

"Come on, Sylk. We can't stay in here forever. Let's go upstairs. I'm getting cold."

"All right." He was hoping things would have chilled out by the time the two of them reached the apartment. "Let's go. It has gotten chilly."

Upstairs, they both went into his room. Sean went into the bathroom, shut the door, and quickly undressed. Talk about needing a cold shower . . . the tiny, icy needles of pulsating water felt good on his skin as his mind wandered back to Tatyana. Suddenly, he heard the shower door slide open and Tatyana stepped in. It was the first time he had ever seen a girl in the nude and she was absolutely beautiful.

This girl doesn't know when to quit, he reasoned, as they began kissing. He felt his body give in but suddenly his mind took over. "Don't let your body be an instrument of unrighteousness," he heard from way deep down inside. "Your body is My temple." He kissed her for a few more seconds before he realized his desire had dissipated. He climbed out of the shower and grabbed a towel.

"Sylk, baby, what's wrong?" Tatyana whispered, climbing out behind him.

"I'm engaged," he sputtered, walking into the bedroom. He was overwhelmed with guilt knowing Rhonda had not been the real reason why he had turned down her advances.

"Engaged? Then why wasn't she over here cooking your dinner instead of me?"

"Tatyana . . . you're really a nice girl, but I can't marry you."

"Marry me? What does making love have to do with getting married?"

"Everything."

"Everything?" She seemed confused. "That's right, I forgot. Your father is a preacher." Her words were mean and cold. "Sylk, don't tell me you're still a virgin." She laughed.

"No, I'm not," he lied, too embarrassed to tell the truth. "I just think people should have some sort of commitment before they have sex together."

"So, you don't want to do it?" She was totally amazed.

"No, I think we should wait. You can sleep in my bed. I'll sleep in the living room on the couch."

"No, you can sleep in your own bed." She was unable to hide the pain from his rejection. "I'm going home."

Sean was embarrassed for weeks but he quickly put the incident out of his mind once the basketball season got underway.

■

"Every move you make out there from now on will be scrutinized for the NBA draft," Coach barked at them one day after a grueling practice. "So I suggest those of you with aspirations to play pro ball remember that."

"You hear what Coach said this afternoon at practice?" Ty asked Sean later that night. They were in the living room devouring cartons of rum raisin Häagen-Dazs and watching *A Different World*. "They're making decisions now. Man, we're in the house. The NBA house. You just keep passing me that ball."

"You got it," Sean replied with little enthusiasm. "Well, time to hit the books." He headed towards his room. "I've got a test in business law tomorrow."

Several days later, U Penn was scheduled to play the University of North Carolina. When Sean entered the gym, he saw his buddy from ESPN, Chuck Zimmerman, talking to a cameraman. "How's the NBA's next major superstar?" he called out to Sean.

"Great." Sean detoured over to the cameras. "How've you been, Chuck?"

"Wonderful." Chuck slipped on his blue blazer. "I'll be ready for highlights after the game."

"Cool." Sean flashed his Pepsodent smile. "Why'd you guys bring so many cameras?"

"They're not all ours. CNN and Prime Ticket are here, too."

"CNN?" Sean tried to remain cool. "Wow!"

"They're all here to see how you fare against the University of North Carolina, my friend." He flipped through a binder of notes. "If you play half the game you played against Michigan last week, Sylk Ross will become a household word."

"You think so, Chuck?" Sean felt the muscles in his jawline begin to twitch.

"I know so. I've got to go over some things with the guys in the production truck. I'll be ready for you after the game."

Sean walked in a trance towards the locker room. "We've got to win tonight," he whispered determinedly. Then he remembered Coach's warning regarding the upcoming NBA draft.

It was risky. Sean was at the three-point line with the ball in his hands. There were only seconds remaining on the clock. He watched his teammates position themselves for the layup with Ty as the open man, and then he focused on the basket and tossed one up. He sucked in his breath and felt every muscle in his body grow taut as the ball continued its flight. He stood frozen in midair as the ball swished through the net, and only then did he take a breath. "Yes!" He threw his hands up in the air in triumph. The gymnasium thundered with applause as the buzzer signaled the end of the half. He looked at the scoreboard. U Penn was ahead by only three points.

U Penn maintained a three-point lead for the duration of the second half until UNC sunk a beautiful three-pointer and tied the score. Sean, in center court, spotted a direct path to the basket. I've got to take it. He pretended not to notice Ty, who was once again the open man. He dribbled, feeling his heart throb to the rhythm of the bouncing ball. Then, he sped across the floor, leaped through the air, and dunked. Magic Johnson, Larry Bird, Isaiah Thomas . . . eat your hearts out, he wanted to shout. He flashed his Pepsodent smile as the crowd shrieked with praise. The final buzzer sounded and U Penn won by three points.

He pretended not to see Tatyana, zipping right by her, on his way to speak to Chuck Zimmerman. He hadn't spoken to her since the night she left his apartment. Crystal, one of the newest cheerleaders, congratulated him with a kiss. Not another one, he groaned. Why can't these women keep their hands off me? Oh, well, there's nothing I can do if they find me irresistible.

CNN's sportscaster pulled him in front of a camera. "Rumor has it that the Lakers, the Knicks, and the Hawks would do anything to get you on their teams. How do you feel about being the number-one draft choice?" He thrust his microphone in front of Sean, anxiously awaiting his comment.

"It feels great, just great," Sean shouted into the mike. "I've dreamt about this day all my life and my dream is finally coming true." All those teams are interested in me? I must be really good. He tried to concentrate on his response to the sportscaster's next question but his mind kept drifting back to his popularity among the teams.

"You played a great game tonight, Sylk Ross," the smiling newsman continued. "You've really taken an obscure Ivy League team and placed it in the spotlight of the NCAA."

I know, Sean answered in his head.

Sean left the locker room on cloud ninety-nine. He hurried

back to the apartment to change and meet Ty. To celebrate their victory they were going to hit several private clubs where they had been given memberships.

"Man, how come you didn't pass me the ball?" Ty demanded as soon as Sean entered the apartment.

"I haven't been able to get it to you, Ty." Sean headed towards his bedroom.

"Sylk, you looked right at me. You knew I was the open man," Ty yelled. His bulldog face was contorted with anger.

"What difference does it make, Ty?" Sean paused in the doorway of his room to speak to him. "The thing is that we win, not how many points you get."

"How many points I get? You've got a lot of nerve." He stormed over to Sean. "You're the one who's getting all the points and I haven't been getting any."

"That's not true, man. I've just been playing the best game I can. When I can get the ball to you, I will. Don't worry. Everything will be fine."

But as the season progressed Sean continued to hold onto the ball. He would shoot it himself or pass it to one of his other teammates. He continually scored the most points and got the most rebounds. Sean heard students discussing the basketball games constantly. More than that, he heard them discussing him—in the library, in the student union, in his classes. An Ivy League team getting major national coverage in the media was a novelty, and the entire school buzzed with excitement.

"Great game" and "Hi, Sylk" greeted him daily from a sea of unknown faces as he strolled about the campus to and from classes.

"I'm having a birthday party at Zanzibar Blue and I'd love for you to come," offered a gorgeous blonde from his marketing class. She pressed an invitation into his hand and smiled. "My phone number is on the invitation. Why don't you give me a call sometime?" Sean watched her get into a BMW and speed off.

"Interesting." He quickly read over the invitation before carefully tucking it into one of his schoolbooks.

"Maybe we can study together sometime," proffered an attractive black girl with a very British accent. "I attend all your games."

"Yo, man, you down for a little one-on-one?" was another constant invitation.

They really think I'm special. He opened a beautifully wrapped package that had been left for him with his coach. He gasped at the sight of the 18-karat gold rope chain with a heart-shaped pendant that was inscribed I LOVE SYLK and embellished with several small diamonds. *It has to be from a girl*, he reasoned. *But who?* He slipped the chain around his neck and ripped open the enclosed gift card. "Let's be friends, Tatyana." He tossed the card, box, and wrapping paper into a nearby trash can. "Not her again," he muttered, fingering the gold chain.

"*Sports Illustrated* wants to include you in an article on NCAA All-Stars. They want to follow you around to your classes and attend the Washington State game," Coach explained one day after practice.

"Cool. It wouldn't be an article on NCAA All-Stars without me."

Sean lay among books and papers strewn across his bed. He was watching ESPN while he studied. He wrote furiously, finishing up a paper for a class in Afro-American literature. *I've still got my 3.5 GPA.* He tossed the completed paper aside for one of the cheerleaders to type.

He opened his binder and glanced up from his marketing notes just in time to record footage of himself running, leaping, and jumping during basketball highlights on ESPN. *That was great*, he grinned, admiring the pretty shot. Once the highlights were over, he searched his library of clips, pulled out a favorite cassette, and popped it into the VCR.

"Now that was a great shot," he yelled, jumping up off the bed. "Can't touch me." He danced and sang loudly until he heard a telephone ringing. He pointed the remote at the VCR and pressed pause.

"Hey, Rhonda." He flopped on the bed and flipped on the speaker phone simultaneously. "I was just going through some of my clips. You know I have copies of all my interviews and games. I've really got some great stuff. I've been out of town or studying . . . I know I haven't been to church since the season began, but I've been busy. Look, you're not my mother. Was there something you wanted to talk about? . . . No, I can't go to dinner

Friday. I'm going to Dr. E's. I've got a game Saturday and some birthday party to go to." He pulled out the invitation from the blonde in his marketing class and stuck it in his Day Runner. "The party's at a club. You don't like clubs, remember? Look, Rhonda, I've been thinking." He switched off the speaker and lifted the receiver to his ear. "We never have time to see each other anymore, and we don't like to do the same things. You don't like my friends and I don't like yours, so why don't we just see other people . . . No, I'm not seeing anyone else. I just think we need to call it quits." He thought he heard the call-waiting tone signal another call. "My other line is ringing. I've got to go. I'll talk to you later." He hung up the phone and sighed with relief. That girl gets on my nerves. Always preaching to me. I'm glad that's over.

"What's up, man?" Sean greeted Dr. E with a hug Friday night.

"Everything's great, Sylk. Where's Sly Ty? I thought he was coming, too."

"He's out on a date," Sean lied.

"No problem. He just phoned earlier to say he was coming over with you. I thought we'd check out a couple of movies." Dr. E headed for the family room that housed the big-screen television. "A friend who works for one of the big studios in Hollywood sent me a box of movies that aren't even on video yet. I sent out for a bunch of Chinese food. It should be here any minute. Make yourself at home, man."

"Cool." Sean flopped down in an easy chair, looked around the comfortable family room, and smiled. A fire crackled in the fireplace. The room contained Dr. E's extensive collection of basketball trophies, shelves of books, and an elaborate audio-visual system. Dr. E really has a nice house. But mine will be a hundred times better. He watched his hero carry in numerous cartons of takeout Chinese food and toss a handful of quarters on the table for the antique Coca-Cola machine that was stocked with a variety of chilled beverages.

"Pick out a movie, Sylk. I'll get the plates." Sean looked at the smorgasbord of Chinese food spread out on the bar before he sifted through the box of videos. I can't wait until I'm in the NBA.

Several hours later Ty stormed into Sean's bedroom in a rage. "Man, why didn't you tell me you were going to Dr. E's?"

"I don't have to inform you of every move I make," Sean exploded. "I'm getting tired of this. Why does everyone want to hang out with me?"

"Hang out with you?" Ty looked him up and down with contempt. "Man, you trippin'. Dr. E thought I was out on a date. Did you tell him that?"

"I might have." Sean, not bothering to look at Ty, flipped open his notebook to a fresh sheet of paper and began writing. "To be honest, I didn't know where you were."

"You would if you'd talk to me, but you're so high and mighty now that you don't have time for nobody."

"Whatever." Sean looked up at Ty for the first time since Ty had entered his room. "Could you close my door on your way out? I'm trying to study."

"Forget you, man," Ty yelled as he slammed the door shut.

Sean, totally unaffected by Ty's outburst, continued writing. He's just jealous because I'm the star and I'm getting all the attention. He flipped on the VCR to watch some of his favorite basketball clips. And I really don't care.

EIGHT

"HEY, PRETTY baby . . ." Germain sang in perfect pitch along with the radio. Topaz tried not to giggle as he attempted some flashy footwork and tripped on the edge of the Persian rug that covered the hardwood floor in her bedroom. He continued singing as he transformed his near-trip into a well-executed spin. Topaz grinned and blew him a kiss. Germain pulled her up off the bed and into his arms, running his hands through her silky mane, which accentuated her tiny waist.

"I love you, Germain," Topaz whispered. She closed her eyes and covered his mouth with her own, gently sucking on his bottom lip. "You really turn me on . . ." she sang softly in his ear.

"Hey," Germain exclaimed as he pulled away from her. "I think we'd better get back to choosing your classes for school this fall."

"Classes? I'd rather kiss you instead of choose classes." She pulled him back into her arms and kissed him again.

"Hey, pretty girl, your mother will be home any minute now. We wouldn't want her to find us making mad, passionate love, would we?"

Topaz grinned wickedly. "We could get a quickie, couldn't we?" She slid back further on the pink-and-mauve satin bedspread, which was the exact same shade as the walls of her room, and gave Germain a provocative look. "You're crazy." Germain laughed. "You are absolutely crazy. And I'd be even crazier if I agreed."

"Come on, baby." She slipped off her T-shirt and exposed firm, healthy breasts.

"You got it, pretty girl," he whispered, barely audible. She closed her eyes and moaned with pleasure as he took her in his arms and covered her upper body with delicate kisses.

"Topaz." She heard her mother yell and the front door close. "Where are you?"

"Oh, no!" Topaz jumped off the bed in a frenzy. "Germain, Mother's here. Where are my clothes?" She giggled nervously and quickly pulled on her T-shirt as she watched Germain scurry to pull on his own clothes.

"We're in my room, Mother. Germain's helping me choose classes for school," she yelled over the music. She opened the Howard University catalogue on her desk, smoothed her hair, and busily started writing on a notepad. Germain flipped open a biochemistry textbook just as Lisa whisked open the door to Topaz's room.

"Hi, baby. Hi, Germain." Topaz followed her mother's eyes as she spotted her rumpled bed.

"Hi, Mother." She stood up and planted a kiss on her mother's cheek. "Mmmm, you smell like Escada."

"Hello, Mrs. Black." Germain stood on his feet, looking like the cat that swallowed the canary.

"Germain's been helping me get my fall schedule together. I've got lots of great classes."

"That's wonderful." Lisa checked her makeup in Topaz's mirror. "Would you two like to take a break from all this academia and join me for dinner? My treat."

"Thanks, Mother, but we can't. I'm meeting Keisha at the mall and Germain's working at the hospital tonight."

"Okay, well, let's do it another night. I'll see you kids later." Topaz watched Lisa leave the room as quickly as she had entered it. Then she burst into laughter. "We almost got caught."

"I know. Girl, you make me so crazy. Did you see her check out the bed?"

"The bed? You know I never make the bed." Topaz laughed. She handed Germain the hairbrush so he could brush her hair. "She didn't suspect a thing, and if she did, tough. I can't wait until we have our own place in Baltimore this fall with you at Johns Hopkins and me at Howard. Then we can make love anytime we want."

"Yeah." Germain brushed her hair until it sparkled. "I don't know how I ever talked you into giving up your singing and going to school, but I'm glad I did."

"Me too, baby." Topaz took the brush from him and sat on

his lap. "It was a silly dream anyway." She wrapped her arms around him and eyed a photo of Whitney Houston on her wall.

"Yeah. Now my baby's gonna be a doctor's wife."

"Germain." She turned to face him and kissed a freckle on his nose. "You sounded good when you were singing earlier. Real good." She got up and rambled in the drawer of her antique bureau and found a pair of rhinestone and jet earrings and clipped them on. Then she reapplied her lipstick and quickly changed into a short black linen dress and black sandals.

"See, that just goes to show you that everyone who can sing doesn't have to be a singer." He watched her spray on perfume and primp in the mirror.

"Hey, are you sure you and Keisha are only going to the mall?"

"Yes, silly, and you're right."

"Right about what?" he mumbled. It had been just a year since they started dating, and her beauty still rendered him speechless.

"Everyone who sings doesn't have to be a singer." She glanced at a photo of Whitney Houston and quickly looked away. "Let's go now, Germain, so we can get something to eat before I go to the mall."

She had agreed to meet Keisha in one of their favorite stores, Contempo. Topaz paused from sifting through a rack of size six dresses to brush her hair out of her face when she saw Keisha enter the store. She had blown her naturally curly hair straight for a change and she had to constantly brush the long locks out of her face.

"Hey, girl," she called to her friend as she went back to perusing the rack.

"Topaz? Is that you?"

"Yeah, girl, what's up?" Topaz looked up from the clothes rack, surprised at Keisha's question.

"What did you do to your hair? I almost didn't recognize you."

"Girl, stop. I just used the blow dryer for a change." Topaz took a hot, fire-engine-red knit dress off the rack and added it to her stack of things to try on. "Keisha, they've got some great things on sale." She spun around to scrutinize a rack of earrings and pulled off several pairs that complimented her outfits. Jody

Watley's "Looking for a New Love" was booming through the shop's sound system and Topaz sang along as she refocused her attention on the clothes rack.

"Your hair . . . it's absolutely gorgeous." Keisha was still in shock. She ran her hand through Topaz's silky blond mane. "I never knew your hair was this long."

"I know, huh." Topaz grabbed a handful of her hair for a closer look. "It needs a trim. Maybe I'll stop by that salon in the mall while we're here." She sang a little louder as she danced towards the back of the store to the dressing room. "Girl, that song is hot."

"You sure are in an awfully good mood. Where's Germain?" Keisha asked, looking around the store. "I just knew he'd be here. He hardly ever lets you out of his sight."

"He's at work, Keisha. But he left me some money." She flashed a wad of cash and gave her friend an impish grin.

"How much did he give you this time?" Keisha wasn't the least bit surprised by the roll of twenties in her friend's hand.

"I don't know." Topaz flipped through the bills. "It looks like a couple of hundred dollars. He's been giving me everything since I decided to go to Howard."

"Boyfriend was giving you everything before you decided to go to Howard. Girl, you've got that man's nose so wide open you could drive a tractor trailer through there." Keisha settled into a chair outside the dressing room to watch Topaz try on dress after dress.

"Keisha, stop." Topaz blushed as she whirled around in the red knit dress. "We're in love. He loves me and I love him," she finished with a silly grin. "How do you like this one?"

"I'll say you're in love. And definitely buy that red dress, girl, because Germain would love you in it." Keisha fussed with her hair in one of countless mirrors as Topaz vanished back into the dressing room. "But I'll never understand how he ever talked you into giving up your dream to sing to go to Howard."

"Germain didn't talk me out of singing." Topaz's tone was serious. "There was no singing career to give up. Besides, I'm going to study music and drama at Howard. You know, Debbie Allen graduated from there." Topaz paid for her dresses and took the shopping bag from the salesclerk.

"So, where shall we go next?" Keisha asked once they were back inside the mall.

"I don't know." Topaz gazed down the corridor of stores. "Let's walk towards the salon and I'll decide if I'm going to get my hair cut."

"Okay. And we can stop in Saks. My mother wants me to pay her charge while I'm here."

"Look at that dress, Keisha." Topaz pointed to a Donna Karan original in Saks. She picked up the black chiffon dress and held it up in front of her. "Girl, I'd think I was too fine in this."

"Think?" Keisha repeated. "Topaz, you already know you're too fine."

"No, I don't, Keisha."

"Topaz, you know you do. Remember, this is me, Keisha."

"Well, maybe just a little bit." She took a peek at the price tag. "This thing is twelve hundred dollars." She glanced longingly at the dress as she returned it to the rack.

"Cheer up, girlfriend. In a minute, Dr. Gradney will be able to buy you lots of Donna Karan dresses."

"That's true." Topaz brightened at the thought. "My baby's going to be a doctor. He'll buy me a big house, diamond rings, and lots and lots of designer dresses."

"Girl, come on, let's get out of here." Keisha took Topaz by the arm. "It's getting late and that man's been following us ever since we came in here. He probably thinks we're trying to steal something."

Topaz turned around to look. "What man?"

"Don't look now," Keisha squealed. "He'll see you." She took a quick glance over her shoulder. "See that strange-looking white guy? He's been following us ever since we left Contempo."

"Really?" Topaz looked puzzled. "I wonder why."

"Let's go to the hair salon and see if he follows us down there." The girls quickly left Saks and walked down to Supercuts.

Topaz spoke with the receptionist as she checked out her reflection in the mirror in the brightly lit shop.

"It'll be a few minutes before a stylist can take you," the receptionist replied over the roar of blow-dryers. The girls were hardly seated before the mystery man approached them.

"Good evening, ladies," he offered, greeting them politely.

"Hi," Topaz and Keisha replied together.

"I guess you must have noticed me following you." Topaz felt Keisha nudge her knee.

"I'm sorry if I startled you. But you're very beautiful. Do you model?" He looked directly at Topaz.

"Yes, I do," Topaz replied in her most sophisticated voice. She heard Keisha stifle a giggle but she pretended not to notice. "I'm Topaz Black." She extended her hand. "Perhaps you've heard of me."

"I'm Mick." He spoke with a hint of a French accent. "I'm a freelance photographer. I do a lot of work for *Vogue*, *Elle*, *Bazaar*, all the high-fashion magazines. I'm on my way back to New York from a job in the Bahamas to do a shoot for *Mademoiselle* and I still need a model. I think you'd be perfect."

Topaz felt her heart pounding. She wanted to scream as she fought to maintain her composure. "That sounds like something I might be interested in." She was cool despite her excitement.

"Have your agent call me." Mick pressed a business card into her hand. "I'll be in Atlanta visiting friends until the weekend." As soon as he walked away, the girls went into a fit of laughter.

"Topaz, you're crazy." Keisha laughed. " 'Perhaps you've heard of me,' " she repeated, mimicking Topaz to a T.

"But did I get the job?" Topaz batted her amber-colored eyes.

"Yeah, girlfriend. *Mademoiselle* is big time. You're gonna get paid."

"I sure am. Now I'll be able to buy that Donna Karan dress."

"Okay," Keisha agreed as the girls hit a high five.

Out in the parking lot, Keisha opened the door of her white Volkswagen Cabriolet. "Topaz, you're going to need a portfolio. Especially since you're supposed to be this professional model with an agent."

"I know, I was just thinking about that." Topaz tossed her bags onto the backseat. "Keisha, let's put the top down. It's so hot out tonight."

"All right." The girls pushed the soft white canvas top back and climbed into the car. "And now for some music." Topaz watched Keisha flip through her bag of cassettes looking for just the right one.

"Whatcha gonna play?" Topaz tried to look in Keisha's box of cassettes to see what her friend would select.

"Just wait and see. It's a surprise." Topaz smiled at her pretty, petite friend with her kind, easygoing, earthy ways. She noticed Keisha wasn't wearing any makeup, but every strand of her short cropped hair was in place. I wish I could be more like her. She's always so carefree.

"Hey," Topaz yelled when she heard the first few notes of their favorite song, "I Wanna Dance With Somebody." Keisha cranked the volume and sped out of the parking lot into the traffic. "You wanna dance?" Topaz yelled to a brother walking down the street.

The girls' laughter floated into the air as they breezed down the street with the humid Georgia heat enveloping them.

"Now, look." Keisha lowered the volume of the car stereo. "We have to get you a portfolio. You know, my cousin Brian is a photographer. He's done some high-fashion stuff. I've seen some of his work, and he's really very good."

"Really? Which cousin is that?"

"Debbie's brother, Brian. You know he's always had the hots for you."

"Brian? You mean I have to give him some to get him to take some pictures? No way." Topaz crossed her arms in defiance.

"Girl, nobody said you had to give up anything, except the opportunity for Brian to photograph your body."

"I don't know, Keisha. What if he tried something?"

"He's not going to try anything. Besides, I'll be there, too. He's not crazy."

"Okay. Let's call him when we get to my house and see what he says."

Keisha hung up the phone and looked into Topaz's amber eyes. "He said he'd do it . . ."

"Yes," Topaz shouted, cutting her off.

"He said he'd do it for three hundred dollars."

"Three hundred dollars? Where am I going to get three hundred dollars?" Topaz wailed, wringing her hands in desperation.

"From the same place you always get it." Keisha calmly inspected her French manicure. "Germain."

"Germain just gave me money tonight."

"And he'll give you money tomorrow. Brian said to be at the studio at nine tomorrow morning. I'll pick you up. Bring lots of clothes. See ya."

Topaz absentmindedly watched her friend get into the car before she closed the front door. I've just got to get that money from Germain. She picked up the phone and dialed his pager number. Moments later, the phone rang. That's Germain. Topaz took a deep breath and picked up the phone.

"Hi, pretty girl. What's up?"

"Nothin' much. Germain, I need three hundred dollars," she pleaded in her sweetest voice.

"Three hundred? What happened? Did you see some fabulous dress at the mall that you've just got to have?"

"Well, I did see this fine Donna Karan dress in Saks but I need the money for something else. I met this photographer at the mall and he wants me to do a shoot for *Mademoiselle*. I need a portfolio to go on the interview."

"Are you sure this guy's for real and not some pervert trying to get you alone with a camera?"

"Oh, no, Germain. He really is a photographer. He works for a lot of different magazines and he's on his way home from the Caribbean. He's just passing through Atlanta."

"Okay, we'll talk about this later. I have to get back to the lab."

Topaz was on the verge of tears. "But I have to take the pictures in the morning, Germain," she wailed. "Can't you bring the money by in the morning on your way home from work?"

"I'll see what I can do, Topaz. I've got to get back to work now."

She hung up the phone slowly. He called me Topaz. He never calls me Topaz unless he's mad. He's not going to give me the money. Now what am I going to do?

But when she heard the doorbell ring at seven-thirty the next morning, she knew he had come through for her as usual.

"Hi, pretty girl." He greeted her wearily with a kiss. "Here's the money." He handed her fifteen crisp twenty-dollar bills.

"Oh, thank you, baby. Thank you." She squealed with delight and covered his face with kisses.

"I'm tired, baby." He yawned. "I've got to go home and get some rest."

"Okay. I'll call you later and tell you everything."

"Maybe I could come by the studio later after I get some sleep."

"No, I don't think that would be a good idea." She twisted her pretty face into a frown. I've got to handle Brian and I don't think Germain should be there. "Keisha will be with me. The photographer is her cousin. I've got to go get ready. I'll see you later, sweetie. You go home and get some rest." She practically pushed him out of the door. "I love you." She waved good-bye and blew kisses.

Topaz tore up the stairs to her room and threw open the closet door. "What do I take?" she asked herself out loud. She quickly flipped through several issues of *Vogue* and *Elle* and studied the photographs of the models. Then she selected evening gowns, sportswear, her new red dress, and a couple of bathing suits. She borrowed her mother's makeup case and raided her jewelry box.

She had just slipped on her favorite pair of Guess jeans when she heard the doorbell. That's Keisha. She zipped up the garment bag of clothing. "I'll be right there," she yelled out of the window.

"Did Germain give you the money?"

"My baby loves me." Topaz flashed a dazzling smile and waved her stack of bills in front of Keisha's face. "I just love the smell of fresh money." She laughed as she sniffed the bills.

"That brother's got it bad, real bad."

Minutes later, Keisha stopped the car in front of a well-kept three-story warehouse. "This is it." Before they could get out of the car, Brian, a handsome honey-colored young man who looked nothing like his sister Debbie, was opening the front door of the studio.

"Good morning, ladies." Topaz saw him zoom in on her right away but she pretended not to notice.

"Hi, Brian. Want to help me with my things? This garment bag is pretty heavy." Topaz was so sweet she was sickening. She saw Keisha give her a look of disgust and tried not to laugh. Brian dashed to the car and grabbed her things before she could say another word.

"I'll put these in the dressing room for you."

"Thanks, babe."

"Oh, gosh." Keisha looked nauseated. " 'Thanks, babe'? You sure are laying it on thick."

"I want some great photos. And I'm going to be very nice to Brian so that I get them."

Brian worked feverishly all day, and by early evening he called it quits. "I've got some great stuff here. You're a natural in front of the camera, Topaz. You should do well in New York."

"Do you really think so, Brian?"

"Definitely. I'll get you some contact sheets to look at tomorrow, but you'll have to choose your photos right away. I'll rush these over to the lab now." Brian held up a plastic bag with twelve canisters of film.

"Thanks, Brian." Topaz was using her sugary sweet voice again. "I can't wait to see everything."

"Me, too. And I get to use whatever I like for my window display."

Topaz phoned Mick, the photographer, the first thing the next morning. "Mick Edinburgh." She spoke through her nose in a thick, New Jersey accent. "This is Aida Foxx, from Images. We represent Topaz."

"Oh, yes, Topaz. I'd like to take a look at her portfolio. I might be able to use her for a shoot with *Mademoiselle*."

"That sounds fabulous. I can have her meet with you on Saturday." Topaz's Jersey accent was perfect.

"Have her meet me in the cafe at my hotel Saturday morning at eleven. I'm staying at the Ritz Carlton."

"She'll be there." Topaz hung up the phone and screamed. "I did it. Now all I have to do is have some fantastic pictures."

It was Friday evening before Brian phoned.

"What happened?" Topaz snapped. "You were supposed to be here two days ago. My appointment is tomorrow morning."

"Just chill, baby girl. Everything's under control. Go out and buy yourself a portfolio case. I'll be by your house at nine in the morning."

Germain insisted on taking her to the interview. Topaz watched him sleeping in her bed while she waited for Brian. "Brian better not mess this up for me." She paced back and forth in front of the bed until she heard the doorbell ring.

"Morning, beautiful," Brian sang. "Where's that portfolio

case?" Topaz said nothing but her amber eyes were like daggers when she handed him the case. She relaxed as she watched him slide photographs under the protective plastic sheets. "There you are." He proudly handed her the black case. "One portfolio."

Topaz's fingers barely worked as she unzipped the case. She paused for a moment before flipping it open. The first thing she saw was a wonderful photo of her in the red knit dress. She had been dancing when he shot it. This is absolutely wonderful. She turned page after page. "Brian, these are absolutely wonderful," she whispered, midway through the book. He had blown up over two dozen photos.

"I knew you'd like them," he replied with the utmost confidence. "There were so many to choose from. I knew you'd never be able to make up your mind, so I chose them for you. I hope you don't mind."

"Brian, they're fabulous. Thank you so much."

"Topaz, that was a thousand-dollar session, easily. But Keisha told me to cut you a deal and it was a pleasure to work with such a gorgeous model."

"Thanks, Brian. I'll let you know how everything goes." Now that she had what she needed she practically pushed him out the door.

"Germain," Topaz yelled. She ran up the stairs to her bedroom. "Wake up and see my portfolio." She was ecstatic when she placed it in front of him. He sat up in the bed and leaned on one arm, flipping through the book.

"These are nice, baby. Real nice."

"Nice? They're incredible. Come on, we have to go."

At eleven o'clock on the dot she sat down at a table in the hotel cafe and calmly handed Mick her portfolio. She pretended to be aloof as she sipped on a diet Coke and watched a waitress pass by with plates of fluffy scrambled eggs, bacon, and waffles.

"Gorgeous," Mick chanted breathlessly as he viewed each photo. "Absolutely gorgeous." Topaz held her composure but her heart was racing. Finally, he snapped the big black book closed and looked at her with admiration. "You're a knockout. You've got the job."

"Thanks," she replied coolly, wanting to scream.

"It's a three-day shoot in Manhattan. You'll be paid a thousand dollars a day and we'll cover all your expenses."

Three thousand dollars! Her head was spinning with thoughts of New York and the shopping spree she'd go on with all that money. "I'll phone you on Monday with your flight information," Mick continued. "You'll leave for New York on Tuesday. I'll see you bright and early Wednesday morning."

Germain was waiting outside in his mother's Mercedes. "I got the job," she yelled across the parking lot. "I got the job!"

"I'm happy for you, baby." He kissed her passionately. He was wide awake now. Topaz cuddled into his arms and sighed. "My sweet pretty girl. This calls for a celebration."

He drove to their favorite Chinese restaurant and ordered them a magnificent lunch—chicken with spinach, fried shrimp in a delectable sweet and spicy sauce, lobster fried rice, and lightly steamed Chinese vegetables. Topaz chatted all through lunch about the shoot and New York City.

Back at his house, Germain placed the remains of their Chinese feast in the refrigerator and pulled out a bottle of Cristal that had been chilling. "I bought this earlier because I knew we'd be celebrating." Topaz rewarded him with a luscious kiss. "Okay, pretty baby, let's go to my room quick before I do you in the kitchen."

Topaz giggled as he poured the champagne into two Baccarat flutes. Germain's mother had impeccable taste and the entire house attested to his parents' lavish income. "Germain," she whispered in his ear, "let's do it." She felt her passion ignite as she watched him sip his champagne.

"Okay, come on." He took her hand and started to walk out of the kitchen in the direction of his bedroom.

"No, Germain, let's do it here, in the kitchen." He laughed out loud and pulled her into his arms. This is the most exciting, beautiful woman I have ever known. No one was at home and no one would be home for a long time. His parents were in Jamaica and this was the maid's day off.

"Okay, baby." Unable to refuse her, he felt himself grow weak the moment her hands touched his body. They made love all over the house that day, ending up in his mother's pink Jacuzzi bathtub in her private bathroom.

Topaz loved the dusty-rose marble flecked with gold, the golden fixtures, the plush pink, mauve, and gold velour towels, the flagons of exotic bath oils, and the crystal apothecary jars filled with bath salts. She glanced up at the small crystal chandelier suspended over the tub and sighed with pleasure as she leaned back into Germain's strong honey-bronzed arms, hypnotized by the warm, spurting scented water.

She turned around to look into his face and saw that his eyes were closed. He looks so peaceful. I wonder if he's asleep. My friends call him a pretty boy. He is. She ran her hand through his wavy hair and kissed him gently on the lips before leaning back into his arms.

Germain's gonna build me a big house with a bathroom just like this, except I'll be able to swim in my Jacuzzi tub. She wiggled her toes in the water and smiled. I'm going to be a famous model, just like Iman. I'll make lots of money and own lots of beautiful clothes. I'll have a closet full of Donna Karan dresses.

There's only one thing, she reasoned, sitting up straight in the bathtub. I'm not going to Howard. I can't. I have a modeling career now. She turned around to look at Germain. His eyes were still closed and he seemed so content. There's just one problem . . . how do I tell Germain?

NINE

"SOME OF my dad's biggest deals were closed on the golf course." Pete pulled out a left-handed putter from a burgundy leather golf bag, which sported his monogram in gold. Gunther casually eyed the bag of shiny irons before he switched his attention to Pete and the nine-foot strip of artificial turf spread out on the floor of their dormitory room. Pete placed a dime on the green and carefully balanced a golf ball on top of it.

"He closed several major deals in Maui, Cancún, and the Virgin Islands over the summer." Pete putted the ball into a Styrofoam cup, retrieved the ball, and replaced it on the dime. "The entire family spent a month at our house in St. Croix and I went with my dad to Hawaii and Mexico. I had a great summer. I golfed and surfed the entire time." He picked up the ball and brushed a tuft of sun-streaked blond hair out of his face.

Pete looks great, Gunther thought for the thousandth time. He had been admiring Pete's swarthy tropical tan from the moment he laid eyes on him. Pete's as dark as I am. Gunther glanced at his cappuccino face in the mirror. His slanted eyes gave him an Asian look, but the healthy sprinkling of freckles across his nose and his reddish-brown kinky hair were definitely African-American. I wonder how Pete got that dark. I should ask him, but I can't. Imagine me asking a white boy how he got so dark. Gunther laughed to himself. That'll be the day.

"I've been playing golf with my dad since I was six." Pete wiped down the iron with a clean white cloth and returned it to the bag of Ping clubs. "I got these for our trip to the Virgin Islands. Tomorrow I'm going to play at the country club. I'll play several times a week until it's too cold to play anymore so I can keep my game up. I have a nine handicap and I can almost beat my dad."

What's a handicap? Gunther wondered, too proud to ask.

"We're going to Palm Beach and back to St. Croix for Christmas. I'll be ready for him then," Pete finished, with a determined look on his face. "Do you play, Gunther?" Pete fixed his cobalt blue eyes on Gunther.

"No . . . I've never played," Gunther slowly admitted. He smiled, but inside he was seething because this was one more thing this white boy had over him. "But I'd like to learn."

"Great." Pete gave him a wide, boyish grin. "I'll teach you. I'll even give you a set of my old clubs. You're a southpaw, too. I'll get my mom to ship them right away."

"Thanks, Pete." Gunther's gratitude was sincere. "Thanks a lot, dude. You're the best."

"No problem. We'll have fun. And you never know when you'll have to close that million-dollar deal on the golf course. Well, I've got a calculus class." Pete tossed his textbook and notepad into a leather briefcase. "Another gift from my dad," he offered, patting the briefcase. "He thought it was time for me to get rid of that old backpack. I'll catch you later, dude." Gunther waited until Pete left the room before he inspected the clubs. He counted fourteen of them, and they were various sizes and shapes. He recognized the putter, slid it out of the bag, and swung it back and forth. He liked the sound it made as it cut through the air.

"Yeah, Pete, teach me how to play golf so I can put together a million-dollar deal," Gunther whispered, angry and envious of Pete's wealth.

Several days later the golf clubs arrived. Gunther was disappointed when he realized they weren't Pings and they had definitely seen better days. White people's hand-me-downs.

"Thanks for the clubs, Pete," Gunther smiled at his friend. "I can't wait to try them out."

It was a glittering, brisk Saturday morning when the boys arrived at the local country club. Pete signed them up for nine holes and then he took Gunther out on the driving range. "I'll show you how to use each club and then I'll teach you how to drive."

"Oh, I already know about the clubs." Gunther had borrowed a book from the library and memorized the name and use for each club. *I can't come across like a complete idiot.* He pulled out the driver from his bag of clubs. "Let's hit some balls, dude." He grinned and swung the putter at a pretend ball.

Pete returned his smile. "Way to go, Gunther."

Gunther worked hard, but he knew he'd have to work overtime before he would be able to beat Pete. He's good, Gunther reluctantly admitted. Real good. But then Pete was always good at everything. His strokes were clean, smooth, and powerful. Pete would complete many of the holes under par.

"You did real well your first time out." Pete wheeled the golf cart up to the curb in front of the clubhouse and stopped. "Your strokes are smooth and strong. You're going to have a real nice game, Gunther."

For Thanksgiving vacation Gunther went with Pete to his family's house in New York. Mrs. Wingate picked them up at Grand Central Terminal in her black Mercedes station wagon the day before Thanksgiving.

"Mom, this is Gunther." Pete slapped his buddy on the back. "Gunther, my mom, Mrs. Wingate."

"Well, Gunther, I've certainly heard a lot about you for the last year." Mrs. Wingate's voice was warm and gracious. She reached for Gunther's hand as she continued speaking. "I'm very pleased to meet you and I'm glad you'll be joining us for Thanksgiving. I understand this is your first trip to New York City."

"Yes, Mrs. Wingate, it is. Thank you for having me." Gunther looked into a pair of cobalt blue eyes identical to Pete's. She was a petite lady and a very attractive brunette with Pete's handsome smile. She was wearing an Anne Klein pantsuit and she reeked of money.

"Well, don't dawdle, boys, let's get going." Her cobalt eyes sparkled with excitement. "I still have to prepare the Thanksgiving dinner menu, and we won't mention the Christmas party on Friday."

Gunther felt like his head was on a swivel as he turned in every direction in order to see as much of the city as he could.

"There's Rockefeller Center," Mrs. Wingate informed him as they drove by.

"And that's the Plaza." Pete pointed out a ritzy hotel. Gunther just stared out the car window, speechless, enthralled by every speck of the city. Minutes later, Mrs. Wingate parked in front of a six-story brownstone directly across the street from Central Park.

"Home, sweet home." Pete was already out of the car.

Gunther hopped out behind him and lugged his garment bag up the stairs behind Pete and his mom. This is a nice apartment building. I know the Wingates live on the top floor. When he stepped inside the brownstone he was standing in the most splendid foyer he had ever seen.

The entryway, paved in charcoal marble, housed a curio cabinet filled with a collection of porcelain figurines. The walls in the house were done in designer wallpapers—deep forest green, ecru, and mauve. Gleaming hardwood floors flaunted colorful Chinese rugs. Fine antique pieces furnished the rooms. Priceless paintings, sculptures, and vases of fresh-cut flowers were in every room. A Steinway grand piano had its own special place in the sitting room, and a crystal teardrop chandelier hung graciously above a dining room table for twelve. Gunther had to remember to keep his mouth closed.

"Come on, dude, my room's upstairs." Pete tugged on Gunther's arm and pulled him toward the stairs. "I'll give you a tour of the house."

House? The Wingates live in the entire building, Gunther realized as he sprinted the stairs behind Pete.

The first level was actually the basement. It contained the laundry, kitchen, and maid's quarters. The boys had entered the brownstone from the second level, where the living room, dining room, parlor, and library were located. The family room and two guest bedrooms were above it. Pete's bedroom and bath and two other bedrooms with bathrooms were on the fourth level. An exercise room, another sitting room, and Mr. Wingate's office were on the fifth level. His parents' suite occupied the entire top floor. Their suite included a sitting room with fireplace, two private baths, and a sauna.

This is the most beautiful house I've ever seen, Gunther marveled. It's like a miniature palace. This is even better than the pictures in Rita's *Architectural Digests*. Someday, he solemnly vowed, making mental notes of every nook and cranny. Someday I'm going to have a house just as fine as this.

Dinner at the Wingates was served in the dining room promptly at seven. Mr. Wingate was present, as well as Pete's younger sister, Jennifer, and his older brother, Skip.

"Skip's home from the Wharton School of Business and Jen attends the school of the arts. You know the one in *Fame*?" Pete explained. "Skip's replacing my uncle in the finance division of our bank when he retires in June. Jen's the delinquent in the family. She's going to Paris to model."

"I am not," she protested. "I'm going to take a year off before college and study art history and French."

"And chase rich young eligibles around the French Riviera." Skip laughed.

"Daddy, make them stop teasing me," Jennifer begged. "They'll have Gunther thinking I'm an awful person." She smiled warmly at Gunther, who returned her smile.

Gunther took several tiny sips from his glass of ice water. Jennifer was gorgeous and she was making him nervous. He had been admiring her ever since she sat down at the dinner table. She had the same cobalt blue eyes and dazzling smile as her mother, but she was tall and blonde like her father and Pete. I'd sure like to chase her around the Riviera.

A maid, wearing the customary black dress and starched white apron, served Gunther a plate of rare roast beef, mashed potatoes, and green peas. Wow, just like in a restaurant. And I thought the Brady Bunch had it good.

Thanksgiving Day dinner was quiet, with just the immediate family and a few friends. The family dressed for an afternoon sit-down dinner at which Gunther and Pete stuffed themselves with roast turkey, oyster dressing, scalloped potatoes, broccoli timbale, and plenty of pumpkin pie and chocolate torte. The boys spent the rest of the day in the family room, watching football games and videos on the big-screen television.

The day after Thanksgiving, the family gave its annual Christmas party. The party had been a tradition in the Wingate family for decades. By the time the boys returned from sightseeing and lunch at 21, the house had been transformed into a yuletide extravaganza. A fifteen-foot Christmas tree had been bought and professionally decorated. It was displayed in a window in the parlor, creating an excellent backdrop for the piano. A staff of caterers had taken over the kitchen. They were preparing a buffet of various pastas; a salad of spinach, opal, basil, and endive; linguini chinoise; lemon-garlic salmon; and ragout of veal.

Mr. Wingate's business associates, members from Mrs. Wingate's various charities, and a host of relatives and friends mingled throughout the second floor of the house. Waiters in black tuxedos offered trays of scallops wrapped in prosciutto, shrimp cocktail, caviar, and sparkling flutes of champagne. A hired pianist tinkled the keys, filling the room with the perfect Christmas sound track. It was a wonderful holiday party.

Gunther and Pete, dressed in their best suits, circulated throughout the living room with flutes of champagne, feeling very grown up. Gunther tried every appetizer offered to him. He almost gagged on the caviar, but he managed to keep a straight face after he used the last of his champagne as a chaser to wash the salty taste from his mouth. That stuff is nasty, he discovered, helping himself to another skewer of scallops and more champagne.

"Gunther, this is Nick Manning, television director and producer extraordinaire. Uncle Nicky, this is Gunther Lawrence, Petey's roommate from school." Jennifer flashed a dazzling smile at them both.

Gunther was in awe. He swallowed a scallop and remembered to extend his hand. "I'm very pleased to meet you, Mr. Manning. I love all of your shows." Gunther pumped the man's hand a few times and then turned his attention to Jennifer. "Jen, I must say you're looking fabulous tonight," he remarked, using his best New York accent.

She was striking in a black alex jersey evening dress that clung gently to her sleek figure. A gold heart encased with perfect little diamonds accentuated her slender neck.

"Gunther, you certainly do have remarkable taste in women," Nick confessed. "Jennifer is my goddaughter and I'm very proud of her."

"Thanks, Uncle Nicky." Jennifer planted a kiss on his cheek. "I'll leave you two to talk. Petey tells me Gunther is absolutely fabulous with a camera." She smiled the Wingate smile and floated off among the guests.

"Is that so?" Nick asked, focusing on Gunther.

"I've done several short sixteen-millimeter films. I did everything, including all the editing and music. My instructor said they were excellent pieces." Gunther's feigned accent was perfect.

The producer plucked a cracker covered with caviar from a tray of appetizers. "That's wonderful, Gunther. Are you considering a career in film?"

A career in film . . . a career in film. I love movies and I love making films and I can definitely make some cash as a director. Why didn't I think of that? "Yes," Gunther lied. He was delighted with his newfound discovery. "I think about it all the time. I've even got an application in at NYU."

"NYU . . . I believe Spike Lee studied there. Good school. But I'm a USC man myself. Like Spielberg and Lucas."

"Spielberg and Lucas." Gunther sighed in awe. "They're incredible filmmakers. I just love the *Star Wars* and *Raiders of the Lost Ark* serials. Lucas's special effects were awesome."

"Are you interested in television or film? You know, they're as different as night and day."

"That's true. But I'm going to do film. Feature film. I've got loads of ideas."

"Any particular genre?"

"Mystery, suspense . . . intrigue." Gunther was getting so excited about his new career he thought he would explode.

Nick chuckled. "You've definitely been bitten by the bug. I look forward to seeing some of your work, Mr. Lawrence. I wish you lots of luck."

"Thank you, Mr. Manning." Gunther pumped his hand. "It was a real pleasure meeting you," he finished in a slightly imperfect East Coast accent. A film director. Gunther smiled his biggest smile as Nick wandered off among the guests. "I'm going to be great," he whispered to himself. "Absolutely great."

Once the Christmas holidays were over, Gunther and Pete took turns marking the days off the calendar. They were counting the days until April. The advanced French class was going to spend four weeks in Paris, taking classes in French at the Sorbonne.

"Paris is magical in April," their teacher had told them.

Gunther could hardly wait for the American Airlines 747 to touch down at Charles de Gaulle Airport. A shuttle bus was waiting to take the group of thirty students to the Hotel Agora St. Germain once they cleared customs. Despite jet lag, Gunther wasn't the least bit tired when he saw the city's ornate mansions and picture-perfect gardens on famous boulevards lined with trees.

The hotel was in walking distance of the Sorbonne, where

Gunther took classes in French literature and cinema. Every morning Gunther, Pete, and several other classmates would stop at one of the nearby outdoor cafes for coffee with hot, frothy milk, fresh croissants, and fruit. There were pinball machines in every cafe and the guys flipped and tipped the silver balls until they had to run all the way to class. Classes ended by early afternoon, which left plenty of free time until evening check-in at the hotel. Gunther and Pete went exploring every afternoon. They took the Metro everywhere. Gunther would never forget the Luxembourg Gardens with the fountains, ponds, flowerbeds, and outdoor concerts, or the Louvre, a palace filled with fabulous art collections. Gunther liked the paintings best. He had a deeper appreciation for the French Impressionists after he had strolled down carefully raked gravel lanes in majestic French gardens where nannies pushed babies in magnificent carriages.

Gunther also loved the ritzy Left Bank with its high-fashion design houses, decadent restaurants, and opulent hotels; however, he treasured the Latin Quarter the most. It was his home in Paris, and he could find his way through it blindfolded. Every afternoon the students gathered at the Fontaine St. Michel when school ended. The assembly was like a small United Nations gathering. They would stand there chattering in a dozen languages, reading books, strumming guitars, blasting radios, or kissing and hugging.

"There's a gospel concert tonight, Pete. Want to go?" Gunther announced. The boys were planning an evening out.

"A gospel concert in Paris? That sounds great, dude. Where is it?"

"I don't know. They have flyers in the Librairie Presence Africaine on rue des Écoles," Gunther rattled off in French, referring to the African bookstore.

"Great. We'll go by there on the way to dinner. I'm in the mood for some shish kebab and baklava." Pete smacked his lips in anticipation of the savory Mediterranean food. "Let's go to the bookstore now so we can have time to browse." The bookstore was an authority on African cultures throughout the world.

"This collection of magazines is fantastic." Pete stopped to investigate a collection of Third World periodicals from Caribbean and African countries. "They even have American magazines." He held up a copy of *Jet*.

"They're supposed to have material from everywhere." Gunther was absorbed in a book of Senegalese short stories when he was interrupted.

"Is there anything in particular you'd like to see?" he heard an accented female voice ask in English.

"No, thank you." Gunther glanced up from his book. A young woman was smiling at him. Waist-length locks of tawny hair framed an exquisite face with green eyes, a delicate nose, splendid full lips, and an olive brown complexion.

Gunther swallowed hard as he felt his heart begin to race. She's beautiful. Absolutely beautiful. I've never seen anyone as beautiful as her. "Hi, I'm Gunther Lawrence," he heard himself say.

"Je suis Aria. Aria Versailles. Let me know if you need anything."

Need anything? I need to know everything about you, he answered in his head. "I will, thank you." Gunther smiled.

Pete walked up just as Aria was about to walk away. "Hello," he called, greeting her with his best smile.

"Hello. I'll be in the front if you require any assistance."

"Who was that?" Pete demanded once she was out of hearing distance.

"Aria Versailles."

"Aria's gorgeous. Did you ask her out? Because if you don't I sure will."

Gunther's mouth dropped open in surprise. Park Avenue Pete asking out a sister? I know she isn't American, but she definitely has African blood, and there's no way I'm letting him get her.

"Well?" Pete demanded.

"Pete, you're crazy." Gunther picked up the stack of books he had been reading and rushed to the checkout counter. "I'll take these, Aria." He placed the books on the counter and gave her his best smile.

"You're from America."

"Yes, Los Angeles, California."

"I've been to New York." Aria placed the books in a bag.

"Where are you from?"

"Rio. I'm attending the Sorbonne."

"I am, too," Gunther told her, pleased because he had something in common with this stunning young Brazilian woman. He spotted Pete walking up to the counter. "Would you like to have dinner with me?" he blurted out.

"Tonight?"

"Yes. And we could go to a gospel concert afterwards." Gunther sucked in his breath. This is the first time I ever asked a girl out, he realized.

Aria looked at her watch. "If you can wait until the bookstore closes in thirty minutes, I'd be glad to join you."

"Great," said Pete, jumping into the conversation. "We'll just hang out until you're ready. Oh, by the way, I'm Gunther's roommate and best buddy, Pete." He flashed the famous Wingate smile and Gunther thought he saw Aria blush.

"Bien. This will be fun." Aria's beautiful smile lit up her entire face.

He's really serious about this, Gunther realized, becoming more perturbed by the minute. I can't believe him, trying to date a sister.

The boys usually took the train everywhere, but this time Pete hailed a cab to take them to the restaurant. Show off, Gunther thought to himself. Pete chatted in French with Aria all the way there. At the restaurant Gunther watched him slip the maitre d' a bill that got them the best table in the restaurant.

"Order anything you like, Aria." Pete was at his charming best. "You, too, Gunther. My treat." Pete ordered salad, shish kebabs, buttered rice, pita bread, and champagne in more perfect French.

Gunther was so angry he could have spit knives. "What are you studying at the university, Aria?" he finally asked.

"I'm a history major, but I intend to study law at Oxford," Aria informed him as she smiled at Pete.

"That's impressive." Pete sipped his glass of champagne. "Have you ever thought of attending school in the States? I'm going to Harvard. They've got a great law school."

"Harvard? Oh, yes. That's a wonderful school. I'd love to attend Harvard."

"You know, you could attend Harvard for undergrad."

Now he's trying to get her to go to his school. Give me a break, Gunther wanted to shout.

"Where will you be attending college, Gunther?" Aria asked.

"The University of Southern California." How nice of you to let me join in the conversation, he thought.

"Gunther's going to be the next Steven Spielberg. He's been accepted to the illustrious School of Cinema." Pete grinned at Gunther, proud of his friend's accomplishment.

"That's right," Gunther bragged, sticking out his chest. "You'll definitely see me at the Academy Awards picking up all the honors." He hoped he was gaining some type of advantage with Aria, who was busy smiling into Pete's baby blues and ignoring him. I hate him. No I don't. I can't hate Pete. He's my best friend, the only real friend I've ever had. He can't help if he was born good-looking, rich, and white.

Pete's whirlwind romance lasted the duration of their stay. He took Aria dancing at Regine's and La Place, to dinner at Maxim's and Taillevent. They strolled hand-in-hand along the Seine and even rented a car to drive to the country for a picnic one weekend.

"A month in Paris went by entirely too fast." Gunther carefully wrapped a Parisian sculpture. The boys were packing for the trip back to Massachusetts.

"I know." Pete was obviously sad.

"What are you going to do about Aria?" Gunther asked, glad because he knew Pete would finally have to leave her.

"I don't know. Write, phone, visit. I think I'm in love with her." Pete closed his suitcase and flopped on the bed.

Serves you right, Gunther thought, looking at Pete's unhappy face. You had no business dating a sister. He was glad their semester in Paris was ending.

Back at school there was no time for anything but studying for finals. Then graduation day, with all its festivities, was upon them. Charles, Charles Jr., and Marshall flew in especially for the big event. Rita penned her congratulations.

"Regrettably, I can't attend. I'm too tied up with work. Congratulations, Gunther. Mother's very proud of you." What else is new? He tore the note into tiny pieces and tossed them in the trash.

The day before graduation, the Wingates and the Lawrences had breakfast together at the local hotel where both families were staying. Gunther's father wouldn't talk, Charles Jr. knocked over a glass of orange juice, and Marshall put ketchup on his scrambled eggs. That's the last time I'll take them anywhere. Gunther tried his best to ignore them as he chatted graciously with the Wingates, using his best East Coast accent.

"Man, I don't see what the big deal is about this place," Charles Jr. commented after Gunther gave them a tour of the campus. "This is the boonies. I can't wait till I get back home."

I can't wait until you get back home, either, Gunther wanted to tell him.

Graduation was held outside on the lawn on a radiant, warm New England day. "Gunther Lawrence, magna cum laude," the headmaster announced. Gunther was so pleased he thought he would burst until he heard the headmaster call out, "Peter Wingate, summa cum laude."

Next time, he promised himself silently, forgetting that he was the only African-American in his class to graduate with honors.

"I'm very proud of you, Gunther," his father told him afterwards. "You made me real proud today, boy." Gunther noticed there were tears in the man's eyes as Charles held him tight.

That's the first time Pops ever hugged me, Gunther realized. They walked back to the dormitory together in silence.

"I know it's not much, Gunther, but I got you a car as a graduation present." He pressed a set of keys into Gunther's hand.

"Really, Pops?" Gunther stared at the VW keys in his hand and then at his father. He was genuinely excited. I can't believe Pops did something special for me. Maybe Pops really does care.

"Yes. Now it's just a little Volkswagen bug."

"Thanks, Pops. Now I won't have to catch the bus back and forth from USC."

Just as Gunther and his dad reached the entrance of the dormitory, Pete walked out of the dorm with his dad. They were carrying the last of Pete's things.

"Well, Gunther Lawrence, we're going to head back to the city before traffic gets bad." Gunther smiled and looked at the ground. "I guess this is it, dude." Pete smiled his handsome Wingate smile.

"Yeah, dude, it's been a lot of fun." Gunther extended his hand to Pete for a lack of anything better to do. He was unable to reveal his true emotions. Pete embraced him and suddenly Gunther felt like crying. It's over. And now it's time to go back home.

"If you're ever in the city, give me a holler." Pete unlocked the door of a spanking-new charcoal 318i BMW. "Graduation present from the family," he explained, waving at the car.

Gunther fingered the Volkswagen key in his hand and looked up just in time to wave as Pete tooted the horn and pulled out behind his father's 735i. He felt a tear squeeze out of his eye and brushed it away quickly.

"White people have everything," he muttered and walked back into the dorm.

TEN

UCLA's Pauley Pavilion was packed with Bruins fans. Sean could hear them stamp, hiss, and boo as the U Penn basketball team ran out on the court to warm up. He felt the muscles in his jawline grow taut and tiny beads of perspiration form around his hairline as he quickly glanced around the stands.

"Bruins fans everywhere," he whispered, taking a seat on the visitors' bench. He noticed a barrage of television cameras. "And major media coverage. Yes!" His handsome smile lit up his face. Prime Ticket, ESPN, and several Los Angeles stations were covering the game. Sean drained his water bottle and peeled off his sweats. He pretended not to notice Ty, who had flopped down on the bench next to him and sprawled his long legs out onto the court.

"This is UCLA, man. Let's kick some butt tonight," Ty whispered through clenched teeth. "Like old times."

"I'm down." Sean gave him a wide grin. He heard the opening lineup announced and sprang to his feet at the mention of his name. "Let's play ball," he shouted. He pranced eagerly onto the court and clapped his hands with anticipation.

The moment Sean hit the court, UCLA's guards were all over him. They were very aggressive players, constantly shoving and double-teaming him and attempting to block every shot. He knew they had been told by their coach to guard him carefully. These are some big dudes. Sean danced around them down center court and slam dunked. There, take that, he wanted to shout. You can't keep a good man down.

UCLA held a consistent three-point lead throughout the second half. Sean, drenched in perspiration, quickly glanced at Ty, the open man, before he dribbled twice and focused on the basket. Sorry, babe, I've got to go for it. He tossed in one of his magnificent three-pointers. He heard the crowd boo as he trotted back up the court for the Bruin's next layup.

"Weak." Sean snatched the ball from the hands of the UCLA point guard before he had a chance to pass it to the lofty center. I'm going to ruin these Bruins. He slammed the ball through the net.

"Ouch." He slapped a high five with Ty. I love this game. He flashed a smile at the gorgeous coffee-colored cheerleader with a body that begged to free itself from the confines of the short, tight cheerleader's outfit. Mmm, baby girl is too fine. He had been aware of her giving him the eye all evening.

Once again, as UCLA's point guard prepared to shoot, Ty stole the ball and hurled it across the court. Sean, positioned directly under the basket, caught it and was attempting to toss in one of his sweet hook shots when he felt his body crumple from the force of a Mack truck. A hefty Bruin guard shoved him so hard that he landed heavily, on his knees. The moment he hit the floor, he immediately felt pain shoot through his left knee.

"Oh, my God," he whispered. Tears welled up in his eyes. "This hurts." He clutched his knee to his chest and writhed in pain. "Oh, Jesus, help me." He sucked in his breath and rocked from side to side to keep himself from crying out. Tears forced themselves out of his eyes and down his cheeks. I've broken my knee, and I'll never be able to play again. Sean heard the sound of running footsteps and opened his eyes to see his teammates standing over him.

"Can you walk, Sylk?" Ty asked.

He reached up to clasp Ty's extended hand and winced at the pain. "Naw, man. I can't do it."

The medics, with a cot, broke through the small throng of spectators. "Just relax, fellow," one of them instructed as they lifted him up onto the cot. "You're going to be just fine."

Sean saw the concern in his teammates' faces as he was carried off the court. In the locker room a doctor was waiting. "All right, Sylk, let's straighten out that knee," the doctor commanded.

Sean yelled as soon as he felt the doctor touch his leg. "I can't, man, I can't." The tears continued to flow.

"Okay." The doctor fixed his eyes on Sean and continued speaking. "You're in a lot of pain." Sean nodded, watching him fill a hypodermic needle with a clear liquid from a small vial.

"Are you allergic to anything?"

"No," Sean whispered, barely able to speak because of the pain.

"Good. Just a shot of Demerol, son." Before Sean realized it, the doctor had given him an injection in his hip. Within minutes he felt the drug take over. The pain subsided, and he slowly straightened his leg. "Get him over to UCLA Medical Center. I'll need a full set of X rays on that knee," Sean heard the doctor command. He felt himself being wheeled out to the ambulance.

"You all right, man?" Ty demanded. "We won the game." Sean snapped his eyes open to find Ty trotting along beside the gurney. Unable to speak, Sean gave him a smile and grasped his hand firmly before closing his eyes again. My knee, he thought, before he floated into deep, unconscious slumber. How will I ever be able to play in the NBA? He was unable to concentrate on anyone or anything. The medicine was too strong. He just wanted to sleep.

Sean opened his eyes again when he felt the cold stainless steel of the X-ray table against his body. He silently watched the technician position the large plates of film for a series of exposures. I never wanted to pose for these kind of pictures.

"I really jammed myself up," he informed Ty and his coach, who were waiting for him when he returned to his bed in the emergency room. He felt a throbbing pain creep back into his knee. "Could I have another one of those shots?" he whispered to the attending nurse.

"You're going to be okay, man," Ty assured him. "Lots of players have knee injuries and they're still able to play."

"I sure hope so, Ty. But I'm in a lot of pain." Their light conversation faded into silence when the doctor entered Sean's room carrying his X rays.

"Hello, Sean, I'm Dr. Levine. I just had a look at your X rays."

Sean swallowed hard as he felt his body tense up. Somehow I know I don't want to hear this.

"You severely tore the cartilage around your knee and chipped the bone. We're going to have to go in to repair the damage."

He talks like he's going to fix a car, Sean thought, becoming annoyed. And he's talking about the rest of my life.

"It's a fairly easy procedure and with lots of physical therapy you should be back on the court in no time."

"How long are you talking about?" Sean demanded, his voice raspy from the medication.

"Anywhere from four to six months." Dr. Levine gave him a plastic smile.

"Four to six months? The season will be completely over by then," Sean hollered.

"You've got a lot of damage there, young man. You need time to heal."

"But I thought you said I'd be able to play again in no time at all?"

"It could be longer or not at all," the doctor continued. "It depends on how well the procedure goes and how quickly you recover. It's best that we get you into surgery as soon as possible. I can probably get you scheduled for surgery in a couple of days."

Surgery . . . Sean fought the urge to cry. My life is over. It's over. I'll never be able to play in the NBA. He sank back onto the small, hard hospital pillow.

"If Sean's able to travel, we'll return to Philadelphia tonight," Coach Dalton informed the doctor. "I know a doctor there who performs this type of surgery on the pros on a regular basis."

"He can travel. We'll wrap that knee and give him something for pain."

Sean remained silent during the entire flight back to Philly. I had to be taken on the plane in a wheelchair. Why is this happening to me? Everything I've worked so hard for has been taken away from me. I'm out of the game and now the pros probably won't want me since I damaged my knee. He flipped open a copy of *Sports Illustrated* to an article on the rising salaries in the NBA, skimmed it quickly and tossed it under the seat in front of him.

I need to talk to Daddy. He stared at the Airphone attached to the back of the seat in front of him. No. I can't call him now. I don't have any privacy. He pretended not to notice Ty watching him. Sean picked up a copy of *People*. He felt a twinge of pain in his knee and gulped down several tablets of Demerol with a swig of Evian. They work fine on my knee, but they can't even begin to ease the pain in my heart.

He was taken straight to the hospital from the airport. The surgery was performed the next morning. When he awakened, he saw his father sitting in a chair beside the bed reading his Bible.

"Daddy," he whispered, unable to restrain the deluge of tears that had been collecting for the past twenty-four hours. "Daddy," he sobbed. "It's all over. My career is finished."

"Son, where is your faith?" his father asked gently, closing his Bible. He carefully plucked several tissues from the box of Kleenex sitting on the nightstand and handed them to Sean. "The Lord has brought you this far. He won't let you down."

Sean cried even harder. "But I let Him down, Daddy, and now He's taken my career away."

"Sean, you know that God doesn't take things away. As for you letting Him down, God is still in the business of forgiveness. Everything happens for a reason. You just continue to trust Him."

"But why did this have to happen, Daddy, why? I may never be able to play pro ball now."

"I can't tell you why this happened, Sean. Our Heavenly Father uses the mountains and valleys in our lives to bring us closer to Him. Just focus on Jesus, son. Take some time to find out what He has to say."

"All right, Daddy, I will." He brushed a tear away. "And if the Lord ever gives me another chance to play basketball, I promise I won't let Him down again."

"I know you won't, son." Sean grasped his father's large, strong hand. "I spoke with your doctor, and he said the surgery went well and you should be able to play again. See, your Heavenly Father has been working already."

Kenneth Ross leaned over and kissed Sean on the top of his head. "I love you, son."

"I love you, too, Daddy. Thanks for being here with me," he whispered through his tears. "You always know how to make things better."

Sean pushed his marketing textbook aside and stared at the pair of crutches propped up in a corner beside his bed. "I messed up," he concluded. "I really messed up." It was a Saturday afternoon in late February. It had been almost four months since his accident. Ty was out of town with the team and the apartment was frightfully empty.

Ty sure turned out to be a real friend. Sean stared out of his bedroom at the dirty, frozen snow along the curb that refused to melt. He came to visit me every day when I was in the hospital. He worked out with me, made dinner or ordered out, and was a constant source of encouragement. Ty's been a better friend to me than I ever was to him. All those times when I took the shot instead of passing him the ball, the interviews I hogged, and the times I went to Dr. E's without him. Sean squeezed his eyes closed in an effort to erase all the painful memories that haunted him. Only during his rigorous workouts did the past vanish temporarily.

Sean spent lots of time alone now. His doctor had advised him not to drive, and unless one of his brothers offered to drive him around, he stayed in his room. Rhonda had visited him once in the hospital, but he didn't want her to play nursemaid to him now. It wouldn't be right and he had hurt her enough already. He stared at the telephone. He had picked it up a thousand times to call her. I don't know what else to say to her besides I'm sorry, and that's just not enough. He hadn't been able to face her since his interlude with Tatyana.

Tatyana . . . he fingered the gold chain around his neck. I never even said thank you. I never should have drunk that stupid champagne and I never should have allowed myself to get into a compromising situation with her. I almost lost my virginity.

He stared at the Bible on the night table beside his bed. I haven't read my Bible for months, he realized, picking it up. A layer of dust had collected on the cover. I haven't prayed very much, and I don't remember the last time I was in church . . . probably Christmas. The tears fell from his eyes one by one and then in steady streams.

I'm sorry, Lord, I'm sorry. I did so many wrong things, because I was the star. It wasn't worth it. It wasn't worth it. Nothing's worth losing my relationship with You. I just can't believe I treated everyone so badly.

Sean sat in silence and flipped through the pages of his Bible. He read an occasional psalm or proverb. Pride goes before destruction, and a haughty spirit before a fall.

"I was an awful person," he whispered. "I don't like the person I was becoming. That wasn't me. I don't know who that was. Daddy was right. You were definitely trying to tell me something." He sighed deeply. "I know You've forgiven me, Lord, now please help me to forgive myself. And if You just give me another chance, I promise I won't let You down again." He closed his eyes and slept peacefully for the first time in months.

It was the end of March when Sean rejoined the team. His knee had finally healed. U Penn had made it to the Final Four, the last stage of the NCAA playoffs, without him. The NBA teams were nearing their playoff season, and the June draft was quickly approaching.

It feels good to be back, even though Coach isn't letting me play. Sean suited up for every game, but his coach only allowed him to play a few minutes before he pulled him out. The team was winning without him, and although Sean's doctor had given him the okay his coach felt he should stay off his leg.

Sean played well during the few minutes he played, but the media was more interested in Ty now. He had really sparkled during Sean's absence from the team. It's amazing how they love you one minute and hate you the next, Sean realized as Chuck Zimmerman from ESPN practically knocked him down after a game one night in order to get to Ty, who was named MVP. Absolutely amazing.

Within days of the NBA playoffs ending, Ty was chosen second during the first round of the NBA draft to play for the Philadelphia 76ers. "They're starting the negotiations at a million dollars," Ty shouted into the phone from his hotel room in New York City where the NBA draft was held. Ty's parents had even flown in from Cleveland.

"Congratulations, man," Sean yelled back into the phone. "I'm really happy for you."

"We're celebrating at Hard Rock Cafe. Why don't you and your brothers meet us there?"

"No, thanks, man. I've got to study for finals. But you have a great time."

"I'm in the house, Sylk, the NBA house," Ty yelled before he hung up.

"Yeah, man, you're in the house. Congratulations." Sean was genuinely happy for Ty despite his own disappointment. His knee injury had placed him at the bottom of the third round draft list. He had very little chance of being selected.

Several days passed with no phone calls, so Sean finally called his agent. "Hey, George. This is Sean Ross. I just called to see how things were going and if you'd heard anything from any of the teams yet."

"I'm sorry, Sean, but I don't have good news. Everyone's afraid to take a chance on you since you busted your knee. I tried to convince them that you were better than new, but they just aren't interested now."

"They don't want me?" Sean couldn't believe what he was hearing.

"No, Sean, I'm sorry. You got a tough break, kid. I'll see what I can work out for you with one of the European teams."

"Europe?" Sean repeated with very little enthusiasm. "I don't want to go to Europe. I want to play here in the NBA."

"Europe," George replied firmly. "You can try out as a free agent for a couple of the teams here, but I wouldn't advise it. Not enough money. I say we get you playing in Europe and the league will be begging to get you back here."

A European team . . . Oh, no. "Okay, George, thanks for everything." Sean hung up the phone slowly. It's over. My basketball career is actually over. "It was a good thing I did choose U Penn." He laughed, trying to cheer himself up. "I did get a nice job offer in marketing from IBM."

Graduation long over, Sean was packing up his things. He was moving back home for a while. Ty was moving downstairs into a one-bedroom apartment. Sean had just placed the last book in the box when he heard a knock at the door. Daddy and the twins are finally here to help me move my things. When he opened the door, he was surprised to see his coach.

"Sylk, I received a very interesting phone call this morning."

"What's up, Coach? Need me to coach one of those inner-city basketball clinics this summer?" Sean asked, hoping that someone would solicit his athletic skills.

"No, Sylk. It's nothing like that."

"Oh." Sean tried to conceal his disappointment. I can't even get a job coaching kids now.

"There's a new team in New York, the Concordes. They've only been in the NBA for two years. No one's given them much thought because they're so new in the league and they haven't won many games," his coach expounded.

"I know the Concordes. Everyone thinks they're a joke."

"That's the team. Their coach thought you had been signed by the Knicks."

"Now that's a joke." Sean laughed.

"I kind of told them that, but not in those exact words." He smiled at Sean before he continued speaking. "They want you to try out for the team as a free agent."

"The Concordes want me for a tryout?" Sean shouted.

"Yes, they're looking for a strong point guard. I know they're not one of the hottest teams in the NBA, but you can put them on the map. And they need a star. You can really help them, Sylk. Look what you did for us. So what do you think? Are you interested?"

"Coach, forget being a star. Of course I'm interested. I'm interested in anyone who's interested in me." He sensed an excitement that he hadn't felt for months permeating his lean body. "When's the tryout?"

"Sometime next month. I have to call them back for all the details. I wanted to check with you first. I'll give them a call and have them get in touch with your agent. Meanwhile, you get down to the gym and practice those hook shots and jumpers you do so well."

"You got it, Coach." Sean said, laughing. "I'll practice all day and night."

Sean was scheduled to attend the team's camp in Virginia Beach for two weeks in July. His father and Kyle went with him for moral support. He was so pumped up he thought he would explode by the time they arrived in Virginia. He played with the Concordes in daily scrimmages for the entire two weeks. Sean met free agents from all over the country and some of them played exceptionally well.

"I never saw so many great players on the same court," he had told his father and Kyle after the first day of tryouts. Sean sank countless jumpers, tossed in hook shots, scored rebounds, and stole the ball every chance he got.

On the last day of camp, Sean's father and Kyle returned to Virginia. They drove Sean back to the Founders Inn in silence.

"I did my best, Daddy," Sean finally confessed. "I even had my first triple double. But there were so many great players."

"I know you played extremely well, son," his father assured him. "You're a great player."

"Thanks, Daddy. But this tryout was the first time I've really played since the injury. It's taking longer than I thought to get my rhythm back."

"Aw, Sean, you know you got it goin' on," Kyle encouraged. "Even if your rhythm was off you still played circles around everyone else. And I'm not saying this because you're my brother, but can't nobody play like you. You are basketball."

"Thanks, Kyle." Sean smiled fondly at his older brother. Sean and the twins had always shared a special bond. They were not only brothers, but best friends.

"I'm glad we decided to stay overnight," his father declared in the hotel parking lot. "I'm not ready to drive back to Philly after all this excitement."

"I know," Kyle agreed. "You'd think that we tried out for the Concordes. I just want to order room service and chill out."

"Yeah." Sean laughed. "A steak and french fries sounds real good to me."

The phone was ringing when they entered the hotel room. "I know that's your mother calling to check on her men." The boys' father smiled.

Kyle picked up the phone and handed it to his brother.

"For me? Who would be calling me? Yes, this is Sean Ross. I made the team?" A smile lit up his handsome face as he continued speaking. "A meeting tomorrow at ten-thirty. Yes, I'll be there. And thanks, George. Thanks for everything." He slammed the receiver down. "Daddy, Kyle. I did it," he yelled. "I made the team!"

"I knew you would," Kyle yelled. His father just grinned.

Sean danced around the room. "I'm going to play point guard and I'm part of the starting lineup. Right now they're talking about paying me a million dollars a year, but George thinks he can get more.

"God's given me another chance." Sean was solemn as he spoke.

"He sure has, son. He sure has," his father agreed, as they each whispered personal prayers of thanks.

Several days later, Sean's attorney pushed the contract across the desk and handed him a pen. "Everything's in order, Sean. Sign it and you're officially a New York Concorde." Sean's hand trembled as he took the expensive ballpoint pen from his attorney. He sat there staring at the piece of paper for several minutes.

"Go on, sign it. Everything you wanted is there."

"I know. It's just that I've been waiting for this moment all my life and now I don't want to rush it."

"I understand. I've got a few phone calls to make. You take all the time you want. I'll be in the conference room if you need me," Sean's attorney offered.

Sean looked over the contract one last time, then he closed his eyes, bowed his head, and quietly prayed. "Lord, thank You for giving me a second chance. I've learned that I don't have to compromise to be recognized. Thank You . . . for everything." He sat in silence a few moments longer, then he picked up the pen and carefully signed his name.

ELEVEN

TOPAZ THOUGHT she would self-destruct by the time the 747 aircraft touched down at New York's JFK International Airport. "Keisha, we're here." Topaz tossed her blond waist-length curls, oblivious to everyone around her who gawked at her exquisite face and leggy five-foot-nine frame.

"There's supposed to be a shuttle to the hotel," Topaz informed her friend, as they stepped into the airport bustling with people scurrying to catch departing flights and to meet arriving passengers. I'm really in New York City for a shoot with *Mademoiselle*, she wanted to scream. I'm actually on my way to becoming a star. An uncontrollable smile found its way onto her face. I'm going to be famous.

Topaz arranged her hair across one eye as they proceeded to the baggage claim area to retrieve their luggage. "Oh, look, Keisha, next time I'll arrange for them to meet us with one of those little carts so we don't have to walk." She pointed to a group of people being transported on a shuttle cart.

"Girl, you buggin'."

"Look, Keisha, if you're going to be a star, you have to act like one. Do you think Diana Ross would walk through an airport?" Keisha rolled her eyes in response and walked off towards the baggage carousel.

"Here." Topaz handed her baggage tickets to the driver who had come to meet them from the hotel without making direct eye contact. "I have a Louis Vuitton suitcase and garment bag."

She watched him and Keisha return laughing several minutes later with the girls' luggage. "You should have let him get your suitcase for you, Keisha," Topaz informed her as they walked out to the car. "And stop talking to him."

"He's a person, too. And stop telling me what to do. Who do you think you are?"

Topaz glared at Keisha as she put on a pair of her mother's Chanel sunglasses. She opened her compact and fussed with her hair momentarily, tossed her curls in Keisha's face, and marched over to the car and climbed in. I'm Topaz, the famous high-fashion model, she wanted to reply, but she knew she shouldn't push things any further with Keisha.

She gazed out the window in silence and drummed her fire-engine-red nails on the armrest all the way to the Parker Meridien. She glanced sideways at Keisha, who was staring out the other window. Keisha sure acts like she's never been anywhere, for her family to have all of that money. I guess it's true, you really can't buy class.

Topaz walked into the hotel lobby like the Queen of Sheba, trailed by a bellboy with her Louis Vuitton suitcases and Keisha's Hartman luggage on a baggage cart.

"I'm Topaz Black," she informed the reservation agent. "You have a reservation for me from *Mademoiselle* magazine." Through her dark glasses she watched him type her name into the computer. Then he handed her a stack of messages and a manila envelope with a *Mademoiselle* mailing label.

"Enjoy your stay, Ms. Black."

Topaz ignored the reservationist, picked up her papers, and headed towards the elevator.

"Who are all those messages from?" Keisha asked once they were inside the elevator.

Topaz sifted through the thin slips of paper quickly. "They're all from Germain." She looked up at her friend completely amazed. "I can't believe he called this many times already."

Keisha burst into laughter. "How many are there?" They slowly walked down the corridor while Topaz counted the messages.

"Ten."

"Ten?" Keisha laughed until there were tears in her eyes. "I can't believe him. Boyfriend's got it bad, real bad."

Topaz opened the door to their room and squealed, tossing off her Queen of Sheba attitude with her sunglasses. "Ooh, girl, we're in New York City."

"Yes," Keisha squealed, equally excited. "What do you want to do first?"

"I don't know. Call Germain?" She glanced at her wrist watch.

"Girl, please. I didn't come all the way to New York City to sit up in a hotel room while you talk on the phone to Germain."

"I wouldn't call him now anyway. He's asleep. You know he's got to be at the hospital by eleven."

"Let's order room service," Keisha suggested excitedly. "With champagne!"

"All right." Topaz agreed, forgetting all about Germain. "Dinner's on me."

"My treat for the champagne," Keisha informed her as she picked up the phone and called in their order.

"Mmmm, this is delicious," Topaz commented. They were both sitting in bed drinking Cristal and eating lobster with pasta. Topaz popped a bite of lobster into her mouth and took a sip of the icy champagne. "This is the life. I could get used to this real fast. People serving you and bringing you things." She dropped a strawberry into her glass of champagne. "I miss Germain." She sighed.

"What?" Keisha sat up and faced Topaz. "Where did that come from?"

"I don't know." She stared into her glass of champagne. "He's always doing special things like this for me, you know. Like the strawberries, whipped cream, and champagne." She sighed again. "I really miss him."

"You really love him, don't you?"

"Of course I do, Keisha. You know that. There will never be anyone for me except Germain."

The *Mademoiselle* layout would feature holiday wear by young designers. Topaz, the featured model, was given the hottest items of clothing. This is the most beautiful dress I've ever seen. "And I thought Donna Karan was something." She slipped into a black silk party dress covered with jet beads. It slid over her body like melted butter.

I look wonderful. She swirled around in front of a full-length mirror admiring herself. Topaz posed in exquisite bugle-beaded gowns and colorful minidresses fashioned out of silk velvet, chiffon, satin brocade, and silk crepe, adorned with rhinestones, sequins, and feathers.

She was fascinated as she watched hairdressers arrange her waist-length hair into styles she had never imagined. She studied the makeup artists while they applied cosmetics until she didn't even recognize her own face. They were playing dress-up and she was the doll.

"You were wonderful, Topaz," Mick informed her when he had snapped the last photo.

"Thanks, Mick." Topaz started off towards the dressing room, but stopped and walked back over to him.

"Mick, uh, I sort of have a confession to make. I really don't have an agent. Could you help me get one?" She smiled her most dazzling smile.

Mick burst into laughter. "I thought that was you on the phone calling from Images, but I wasn't sure."

"Images is legit. It's my mother's personal-image consulting business." Topaz laughed.

"You fooled me. Aida Foxx." He shook his head, completely amazed. "You were really good. Have you ever considered acting?"

Topaz flashed another brilliant smile. "No, I've never really considered acting. But I do sing."

"Really?"

"Yes." Topaz laughed. "I really do sing, Mick."

"Are you any good?"

"Yes."

"Who would you say you sound like?"

"Whitney Houston."

"Really?"

Topaz sang several lines of "How Will I Know?" Mick seemed perplexed. "An absolutely gorgeous young woman who sings like Whitney Houston. That's definitely a marketable act. So, what have you been doing about this singing career?"

"Nothing." Her smile disappeared as her face clouded over with disappointment. "There's not a whole lot to do in Atlanta. Everyone says I have to be here or in Los Angeles."

"That's true. So, have you made plans to move to New York or L.A.?"

"No. I'm supposed to move to Baltimore with my boyfriend and attend Howard University in Washington. He's going to Johns Hopkins for medicine."

"College is good, but is that what you want to do?"

"I did until I met you. Now I know I want to be out there singing more than anything."

"So, what do you intend to do about your career? With your face and voice you should be able to do big things in music."

"You really think so, Mick?" Topaz asked, hanging onto his every word.

"Definitely. I'll give you a couple of names of people I know. The rest is up to you, Topaz. If this is your dream, you'll have to give it everything you've got and you can't let anything or anyone stand in your way. Not even your boyfriend."

"I know. Thanks, Mick. Thanks for everything."

Topaz couldn't think about anything but her singing career and the advice Mick had given her. "Don't let anything stand in your way, not even your boyfriend." His words echoed throughout her mind as she rode alone in a taxi back to the hotel. I need to think, she decided.

In the hotel's marble bathroom she turned on the water in the bathtub full force, poured in all the complimentary containers of bubble bath, and stared dreamily at the swirling water as the scented foam quickly rose to the top. I could actually become a singer. But I have to do something about my singing career, Topaz concluded, easing herself into the tub. She had carefully wrapped her hair up in one of the hotel's big, fluffy towels, and now she leaned back and relaxed.

"Ahh, this is nice." She stretched her long body in the warm, fragrant bath water. I'm moving to New York. That's it. I have to. I'll only be a couple of hours away from Germain in Baltimore, and I can visit him on weekends. For a moment, her mind drifted to Germain and their escapades in his mother's bathtub. She had at least half a dozen new messages from him today. They were playing phone tag. She had missed him every time she tried phoning him.

I wonder how Germain's going to take the news about school and me moving to New York. She wiggled her freshly painted toes that were peeking through the suds. She heard a door slam. "Keisha?" she yelled. "Is that you?"

"Yes. I got the outfit of life to wear to the club tonight, girl."

"You went shopping?"

"Look." Keisha entered the bathroom with a little black dress still on the hanger with tags. "Versace!"

"Keisha, I can't believe you went shopping without me."

"I told you I wasn't going to sit around the hotel while you were at the shoot. And I couldn't come to New York and not go shopping."

Topaz heard her back in the other room rattling shopping bags. "You cow," Topaz pouted.

"Cow? Did you call me a cow?" Keisha pretended to be angry.

"Yes." Topaz giggled.

"That's it, I'm pouring ice in the bathtub."

"No, Keisha," Topaz screamed. "If you do, I won't let you move to New York with me."

"You're moving to New York? Topaz, what happened today?"

"I'll tell you all about it later."

"Okay, and hurry up," Keisha pleaded. "I need to take a shower."

Topaz turned on the cold water and stood up in the tub.

I'm going to be a star. A famous singer . . . The cold water pelting her body felt good. She imagined she was standing under a rushing waterfall on a remote tropical island.

"To-paz!" Keisha was banging on the door. "Hurry up."

Topaz turned off the water, got out of the tub, and picked up the bottle of Neutrogena body oil. She squeezed a few drops into her palm and began to massage the oil into her skin. Finally, she wrapped the large body towel around herself, opened the bathroom door, and stepped out.

"Well, thank you, Princess Topaz," Keisha barked. She walked into the bathroom and screamed. "Topaz, you left the bathroom a mess." She had left her towels and dirty clothes all over the floor. There wasn't one clean towel in the bathroom. "Topaz, I'm not cleaning up your mess."

Topaz took a dainty mouthful of the lobster salad she had ordered for dinner and switched the channel on the television. "You don't have to. That's the maid's job. I'll call her for you." She picked up the telephone and dialed housekeeping. "I need fresh towels and my bathroom cleaned right away," she ordered and hung up the phone.

"I can't believe you," Keisha fumed.

Topaz watched Keisha go into the bathroom and toss Topaz's clothes out onto the bed. "Keisha, let the maid do that. You know you're really into assisting the servants."

"You really do think you're Diana Ross, don't you?"

Topaz rolled her eyes. "Please . . ." A knock at the door interrupted her. A maid arrived with fresh towels. The woman gathered the soiled towels, tidied up the bathroom quickly, and left. Keisha disappeared into the bathroom, slamming the door behind her.

This is my hotel room, Topaz reminded herself. Next time, I'll come by myself. She put on new Victoria's Secret underwear and once again her thoughts drifted to Germain. He had bought them for her. She glanced at the phone and then at the clock. It was nine-thirty and he would be sleeping. Besides, he'll want to hear all about everything and keep me on the phone and I still have to put on my makeup and do my hair. The girls were going out to Tatou, a club that Topaz had read about in a magazine. I can't call him now. I don't have time. Besides, I'm not ready to tell him that I'm not moving to Baltimore with him.

She pulled the towel from her head and watched the thick mass of golden curls tumble down her back. She smiled at herself in the mirror, pleased with her own reflection. I love my hair. She brushed and brushed until her hair was glistening. Keisha's still in there. Topaz had heard the water from the shower stop some time ago. She must be dressing in there. Yuck. How could anyone dress in a bathroom. Unless it was like Mrs. Gradney's. You could do anything in that bathroom.

Keisha stepped out of the bathroom fully dressed. Her demeanor was cool. "You look nice," she offered politely.

Topaz was wearing the red knit she had purchased at the mall with Keisha. She looked fabulous but her Contempo special made her feel cheap in comparison to Keisha's designer garb. I wish I had one of those party dresses from the shoot. She turned to fuss with her hair in the mirror hoping Keisha wouldn't see the envy she always tried to hide when it came to Keisha's wealth.

"Thanks, Keisha. You look great, too." She didn't want to be jealous, but Keisha had everything. And Keisha did look gorgeous. Her voluptuous curves were nicely tucked into her new Versace dress and her short haircut called attention to a splendid pair of Chanel earrings.

"So, what's this about you moving to New York?" Keisha asked, sitting on the bed.

"I have to start my singing career, Keisha. I can't do that in Baltimore, Washington, or Atlanta. I should be here or in L.A. Mick gave me some numbers for people here in New York. He said I could get an agent. I could work on my singing and model," she continued excitedly. "He said I was a marketable act."

"What about your plans with Germain?"

"I won't be far from him. I can go visit him every weekend," Topaz explained.

"Topaz, you won't have time for that. You'll be too busy."

"Not for Germain," she wailed.

"It's him you have to convince, not me."

"I know, but I want you to come with me. You'll come with me, won't you, Keisha?" Topaz pleaded. "We'd have so much fun living in New York City. And you've been saying you want to do something else besides work for your dad. You could go to school or get another job for some big company. You're so smart you could do anything. I'm not like you and Germain. You guys are smart. I've never been big on school. That's not me." Her tone was sincere. "But I can sing and I do great face. Besides, I'd be afraid to come alone," she added softly.

"You're right, Topaz, you can sing. And you should pursue your singing career. You'd be great. You can model, too. That might help you get a record deal and pay your half of the rent."

"You'll come with me?"

"I'm not making any promises yet. But, I like New York," she added slowly. "And I have been wanting to do something new. Maybe I'll work part-time and take a class or two."

"Oh, yes! I promise I'll keep the bathroom clean."

"I'll put together a resume and see what happens." The girls were equally excited.

"Thanks, Keisha." Topaz gave her friend a hug. "I don't know what I'd do without you."

"Move to New York anyway." Keisha laughed. "And girlfriend, that sad little story about school and books . . . I'm not buying that for one minute. Because when it comes to you getting what you want, you're a genius."

TWELVE

GUNTHER OPENED the door of his battered black Volkswagen bug, tossed his bookbag on the badly ripped backseat, and retrieved his Walkman and headphones. Stupid car doesn't even have a radio. He pumped the gas a couple of times, started the engine, and puttered out of USC's parking lot. He was beginning the final semester of his senior year.

Now I wonder where I can check out Spike's new flick? It's probably playing at the theater across the street. Gunther pulled into a parking space in the shopping center. He slammed the car door closed, then sprinted off towards the theater. Once inside, he shoved past a bunch of young black teenagers who were chewing bubblegum and giggling. Oh, joy, the natives are out. That's just what I need. He stood in line behind the teenagers to purchase a tub of buttered popcorn and a Pepsi. A theater full of gang bangers. I should have known to expect this at a theater in South Central.

"Watch it," he yelled, as one of the teenagers stepped on his foot.

"Sorry," the young man apologized.

Gunther glared at him and walked into the theater. Why are young black kids so ignorant? He found a seat in the middle section towards the front of the theater, his favorite place to sit. He took a swig of Pepsi and began shoveling popcorn down his throat.

"What?" Gunther exclaimed after the first fifteen minutes of the movie. "This is whacked," he shouted through a mouthful of popcorn. I thought this was going to be a movie. Why doesn't Spike run for office instead of always trying to make some sort of political statement on film. Gunther tossed the empty popcorn tub on the floor and left. "I've had enough of this."

The Volkswagen coughed and sputtered away from USC and

onto the Santa Monica Freeway. I can't wait until I get a deal with a major studio. Gunther struggled with the clutch and switched gears. Then I'll show Hollywood what real moviemaking is all about. He turned onto Sunset Boulevard and pulled up next to a burgundy Range Rover stopped in traffic. "Nice," he exclaimed, giving the car his stamp of approval. One day, one day, he promised himself.

He found a parking space on the street near Spotlight, the music video production company where he worked. Spotlight produced videos for many major recording artists. Gunther sighed as he pulled open the door to the production studio and headed towards the editing room. He would spend the next eight hours splicing together reels of raw footage into a four-minute video for broadcast on television.

"I hate this job," he grumbled to himself. He positioned a reel of film on the projector. But editing will help me become a better director. He quickly read over the script and tossed it aside. A moron could figure that out. He started the film rolling, along with the music track, and carefully monitored the time code at the bottom of each frame.

"White boys and their rock music," he remarked, making a face. "I don't see how they can stand this awful stuff." A clean-cut Brit with hair the color of a bright copper penny, wearing a Tokyo Hard Rock Cafe T-shirt, walked into the room. He silently stood behind Gunther, watching him work.

"Hey, man, how's it going?"

"I'll have it finished tonight, dude," Gunther replied.

"Great. Virgin is waiting for this one with baited breath. They're going to use it to launch some heavy promotion for the band."

"Cool." Gunther continued monitoring the time code. The director, imported from London, stood there for several more minutes to view the footage with Gunther.

"You did a great job on this, Gunther. You put those shots together just like I wanted. I never have to sit in the lab when you're doing the editing."

That's because I'm great, Gunther thought smugly. And I make you look good. "Thanks, dude."

"Say, we've been asked to do videos for a couple of R&B artists and some rap groups. We've found that a lot of the black acts are more comfortable with a black director. Josh and I were talking it over, and we think you'd be great. We'll pay you the same salary as our other music video directors. Are you interested?"

I've been to at least a hundred shoots over the last few years. Who knows, I might even get a chance to work with somebody hot like Janet Jackson. "Sure, why not," Gunther finally replied.

"Great. I'll set something up for you next week."

Gunther's first video directing job was with a bunch of young rappers called Da Phat Pak. He bopped around his room to their music every night after he finished his homework, trying to create a concept for the video.

"Hey, man, what's that?" Charles Jr. demanded, bursting into his room.

"Can't you knock?" Gunther glared.

"Sorry, man, but that track is dope."

"You really like it?" Gunther forgot his anger for the moment and an easy smile broke his frown.

"Yeah, man. What's it called?"

" 'Step 2 Da Mik.' It's the upcoming premiere release for a new group of rappers called Da Phat Pak," Gunther rattled off. "I'm directing their music video."

"Really? When?"

"Next Saturday."

"Yo, can I come check it out?"

"Sure, Charles Jr. You can bring a friend if you like."

"Slammin'. I'll be there, man."

"It's about time I get some respect around this house." Gunther smiled, pleased because his brother had been impressed with him. He bopped around to the music and cabbage patched. They really have a good dance track on that song. Even though it's a rap song it makes me want to go out and party. "That's it!" he yelled out loud, clicking the CD back to the beginning. "A house party." Only I won't do an indoor house party, I'll do it outdoors on some vacant lot in South Central . . . no, in Compton. Rappers like that outdoor urban look. The set will be easy. I'll just throw around a lot of old junk. "This is going to be great. Cause I'm just too good."

Gunther presented the concept to Da Phat Pak and his boss. Everyone loved it. But how couldn't they? It was a great idea. He chose an old abandoned lot near Nickerson Gardens in Compton as the location. I sure hope I don't get killed down there. He laughed to himself. But even major pop artists are shooting videos on abandoned lots now, he realized as he flipped from BET to VH1 to MTV comparing videos.

The video shoot took place on a balmy Saturday night in March. Gunther jumped out of his Volkswagen and strutted onto the set with his head held high, dressed in jeans, a polo shirt, and a pair of brown Top-Siders. A black baseball cap that said FILMMAKER covered his sandy hair. He gave the crowd of a hundred-and-fifty teenage extras who would be dancing in the video an insignificant glance and entered the production trailer with his clipboard of notes feeling real important.

"All right, everybody," he shouted, clapping his hands. He watched the crew scurry to their positions. "Let's get busy. What's happening, brothers?" he yelled as he stepped inside the artist trailer. "You dudes ready to make a slamming video?"

"Yeah, man," the three teenagers cheesed and chorused. They stood to their feet to shake his hand.

"Cool. I'll send the A.D. in for you after he gets the crowd going." Gunther went back outside and quickly inspected the set, making sure the trash cans were burning and the barbecue pits were set up. He could smell the barbecue already. He had requested an official soul food dinner of ribs, chicken, links, macaroni and cheese, and collard greens for the video. Black people sure love barbecue and they sure love to eat, he reasoned, although he had given Kraft Services a special order for California rolls and several bottles of Pellegrino for himself. I'm not eating that soul food crap.

Stacks of red bricks and old rubber tires were the only props on the weed-infested lot that still housed the remains of a partially demolished building. "Perfect," Gunther whispered. Everything's perfect. He walked past the Chevy Impala low riders that were bouncing on the side of the set. I hope this is black enough for them.

He shook his head in disgust as a group of buxom black girls with thick braids and long flowing weaves sauntered across the lot in front of him. The girls, a rainbow of chocolate, were dressed in tight Spandex dresses, biker shorts, and bustiers. I don't see how men find them attractive, he thought, while he mindlessly ogled their fine, shapely bodies.

"Get them on the set and dancing," he commanded his assistant director. He pointed to a group of young men attired in hip-hop regalia—dark sun glasses, saggin' black khakis and plaid shirts, bomber jackets, bandannas, baseball caps turned backwards, and thick, gold rope chains. Do they really go around looking that way, or did they go out and buy that stuff for the video?

"Hey, Gunther." Charles Jr. ran up grinning. Gunther could tell he was excited.

"What's up, dude?" Gunther replied, playing it cool.

"Rick, this is my brother Gunther, he's the director." Charles Jr. was obviously very proud of Gunther.

"We're just about ready to start, dudes. There are some seats over there with the crew." Gunther motioned to some chairs on the side of the set near the bouncing Chevys.

"Can we be in the video, Gunther?" Charles Jr. pleaded.

"No. Maybe some other time, dude. I've got to go." They could have danced, Gunther realized as he walked away. Oh, well . . . The party was in full swing when the rappers walked out onto the set.

Gunther felt waves of electricity flow through his body as he picked up the bullhorn. "Quiet on the set." He watched everyone come to a halt and look to him for his next instruction. This is great. He tried to restrain the grin that wanted to possess his face. Slamming. "All right, when the music starts, I want everyone dancing. I want to see lots of energy out there, and Rat Pak, I mean Phat Pak, do your stuff." He watched as the dancers and rappers readied themselves. Then Gunther signaled for playback. "Action." Gunther scrutinized every inch of the set as the cameramen zoomed in for close-ups of the Phat Pak. "Cut," he yelled several minutes later. "Send the guys back to the trailer while they reset the lighting." He quickly left the set for the production trailer. I can't be out there with them, I'm the director.

He gulped down an icy Pellegrino, sprinkled soy sauce on a spicy salmon roll, and devoured the entire Japanese morsel in a bite.

Gunther stepped out of the trailer thirty minutes later to prepare for the next sequence of shots. A gorgeous, caramel-colored beauty stepped directly in his path. Her hair was slicked back, and she was dressed in a red Spandex mini so tight that it had to have been sprayed on. She wore five-inch red pumps, no pantyhose on her big legs, makeup so thick you could scrape it off with a spatula, and huge golden hoop earrings.

"You the director, huh?" Girlfriend knew she was fine. Her bright red lips were parted suggestively, and her cracking chewing gum made loud popping sounds. She stood so close to Gunther he could feel her warm breath on his face.

"Excuse me?" She was making him nervous because for some strange reason he found himself attracted to her. Gunther took several steps away from her.

"I'm an actress and I wanna be on TV." She cracked her gum and took another step forward.

Get some class, Sapphire, he almost yelled. "Well if I ever need someone like you, I'll call your agent," he informed her in a businesslike manner.

"I ain't got no agent," she replied, sticking her chin out. "I'll give you my beeper number." Gunther was impatient while she carefully wrote her number on a tiny scrap of paper. "Give me a close-up and I'll give you some." She licked her lips and blew Gunther a kiss as he walked away.

"Not in this lifetime," he muttered under his breath, tossing the scrap of paper on the ground.

Gunther edited and spliced the footage into a tight, slick finished product. "This is fabulous," he yelled, viewing it for the hundredth time in Spotlight's screening room. "Fabulous."

"Just the thing we need for urban radio," the vice president of A&R commented when he saw the video. "You did an exceptional job, Gunther."

"Yeah, man," Da Phat Pak agreed, jumping to their feet. "It's phat."

I know, Gunther replied in his head. He checked out a collection of platinum albums on the wall while Da Phat Pak and their manager viewed the video a second time in the VP's office at the record company. They'll never see me sweat, Gunther vowed. But then I have no reason to sweat.

"We want you to direct all our music videos," the three cuties cheesed after they had viewed the video a third time.

"I'll be on the set of my first film by the end of summer," Gunther bragged. "But give me a call. If I'm not too busy I'll try and work you in."

Gunther was very proud of his film that he had made for the final project for his film-directing class. He snapped on the lights in the editing bay at USC and slowly exhaled. I like it, he smiled. I like it a lot. It was a silent, thirty-minute, black-and-white film entitled *Jealousy*. Gunther had been heavily influenced by his favorite mystery and suspense writer, Alfred Hitchcock. With equipment from school and Spotlight, he was able to produce a superb piece.

"Gunther." The professor from his directing class tapped him on his shoulder. Gunther looked up from the music video he had brought in to work on, surprised to see his professor in the editing lab.

"Oh, hi, Mr. Dietz." I wonder what he wants.

"Gunther, do you realize you produced the best film in class?"

"Really, Mr. Dietz?"

"You did a fine piece of work. I wanted to be the first to tell you that it's been selected for screening at the Academy of Motion Picture Arts and Sciences this year."

"The Student Academy Awards? Yahoo!" Gunther shouted.

"I thought you'd be pleased." Professor Dietz smiled. "Congratulations, Gunther."

My film's going to be shown at the Student Academy Awards. All the major studios will be there looking for new talent. I can taste that deal now. He laughed, smacking his lips.

Gunther went to Kinkos, where he had special announcements of the premiere of *Jealousy* printed. He mailed them to the development departments at Universal Pictures, Columbia Pictures, Warner Bros., and New Line, as well as to talent agents at William Morris, ICM, and CAA. I'm only sending seven. That's my lucky number. Besides, I don't need to have my name all over the place. After the awards all of them will be looking for me anyway.

Gunther purchased a new Armani suit and rented a black 535i for his big night with the Academy. He strolled inside the Samuel

Goldwyn Theater on Wilshire Boulevard in Beverly Hills feeling like a million dollars. The room buzzed with conversation. Parents and friends of the other nominees and film industry executives milled about sipping champagne and eating hot appetizers.

"Hello, Gunther, baby." His mother greeted him crisply with a small peck on the cheek.

"Hello, Rita." He gave her a lifeless hug. It figures she'd be here.

"Gunther, we can't wait to see your film," his little sister Rosalyn chirped. Gunther's heart melted as he looked into Rosalyn's brown eyes. She was barely a year younger than he. She had been his playmate when they were kids, and now she had grown into a very pretty young woman.

"Thanks," he said, with a hint of a smile. "I hope you like it."

"You look real handsome in your suit, Grunt." Rosalyn smiled into his eyes.

"Grunt? I haven't heard you call me that in years." He laughed. "But then I haven't heard from you in years."

"I know, Grunt. I'm sorry. I really wanted to come to your graduation from Bridgeforth, but Mother wouldn't let me. She said I didn't need to be traveling across the country with a bunch of men."

"A bunch of men? But they're your father and your brothers."

"You know that and I know that. But you know Mother. Sometimes I think she hates men."

"She certainly hates me."

"No, she doesn't."

"Rosalyn, she does. I gotta go." The conversation had struck a raw nerve. He turned to leave.

"Gunther, wait." He stopped in his tracks and turned back to face his sister. "I'll call you, okay?" She planted a kiss firmly on her brother's cheek.

"Yeah. Whatever." He didn't want her to see how much he cared. Now that I'm becoming famous all of my family wants to be around. He glanced at his mother who was nursing a glass of Chablis. She was mingling with the other guests and doing most of the talking. She's probably telling the whole world I'm her son. She couldn't come to my high school graduation, but she sure made it here. Why did Pops have to invite her? he wondered, growing angrier by the second. He should be glad I invited him.

"Gunther, darling," his mother called sweetly. He spotted his directing professor, and acting as if he hadn't heard her, he hurried across the room to do his own mingling. I've got more important things to do.

Gunther tried not to fidget while he viewed the other films. Most of them were pretty boring, but the animated films and the documentaries were exceptional. Gunther received a gold medal, the highest honor in the dramatic category. He also won the Directors Guild of America Student Award, but he lost his cool when his idol, Steven Spielberg, presented him with the award.

The dramatic films were shown after all the awards were given out. When Gunther heard the first few bars of the concerto he had used in the opening, he crossed his legs and grinned in the darkened theater. It was finally time for *Jealousy* to begin. He thought he would lose it completely before the closing credits rolled by in silence thirty minutes later. Gunther heard the room thunder with applause and he slowly exhaled. They loved it. They really loved it.

"I'm a VP in Development at Touchstone," a smiling black-haired lady informed him after the screening. "I loved your film."

"Great piece of work, young man. Congratulations on behalf of Mr. Ovitz and CAA." Gunther scrutinized the distinguished gentleman wearing a fine tailored suit who was obviously there on behalf of Michael Ovitz, superagent to the superstars. And so it continued for the entire evening. Gunther floated home that night on cloud ninety-nine.

The next day, between every class, he rushed to the pay phone to call his answering machine. The only message was from Josh at Spotlight with an offer to direct a music video. After several days of no phone calls, he decided to phone all of the people he'd met at the screening. "Good morning, this is Gunther Lawrence," he began, using his best New York accent.

"She's not available," said the secretary to the VP at Touchstone. "May I take a message?"

"Certainly. I'm Gunther Lawrence, recipient of the Gold Medal Award for my dramatic piece *Jealousy* at this year's Student Academy Awards. I met Ms. Eisenstein several nights ago at the awards."

"Right," the secretary replied with little enthusiasm. "I'll give her your message."

Gunther left his number and sighed with relief as he hung up the phone. Now they'll start calling. But no one ever returned his calls, or if they did, they told him there was nothing available.

I can't believe it. Gunther sat in his bedroom staring at his diploma the day after his graduation from USC. I graduated summa cum laude, I won the DGA Student Award, and I won a scholarship for special studies at the American Film Institute, but I haven't received one freaking job offer. He hurled the crimson University of Southern California diploma case across the room.

What good is this thing if I can't get a job? All I've got is an offer to do those crappy videos. Directing music videos won't get me the power I need to make the kind of movies I want to make in Hollywood. I need a deal with a major studio. What am I going to do?

Several days later Gunther was clearing his things out of the cinema school editing lab when several other students came in to clear out their things.

"That job at Majestic sounds real good, Elliot. How'd you get that?" he heard one of them say.

Why don't they just shut up? White boys—always bragging about what they have.

"Well, I don't have the job yet, but I know I'm going to get it."

"It's in development, right?"

Development . . . Gunther quietly sat on a stool a little closer to them, taking in every word.

"Yes. It's a creative position, writing synopses of scripts, meeting agents, talent. I'll be assisting the VPs of production and development. It's a good way to get into development."

How did this nobody get a contact for a job like that? He's probably somebody's godson or nephew. I've worked my butt off and won all kinds of awards and all I can get is a few lousy offers to direct music videos. He slammed a reel of film on the floor.

"Darn," Gunther muttered. He gritted his teeth as the fire of determination raced through his body. These rich white boys always get everything. Not this time, he swore, shaking his head. No, not this time.

He ran to the pay phone in the building next door and dialed information for the number of Majestic Entertainment. "Development, please. I'm Gunther Lawrence, a graduate from the USC

School of Cinema. I understand you have an opening for a creative assistant."

"Yes," the secretary replied. "That would be Bob Wiseman's office. I'll connect you."

"Bob Wiseman," Gunther demanded.

"Who's calling?"

"Gunther Lawrence. I'd like to arrange an interview for the creative assistant position. I'm a director for Spotlight. I've got a reel of over a dozen music videos that have been in heavy rotation on MTV. My dramatic film won a gold medal at the Student Academy Awards and I just graduated summa cum laude from the School of Cinema."

"One minute please," she replied, unimpressed. It seemed like an eternity before she returned to the phone. "Mr. Wiseman will see you at eleven on Friday."

"Yes." Gunther hung up the phone and rushed over to the lab to edit portions of his videos and student films onto one reel. At three the following morning, he packed up his editing notes and the excess footage, pleased with the final result.

On Friday morning, he showered and put on his best C&R Clothiers suit and Stacy Adams shoes. He placed the reel of film clips, a resume, a notebook, and a designer ballpoint pen in a sleek, black, Italian leather briefcase. He drove his battered Volkswagen to Majestic Entertainment in Burbank and parked it a block away on a side street.

Gunther was cool as ice while Bob Wiseman carefully viewed his director's reel.

"This is quite impressive, Gunther. Quite impressive." He placed the video in the black plastic cassette box from Dubs and handed it back to him.

"I wrote, directed, produced, and edited every music video as well as my films," Gunther bragged.

"This is a development position. I don't need a director. I need a right-hand man. I need someone to read scripts and interact with talent and agents," Wiseman barked.

"I understand, Mr. Wiseman, and I'd still like to be considered for the job," Gunther pleaded.

"Wonderful. Because I think you're just what I've been looking for." Wiseman smiled for the first time since the interview began. "You'll start at forty-five thousand a year."

THIRTEEN

THE APPLAUSE was deafening in Madison Square Garden. Sean felt currents of energy bombard his body as his eyes swept the loges filled with thousands of enthusiastic Concorde fans.

"Number twenty-three, Sylk Ross," he heard clearly over the din of the crowd. He sprang to his feet and carefully placed the toes of his Nikes on the boundary line of the court as the announcer began to call out the starting lineup for the opposition.

Sean strained his eyes to see if his father or any other member of his family was seated in the VIP seats reserved for them during home games. "I hope Daddy's here," he whispered as he jogged over to his position on the court.

Sean watched his teammate smack the ball before he lunged through the air and quickly retrieved it. He sped down the court and deftly tucked one of his famous sweet hook shots through the net. The crowd stamped, screamed, and applauded. I love this game. He smiled.

With only minutes remaining in the game, Sean had already scored thirty-three of the 101 points on the scoreboard. He waved at the audience as they applauded him before he exited the game. The Concordes were winning, as usual, and he was going to sit out the rest of the game.

He drained his sports bottle, which had been filled with Evian, and pulled on turquoise and teal Concorde sweats. When the final buzzer sounded, he headed in the direction of the locker room only to be intercepted and surrounded by a battalion of sports media.

"Sylk Ross, since you joined the team, the Concordes have become a household name. Any comment?"

"I'm very proud to be a member of the team." Sean was sincere and humble as he stared into the lens of the television camera.

"But Sylk, you are the Concordes . . ."

"It takes five players to win a game."

"*Sports Illustrated* proclaimed you a rookie sensation . . ."

"I love basketball and I'm just thankful to be playing the game."

"Will you be renegotiating your million-dollar contract since you carried the Concordes to the playoffs?"

"Good night, everybody." Sean was cordial but firm. He pushed open the door to the locker room. The cheerful postgame banter ceased the moment he entered the room. He swallowed hard and took a deep breath.

"Great game, huh, guys?" He hung the jacket to his sweats in his locker and ignored their silent glares. They headed for the showers and completely ignored his comment.

"It was a great game, Sylk," replied a handsome honey-colored player in a thick Brooklyn accent.

Sean smiled, glad to see Eric Johnson, the team's other guard. "Thanks, E."

"You have to ignore them, man. They're just buggin'. If it was one of them the press was after, then everything would be different."

"I didn't ask for this. I just want to play basketball," Sean protested.

"I know that, man, but the brothers are jealous. Nobody knew who we were the last two years until you came along. Why wouldn't everybody want to talk to you?"

"They could talk to some of the other players, too."

"Yo, money, everybody wants a piece of a winner. I'm glad they want to talk to you. Before you came they didn't talk to nobody. Man, you gave this team some respect."

"Yeah, but my teammates can't stand me. It's not worth it, E." Sean flopped down on the bench.

"They'll get over it. Later for them." Eric started towards the shower. "You down for some dinner?"

"Shark Bar?" Sean's matinee-idol smile lit up his face.

"Do we ever go anywhere else?"

"No." Sean laughed.

"Want to try something else?"

"Naw, man. You know how I love soul food."

"No problem." Eric laughed. "You don't hear me complaining."

Thank you Lord for giving me Eric. Sean watched his friend head for the showers. I'm glad he doesn't think like the rest of them. If it wasn't for him, I wouldn't have any friends on the team.

"That was good, E." Sean drained his second glass of lemonade, tossed his napkin on the table, and leaned back in his chair. He was oblivious to the patrons at nearby tables taking repeated glances in his direction.

"I know." Eric finished off a large glass of iced tea. "Why do you think I let you drag me here whenever we're in town?"

"I thought it was the other way around." Sean peeled off a couple of twenties from a wad of cash and placed them on the bill. "I got it."

"Thanks, Sylk." Eric rolled a toothpick around in his mouth. "You down for a little late-night dancing?"

"I pass, man." Sean yawned. "I'm tired. The only thing I'm down for tonight is my bed."

"Aw, Sylk. We go to movies, we go to restaurants, we go bowling, we go to concerts, or we just sit up all night and talk and the only time you get sleepy on me is when I mention going to a club. What's up with that?"

"I'm not really into clubs. I don't care for the music, alcohol, or cigarette smoke."

"Forget all that, Sylk. What about the honeys, man, the honeys?"

"What about them?" Sean tried to keep a straight face. He knew what Eric was getting at.

"Man, we could just slip in there, make that love connection, and slip on out."

"Love connection?" Sean repeated, laughing. "No, Eric," he replied, shaking his head. "I don't think so."

"Aw, man, you act like you afraid of women." Eric was frustrated with him.

"Afraid of women?" Sean burst into laughter. "Not hardly."

"Then what is it?" Eric demanded.

"All right, E, I'll level with you. I ain't gay or nothin' like that now. Believe me, I like women . . . a lot."

"Good." Eric breathed a sigh of relief. "You had me worried there for a minute. A good-looking brother like yourself not interested in women . . ."

Sean drank his glass of ice water and signaled for the waitress. He was trying not to laugh. He couldn't believe Eric was wondering if he was gay.

"Okay, man." Sean took a deep breath, knowing he was about to unload a heavy burden. "This is what happened . . . when I was in college I had this sweet, fine lady named Rhonda. We had been going out since high school."

"What happened to her?" Eric cut in.

"Would you let me tell you?" Sean continued, pleased because Eric was interested in what he was saying.

"All right, all right. Tell the story, Sylk."

Sean shook his head and laughed. "You crazy, E." He took a drink of water. "Anyway, Rhonda was the girl for me, and when I graduated from college we planned to be married." Eric nodded, encouraging him to continue. "Well, during my junior year, things began to get a little crazy. The team had been on a losing streak and then we started winning. The press went crazy, and I was the center of attention. I loved it, man. I had this roommate, Ty Williams. He was wild. He's playing for the 76ers now."

"Yeah, I know who Ty Williams is."

The waitress placed a slice of pie in front of Sean and Eric, along with a pitcher of water and Eric's glass of iced tea.

"Thank you." Sean smiled.

"Go on, man," Eric prompted as Sean took a bite of pie and ice cream.

"Well, Ty used to throw these wild victory parties with women galore and lots of alcohol."

"I know the type."

"Rhonda and I were raised in the church and we had never been around that type of stuff."

"What?" Eric was in shock. He dropped his spoon into his plate.

"Yeah, man. I handled it pretty well at first, but Rhonda hated it."

"What do you mean at first?"

"We partied but we didn't drink. But that wasn't the real problem. There was this girl, Tatyana. Talk about a fine honey?

This girl was gorgeous. She was on our cheerleading squad. And Tatyana had it out for me. To make matters worse, I was very attracted to her."

"So what was wrong with that?"

"I'm in love with Rhonda and this girl is way too experienced for me, man."

"What? What do you mean too experienced?" Eric practically shouted.

"Keep your voice down, man."

"Oh, yeah, sorry," Eric apologized, looking around to see if anyone had overheard them.

"I . . . well, I . . ." Sean felt himself blushing. I'm not going to be ashamed, he told himself. "You know I'm a Christian and I don't believe in sex before marriage, man," he confessed quickly. "I'm still a virgin."

"What?" Eric almost choked on his drink.

"I'm still a virgin and I intend to stay that way until I'm married." That wasn't so bad. He sighed with relief.

"Wow." Eric was completely amazed.

Sean watched Eric sit in silence, shaking his head. Oh, well. Now I've lost my only friend on the team.

"I couldn't do it, man," Eric finally said. "But I have a lot of respect for you. That's all right."

Sean's handsome smile lit up his face again. "Like I was saying, this girl had it out for me. She wasn't shy about letting me know it either . . . even with Rhonda around."

"You guys broke up over that?"

"No. I lost my mind senior year. Me and Ty had this really nice apartment off campus and Coach got me that Mercedes I drive, too. We really got the big head. So Ty sets up this little private party for four and Tatyana was my date. Things got a little hot and heavy, and after I cooled them down I couldn't face her or Rhonda."

"Wow." Eric stared in silence.

"So you see it's not that I don't like women, I like them too much. A pretty girl is my weakness and I'm not ready to subject myself to that again."

"How long ago did all this happen?"

"It's been about two years now."

"Two years? You mean you haven't had a lady's companionship for two whole years?"

"Nope." Sean finished off the rest of his pie.

"Man, you really have a lot of strength."

"I tried to patch things up with Rhonda, but she wanted me to give up basketball, and I just couldn't do that."

"I heard that, Sylk. I wouldn't give up my basketball career for some babe either, no matter how fine she was."

"Well, it's a lot deeper than that. I hurt myself, E, and I thought I would never be able to play ball again let alone have a career in the NBA. But God gave me a second chance, man. He healed my leg and gave me another chance to play ball, and I'm not giving that up for anyone," he proclaimed. "There's a lady out there for me somewhere who will love God and me with my career in basketball."

"Wow, man, that's deep." Eric was completely at a loss for words.

"So you see all the press and all the money . . . that stuff don't mean nothin' to me . . ." He focused momentarily on some invisible object. I've never shared this with anyone, he realized. He felt a surge of new strength permeate his body. He made eye contact with Eric and continued speaking. "This fame stuff ain't about nothin'. Me, I'm thankful every time I run out on the court for the starting lineup because I know I don't have to be there. I'm thankful for having Jesus, my daddy, my family, and the few friends that I do have in my life. That's what's important. Love and relationships." Sean finished off the pitcher of water and placed ten dollars in the brown leather check case for the waitress.

"That's a wonderful story, Sylk. God bless you." Eric rose to his feet. "Well, I think all the good food and conversation just chilled me right on out. I'm going home. I guess I won't be making that love connection tonight either."

Love connection. Sean smiled as Eric's words echoed in his mind. That's too funny.

The guys found a path outside through the sea of people gathered around the bar. It was a warm June night in Manhattan and the Concordes were in the playoffs.

"Don't get quiet on me, Eric," Sean scolded as they drove home. They both lived in loft apartments in the same neighborhood.

"I'm cool, but that was some deep stuff you dropped on me."

"I tell you what," offered Sean. "My birthday's next month. How about we go out to a club then?"

"You sure, Sylk?"

"Yeah. I'll be okay. I can't stay away from women forever."

"All right, man, I know just the place."

Sean paced nervously back and forth in his apartment. He was dressed in black Armani trousers and a crisp, white silk shirt. Maybe I shouldn't go, he thought for the hundredth time. He peered out the vertical blinds to see if Eric had arrived yet. "Too late," he mumbled. Eric's black Range Rover rolled to a stop in front of his building. "I can't back out now." He tucked a black Gucci wallet in his pants pocket and picked up his keys and jacket.

"Yo, man, happy birthday."

"Thanks, E. Let's go party." Sean was trying to be excited about the evening despite his apprehension.

"Sylk, tonight I'm taking you where the most beautiful women in town are," Eric announced.

"And where's that?"

"It's a place uptown. You'll like it."

Eric left the car with the valet, and the guys strolled up to the front door of a nondescript building. "Good evening, Mr. Johnson." The door attendant held the door open for them.

Eric paused to speak to the doorman as he entered the building. "Are the ladies in the house?"

"Yeah, man, and they're all waiting just for you."

"Cool." An easy smile graced Eric's face. "This is my boy, Sylk Ross."

He grasped Sean's hand excitedly. "You really played some great games last season."

"Thanks, man."

The doorman ushered them inside an elegant club that had great sound and lights. Multicolored high-tech lighting flashed in sync to the pulsating beat in "Diamonds." Eric's tall, lean body swayed with the music. "Yo, Sylk, what do you think?" he yelled to Sean over the music.

"It's loud," Sean yelled back. He followed Eric over to the bar. I know I should have stayed home.

"You want something?"

"Juice. I'll have some cranberry juice, man."

Eric nodded and placed the order. Moments later he handed Sean a glass and led him over to a reserved table. "They keep one for me if they know I'm coming," he explained as "The Finer Things" kicked in. Sean watched Eric's eyes follow a curvaceous blonde as she passed their table. "You ever dated a white girl, man?"

"There was this girl in a class, but she was just interested in me because I was on the team." Sean watched a butterscotch beauty in tight jeans stroll by. "But there ain't nothing like a beautiful black woman."

"I know. But you have to be careful with women, period. How do you know when they're really interested in you for you and not because you play basketball?"

"You don't. That's why I pray, because people are crazy." Sean laughed. "You want another drink?"

He glanced towards the bar trying to find a waitress and did a double take. Wow, she's the most beautiful woman I've ever seen. He took a third look. She was a black blonde with a creamy butterscotch complexion, exotic looks, and a statuesque body. She was wearing a red minidress that made her long legs appear endless. She was standing near the bar, gazing around the room as though she were looking for someone.

"Yo, man, you see that honey in the minidress?" Eric inquired.

"How could you not see her?" Sean took another look. "I wonder who she is?"

"She's got to be somebody famous because baby got it goin' on!"

Should I ask her to dance? Sean wondered as he signaled the waitress. He rattled off the order while his mind traveled back to the black blonde in the minidress.

"You like her, don't you, man?" Eric grinned.

"I don't know her, E." Sean knew he was blushing. "But I can't deny the fact that she's definitely a beautiful woman."

"Ask her to dance, Sylk."

"I don't know."

"What harm can one little dance do? Then you can see if she's got some conversation to go with those looks. Look, there's my boy." He waved at the handsome young actor standing on the side of the dance floor. "Come on, I'll introduce you." Sean recognized him right away. He was the only son in NBC's number-one sitcom.

Sean noticed the beauty in the red minidress walk onto the dance floor. He pretended to be interested in Eric's conversation, but he was captivated by her dancing. He watched her spin and twirl. When he saw her flash a dazzling smile directly at him, he quickly turned away, realizing he had been staring. She smiled at me, he realized, as a smile lit up his face. But who's that guy she's dancing with? She flashed another brilliant smile at Sean as she left the dance floor. And why is she giving me the eye? Before Sean knew it, he had followed her to her seat and touched her gently on the arm. "Would you like to dance?" he heard himself ask.

"Sure," she replied softly, glancing up at him through lowered lashes. "I'd like that."

Sean relaxed, gave her a handsome smile, and escorted her onto the dance floor. "I Wanna Dance with Somebody" had brought everyone back out on the floor.

Sean smiled as he watched her move with great sophistication and ease. "I'm Sylk Ross. What's your name?"

"Topaz. Topaz Black." She spoke loudly over the music.

She is so gorgeous. I'd like to know more about her, but I'm tired of yelling over this music. "Have you had dinner?"

"I am a little hungry," Topaz lied, not really hungry but not wanting to leave him yet. He's really nice looking, she admitted. And I might need a friend or two when I move to New York.

"Great. I know the perfect place." He led her off the dance floor towards the table where he and Eric had been sitting.

"Wait . . ." Topaz stopped dead in her tracks. "My girlfriend Keisha's with me."

"No problem. Do you think she'd like to come, too?"

"She mentioned she was getting a little sleepy. She may be tired," Topaz lied. "But I'll ask her anyway." I know she'll want to come although I don't want her to. There's no way she's going to dinner with me and this fine brother. I'm sending her back to the hotel.

"Cool." Sean smiled. "This is turning out to be a party after all. Topaz, this is my friend Eric. Now where's Keisha?"

"I'll go get her." Good, he has a fine friend for Keisha. She couldn't help admiring Eric's light brown eyes. We're going to have some fun now. Two cutey pies.

"Do you know who they are?" Keisha whispered to Topaz while they stood outside waiting for the car.

"Two fine brothers." Topaz was pleased as punch with her catch. "See, I even got you one, too."

"That's Sylk Ross and Eric Johnson from the New York Concordes. You know . . . the basketball team."

"You're kidding?" Topaz grinned.

"They're both real good players but that Sylk Ross is big time. He's the Kidd Maxx of basketball. He's always on television and he has tons of endorsements."

Topaz covered her mouth to stifle a scream. "Ooh, girl, I knew if we came to this club I'd meet somebody famous."

"Ladies." Sean was holding open the back door of the Range Rover.

"Keisha, girl, look at their car . . . a Range Rover," Topaz squealed. She held onto Keisha's arm in an attempt to maintain her cool.

"Girl, chill," Keisha ordered in a whisper. Sean helped them into the SUV, closed the door, and climbed in the front with Eric.

"I hope you ladies like soul food. Sylk would have me shot if I tried to suggest something different. And we really have to go there tonight because it's his birthday."

"It's your birthday, Sylk?" Topaz inquired.

"Happy birthday," Keisha offered.

"Thanks. But Eric likes this place as much I do, if not more," Sean explained, laughing. "He just won't admit it."

Over fried chicken, short ribs, yams, macaroni and cheese, potato salad, collard greens, rice and gravy, crispy hot corn muffins, and lots of lemonade, Sean and Eric entertained the girls with funny stories about different games.

I can't believe he's such a famous basketball player. Topaz took a tiny bite of her fried chicken and stared into space.

She's beautiful, and she seems like a really nice person, but she lives in Atlanta, Sean reasoned.

"Happy birthday to you." Eric, Keisha, and Topaz sang together in unison.

"Happy birthday to you." Everyone in the entire restaurant joined in.

A waitress placed a cake complete with candles in front of him.

"Make a wish," Topaz reminded him. Sean closed his eyes and blew out every candle. Everyone in the restaurant cheered.

"Thanks, everybody," Sean called out. "Man, when did you do that?" He punched Eric lightly on the arm.

"Do what?" Eric questioned, feigning innocence.

"Thanks, E, thanks for a real nice birthday."

"Sylk, where's the ladies room?" Topaz asked sweetly.

"It's downstairs."

"Thanks." She flashed him a dazzling smile. "Come with me, Keisha." Sean and Eric stood as the ladies left the table.

"Yo, man, I think she likes you." Eric placed a platinum American Express card on the table. "You better get with that."

"She's a nice girl, man. We'll see where it leads. What do you think about Keisha?"

"She's nice. Real nice. There's just one problem. She lives in Atlanta."

"Sylk is so cute and he's nice." Topaz took out a tube of lipstick and carefully reapplied it to her lips with a brush. She stared at her reflection in the powder room mirror. "Doesn't he look like Denzel Washington?"

"He is cute." Keisha placed her lipstick back in her purse and ran her fingers through her short hair. "But what about Germain?"

"Oh, Keisha, it's only dinner and Germain's in Atlanta."

"Seems like more than dinner to me the way you and Mr. Ross have been making eyes at each other all night."

"Keisha, stop. We have not and what about you and Eric? I think he likes you."

"He is nice." Keisha tried to conceal a smile. "But I don't have a boyfriend, you do."

On the ride back to the Parker Meridien, Keisha sat in the front with Eric and Sean sat in the back with Topaz. Eric double-parked the Range Rover at the hotel and left Topaz and Sylk in the car while he walked with Keisha into the hotel lobby.

"So you're leaving tomorrow?" Sean questioned, stalling for time.

"Yes." Topaz didn't want to get out of the car. "I was here on a shoot for *Mademoiselle*. Keisha came with me."

"So, you're a model?" Sean was impressed.

"No, actually, I'm a singer."

"Really? So, what else do you do, Ms. Black?" Sean asked just as Eric pulled open the car door, interrupting their conversation. "Topaz, are you tired?" Sean smiled into her amber eyes.

"No."

"Great. Eric, you go on home. I can catch a cab later."

"You sure, Sylk? I can hang out for a minute."

"Yeah, E, you go on home. I'll talk to you tomorrow. And thanks again for everything."

"All right, man. You guys be cool. Tell your girlfriend Keisha I think she's really special." Eric waved as he drove off.

Countless taxis paraded up and down the brightly lit street. The night air was still warm. "Since this is your last night in New York, we'll do something special. We'll hire a carriage."

"A carriage as in horse and buggy?" Topaz was skeptical.

"I'm sorry, I keep forgetting you're not from New York City. Well, now we have to find a carriage because there's no way I'm letting you go back to Atlanta until we do." He took her hand in his and strolled down the block to Sixth Avenue and hailed a cab to Central Park. As soon as they stepped out of the cab, a horse trotted down the street pulling an unoccupied Cinderella-type coach.

"See," Sean whispered. "It's magic." He whistled to get the driver's attention.

Topaz stared dreamily out of the carriage as the warm night breeze blew through her hair and gently caressed her face. I'm a fairy tale princess and he's Prince Charming, she imagined. She stole a quick glance at Sean, who was equally silent, and tried to think of something cute and witty to say. I don't want to sound stupid, so she continued to stare out of the carriage and fantasize.

She's so quiet. Sean was in a world of his own. I wonder if I should hold her hand. She is so beautiful. He noticed how the light reflected in her hair. Absolutely beautiful. No, he told himself, returning to the view from his own window. I don't want things to move too fast.

The magical journey ended entirely too soon. Sean and Topaz walked in silence up 57th Street to the hotel. I'll never forget this night as long as I live, Topaz decided.

"So, Princess Topaz, when will I see you again?" The carriage ride had obviously sparked a bit of fantasy in him as well.

"I'm making plans to move to New York, Sylk."

"Sean," he corrected. "My family and my real friends call me Sean. When are you moving to New York, Topaz?"

"As soon as I can make all the arrangements. Hopefully by September."

"It's really hard to find a place in New York . . ."

"I'll find one," she said with determination.

"And I'll help you." He was smiling that irresistible smile again. Topaz thought she noticed a dimple.

"My brother's in real estate," Sean added.

"Great. Things are really falling into place."

They were standing in front of the hotel now. Should I kiss her? Sean fingered a lock of her hair.

"Thanks for a wonderful evening, Sean." Topaz took his beautiful chocolate face in both of her hands and kissed him gently on the lips. There, I've been wanting to do that all evening.

Sean smiled and kissed her again. "You'll be hearing from me soon," he promised.

Topaz turned to wave one last time. "Sean." That's right, he told me to call him Sean. "Tell Eric that Keisha's moving to New York, too."

"Cool. We're all going to have lots of fun." He gave Topaz a matinee-idol smile and she thought she would melt. "And Topaz . . ."

"Yes," she replied, hanging on to his every word. Maybe he wants me to come home with him.

"Thanks for helping me celebrate my birthday."

FOURTEEN

TOPAZ WAS completely absorbed in thoughts of New York City, Sylk Ross, and her singing career as she wandered down the jet way into the Atlanta airport. She had pretended to be asleep during the flight back from New York in order to avoid Keisha's irritating questions about Germain and Sylk. Sean, she reminded herself with a smile, Sean.

"Topaz!" It was Germain's voice shouting her name that summoned her from her thoughts. She looked up and saw him rushing towards her. He was dressed in an old pair of faded blue jeans that hugged his slim hips like a glove and a pink polo shirt that accentuated his biceps and pecs.

"Hi, pretty girl." He kissed her passionately, relieving her of her overnight bag at the same time. "I missed you." He ran his finger gently across her high cheekbone.

"Hi, Germain." Topaz gave him a quick peck on the lips.

"Hello, Germain, and how are you?" Keisha waved a hand in front of his face. "Remember me? I'm Keisha," she teased.

"Oh, hey, Keisha," Germain grinned, embarrassed because he had forgotten to speak to her. He led the girls towards the baggage area.

"So how was New York, ladies?"

"Fabulous," Keisha responded.

"Topaz?" Germain focused his attention on her.

"Huh?" She was trying to remember the way Sean said her name. When he said it, it sounded musical. Not boring and flat the way Germain said it in his ever-so-slight Southern drawl.

"How was New York?"

"Oh, it was nice." She saw Keisha give her a dirty look and tried to think of something else to say.

Something's up, Germain concluded. He had been watching

her ever since she got off the plane. Something's definitely up. I could tell as soon as she kissed me.

Topaz climbed into Germain's new white Mercedes and immediately changed the radio from his favorite news and talk station to her favorite urban pop station. "Germain, guess what?" She sucked in her breath, bracing herself for what she was about to reveal.

"What?" he demanded, hoping to receive some sort of explanation for her aloofness.

"Me and Keisha are moving to New York so I can begin my singing career." Topaz had decided to tell him with Keisha in the car because she knew he wouldn't start an argument as long as Keisha was around.

I'm glad that's all it is. Germain sighed with relief. For a minute, I thought she had met someone else.

"I knew you were going to come back and tell me that." He spoke softly as he gazed into her tawny eyes.

"Baby, you're not mad at me because I'm not going to Howard?" Topaz couldn't believe what she was hearing.

"No, Topaz. I remember the night we met. You were on stage singing. You were wonderful." He paused as the memories of that evening filtered through his mind. "Baby, I know you could be big in music, and if that's your dream then I'll be right there with you."

"Oh, Germain, thank you, thank you." She covered his face with kisses.

"Topaz," Keisha interrupted from the backseat. "Would you let the man drive?"

"I'm glad you're back, pretty girl." Germain pulled to a stop in front of Topaz's house. "Always" was playing on the radio and Germain sang along as he ran around the car to open the door for Topaz and Keisha.

"You're so sweet." Topaz giggled and kissed him on his full lips. She tucked her arm through his and walked up the stairs to her house with him. "Mother, I'm home," she yelled. She glanced at one of her mother's favorite Kathleen Wilson prints hanging in the foyer. Then she screamed.

"Keisha, look!" Topaz stared in disbelief at dozens and dozens of long-stem roses in red, pink, and white. Tulips and fabulous exotic arrangements covered the tables and the floor. The fragrant bouquets had perfumed the entire house. The living and dining rooms looked like the inside of a florist shop.

"Can you believe it?" Lisa came out of the kitchen and joined the girls and Germain in the living room. "Hello, ladies." She kissed Topaz on the forehead. "They all arrived first thing this morning. The florist had to rent a truck to deliver them."

"I've never seen anything like this in my life," Keisha uttered, totally amazed. Topaz was in a daze as she gently touched and sniffed each arrangement to see if it was really real.

"Oh, Germain," she squealed, throwing her arms around him. "Baby, this was so sweet of you. I can't believe you bought all of these just for me." She kissed him playfully on the tip of his nose.

"I didn't buy them, Topaz," Germain mumbled, wishing he had. Who could have sent her this many flowers?

"Baby, you didn't buy them?" She saw the hurt in Germain's eyes, and her thick eyebrows drew together in a frown. "Then who did?" she wondered out loud. Sean . . . She was unable to conceal her smile. They're from Sean.

She ran over to an arrangement and tore open one of the enclosed gift cards. "Counting the days until I see you again, Sean." I knew it. She smiled. I knew it. Oh, my goodness. She could feel every eye in the room on her, watching as she basked in pleasure. Embarrassed, she clasped a slender hand to her face. Germain . . . How am I ever going to explain all of these flowers to him? She slipped the card into the pocket of her jeans.

"They're from *Mademoiselle*," she lied, hoping everyone would buy her story. "To congratulate me for doing a really great job."

"Oh, how nice," Lisa exclaimed. "I'm so excited. My little girl on the cover of *Mademoiselle*."

"Mother . . ." Out of the corner of her eye, Topaz saw Keisha give her a dirty look. "Germain, I'm sure Keisha wants to go home now. And I'm hungry. Can we go get some dinner, baby?" She fixed her amber-colored eyes on his boyish face.

"Sure, baby." He swallowed hard, trying to contain his mounting desire as he gazed back into her eyes, knowing in his heart there was nothing he wouldn't do for her.

"Great." She smiled her prettiest smile and kissed him softly on one of his favorite places, the back of his ear. "I'll get changed."

Topaz gazed up at the red embossed wallpaper in their favorite Chinese restaurant and sighed. I can't believe Sean sent me all of those flowers. She deftly picked up a large chunk of lobster with a pair of black-lacquered chopsticks. Germain watched her as he sipped a glass of ice water, catching a few pieces of the crushed ice on his tongue. He pushed away the remains of his lobster fried rice, spicy shrimp, and egg roll, unable to eat.

"That must have been some shoot," he commented, crunching the ice between his teeth. "You must have really done a good job for them to send you all those flowers."

"I really did." I can't tell him the truth, Topaz told herself. She swirled a jumbo shrimp through dark, savory, spicy sauce and popped it into her mouth. "I can't wait to get back to New York. Mick gave me phone numbers of people who can help me with my singing, and Sean . . . I mean, Shaunda's going to help me find an apartment." Oops, I've got to be careful.

"Who's Shaunda? One of the other models?"

"Yes. So what have you been up to?" Topaz wasn't really interested but she wanted to change the subject.

"Same old stuff," he replied flatly, mashing the edge of his eggroll with his fork. "Just working in the lab and studying. I've got to be ready to hit the books seriously this fall."

He is so boring. Topaz picked out another chunk of lobster from her fried rice with her chopsticks. Always studying. I wonder if I should tell him about Sean. No, it's too soon, she concluded, taking a sideways glance at him. Too risky. I'll see how far things go with Sean first.

"So, when do you think you'll be going back to New York?" Germain searched her eyes, hoping to find some new response that he hadn't seen before.

"As soon as I can." She gathered up her purse and sunglasses from the table. "Babe, can we go now? I'm starting to feel a little tired." His questions were making her uncomfortable.

"Sure." Germain sprang to his feet. He tossed some bills on the table and walked swiftly behind her. When he caught up with her, he locked his arms gently around her waist. "What's the big hurry, pretty girl?"

"Nothing." She pulled away from him. "I'm just ready to go."

"Oh, I know you can't wait to get me home, right?" He laughed and opened the car door.

"Not tonight, babe, I'm tired." She gave him a little kiss to pacify him before she slid down into the cool leather seat. I don't have time to hang out with him. I have to get home to see if Sean called. I know he called. "We can spend the whole day together tomorrow, babe. I promise," she vowed solemnly, giving him a look that tugged on his heartstrings.

"All right," he agreed halfheartedly. "I guess you are tired."

"Exhausted." Topaz watched him put the key in the ignition and start the car. Her mind wandered back to Sean as she stared at Germain's huge bunch of keys. "I couldn't even love you the way you like tonight," she confessed as she tucked her arm through his and fixed her amber-colored eyes on him.

"We don't have to make love." Germain's voice was soft and vulnerable. "I just want to be with you."

"No." She shook her head and tossed her tawny curls. "I want to sleep in my own bed tonight."

This is the first time she ever said no, Germain realized. He was distraught by the time he stopped the car in front of her house. The only time she never wants to make love is when she's on her monthly and it's not that time of the month.

"You don't have to get out, babe." Topaz was already opening the door. "I'll call you in the morning when I get up." She gave him a light peck on the cheek before she sprinted the stairs to her house, her long legs easily taking two steps at a time. She waved good-bye and carefully closed the front door behind her and sighed with relief. I thought I'd never get rid of him.

"Mother, I'm home." She tossed her purse and keys down on the table in the foyer and smiled when she saw all of the floral arrangements in the living room. She paused to stroke the petals of a fragrant white rose with her long, slender fingers as she brushed a handful of tawny curls out of her right eye.

"I still can't believe Sylk sent me all these flowers." She picked up the crystal vase that held two dozen white roses, carefully went upstairs to her bedroom, and placed the vase on her dresser. "Those will look real nice there." She glanced at her answering machine and frowned when she saw the red message indicator wasn't blinking. I wonder why he hasn't called.

She pulled off her jeans and T-shirt and jumped into the shower, sighing contentedly as the cool water pelted her body. For a moment, her mind went blank as she allowed the water massage to caress her body in all the right places. I can't believe he didn't call. She turned off the shower, patted herself down with baby oil, and pulled on an oversized Atlanta Hawks T-shirt. She brushed her curls up into a lopsided bun, scooped up a stack of fashion magazines, and sat with her legs crossed in the middle of the bed. She flipped through a *Vogue* and tossed it aside to stare at the telephone.

"Ring," she commanded. She placed the telephone directly in front of her. "Ring." Restless, she continued flipping through the magazine, not really focusing on anything. "Forget it." She jumped off the bed and dashed downstairs for her purse and found his telephone number written on a Parker Meridien notepad.

"I'm calling him. I have to thank him for the flowers." With the tip of a fire-engine-red nail, Topaz carefully punched the numbers on the telephone. While the phone rang, she drummed her nails on the cover of the June *Essence*. Finally she heard him answer. It's him, Topaz wanted to scream as a smile took control of her face. But he sounds like he was sleeping. And it's not even midnight.

"Hi, Sean. This is Topaz."

"Hi, Topaz. How are you?"

"Fine, now that I've spoken to you. I just wanted to thank you for all the beautiful flowers."

"Beautiful flowers for a beautiful lady." He spoke softly into the receiver. Topaz smiled as she kicked the magazines off the bed onto the floor, stretched out comfortably on her back, and stared dreamily at a crack in the ecru ceiling.

"I can't wait to get back to New York. I miss it already."

"It's a fun place. And it's real close to my hometown, Philly."

"So what's it like to be a big famous basketball player?" Topaz questioned, ignoring his previous comment. "It must be great to have people recognize you everywhere you go."

"I love to play basketball. But I could do without all the fanfare.'' I guess it's only natural that she would be a little curious about those things, he convinced himself.

"You mean you don't like being famous?" Topaz was so shocked, she sat up straight in the bed.

"It has its moments. I get to do a lot of special things and I get to help people, but then I usually can't go to a restaurant or even the grocery store without being recognized."

"I would love for people to recognize me everywhere I went."

"Topaz, you're so pretty that people would notice you even if you weren't famous."

"You're sweet," Topaz whispered in the phone. She etched herself a perfect spot amidst the mound of pink satin and lace pillows on her bed.

"So tell me about yourself. What's Topaz all about?"

"I'm going to become a famous singer." A lock of hair had worked itself out of the bun. As she talked, she twisted it around her index finger. "I'm going to make lots of money and live in a big house. Would you like to live in my house with me, Sean?" she asked coyly.

Sean blushed. Although he wasn't ready to respond to her question, he wasn't turned off by her flirtatious remark. "I've got an exhibition game in Orlando next Saturday at Disney World for Nickelodeon. Would you like to meet me there?"

"Yes," Topaz practically shouted into the phone.

"After the game we could hang out at Disney World for a while."

"That sounds wonderful. I love amusement parks and I've never been to Disney World. Is Eric coming?"

"Yeah, he'll be playing in the game, too."

"Oh, good, then I'll bring Keisha."

"Cool." Sean's voice was smooth and sweet. "This is going to be fun. I'll call you in a couple of days with all the details."

"Okay, Sean. I can't wait to see you," she whispered into the phone. Topaz pressed the disconnect button several times until she heard the dial tone. Then she punched her speed-dialing code for Keisha.

"Hello," Keisha answered sleepily.

"Keisha, I can't believe you're in bed already. Wake up," Topaz commanded. "I have the most fantastic news."

"What?" Keisha groaned.

"I talked to Sylk."

"What?" Keisha was sounding more interested. "He called you already?"

"No, I called him. Anyway, he wants me to meet him at Disney World."

"Disney World? You're kidding." Keisha was fully awake now.

"And guess what else?"

"What?" Keisha screamed.

"You're coming, too. Eric's gonna be there."

"Eric? Oh, yes! When are we going?"

"Next weekend. Sylk, I mean Sean's setting up everything."

"Wow. Hey? What are you going to do about Germain?"

"I don't know. I'll think of something. I'll tell him I have another shoot."

"What if he wants to come?"

"I'll tell him he can't."

"Topaz. You can't do that. Say, where are you, anyway?"

"At home."

"At home? You've been out of town for five days and he let you go home? How did you get away with that?"

"I told him I was tired and I wanted to sleep in my own bed." Topaz inspected a tiny chip on the nail of her index finger.

"Topaz." Keisha was shocked. "I thought you loved Germain."

"I thought I did, too, until I met Sylk."

"But you don't even know Sylk."

"I know all I need to know. He's fine, he's sweet, he's rich, and he's famous."

"So are you saying you and Germain are through?"

Topaz reached in her nightstand for the tube of Krazy Glue she kept on hand for her nails. "I'm not saying anything yet. Germain will be at Johns Hopkins soon and Sylk is in New York. Maybe I'll see them both until I make up my mind." She carefully squeezed out a tiny drop of glue onto the chip in her nail.

"I can't believe you."

"Believe it," Topaz snapped, irritated by Keisha's apparent disgust for her decision. "It's my life, anyway. Besides, you should be grateful that I hooked you and Eric up."

"But I don't have a boyfriend. You do."

"That's your problem. You need a boyfriend. Why don't you get a life and stay out of mine?" Topaz slammed the phone down before Keisha had a chance to say another word.

"Always telling me what to do." Topaz stared at the phone as her anger subsided. I shouldn't have said that. She picked up the phone and pressed the redial button but the line was busy.

"She's pissed." Topaz returned the receiver to the cradle of her hot-pink and gold princess phone. I'll make it up to her and take her to lunch or something tomorrow. She tossed the decorator pillows onto the floor and climbed into bed between fresh, crisp sheets.

"Mmmm," she purred as she caught a whiff of Escada. Mother had the cleaning lady change my linen while I was gone and she put Escada powder on the sheets. She yawned and stretched her long legs luxuriously until she found the perfect spot. I'm meeting Sylk at Disney World, she reminded herself with a smile as she drifted off to sleep.

The sound of a ringing telephone summoned Topaz from a deep sleep. She squinted at the digital clock as she picked up the phone. Twelve-thirty? "Hello," she answered, trying to sound fully awake.

"Good afternoon, pretty girl."

"Hi, Germain," she replied with very little enthusiasm.

"Wake up, baby. You promised to spend the entire day with me. I'm on my way over with breakfast. I'll see you in a few."

"Germain, wait," she yelled as she heard the receiver click in her ear. He was calling from the car. "Darn. Oh, well, I did promise."

She dragged herself out of bed and into the bathroom where she brushed her teeth and braided her hair into a single braid. It's going to be hot today, she groaned, as she rinsed her face with cool water. Downstairs in the kitchen she poured herself a glass of orange juice and dabbed her face with a cottonball wet with chilled Chanel astringent from the bottle that her mother kept in the refrigerator during the summer. I wonder what Germain's bringing for breakfast.

"Hey, baby, I'm here." She heard Germain call from the front porch as she finished her glass of juice.

"What's for breakfast?" She opened the door and relieved him of the paper bag full of fresh berries and cream, ham-and-cheese croissants, and iced mocha drinks from the gourmet shop.

"All your favorite things." As he kissed her on the mouth, he expertly ran his hand under her T-shirt and caressed her breast at the same time.

"Germain," she squealed, stuffing a handful of raspberries into her mouth. "Stop." But it was too late, he had already ignited her desire and the look in her eyes told him everything he needed to know.

"Come on, baby," he whispered in her ear. "Stop playing hard to get. You know you missed me." She kissed him passionately as excitement licked throughout her body. Her hands tore his clothing away from his lean, hard body as though her life depended on it. He freed her from her T-shirt, and kissing her fervently in all her favorite places, set her body ablaze.

"Oh, baby," Topaz whispered later as they lay intertwined in her bed, "I missed you so much."

"How are we ever going to make it with you living in New York City and me in Baltimore?" Germain rolled a strawberry in light cream and powdered sugar and popped it into Topaz's mouth.

"I don't know, baby. But I don't want to talk about that now. I just want to make love to you over and over and over," she whispered as she covered his face with delicate kisses.

"Hey, Keisha, girl," Topaz sang into the speaker phone in Germain's Mercedes. "I've got the car tonight. I'm on my way to pick you up so we can go out to dinner."

"No, thanks. I'm busy."

"Busy doing what?"

"Getting a life."

She's still pissed. "Look, I'm sorry about last night but you were making me feel guilty. Besides, I spent the entire afternoon with Germain."

"Gee, an entire afternoon. Did you tell him about Sylk?"

"No." Topaz drove in silence, listening to "Songbird" and waiting for Keisha to say something. "So, do you want to have dinner or not?" Topaz finally asked. "I'm in front of your house."

"Yeah, okay. Hey, Topaz?"

"What?"

"You know, one of these days you're going to go off on me one time too many."

"I said I was sorry."

"You're always sorry. Just remember what I said. I'll be down in a minute."

"You know I'm your best friend." Topaz laughed, happy because Keisha had given in.

"No, Topaz." Keisha's tone was serious. "I'm your best friend."

"You don't look so good." Keisha sat on the bed beside Topaz at Disney World. "What's wrong?"

"I feel nauseous. It was probably that nasty airplane food," she moaned, making a face.

"You'll be fine." Keisha was used to her friend's heavy drama over broken fingernails, so she had assumed this was just another one of Topaz's moments. "Aren't we supposed to meet the guys for dinner at seven?"

"Yes." Topaz nodded.

"Do you think you'll be able to make it?"

"I'll be okay. I just need to lie here for a minute."

"That's them," Keisha whispered, several hours later. She quickly checked her makeup one last time in the mirror. "I'll get the door."

Topaz nodded and followed Keisha into the living room. She felt somewhat better after she had showered and dressed in a vanilla linen blazer and black-and-white striped georgette pants. Her freshly washed hair hung in damp curls around her face and down her back, and she had chosen to wear a golden bronze lipstick and matching eye shadow.

"Hi, Topaz." It was Sean's voice and she was afraid to look.

"Hello, Sean." She struggled to maintain her composure. He is too fine, she told herself for the thousandth time. He was smiling and wearing white linen slacks, a teal green shirt of raw silk, and white slip-ons with no socks. His black curly hair was still slightly damp, and his chocolate skin glowed as though it was illumined from within.

Dang, he's fine. She watched him walk over to her; his stride was long, sexy, and confident. I'm going to melt right here, she realized, as he bent down and kissed her gently on the cheek. She could smell his Gucci fragrance and she felt her head go light. Oh, no. She felt herself falling through space in her mind. I'm going to faint.

"Topaz, are you okay?" Keisha demanded.

Topaz opened her eyes and saw the three of them standing over her and looking quite concerned. "I'm fine," she smiled. "I just felt a little lightheaded. It's warm in here."

"Man, I didn't know you had it like that. Got women fainting at your feet," Eric teased.

"Aw, be cool, E." Sean blushed.

Keisha stifled a giggle. "Yeah, Sean, you definitely got it goin' on like that."

"Are you okay, Topaz?" Sean was very concerned. Eric and Keisha laughed so hard they were crying.

"I'm fine." Topaz was embarrassed. "I can't believe I fainted."

The entire front wall of the Black Swan opened out onto a water garden courtyard. The couples were seated at a center table right by the water. Topaz could hear waterfalls gently trickling and was enchanted by the elegant swans that swam right up to the table begging for bread. The restaurant, lit solely by flickering candles, was something straight out of a romance novel. "This place is fabulous," she whispered to Sean. "Thank you so much for bringing me here."

"It is special," Sean agreed with a handsome smile. "Did I tell you that you look beautiful tonight?"

"Thank you, Sean." She kissed him gently on the lips. "You look incredible, too." She could feel Keisha's leg nudging her under the table and glanced at her friend to see her give her an I'm-ready-to-scream look that made Topaz laugh. Keisha is too funny sometimes.

Topaz was practically speechless throughout the entire dinner. Germain's never taken me anywhere like this, she recalled.

Later, Sean kissed her at the door of her hotel suite. "I'll see you after the game." He kissed her again and helped her open the door. "Good night."

"Darn," she muttered, closing the door behind her. I thought I was going to get some tonight. I know Keisha will. Keisha and Eric had taken off in another direction as soon as they entered the hotel.

Topaz awakened to find Keisha sleeping in her bed the next morning. "Maybe she didn't get none." Topaz laughed. She picked up the phone and ordered herself eggs, bacon, juice, croissants, and fruit for breakfast.

"I'm hungry." She lifted the shiny cover from the plate of food, tossed the cover aside, and flipped on the television in the living room. But as soon as she smelled the greasy bacon she was in the bathroom bent over the toilet bowl.

"What's wrong with me?" she asked her reflection in the mirror as she dabbed her forehead with a cool towel. I can't be. She shook her head vehemently as she rushed to pull on her jeans. She could barely zip up her favorite Guess jeans anymore. I just need to take off a few pounds and stop eating all those sweets. She pulled off her pajama top, pulling on her brassiere, noticing for the first time that her breasts were tender and spilling over the top of her bra.

"No way," she convinced herself as she grabbed her wallet. She closed the door gently behind her and dashed down the corridor to the elevators. She tried to remain calm as she paid for the home pregnancy test in the drugstore. "I'm just buggin'," she whispered. "I'm not pregnant."

Back in the bathroom, she took the test, trying to convince herself that the positive sign was a mistake. "Darn," she muttered out loud, trying to recollect when she'd had her last monthly. It's been awhile, she realized. Stunned, she dumped the remains of the kit back into the box and walked slowly out of the bathroom and into the bedroom where Keisha was just waking up.

"Girl, last night was the bomb," Keisha began, but was unable to complete her sentence when she saw Topaz's face. "Topaz, what's wrong? Did you and Sean have a fight?"

"No." Topaz shook her head and sat down on the bed. She made a valiant effort to fight back the tears.

"Then what's wrong?"

Topaz glanced up at Keisha through lowered lashes. Tears streamed steadily down her face. "I'm pregnant," she mumbled, barely audible. "Keisha, I'm pregnant," she sobbed.

FIFTEEN

"GOOD MORNING, Mr. Lawrence." The Majestic Entertainment security guard greeted Gunther warmly and waved him onto the studio lot. Gunther looked right past the uniformed studio guard and drove through the gate onto Majestic's lot. He looked into his rearview and watched the gate close behind him. He saw the security guard search his clipboard before he denied the next passenger and vehicle admittance to the studio lot.

"Peon." Gunther laughed. He pulled his old Volkswagen bug into his assigned parking spot adjacent to the Blue Tower, which housed the studio's chief executive offices. Why are these nobodies always trying to park on the lot with us VIPs when they know they're supposed to park across the street with the rest of the riffraff?

Gunther picked up the stack of scripts and his black Italian leather briefcase from the passenger seat and kicked the car door closed with his foot. No need to lock it, he reasoned, admiring the Mercedeses, BMWs, Range Rovers, Porsches, and Jeeps parked nearby. Who'd want to steal this piece of trash with these babies around?

He caught a glimpse of himself in the mirrored lobby of the tower and smiled. With his crisp, white Eddie Bauer shirt, black Dockers and a conservative black printed tie, he had that young-executive look. That black hair dye was just what I needed. He took a closer look in the mirror at his freshly dyed hair while he waited for the elevator. He had purchased the dye to cover his sandy hair. Now my hair and skin aren't the same color. And my black hair makes my skin look even lighter. I like it. He smiled into the mirror. Suddenly, the elevator doors opened and Gunther forgot his hair and stepped inside. He flipped through a *Daily Variety* while he rode up to the eleventh floor.

"Good morning, Marilyn." Using his best East Coast accent, he spoke to a well-dressed strawberry blonde. She had stepped inside the elevator just as the doors were closing.

"Good morning, Gunther." Gunther smiled as he admired her impeccable taste and cool demeanor. Marilyn, somewhere in her early forties and the executive assistant to Joel Zwieg, Majestic's CEO, exuded power. Marilyn had juice. She answered Mr. Zwieg's phone and no one spoke to or saw Mr. Zwieg without going through Marilyn.

"Have a nice day, Marilyn." Gunther stepped out of the elevator on the eleventh floor. She smiled a plastic smile in response before the elevator whisked her away to the twelfth and final floor, where Majestic's mogul trinity held court. Gunther had already been to several meetings with Mr. Zwieg, with recommendations for future projects. An action-packed adventure, *Hardly Dead,* had been proposed by Gunther, and it was currently in production.

"Good morning, Mr. Lawrence."

Gunther breezed into his office without bothering to greet his secretary. He snapped open his briefcase and pulled out several pages of carefully handwritten notes.

"I need these typed for my two o'clock meeting with Bob," he barked, dropping the pages on her desk. "See me if you have any questions. Oh, yes." He paused briefly in the doorway of his office. "I'm expecting a call from Dick Mason from CAA. Otherwise, I'm not taking any calls. And have lunch sent up for me from the commissary. I have a script I need to finish reading for my meeting, so I'll need you to type those notes as well. You'll either have to take a late lunch or order something in."

Finished with his orders for Beth, he stopped at the credenza to place a Karyn White CD in the player. There, a little music to read by.

"Mr. Lawrence?" Beth stood in the doorway looking timid. "Will you be having the usual for lunch?"

"The usual?" he repeated, looking totally confused. "What are you talking about?" His brow wrinkled into a frown.

"The thing you usually order, sir, pineapple and cottage cheese."

"Oh, yeah." The frown vanished from his face. "And a large diet Coke." Got to keep my body fine-tuned.

He closed his door and flipped through his Rolodex. I'm the man, he grinned. I've got private numbers for every agent and star in town. He took a script from the pile on his desk and settled down on the settee to complete his reading. He yawned as he opened the heavy blue paper cover. I'm sleepy. I've been up until three every morning this week reading scripts and that trash they send up from the story department. He yawned and picked up the phone. "Beth," he summoned over the intercom. "I need some coffee."

Just as he returned to his reading, his phone rang. "Beth," he called after the phone had rung several times. "Where is she?" He snatched the door open, but she was nowhere in sight. "Gunther Lawrence," he barked into the receiver.

"Dick Mason from CAA. How are you?"

"Oh, Dick. I'm great. How can I help you?" he continued, using his best telephone manners.

"I've got a fantastic project I'd like to discuss with you. Can we meet for lunch this week?" Gunther shuffled through the mail and papers on Beth's desk and found his schedule.

"How about one o'clock at Columbia Bar and Grill?"

"Great." Gunther wrote the appointment on his calendar as he watched Beth, a petite, mousy brunette, walk up with his coffee. She'd look a thousand times better if she got rid of those Atom Ant glasses and took that perm out of her hair. He had interviewed a dozen secretaries before hiring her and had chosen her because she had worked for Amblin Entertainment, Steven Spielberg's production company at Universal. He took the steaming black coffee in a Majestic Film mug from her and went back into his office to finish his reading.

Trash . . . this stuff is trash. I can't believe these people get agents to pitch this crap to major studios. He tossed the script on his desk and turned on his computer. Maybe one day I can get them to make one of my films. He scanned the index of files until he came to *Intrigue* and pulled it up on the screen. "Now, this is a film." He sighed. He quickly ran page after page across the screen, pausing to make a correction from time to time. "*Intrigue*," he whispered, leaning back in his chair. "Even the title is great." He saved his changes, brought up a blank page on the screen, and began typing a synopsis of the script he had just finished reading.

"Gunther." He glanced up to see his boss, Bob Wiseman, pacing nervously in front of him.

"Yes?" Gunther leaned back in his chair and focused on his boss. Judging from the tone of his boss's voice, Gunther knew that some catastrophe was about to be dropped in his lap.

"I just got a call from Marilyn," Bob shouted.

I knew it . . . Marilyn. Gunther raised an eyebrow of interest. I wonder what's up.

"The big guy wants a synopsis right away on that property CAA has been shoving down our throats. It seems like this is one hot property and he's gotten several calls on it already from talent."

Gunther watched Bob, somewhere in his midforties, wear a path in the carpet in front of his desk with his pacing. White people have no behind, Gunther observed, as he mindlessly watched Bob's black trousers sag in the rear. Now how did I go there? He wanted to laugh but he quickly switched his attention back to Bob's stressed, pallid face. I sure hope this fool doesn't have a heart attack in here.

"No problem," Gunther finally responded. "Beth has that synopsis on her desk. I'll have her make a copy for you." Gunther picked up his phone and barked out another order to his secretary.

"You're a lifesaver, Gunther."

I know. Gunther watched the color ease back into Bob's face. I should have let him sweat it out a little longer. He'll just take my work upstairs and pass it off as his own.

"No problem, Bob. That's what I'm here for."

Bob started out of Gunther's office but stopped in his tracks. "Oh, by the way. The two o'clock development meeting is cancelled. I'll be upstairs with the big guy."

All that work for nothing, Gunther wanted to shout. Well, I'm going home.

"Better stick around just in case Mr. Z needs you," Bob commanded, as if he could read Gunther's mind.

"I'll be right here."

Beth had brought in Gunther's lunch while he was talking to Bob. Now Gunther placed the tray of food on the end table by the settee and grabbed his mail. He sifted through the envelopes quickly, pulling out the *Hollywood Reporter* and an advertisement from Zipper BMW.

Chow time. Gunther removed the Saran Wrap from his fruit and cottage cheese. He finished his entire lunch while he devoured the contents of the *Hollywood Reporter*. "Spike's making another film. I have got to get started." He flipped open the BMW mailer. "Nice," he whispered, admiring a 735i. He started to toss the brochure in the trash when he spotted a photo of a convertible 325i. I could work with that. I need a new car, too. I can't keep driving that old bug around. It doesn't fit my image. He placed the mailer on the desk and searched in his briefcase for his checkbook. I've been working here for six months now. He smiled when he saw his two-thousand-dollar balance. And that's just my checkbook. He pulled out his savings passbook and almost shouted when he saw his balance was well over ten thousand dollars. I didn't know that I had managed to save that much money. Living at home has been good for something, after all. That settles it. I'm getting rid of that piece of junk tonight.

Gunther glanced at the clock. Almost four. I wonder if Bob's back. He picked up the phone. "Vanessa, it's Gunther. Is Bob back?"

"Hi, Gunther, how are you today?"

Don't answer a question with a question, he wanted to shout. Vanessa, Bob's executive assistant, was an extremely attractive black girl, the color of light toast, who had the hots for him. Why does she take me through these changes? Doesn't she realize I'm not interested?

"I'm fine, Vanessa, how are you?" He made an effort to be polite.

"Pretty good. I've been reading your synopses. You're such a good writer, Gunther. Oops, hold on. I've got to catch the other line."

"Heifer!" Gunther put the call on the speaker phone and slammed the phone down. "How dare she put me on hold!" Several minutes later, Vanessa picked up the phone.

"I'm sorry to keep you holding, Gunther. Bob's still upstairs. I'll tell him you phoned. I've got to go now. Bye."

"Ugh," Gunther growled, ready to tear his hair out. "Black women. Totally unprofessional and always thinking they're so fine that somebody has the hots for them. I don't see why Bob hired her."

He poured himself a glass of ice water and slowly sipped it while he gazed out his office window. It didn't offer him a clear view of anything except the mountains he traveled over every day to get to work, but staring out of his window always had a calming effect.

"Gunther." It was Bob again.

"Yes," Gunther replied, turning to face him.

"I think we're going to pick up the CAA property. And Mr. Z said if you recommended it he knows it's a winner," Bob finished happily with a grin.

"Good." Gunther maintained his composure although he was too pleased with the compliment. "It's a great story. If it's made properly, it should bring in a lot of money for the studio."

"You know, Gunther, I'm glad to see you're interested in films that make money and not just some cutesy idea."

Isn't that the point, making money, he started to reply but quickly decided this wasn't the time to be flip or to talk.

"Mr. Z and I were discussing sending you out on location. He really likes your work and wants you to become more involved in production."

Production? Gunther repressed a scream. "That sounds really interesting, Bob." Gunther made an effort to look Bob straight in the eye without blinking in order to maintain his cool.

"We'll talk about it later, pal. Right now, I've got a plane to catch. I'm taking the red-eye to New York tonight."

I can't drive this piece of crap up there or they won't take me seriously. Gunther parked his old Volkswagen a block away from the BMW dealership. He grabbed his briefcase, straightened his tie, put on his shades, and strutted into the showroom like a million dollars. He swallowed hard and took a deep breath to maintain his composure when he saw the cars.

"The ultimate driving machine," he read from a placard in the rear license plate frame of a champagne 525i. "Sweet," Gunther whispered, running his fingers lightly across the hood. "Real sweet." He felt his adrenaline surge and pressure begin to mount in his groin. I've wanted one of these babies for a long time.

"Nice, isn't it?" An attractive blonde interrupted his mental escapade.

"Real nice." Gunther replied coolly, without taking his eyes off the car.

"I'm Greta and I'd be more than happy to assist you this evening."

"Wonderful, Greta. I'm Gunther." He removed his shades and made piercing eye contact. "I'm an exec with Majestic Entertainment and I need one of these babies to get back and forth to work in."

"Well, this 525i could certainly do the job."

"It's nice . . ." Gunther stole a quick glance at the sticker price and nearly cursed. "But I think I'd like a convertible. You know, something cute to take the ladies out for a spin at the beach."

"I know just the thing. Come with me outside."

"I'm at your mercy, Greta." Gunther followed her through the showroom to a side door exit, admiring the blunt cut on her long blond hair. Nice bod, he concluded, noticing the way her silk dress clung to her hips.

"How do you like this?" She stopped in front of a shiny red 325i with chrome rims and a black convertible top already dropped.

Is she kidding? Does she think I want this flashy red car because I'm black? Black people and their red cars, red suits, and red shoes. Please . . .

"Greta, Greta, this is just a little too red." He turned and started strolling through the car lot past various models in an array of colors. "Wow." Talk about Beamer heaven.

"Gunther, perhaps you'd like the same thing in white?" Greta's high heels tapped softly behind him on the asphalt.

White? Do I look like Bozo the Clown?

"No, Greta. I'm afraid white won't get it."

"Well, perhaps—" she began anxiously.

"That's the car I want," Gunther declared excitedly, cutting her off. He pointed to a black-on-black convertible 325i with chrome rims. Carefully, as though he might disturb the magic of the moment, he opened the door, sat inside, and clutched the steering wheel. He exhaled slowly, unaware that he had been holding his breath. I'll have to get a pair of BMW driving gloves. He leaned back into the seat, savoring every inch of the car's interior. Black leather seats, black tinted windows, a CD player. I'll have a phone put in, too. I've got to have a cellular phone. He could already imagine himself driving out to Malibu with the top down in the company of some gorgeous curvaceous blonde, her hair flying in the wind . . . Yep, this is the one.

"I'm sorry, but this car isn't available, Gunther. Someone left a deposit on it just this morning," Greta informed him, intruding once again into a fantastic daydream.

"What?" He couldn't believe what he was hearing.

"This car has already been sold."

Gunther sat in silence collecting his thoughts. Sold. Then why is this car still on the lot? No, he decided. I'm not taking no for an answer. Money talks. He got out of the car and carefully closed the door.

"Greta, if this car is sold, why is it still here on the lot?"

"The car is on hold . . ."

"So the car is on hold and not sold," Gunther repeated. "Greta, I want to buy this car tonight. Now, I suggest you find another car for the person who left that deposit, because I want this one."

"We may have to order . . ."

"Do you want to sell this car or not?" He fixed his eyes on hers in an intimidating glare.

"I'll be more than happy to sell you this car, Gunther. Would you like to take it out for a test drive?" she asked politely.

I've got her right where I want her. Gunther fought the urge to smile. She's going to give me a great price, too.

"No. There's no need for a test drive when you know what you want," Gunther replied coolly.

"I like a man who knows what he wants." Greta smiled and licked her lips.

"I'm your man." Gunther was definitely feeling his Cheerios. "Shall we step inside for a little small talk?" He placed his hand around her waist just above her behind.

Exactly one hour later, Gunther drove out of the showroom in his black 325i with the top dropped. "Jump to It" came on the radio and Gunther cranked the volume. It was a warm summer evening in Los Angeles and he was in no hurry to get home. He glanced at his watch. It's only seven. The night is young. And for once I don't have to sit up all night reading scripts. I'm going shopping.

He pulled into the Fred Segal parking lot on Crescent Heights and Melrose and left his car with the valet. As he entered the store, he noticed several people staring at him. They're trying to figure out if I'm somebody famous. They know I have money since I'm driving a BMW.

Gunther sprinted the back stairs to the men's department. I'm sick of cords, Dockers, and Top-Siders. I'm not a preppie anymore. I'm a creative executive at Majestic Entertainment. He pored over the racks, selecting gabardine and denim slacks, crisp shirts in various colors, and coordinating blazers and ties. He tried them all on, styling each outfit down to the smallest detail.

I look good, he decided, observing himself in a three-way mirror. Real good. I should have dyed my hair years ago. He patted his short-cropped black hair, making sure it was even all over. Now what should I purchase? He stood in silence staring at the clothes.

"I want them all," he whispered. I need them all. Heck, I can't drive around in a Beamer and look like a tack. He grabbed the clothes and strutted over to the cashier. "I'll take all of these."

"Great," she chirped.

Gunther watched her carefully remove each price tag and place them in one neat little pile, while she carefully folded his precious new wardrobe and tucked it into three Fred Segal shopping bags. "That'll be two thousand fifty-three dollars and forty-five cents."

Two thousand fifty-three dollars. "No problem." Gunther reached into his back pocket and pulled out a Louis Vuitton credit-card case. He flipped through the credit cards, pulled out a gold American Express card, and handed it to her. He watched her slide it through the register and give him a halfhearted smile while she waited for clearance on the card.

She probably thinks it's stolen or that it won't go through. Impatient, Gunther drummed his fingers on the countertop until she finally wrote a number on the charge slip and passed it to him for his signature. He scratched his signature on the slip, tore off his copy, and pushed the slip back across the countertop to her.

"Enjoy." She smiled and handed him the bags.

The help these days . . . Gunther took his bags without another word and left.

"It's the black Beamer," he barked at the valet parking attendant. He was wearing his Ray Bans even though the sun had long set. Gunther pressed several singles into the parking attendant's hand when he returned with the car. Never let it be said that Gunther Lawrence doesn't tip.

He pulled over at La Brea and Venice to put the top up on the car. I'm not driving into the hood with my top down. At La Brea and Adams, where he was preparing to make a left turn, he glanced in his rearview mirror just in time to see a battered white Pinto with a family of Mexicans nearly pile into him.

"Go back to Tacoville you bean-burrito-eating, tequila-drinking, nondriving, illegal aliens," he yelled out of the window. Mexicans. No you won't run into my Beamer. He made his turn onto Adams Boulevard. "I'm moving out of this neighborhood." There's no way I'm going to drive a BMW and live in South Central. People will think I'm a drug dealer.

He pulled his car into the backyard and locked the gate. Yep . . . I'm definitely moving. Besides, people know I live in South Central whenever I give them my phone number. You can always tell where someone lives in L.A. by the first three digits of the phone number. Maybe I'll look in Westwood and Brentwood. Who knows? Maybe I'll even find something at the beach. I know one thing . . . a creative executive for Majestic Entertainment with a 325i definitely does not live in South Central. He glanced at his car one last time before he entered the house. I finally got it, he smiled.

"Hi, Pops." He spoke to his father, who was in his usual horizontal position on the living room couch in front of the television.

"Hello, Gunther," his father replied without bothering to look at him.

"I got . . ." No. I'm not saying anything about the car. They'll find out soon enough.

"There's some dinner on the stove if you're hungry."

I am hungry. I forgot all about dinner with all my shopping.

"Thanks, Pops." He went into the kitchen and lifted the lids on the pots. Black-eyed peas . . . I should have known it would be soul food. Oh, well, when in Rome do as the Romans . . . He dished up a plate of peas and rice and found fried chicken and cornbread in the oven. He devoured everything in a matter of seconds. That was pretty good, but you'll never find a black-eyed pea in my apartment.

Gunther strolled onto the set of the studio's latest untitled project, which had just commenced production. He had already successfully served as associate producer on several films, and Bob had dangled a juicy carrot in front of him: to oversee the production of a low-budget, five-million-dollar film.

Dressed in black pants and a black designer jacket he had picked up at Maxfield's, Gunther reeked of power and intelligence. He wore his clothes well and with his expensive Melrose outfit he definitely had that money glow. His hair had been freshly dyed and he had even let the barber give him a fade after he saw a white guy at the studio with his blond hair shaved on the sides.

"May I help you?" Gunther fixed his Ray Bans on the young lady standing in front of him. She was casually dressed in jeans and a sweater. What incompetent is this? he wondered.

"Where's Dave Collier, the producer?" Gunther growled.

"Over there." She pointed to a young guy standing on the edge of the set who was in a heated discussion with a young lady with a clipboard. "Are you here for casting?"

"Yeah, I'm Eddie Murphy," he replied without a hint of a smile. He started across the lot towards the producer.

"Are you really?" she called after him. Casting . . . Why do black people always have to be the entertainers? She thinks I'm here for casting and I'm the executive producer for this project.

"Dave, I'm Gunther Lawrence," he barked, cutting into the conversation.

"Oh, hi, Mr. Lawrence." Dave gave Gunther his immediate attention.

I love watching them squirm, Gunther mused.

"Mindy, this is Mr. Lawrence, our executive producer. Mindy runs our production office."

"It's a pleasure to meet—" Mindy began, thoroughly excited.

"What's going on around here, Dave?" Gunther barked impatiently, looking around the set and not bothering to acknowledge Mindy.

"Everyone's at lunch right now," Dave informed him.

"I need you and the director in a meeting right away. I want to go over the budget and the script." Gunther gave out orders like a drill sergeant.

"Mindy, go tell Paul that Mr. Lawrence is here and he needs to meet with us right away," Dave ordered. It was obvious that Gunther's no-nonsense attitude was starting to affect the producer.

"Dave, my secretary left specific orders that an office be set up for me. Where might that be?" Gunther demanded with a piercing stare.

"Right this way," Dave practically whispered.

Gunther wanted to laugh. He's upset because a black man is ordering him around and he can't do a thing about it. I love it. He followed Dave in silence to a trailer with a sign that said PRODUCTION on the door. Dave opened the door and motioned for Gunther to enter first.

"We set up a spot for you in here."

Gunther stepped up into the trailer. It was air conditioned and the cool air felt good after the arid Los Angeles heat. Three desks were positioned in a T. Each desk held a telephone, an IBM personal computer, and a ten-key adding machine. Gray berber carpeting cushioned the floor and "You Make Me Feel Like a Natural Woman" was playing softly in the background. There was also a compartment that housed an IBM copier, a cabinet of supplies, and a fax machine. This will work, Gunther decided, giving the room his stamp of approval.

"This is your desk, Mr. Lawrence." Dave patted the chair of the desk that stood alone. "If that's okay with you," he quickly added.

"This is fine." Gunther took a seat at the desk and snapped open the locks on his briefcase. Its contents were neatly arranged in rubber-banded stacks labeled with yellow Post-its. He tucked his sunglasses in a case and placed them in the briefcase. Then he removed the script, budget, and a yellow analysis pad covered with carefully written notes.

"Have Mandy type these rewrites and my notes. I'll need three sets of everything for our meeting. And these are budget changes that need to be copied as well." Gunther handed Dave a stack of paper and opened his issue of *Daily Variety*. "Have Mandy bring in some lunch, too, and a couple of diet Cokes."

He pretended to be busy reading as he watched Dave summon Mindy over a Motorola walkie talkie. He's mad. Gunther laughed to himself, but not as mad as he's going to be when he hears all the other changes I'm about to make around here.

"You practically rewrote my entire script," Paul Weinstock, the director and writer for the project, yelled at the top of his lungs.

"It needed to be rewritten," Gunther informed him quietly.

"But there was nothing wrong with it," Paul ranted.

"That's your opinion," Gunther practically whispered. "It's much tighter now." And it was. It read a hundred times better. How dare you challenge me? I sure hope you're a much better director than you are a writer. How he ever got a script sold is beyond me. Gunther gave him a menacing look and focused his attention on Dave. "Dave, you had a lot of fat in the budget. I was able to trim five hundred thousand dollars off the top."

"What? Five hundred thousand dollars? This is crazy," Dave sputtered. He quickly read over the pages. "We can't possibly make this project with these cuts."

"There are dozens of well-made films being made on budgets half the size of this by extremely talented producers. I'm sure one of them would be more than willing to take over this project if you think these changes will render it impossible for you to bring this project in on schedule and within the budget," Gunther replied icily.

"I don't foresee any problems, Mr. Lawrence." Dave was so intimidated by Gunther that he was whispering. Gunther glanced over at Paul, now a bright shade of red, who was still fuming as he silently skimmed the script.

"Wonderful." Gunther smiled for the first time since he arrived on the set. "I'll see you both first thing tomorrow morning at dailies."

"Do you people know anything about filmmaking?" Gunther yelled as soon as the projector clicked off. "We won't be able to use any of this footage. You people are wasting film, and wasted film means you've wasted the studio's time and money."

Gunther glared at the director and his leading man, a lesser-known actor, who would have a booming career once the film hit the screen. Actually, the footage isn't that bad, Gunther noted. I just want them to work harder, and if I go easy on them they won't give me their best.

"I hate waste." He slammed a reel of film on the floor and left the screening room. That ought to get me the footage I want.

Six months later Gunther smirked while his boss and Joel Zwieg ranted and raved over his first executive producing effort. The finished product was slick, on schedule, well under budget, and a booming financial success at the box office.

SIXTEEN

TOPAZ TOSSED a copy of *Brides* magazine on the bedroom floor and stretched out on the plum and charcoal wool throw rug. "I can't believe I'm getting married, Keisha." She bit into a shiny Red Delicious apple and chomped hungrily as she opened up the latest issue of *Modern Bride* and stared at each page.

"I can't believe you're getting married, either." Keisha sorted through a pile of magazines and pulled out a copy of *YSB*. "So Germain just asked you to marry him after you told him you were pregnant?"

"Yep." Topaz nodded her head in agreement and turned a page in the magazine.

"All right girlfriend . . . I want details." Keisha settled back against the bed and peeled an orange.

Topaz laughed and smiled. "There's really not much to tell. At first I said no."

"Girl, you didn't."

"I sure did. I didn't want to be married, especially not to Germain."

"Then why are you marrying him?"

"Because I love him and he is the father of my baby."

"Well, I guess that's a good enough reason." Keisha was hoping that Topaz would finally settle down and enjoy her marriage and baby. Why doesn't she realize how fortunate she is to have someone who loves her like Germain? "Okay, Mrs. Germain Gradney." Keisha laughed. "It sure sounds like somebody important."

"Yeah, like some stuffy old doctor's wife." Topaz laughed.

"Topaz."

"I'm just playing. Keisha, you know I love Germain." She felt herself blushing. "What do you think about this one?" She held up the magazine so Keisha could see a picture of a wedding gown.

"No," Keisha frowned, shaking her head. "Too frilly."

"I don't like any of these things." Topaz tossed aside the magazine. "Maybe I should have something designed."

"So what are you going to do about Mr. NBA?"

Does she ever let up? "I haven't decided yet." The warmth disappeared from her voice. She stole a glance at Keisha out of the corner of her eye to see her response.

"I don't believe you."

"What?" Topaz fixed her amber eyes on her friend.

"Don't play innocent. You know exactly what I'm talking about," Keisha chided.

"We're just friends."

"That might be true, but he likes you for more than a friend and you know it."

Topaz let out a long sigh. "That's not my problem. Besides, he's famous and he knows famous people. He might be able to help me get a record deal."

"Topaz." Keisha was in shock. "I can't believe you."

"Well, who am I supposed to ask, Germain?" she yelled, glaring at Keisha. "I suppose him or one of his boring intern friends has connections in Hollywood."

"I thought you had some leads on a couple of agents in New York who were going to represent you for modeling. That should get some doors open."

"Keisha, read my lips. I'm having a baby," Topaz wailed with exasperation.

"So you won't be having a baby for the rest of your life. You can get your figure back. Beverly Johnson and Christie Brinkley did. And girlfriends look good. Now what's up with the agents?" She gathered the orange peelings and tossed them into a wastepaper basket covered with pink roses.

"That's too time consuming. I don't want to be a model. I want to sing. Besides, I sent those agents my pictures. They all said they were beautiful and sent them back. One agent came right out and told me they wanted girls with Naomi Campbell looks and not somebody who doesn't really look black."

"You're kidding. Someone really told you that?"

"Yes. But when this other agent found out I could sing, he told me I could be the next Whitney Houston."

"So what did your mother say when you told her you were pregnant?"

"Mother said that I was going to be just like her until she found out Germain wanted to marry me. Then she was happy. She likes Germain but she also likes the Gradneys' money and status," Topaz finished sarcastically.

"Hmmmm . . ." Keisha left her comment unspoken. "So when are you guys getting married?"

"The Saturday after Thanksgiving."

"What? You're kidding."

"Nope." Topaz shook her head and patted her stomach. "Baby will be here in March."

"But Thanksgiving's only a little more than two months away."

"I know. But it's a good time for Germain because he'll be off from school, so we can have a few days for a honeymoon." Topaz grinned.

"Honeymoon? It looks like you and Germain have had enough honeymoon. That's how that baby got here in the first place."

"Girl, stop." Topaz burst into laughter. She was really enjoying herself. But then she always did with Keisha. "We're only going away for the night and then we'll go back to Baltimore. But we're going to Jamaica for Christmas for a real honeymoon," she sang happily as the little girl in her came out to play.

"Bad, the girl's got it bad." Keisha shook her head, grabbed a pink notepad from Topaz's desk, and started writing. "Well, let's get down to business. We've got a lot to do to get you and Germain married by Thanksgiving."

"We're getting married at Germain's church and then having dinner at the Gradneys' and then we're going partying in New Orleans," Topaz finished with a triumphant grin.

"Maiden of honor and best friend?" Topaz spoke in an excellent British accent into the telephone.

"Yes." Keisha giggled. Topaz was quite good when she was pretending to be someone else.

"The fair and lovely Princess Topaz needs a big favor," she continued in her English dialect.

"What?" Keisha laughed. "It must be big because you're laying it on awfully thick."

"I need a ride to the airport." She spoke softly in her own voice.

"A ride to the airport . . . wait, where are you going?"

"L.A." She heard Keisha suck in her breath.

"Who's in L.A., Topaz?"

"The Concordes are playing the Lakers the second week in November."

"And you're actually going to see him?"

"Yes, I told you I need him to help me get a record deal . . ."

"I cannot believe you. You're getting married in three weeks, and you're going to see another man."

"Business, Keisha, business. That's all it is."

Topaz tried to remain cool during the limo ride from LAX to Marina del Rey. It was her first trip to Los Angeles, and Sean had even arranged for a limo to pick her up from the airport. It's such a beautiful city. It's so pretty and it's so bright. I would love to live here.

She smiled when the limousine pulled into the circular drive in front of the Ritz Carlton in the marina. Sean had said he'd get her a room in his hotel. And this is some swanky hotel, she noticed as she informed the desk clerk of her reservation.

She handed the bellboy two crisp one dollar bills and closed the door to her room quickly behind him. She wanted some time alone to bask in the magnificence of it all. I'm in this fabulous hotel in Los Angeles waiting for Sylk Ross of the Concordes to arrive so we can spend the weekend together. She frowned momentarily. Why couldn't Germain be a Concorde and I be waiting for his charter jet to arrive at three?

"Oh, well," she exclaimed to her reflection in the bathroom mirror. "I can't have everything. But I'm going to get my singing career."

She was in the hotel bar drinking orange juice and sparkling water and waiting for Sean to meet her for an early dinner. Although she was almost five months pregnant, she was more radiant and more beautiful than ever. Her blond locks glistened like fire against the black wool dress she was wearing. Her mother's black Chanel sweater and tasteful gold jewelry gave her the illusion of being extremely wealthy. She was also wearing a splendid pair of Joan & David shoes that she had found on sale. No, it wasn't the hip, upscale, body-conscious look she usually went for; tonight she was conservative and elegant.

"Princess Topaz," she heard Sean say over her left shoulder.

She turned around to gaze into his smiling face. He was wearing black trousers and a crisp, white silk shirt. His flawless chocolate skin glowed as though it had been scrubbed to perfection, and his eyes were kind and smiling. What is it about this man? she wondered as he assisted her off the stool. He's gorgeous. I just need to give him some so I can get over this thing I have for him.

"Hi, Sean," she managed to say.

"So how's everything?" he inquired over dinner at Benihana.

"Things are going well." She picked up some of the Japanese-style lobster with a pair of chopsticks, squeezed a slice of lemon into her steaming cup of hot butter, and dunked the lobster thoroughly before it disappeared into her mouth. "The food is fabulous."

"Good, I'm glad you like it. I usually try to get over here whenever I'm in the city. Say, you're good with those chopsticks. Can you show me how to use mine?"

"Sure." Topaz took the red lacquer chopsticks and positioned them between his strong, long fingers. "See, this one does all the work and this one keeps still." She demonstrated with her own and cheered softly when Sean successfully picked up a piece of mahi-mahi.

"But I'll probably never be as good as you."

After dinner, they walked arm-in-arm out to the limo. Sean had retained one to drive them around the city. "I really hate driving here. Everything is too spread out and people drive crazy in Los Angeles."

"I don't mind." Topaz gazed out of the window. "I just love riding in limos. What are we doing next?" She snuggled under his arm.

"I thought we'd check out Luther and En Vogue."

"Luther Vandross and En Vogue? You mean we're going to a concert?" Her amber eyes grew wide with excitement.

"Yes . . ."

"Oh, I just love concerts," Topaz squealed with delight. "I love you so much for bringing me here." Sean laughed out loud as she began covering his face with delicate kisses.

"If you like concerts this much I'll take you to hundreds of them," he smiled.

The limo stopped in front of the green room backstage at the Universal Amphitheater. They had entered through a Universal Studios Tour entrance and Topaz hadn't realized they were at the concert until she thought she saw Nick Ashford and Valerie Simpson being ushered inside.

"Is that Ashford and Simpson?" she asked, as Sean helped her out of the car.

"Looks like it to me. Hi, Nick, Val." The couple was in the greenroom drinking Perrier. "This is my friend, Topaz." Topaz grabbed Sean by the arm and pulled him closer so she could whisper.

"Are we backstage?"

"Yes." He handed her a colorful backstage pass that said LUTHER VANDROSS. "I guess we better put these on so they don't throw us out of here." He removed the back and applied the pass to his jacket.

"I've never been backstage at a concert before." Topaz followed suit and stuck the badge on her sweater.

Sean's easy smile exposed his matinee-idol charm. "It's no big deal. I'm only invited back here because I'm a Concorde. I come to see the show. And we have to go out front to do that."

Topaz didn't hear anything else he said. She was too busy gawking at Ronnie DeVoe, Ricky Bell, and Johnny Gill from New Edition. She quietly scoped the room and located Vesta, Denzel Washington and his wife, Pauletta, Martin Lawrence, and Kadeem Hardison. And they all knew Sylk. The moment they spotted him, they rushed right over to speak to him, and Sean was wonderful about introducing her to everyone. Finally, Luther came out and spoke to all his guests.

"Let's go to our seats so we don't miss anything," Sean suggested.

I'd rather stay back here with all the stars instead. Topaz reluctantly followed Sean out of the greenroom and up the stairs into the amphitheater. But she had heard him tell Denzel that he would probably show up later at a place called Roxbury. Maybe

I'll get to see more of them later. An usher showed them to front row seats in the pit. Front row seats, she realized as they were seated. I'm going to die.

The next night, Sean led the Concordes to victory over the Los Angeles Lakers. He scored the most points and tossed in numerous gorgeous jumpers. But Topaz couldn't focus on the game. She could barely sit still once she spotted avid Laker fans Arsenio Hall, Jackie Jackson, and Jack Nicholson.

I swear Arsenio's looking at me. She watched the game momentarily while Magic Johnson had the ball. I just know Arsenio's looking at me.

"You were great and you're the best basketball player of all," she told Sean after the game, lavishing compliment after compliment on him. She kissed him and gently stroked his cheek. There, that ought to get me off the hook since I paid very little attention to his game.

Sunday morning, the limo took them up the coast to Santa Barbara. Topaz was enchanted by the magnificent blue Pacific Ocean. "It's the most beautiful thing I ever saw." She sat in Sean's arms, holding his hand, just taking in the splendidness of it all. "Los Angeles has got to be the most beautiful place in the United States."

"You really like it that much?" Sean seemed surprised.

"Oh, yes," she informed him as he helped her out of the car at the Santa Barbara Biltmore. "Very much."

"I like it, too. I'll have to take you to the Caribbean one of these days. Now that's a beautiful place."

"This is the most wonderful brunch I've ever seen." Topaz couldn't decide what to choose first as she stared in disbelief at the tables laden with fresh sliced bananas, pineapples, strawberries, melons, grapes, kiwi, oranges, peaches, and pears. There was a cook making Belgian waffles and serving them with creamy whipped butter and hot maple syrup or fresh fruit compote. Another table held ham, bacon, sausage, hash browns, and chicken wings, beef burgundy, rice, various pastas, and salads. Another cook was serving made-to-order omelettes, filled with various types of cheese, mushrooms, tomatoes, onions, peppers, spinach, bacon, or ham. Every kind of pastry imaginable, various types of toast, pats of butter inscribed with a "B," champagne, and fresh-squeezed orange juice.

"Ooh." She took a bite of an omelette with spinach, cheese, and mushrooms. "I'm in heaven." She cut into a Belgian waffle piled high with strawberries and whipped cream. I probably gained twenty pounds this weekend the way I've been eating. But Germain won't care. He'd love me anyway. She gazed at Sean who had been the perfect host the entire weekend. Oh, why couldn't I be in love with you? You're so gorgeous.

"Is everything okay?" Sean asked, ever the gentleman. "Can I get you more of anything?"

"No, thanks." She smiled. "I couldn't eat another bite."

Sean smiled and finished his water. "Well, pretty lady, we're going to have to get back. I've got a plane to catch and so do you."

She nodded in agreement, tossed her napkin on the table, and tucked her arm through his as they left the restaurant. Now we'll talk about my singing and I'm going to lay it on thick.

"Sean," she called sweetly, once they were in the limousine. "I told you I sing, right?"

"Yes."

"When I decided not to move to New York, I kind of shut the door on my singing career. You know I told you my mother wants me to go to D.C. with her because we're going to open another branch of her business in Washington," she lied. This was the reason she had given him for her upcoming move to Baltimore.

"I bet your mother is real happy you're doing that."

"Yes, she is, but now I don't have any leads on getting a record deal." She focused her amber eyes on him imploringly. "Do you have any friends in the business who might be able to help me?" she asked, using her sweetest voice.

Sean gazed up at the light fixture in the car before responding. "I know some people. Let me see what I can do."

"You'll help me?" she asked in the same soft voice as she tried not to scream.

"Sure, I will." His gorgeous smile lit up his face. "There's nothing I wouldn't do for my girl." She thought she saw him blush when he smiled. I knew Sylk would help me, she told herself in the first-class section of the plane. I just knew he would.

Topaz studied herself in her mother's full-length antique mirror. The long, white, silk-beaded dress was beautiful, simple, and elegant. It was fitted and draped in all the right places. Her hair had been blow-dried and brushed until it glistened, then carefully tucked into a French roll and pinned with her grandmother's antique gold-and-pearl hairclip under the antique lace veil. She had found a pair of plain white Joan & David shoes and had them covered with the same lace, pearls, and crystals that had been used for her veil and gown.

"You look beautiful," Keisha told her. "Topaz, you're a gorgeous bride."

"Thanks." Topaz smiled, pleased with the reflection she saw in the mirror. Topaz slipped on a blue garter and glanced at her best friend who was standing behind her. "Can't forget that or Germain would have a fit. You look pretty too, Keisha."

Keisha, her maid of honor and the only bridesmaid in the wedding, was stunning in a mauve moire gown. Her shiny black hair peaked out around the sides of her veil. She was simply radiant in the variations of plum makeup that Lisa had applied.

"All right, ladies, smile prettily." Lisa stepped in front of them with a camera.

The girls hugged and squinted as the camera flashed in their eyes. They posed for several more photos by Brian, who had been hired to photograph the wedding.

"You're actually marrying Germain Gradney," Keisha whispered in the limo on the way to the church. "I never thought this day would come."

I didn't think it would, either. Topaz smiled and tried not to hyperventilate. "Keisha," she wailed. "The baby's kicking up a storm. Do you think Baby knows Mommy and Daddy are getting married today?"

"Baby probably does. They can hear and they know voices already."

"That's amazing." Topaz watched a tiny limb punch on her stomach from within. "Oh, Keisha, Baby's coming to Mommy and Daddy's wedding. That's so special." She pouted like a little girl. "Keisha, I think I'm going to cry."

"Oh, please." Her maid of honor laughed. "You'll ruin your makeup."

Germain looks so handsome in his gray tux. Topaz walked down the church aisle on the arm of Lance, her mother's younger brother. She smiled radiantly when she reached the altar and took Germain's hand.

"Beloved, we are gathered here today . . ." she heard the minister begin.

I can't believe she's finally going to be my wife. Germain was elated. I've been in love with her since the night I first laid eyes on her when she was eighteen. "I, Germain, take thee, Topaz," he repeated after the Episcopalian minister, staring into Topaz's amber eyes.

"I, Topaz, take thee, Germain," Topaz repeated, gazing into Germain's hazel eyes as the tears slowly streamed out of her own eyes and down her face. I can't believe he really loves me this much. No one else ever has.

"May I present Mr. and Mrs. Germain Gradney," the minister proclaimed at the end of the ceremony.

Germain took Topaz in his arms and kissed her until he felt his soul ignite with a passion he had never felt. She's mine, all mine, he wanted to shout from the rooftops. She's my wife and the mother of my child.

He's going to have to pick me up off the floor if he doesn't stop kissing me. Topaz felt herself falling through space. It was like they were kissing for the very first time. Just when she was about to faint, she felt a swift kick inside, jolting her back to reality. Thanks, Baby.

They posed for countless photos. Then, Germain, Topaz, Keisha, and Germain's best man and best friend, Allen, an intern from the hospital, climbed into the limo that had been decorated with Just Married paraphernalia for the ride to the Gradneys. Germain opened a bottle of Cristal that had been chilling on ice in the beverage compartment and poured glasses for everyone.

"To the most beautiful woman in the world, I love you." Germain toasted his new bride sincerely.

"I love you too, baby." They kissed for several minutes until Keisha interrupted.

"All right, you two, enough of that. That's how Baby got here in the first place."

The wedding guests were served a buffet of prime rib, gumbo, rice pilaf, mashed potatoes, asparagus, potato salad, yams, and string beans by a staff of caterers who were set up in a large white tent in the backyard. There was an assortment of breads, fresh green salad, chilled beverages, and lots of Cristal. The furniture in the house had been removed and white folding chairs were set up. An area that would be utilized as a dance floor had been roped off in the dining room.

Topaz and Germain posed for picture after picture. After dinner, they fed each other wedding cake. This is the happiest day of my life. Topaz looked into Germain's eyes as he twirled her around the floor to "Endless Love," which she had chosen for the first dance.

Afterwards, Topaz danced her heart out until early evening, when she disappeared upstairs to change into a gorgeous white suit that Lisa had made especially for the journey to New Orleans.

After carefully removing one rose to dry and keep for herself, Topaz tossed her bouquet of long-stem white roses to bridal hopefuls. She tucked the rose into the white Chanel bag she had received on the night of her debutante ball.

"Be cool, fools," Germain warned his male guests. He proudly displayed the garter around Topaz's long, shapely leg. "Stop drooling." They were making cat whistles the moment he touched her leg. He peeled off the garter and tossed it to one of his young cousins. "Don't think I'm going to let any of you older dogs go home with my woman's undergarments," he laughed. "I know she's fine and she's all mine."

I'll never forget this day, Topaz promised herself. Keisha pelted her with grains of rice that had been spray-painted silver as the couple dashed outside to the limo. Topaz waved good-bye and climbed into the limo next to Germain, who took her into his arms and kissed her as they drove away. Not ever . . .

SEVENTEEN

THE OFFERS never stopped coming in. Sean glanced at the thick stack of letters in his incoming mail folder, letters requesting interviews and personal appearances. He sighed and placed them aside. He skimmed a stack of lucrative offers from advertising agencies and commercial agents requesting him to do television commercials and endorsements for Pepsi, Coca-Cola, Wheaties, Kellogg's Corn Flakes, Total, Taco Bell, McDonald's, Seagrams, Coors, and Budweiser. He stuck the letters from the alcohol vendors in his paper shredder and turned the machine on.

"I won't be doing any commercials for you, no matter how much you pay," he informed the trash can. He flipped through the remaining pile of letters, which included offers for cologne, deodorant, shaving cream, and sportswear. "Mo money, mo money, mo money . . ." He picked up a script and laughed. "Me in the movies . . . now, that would be funny."

He glanced at the clock on his office desk and groaned. Six o'clock already? There's no way that I'm going to be able to go out tonight. He clicked on the speaker phone, pressed the speed-dialing code for Eric, and turned on "Addictive Love."

"Yo, E-man, what up?" Sean grinned at the phone.

"Ain't nothin' but a thang, man. Just chilling at the pad until we roll up out of here for a little chow and a flick. What time do you want to go?"

"Well, that's why I was calling you, E. I'm going to have to take a rain check."

"What? You mean you're standing me up?"

"Aw, man, it ain't like you ain't got a string of honeys ready to relieve you of some of your time."

"Word," Eric laughed. "All right, Sylk, what's her name?"

"Paperwork."

"Paperwork?"

"I've got a ton of mail over here to go through that my agent sent over. Everybody wants something. I just have one thing to say. What does all this stuff have to do with basketball?"

"I don't know, G. Nothing really and then everything. You know, when you're hot, you're hot. People can't seem to get enough of you."

"I guess you're right, man. Can you believe somebody even wants to put me in a music video?" He picked up the treatment for the video and flipped it open as he leaned back into a comfortable desk chair.

"Yo, money, go for it. Give Denzel Washington and Wesley Snipes a run for their money," Eric encouraged. "I would."

"I know you would. E, I gotta get through this mail. I'll see you tomorrow." Sean clicked off the phone and settled back in his chair with the treatment.

"I want to do the video," he informed his agent, George, several days later.

"You do? Great. It's just a cameo and Spotlight will pay you half a million dollars for your time."

"Half a million for five minutes on film?" Sean was in shock.

"That's the bottom line."

"Fine, set it up," Sean commanded.

"Great. I believe this is a wonderful thing for you. We want to take advantage of every key move that will keep you busy working when you're not playing basketball."

"That's true. I won't be playing basketball for the rest of my life."

"You're a very wise young man, Sylk. Did you take a look at the commercials?"

"Oh, yes. I intend to do a few more of those, too."

"Wonderful, Sylk. I'm going to enjoy making you money." George laughed.

"I'm sure you will."

"I'll fax you the details. It's a one-day shoot in Los Angeles. You're in and out of there in a day," George informed him.

"Great. Meanwhile, I'll start learning my lines."

"Lines? You really don't have any lines to learn. Did I neglect to tell you that you'd be playing basketball with Kidd Maxx?"

"Kidd Maxx! Wait, I don't have to dance, do I?" Sean had pictured his video debut a little more romantic.

"No, they just want you to play basketball while the dancer of dancers sings and dances."

"I don't know, George . . ." Sean began skeptically.

"Come on, Sean, it'll be fun, and just think about what a video with Kidd Maxx will do for your career off the basketball court."

"Wow, Kidd Maxx," Sean repeated. *I've watched him since we were both little kids. I can't believe I'll be working with him.*

Sean's limo took him from the airport straight to the set. The shoot was in an old abandoned warehouse in the San Fernando Valley. Gravel crunched under the car tires as the limo pulled to a stop in back of the warehouse.

"Gunther Lawrence." A meticulously dressed black man with an air of confidence was waiting for him by the limo. "I'm the director of this music and sports extravaganza."

"Word." Sean smiled as he admired the articulate young brother for his accomplishment. "I'm really excited about being here."

You should be, you overpaid jock. Gunther looked up at Sean to make eye contact. "Kidd Maxx should be here any minute," Gunther barked.

"Great, I'm looking forward to meeting him." Sean placed a hand on Gunther's shoulder and lowered his voice, as though he were about to reveal a secret. "Gunther, you've got to make me look good in this video. I've got an image to maintain." He laughed. "I don't want to look silly in a video with the Kidd."

"No chance of that happening. I don't make silly videos," Gunther bragged.

"Cool. I'm sure you got it going on like that."

Gunther grinned and escorted him to a trailer. "You've got this one all to yourself, Sylk. You can just hang out until Kidd gets here."

"What's going on inside the warehouse?" Sean glanced in the direction of the building.

"Nothing much right now, dude. We were waiting on the stars to arrive."

"Would it be okay if I come in now and shoot some hoops?" Sean was humble and gracious. "I need to warm up and I don't want to sit around in here, if that's okay with you."

"Sure, dude, whatever you like. There's a bunch of bratty kids here, too, hoping to get autographs from you and Kidd."

"Did you say kids, Gunther?"

Gunther nodded and tried to understand why Sean would be interested in kids. "Cool, man, I'll be glad to talk to the kids."

"Sure, dude. I'll be more than happy to take you out to them." Sylk Ross wants to talk to kids? Whatever for?

Sean tossed his teal-and-white sweat jacket over a chair and followed Gunther out to a police barricade where a group of children, all ages, sizes, and colors, were gathered.

"Look, it's Sylk Ross," Sean heard one of them say as he and Gunther approached the small throng.

"Sylkman, Sylkman, Sylkman." The kids all began to shriek at the top of their lungs. Sylkman, that's a new one. Sean laughed to himself.

"Hi!" He greeted the children happily with his best smile. He stood there relishing the innocence and joy on their faces as they all clamored for a closer look. A little chocolate girl with ponytails almost as long as she was tall caught his eye. She's gorgeous, he thought, admiring her pretty little face. She could be my daughter.

"Can I have your autograph, please?" she asked sweetly.

"Yeah, me too, me too," the others pleaded. Sean felt his heart melting within him. He stepped over the barricade and the children swarmed around him like bees after honey, thrusting autograph books and pens towards him. He smiled, reaching out to tug a braid, tweak a cheek, and remove a baseball cap from a shaved head. He loved the energy and joy he always received from children.

"How you guys doing?" He signed book after book.

"Fine." They grinned sheepishly, awed by the presence of their favorite basketball player.

"You guys here to see Kidd Maxx, huh?" Sean inquired.

"Yeah," they chorused.

"Me, too." Sean laughed.

"But we came to see you, too."

Sean smiled warmly. "You guys are precious. You guys know Jesus?"

"I know Jesus . . . I know Jesus. I'm saved," many of them squealed, delighted that they had something in common with their basketball hero.

"Good. That's real good. Keep believing in Jesus and you can be anything you wanna be," he encouraged. "I gotta go now."

Someone had brought him a basketball and he dribbled it over to the warehouse. He stuck his head in to see what was going on and was surprised that it was so cool inside.

"The basketball hoop is over here." Gunther lead him around a maze of Arriflex cameras positioned on the floor.

Sean glanced around at the camera equipment, lights, and crew. Wow. I still can't believe I'm doing a video with Kidd Maxx. He tossed in several sweet jumpers and then he slammed one in. "Ouch," Sean laughed to himself. I'm just too good.

"Sylk Ross, it's a pleasure meeting you," he heard a voice call out. He turned around to see who was speaking. It was Kidd Maxx. He had quietly walked onto the set, but he had a presence about him that immediately captured everyone's attention. Kidd was wearing dark glasses and a red shirt, and his shoulder-length hair was pulled back into a ponytail.

"Hey, Kidd, what up, man?" Sean was truly elated. There was nobody more famous than Kidd Maxx. "Did you see all those kids out there?"

"Yes, aren't they incredible?" An easy smile graced the star's face.

"Yeah, man. I love kids." Sean was earnest. "One of these days I'm going to get married and have a family."

Kids and families . . . how nauseating, Gunther mused. "Yo, dudes, we'd better get started. Sylk has a plane to catch," Gunther cut in. I am the director for this shoot, he reminded himself. I don't care how famous they are. Without me, they'd be nothing.

Dudes? Sean repeated in his head. Where did this guy come from? He glanced at Kidd to see if he could tell what he was thinking and practically laughed out loud when the star shook his head and smiled a radiant boyish grin at him. Kidd's really cool, Sean observed. He thinks this director is a joke, too. He could tell the star was trying real hard not to laugh. I guess the brother's seen a little bit of everything, too.

Sean and Kidd had a good time working together on the set.

Sean taught him his special hook shot, and Kidd taught Sean one of his favorite dance steps.

"It was a lot of fun, man," Sean informed him when the shoot was over.

"Thanks for coming, Sylk. My manager told me that you were a bit skeptical of even doing the video at first." Kidd spoke easily to Sean although he was still wearing his dark glasses.

"Man, I wanted to come. I just didn't want you dancing circles around me." Sean kicked at a crack in the concrete of the warehouse with the tip of his white Nike.

"I wouldn't do that." Kidd laughed.

"It wouldn't take much effort, man. I'm no dancer."

"Well, thanks for coming, Sylk," Kidd repeated.

Sean clutched his hand warmly and smiled. "Thanks for asking me. God bless you, man."

And I can't believe either one of you overpaid clowns makes the money you make. Gunther had been standing nearby listening to their conversation. But then that's show business. Gunther walked Sylk out to his limo.

"You were great, dude," Gunther told Sylk for the thousandth time that day as the driver shut the back door of the limousine.

"Dude." Sean shook his head and laughed. "Only in L.A." That brother was some character. He glanced out of the window as the limo pulled into traffic on the Hollywood Freeway. I actually shot hoops with Kidd Maxx, Sean kept telling himself all the way to the airport. And he's really a great person.

Sean's days off were filled with work. He did the talk show circuit with appearances on *Arsenio*, *Oprah*, and *The Tonight Show*. He did interviews and photo shoots for *Sports Illustrated*, *Inside Stuff*, *People*, *Ebony*, and *Essence*, and fashion layouts for *GQ* and *Ebony Male*.

In addition to the offerings he sent to his father's church, he set aside a portion of his income and established the Smooth As Sylk Foundation, which kept him busy in schools talking to kids, feeding homeless families, and donating large sums of money to other projects like the United Negro College Fund, the Sickle Cell Anemia Foundation, and Pediatric AIDs.

■

He flew into Cleveland to meet the team for a game against the Cavaliers. He had left them several days ago after a game in Seattle in order to fulfill some of the obligations on his hectic schedule.

"What up, G?" It was Eric calling from his room in the hotel.

"Yo, man." Sean grinned, happy to hear his buddy's voice. "Why don't you come down and I'll order up some room service or something?"

"You sure, man? I thought you might want to catch some z's."

"Naw, I'm hungry, E. Come on down here so we can grub."

"So, G, how does it feel to be a big music video star?" Eric inquired once they had polished off the New York strip steaks, salad, steak fries, hot apple pie, and ice cream.

"I don't know, dude." Sean laughed as he jumped up for the phone. "Hello? Who is this?" He frowned as he spoke into the receiver.

"Uh-oh, honeys on the line," Eric softly sang.

"I'm having dinner right now," Sean informed his caller politely. "I've got to go." He hung up the phone and shook his head. "How do they know how to find us?"

"Radar." Eric laughed. "Yo, G, so the video with Kidd Maxx, it premiered on MTV today."

"You're kidding. Did you see it, man?"

"Yep."

"How was it?"

"It was dope. You guys looked like you were having fun."

"We were," Sean reminisced. "Kidd is cool. People should give the brother a chance and stop doggin' him all the time."

"The Kidd can dance his behind off. Nobody can touch him. Not even Hammer, but he's weird," Eric declared, making a face.

"No, he's not, he's a good brother," Sean finished defensively. "People just need to give him a chance."

"You're right, G, but black people won't ever stop doggin' each other."

Sean got up to answer the phone again. "Yes?" he answered in a not-so-friendly tone. "Listen, I don't care if you are downstairs, I'm very busy right now." He slammed the phone down and

stared at the receiver for a moment and then took it off the hook. "I hate to take my phone off the hook, but those girls are starting to get on my nerves."

"Man, they just want a piece of a superstar."

"But they don't even know me," Sean protested.

"That doesn't matter to them. They just want to tell all their girlfriends that they slept with you."

"Do you know I have to change my home phone number at least once a month? And I don't know how they get it."

"They get it from people they know who work at the phone company."

"Really? All I know is that it's a pain in the butt every time I have to call everyone again and give them the new number. Man, I gotta find me a wife."

"A wife . . . say, what's going on with Topaz?"

Sean smiled. "Things are good, but we haven't spoken for a while. I've been so busy. She moved to Baltimore to help run her mother's business, so she's been busy, too. How are things going with you and Keisha?"

Eric smiled and tried to be cool. "Good . . . real good. I like that girl, man. She's all right."

"Yeah, she seemed to be really nice. Are things getting serious?"

"Well, you know, when I want to be with someone, she's the one I want to be with. Why else do you think I'm sitting here chewing the fat with you?"

"Because you're not interested in being the topic of conversation of some babe who got lucky last night?"

"Word. You know that stuff gets old real quick. I really admire you for sticking to your convictions, Sylk."

"Thanks, man, but it's not all me. Besides . . . it's not hard when I remember I have a savior that stuck by His."

Sean walked into the visitor's locker room in Detroit dripping with perspiration. They had just defeated the Pistons 101 to 90. As usual the locker room banter ceased the moment he entered the room. Why do they dislike me so much? He sighed as he watched his teammates gather up their bags and head for the bus back to the hotel.

"Yo, man, where you been?" Eric was fully dressed and looking extremely handsome in a new pair of sweats.

"Where else but doing postgame interviews?" Sean's matinee-idol smile was missing from his face. "What you about to get into, all suited up and smelling good?" he asked, brightening.

"Keisha's in town. We're going to the neighborhood to get some ribs. Want to come with us?"

"That sounds like fun, but I've got to go back to New York tonight. I've got some big meeting in the morning and then I'm flying right back out to meet you guys in Chicago."

"That's crazy, Sylk, but it's really cool the way the organization lets you jet off to handle your business," Eric offered. "I know you're getting paid."

"Word, you do what you gotta do."

"All right, Sylk. I gotta run. Keisha's waiting. We rented a car just so we could get some barbecue."

"Not a Mercedes, I hope."

"Naw, man. Keisha got some kind of Ford so we could be incognegro, she said." Eric laughed.

"Good." Eric had finally said something to make Sean laugh. "I like Keisha. You keep her around."

"I intend to, man. I certainly intend to."

I sure wish I could have gone out with E and Keisha. That would have been fun. I never have time to just hang out anymore. He gathered his things and headed for the showers. It's only eleven and my flight doesn't leave until twelve-thirty, he realized after he checked his watch. He glanced around the still, empty locker room. He was the only player left.

It seems like I'm always by myself now. I hardly ever get to travel with the team anymore, not that they miss me. I'm always so busy. He gave himself a once-over in the mirror, straightened his tie, and tossed his remaining things into his oversized Louis Vuitton carry-on and zipped it up.

A knock on the locker room door summoned his attention. He looked up to see Palace security usher in a uniformed limo driver. Sean picked up his bag and slowly strolled out of the room, wishing he had somewhere to go besides home.

Inside the limo he picked up the phone and dialed, gazing out of the car window into the dark night. He smiled when he heard the familiar voice.

"Hi, Daddy. What'cha doin'?"

"I was just sitting here talking to your mother. How are you, son?"

"Fine, Daddy. I'm in a limo on my way to the airport. We just gave Detroit a nice spanking."

"I know. We saw the game on television. I liked those three-pointers, Sean."

"Thanks, Daddy." Sean tried to think of something else to say. He sat there in silence holding the phone.

"What's wrong, son?"

"Nothing, Daddy. I was just calling to check on you and Mommy." Sean tried to conceal the pain in his voice.

"Sean . . ."

"Well, I was just feeling kind of alone and missing everybody, that's all."

"There's nothing wrong with that. We miss you, too."

"I know, Daddy."

"Nobody special in your life yet?"

"Nope . . . well, there is somebody, but I don't know . . ."

"I'm praying for you, Sean. You'll find that special person. And when you do, you'll know she's the one that God sent for you."

"Okay, Daddy. I've got to go now." He wasn't ready to get into a conversation with his father about the state of his love life.

"All right, Sean. I love you."

"I know, Daddy. I love you, too. Kiss Mommy for me."

Sean hung up the phone and stared out of the window into the darkness. An occasional headlight broke the monotony of the dark highway. Why am I feeling so down? Because I'm lonely, he realized, sighing sadly. All I ever wanted to do was play basketball. I never asked to be alone. But in the NBA, life isn't just basketball. It's a business with plenty of money to be made for the key players. And I'm not a player, he reminded himself. I'm just the commodity in this game. He yawned sleepily. And right about now demand is definitely starting to exceed supply.

He reached into his carry-on to retrieve his Walkman and was surprised to find the bottle of Demerol painkillers that had been prescribed for him when he had injured his knee in college. I can't believe these things have been in here all this time. The memories of that night quickly resurfaced. Seems like I've had nothing but pain since that night, he suddenly realized. I don't like being in pain.

He unscrewed the childproof cap and shook two tablets into his hand, which he gulped down with a swig of water. Before the limo arrived at the airport the drug had already taken affect. He was more relaxed and chilled out than he had been for months. Instead of kicking it in the VIP lounge, Sean boarded the plane to JFK. A flight attendant escorted him on early. He took his seat in first class, stretched out his long legs, and kicked off his shoes. He was asleep before the aircraft left the ground.

EIGHTEEN

"JAMAICA, JAMAICA, I'm in Jamaica . . ." Topaz rapped, making up new words to a House of Pain song. She gazed out onto tranquil turquoise waters framed by white sand beaches. Pausing to take a healthy bite from a stick of savory smoked jerk pork, she turned to her left and gawked at the brilliant flowers, rejoicing in splashes of color on a lush green hillside. The sun was radiant against a vivid, electric blue sky. Beams of sunlight spilled into the sea, causing it to sparkle like a well-cut diamond. A cool light breeze, just enough to temper the warmth of the sun, fluttered through lofty palm trees.

"Germain, this is truly the most beautiful, beautiful place I've ever seen." She was delighted. "Thank you so much for bringing me here, baby." She smiled at Germain, who was chilling on a comfortable chaise next to her, wearing a pair of banana-yellow and apricot trunks. He grinned in response from behind a pair of dark sunglasses.

"Paradise, pretty girl, paradise. That's what it is." He leaned over and rubbed her stomach before kissing her. "Hi, Baby," he whispered softly to her protruding belly.

I don't know when I've been happier. Topaz was stunning in a black and metallic gold swimsuit and cover-up. Her curly locks had been carefully twisted into dozens of tawny braids and adorned with gold beads by one of the Jamaican ladies who braided hair on Port Antonio's Boston Beach. Wearing sunglasses and a black straw hat, Topaz fit right in with the upper-crust Europeans and American celebrities who frequented the ritzy resorts and beaches of northern Jamaica.

She plucked another stick of the pungent island barbecue from the plate of food she and Germain were sharing. "This jerk is so good." She licked drops of sauce from her fingers.

"I noticed," Germain replied, without a hint of a smile. "You've practically eaten both our orders."

"Oh, be quiet." She balled up a napkin and tossed it at him.

"But that's okay." He laughed. "When you're big as a house I'll still love you."

"Germain . . ." She pouted and tossed the half-eaten stick of meat back onto the plate.

"Aw, girl, you know you look good. You're gorgeous." He got up and made a spot for himself next to her on the chaise. He took her into his arms, removed her hat, and kissed her gently on the back of her neck. She moved over to make more room on the chaise for him and cuddled into his arms while she watched the jet skiers skim across the sea in front of them.

"It is the Blue Lagoon. This place looks just like the island in that Brooke Shields movie."

"There's a legend that says the lagoon has a spring flowing into it that has the power to increase virility." Germain kissed a tiny mole on the side of her neck. "Speaking of which, why don't we go back to the hotel now and take a nap?"

"All right." She giggled. "I am sleepy. But I'm going to sleep."

"Sure you are."

Topaz smiled when she saw the Trident Villas strung along the rugged coral seaside. Her eyes followed a peacock strutting down the road in front of their rented Suzuki, his dazzling royal blue, emerald, and purple plumage displayed in all of its glory. A uniformed, white-gloved Jamaican doorman helped her out of the car in front of the hotel. This was home for them while they were on the island. They had left Baltimore right after Germain's last final to spend two magnificent weeks in paradise. And tonight was Christmas Eve.

"I'm never going home." She plopped down on a magnificent antique four-poster. The bedding, drapes, sofa, and chairs were all covered in the same pink and mauve chintz fabric, and there were fresh-cut flowers throughout the suite. She stepped out onto the balcony, where they were served breakfast every morning by a waiter, to take another look at the sea crashing beneath her. I'm never going home.

■

Although it was only four in the morning, it was already quite warm and the streets were alive with activity. Topaz could feel the island vibrate with the pounding drum rhythms, and her adrenaline began to surge from all the excitement. It was Christmas morning and they were in MoBay for Junkanoo, a traditional island street carnival. They walked along the main street, where vendors were selling patties, drinks, mangoes, papayas, orantique, and bananas, and found a place to set up their folding chairs so Topaz wouldn't have to stand for the parade.

"Where's the parade, Germain?" Topaz squealed with excitement, unable to remain seated. "Where is it? I can hear them coming but I don't see anyone." It was hard for her to keep still. Her body followed its own mind, swaying to the pulsating rhythm of drums, cowbells, and whistles that drew closer by the minute.

"Germain, look!" She pointed to masked dancers, musicians, and other colorfully costumed participants that had finally come into view.

"It's great, isn't it, pretty girl?" Germain was just as excited. They were like two kids in a candy store. They watched the entire parade, until the sun came up, before driving back to Port Antonio. They munched spicy patties and drank icy tropical juice in the Suzuki on the way back to the hotel. They were so tired, they slept all afternoon, waking by early evening to dress for dinner.

"You look so handsome, baby." Topaz paused while dressing to admire the way Germain's white dinner jacket hugged his slim hips. "You're gorgeous," she said with a kiss. His skin, tanned a dark golden brown by the tropical sun, was glowing, and his black hair was still damp from the shower they had taken together.

"So are you, Mrs. Gradney." Topaz was wearing a short, red crepe slip dress with an Empire bodice that covered her stomach perfectly and made her long tanned legs appear endless. With a pair of matching red-and-rhinestone sandals and her braids pinned up, she was the epitome of elegance. "Pretty girl, you are wearing that red dress . . . you look so good you got me singing, baby."

There was a calypso combo playing softly on the terrace where they sipped frothy fruit drinks. An antique brass candelabra on the table cast wonderful glowing shadows on their ecstatic faces.

"I love you, Topaz." Germain took her slender hands into his.

"I love you, too, Germain." She beamed radiantly.

"Merry Christmas, baby." He slid a diamond baguette band on the ring finger of her right hand.

"Oh, Germain." Topaz held her hand near the flame of the candle to admire the ring. It sparkled magnificently in the light. "It's so beautiful. Thank you."

He smiled into her eyes, happy because she was pleased. They sat there just staring at each other until a white-gloved waiter interrupted to serve smoked marlin and lobster. The seafood had been slow-cooked over a pimento wood fire, and it was served with rice 'n' peas, vegetables, and champagne.

"Paradise," Topaz whispered softly. "I know I'm in paradise . . ."

"Baby, where you going?" Topaz whined, watching Germain screw the red lid on a thermos of coffee. They were back in Baltimore and Germain was back in school.

"To the library to study." He stuffed the thermos into a bag of his medical textbooks.

"But you can study here," she protested.

"No, I can't because you won't leave me alone. I've got a big exam next week."

"But you just had one last week," Topaz wailed. "Do you have them every day?"

"Yes. I've got to go." He kissed her and headed for the door.

"What time are you coming home?"

"You'll be asleep. We'll go to a movie or something tomorrow."

Dang. Topaz watched him close and lock the door before she waddled back into the family room. There was a fire crackling in the fireplace, a large-screen television, an elaborate sound system, and several comfortable sofas. With the baby only a month away, they had moved into a rented house in Baltimore. With Germain's part-time job at the hospital, his parents taking care of his tuition, and several stipends for research projects, they were able to live nicely for such a young couple.

Topaz felt the baby give her a swift kick as she curled up on the sofa under a vivid patchwork quilt. "Ouch, Baby, you're starting to get a little rough." She flipped the television from channel to channel and finally back to *MTV Jams*. Bill Bellamy is so cute. I can't believe I can't find anything on with all of these channels. She moaned.

An upbeat Paula Abdul music video caught her attention on VH1. "I could do that." She sat up straight on the couch to take a better look. "Hey, I could be better than that. I can sing." She watched video after video, taking note of the things she liked and disliked about them, imagining what her own video would look like if she were out there. But I'm not out there, she realized sadly. She switched off the television and felt her enlarged abdomen. "That reminds me," she whispered. "I'd better get some more cocoa butter."

She went upstairs, pausing for a moment in the baby's room. Germain had painted it the palest mint green. She had picked out a colorful wallpaper border, and with the white baby furniture and gleaming hardwood floor, the room was perfect. "It won't be long now." She clicked off the light and headed into her master bathroom for the jar of cocoa butter. She sat on the bed and massaged her enormous belly with the balm before changing into a nightie.

Now what can I do? She glanced at the stack of fashion magazines by her side of the bed and picked one up. She perused the pages thoroughly, taking in every detail of the models' clothing, makeup, and hair, tearing out the pictures she liked and sticking them in an old Johns Hopkins Medical College folder. After she had scoured several issues of European *Vogue*, *Elle*, and *Harper's Bazaar*, she was restless again. She stared at the phone for several minutes.

"I'll call Keisha," she mumbled softly, picking up the phone. But I can't. Germain would kill me, especially after that last phone bill. "Why don't you call me, you cow?" she yelled at the phone. She's probably off with Eric somewhere.

"Look at all those fine clothes. Just look, and I can't wear any of them, how depressing . . . I'm bored." She angrily tossed the magazines across the room, picked up the telephone, and dialed Germain's pager number. She grinned when the phone rang several minutes later.

"Is everything okay? You're not having the baby or anything, are you?"

"No. I'm not having the baby, Germain. Why are you always thinking about the baby instead of me?"

"I gotta go," he announced flatly. "You're tripping."

"I'm bored, Germain," she wailed.

"Read a book."

She heard the phone click in her ear and threw the telephone across the room, then she cried herself to sleep.

It was after four in the morning when he finally climbed into bed next to her. She squinted at the digital clock on his side of the bed twice to be sure.

"Hi, baby," she whispered, snuggling up next to him.

"You're awake." She could tell he was smiling.

"You know I can't really sleep without you here next to me."

"I brought you something," he whispered in her ear.

"What?" she whispered back.

"This." They made love until the sun came up, then he brought her breakfast in bed.

"You did all of this for me?" She squealed with delight at the French toast sprinkled lightly with powdered sugar and cinnamon, scrambled eggs with cheese, bacon, sausage, grits, and orange juice.

"I did it for us." He helped himself to a hearty bite of French toast as he patted her belly. "All of us."

She let her fork fall into her plate. "You never do anything for me anymore. It's always about the baby."

"What?" He was unable to believe what he was hearing.

"You heard me," she snarled. Topaz threw back the heavy comforter and climbed out of bed. "You said you loved me, but you don't, and you probably wouldn't have even asked me to marry you if I hadn't been pregnant."

"What?" he repeated with a frown. "Topaz, you know that's a lie. What is your problem?" he asked, trying to figure out what this fight was about.

"You." Her eyes were amber daggers.

He watched her go into the bathroom and slam the door, and then he heard her running water for a bath. He shook his head, gathered up the breakfast dishes, and took them back down to the kitchen. By the time he had cleaned the kitchen and put all the dishes into the washer, she was downstairs fully dressed.

"Where are you going?" he demanded.

"Out."

"Out where?"

"Germain, leave me alone. You're getting on my nerves." She flipped her hair, which she had blow-dried silky straight, took the key to the Mercedes, and left the house without another word.

"Now where can I go?" she whispered once she was in the car. "I have to go somewhere. I know, I'm going shopping. I need some new clothes." She backed out of the driveway and drove to Nordstrom in Tyson Corners.

"Spoiled brat." Germain yelled, hurling the dishcloth into the sink. "Dang, she look good." He went back upstairs to take a nap but was unable to sleep. His mind kept drifting back to his argument with Topaz. That was about attention. That was all about attention.

"Topaz never had a father," his mother had warned him. "So she'll expect you to be her father, husband, lover, and friend. Can you handle all of that?"

"I love her, Mother," he had replied. "And I still do," he whispered. "More than life itself . . ."

One morning in the middle of March, while she was watching *The Young and the Restless*, she felt a sharp pain in her abdomen that took her breath away. "What was that?" She clutched her stomach and sucked in her breath. Germain, who had been studying all night, was in class taking a midterm.

"You trying to tell me something, Baby?" She slowly exhaled and rearranged herself on the couch. Minutes later, she realized the quilt was wet. My water broke. What should I do? She changed her clothes and tossed the soiled quilt and clothing in the laundry room for Linda, the cleaning lady, who came twice a week, and glanced at the clock. It would be another thirty minutes before Germain would be out of class. I can't disturb him during his midterm, she reasoned, thinking of someone besides herself for once.

Carefully, she climbed back onto the couch and switched to an old black-and-white movie on cable. "Ouch," she yelled. The pain was so intense it brought tears to her eyes. She picked up the phone and dialed Germain's pager number.

"What's up?" he inquired several minutes later.

"Germain, I'm having pains and my water broke," she wailed into the phone.

"No problem, pretty girl. You're just having a baby."

"I am?"

"Yes. Did you call the doctor?"

"No. I called you. You're a doctor."

"Topaz, call her on the other line so I can listen." She clicked over and dialed her obstetrician, Dr. Crews, an attractive, African-American woman in her midthirties, and clicked Germain back in.

"Topaz, you come into the hospital when those pains are an hour apart," Dr. Crews admonished.

"They're an hour apart now," Topaz moaned. "Ow," she screamed. "I just felt another. Germain . . ."

"I'm on my way, pretty girl. Dr. Crews, we'll see you shortly."

It was around seven-thirty that same night when Christopher Black Gradney entered the world, weighing seven pounds and one ounce. Germain was by Topaz's side the entire time, coaching her through the natural childbirth and holding her hand.

"Look." He placed the tiny baby in her arms. "We have a son."

"He's gorgeous," Topaz whispered. "He looks just like you."

"No, pretty girl. He looks like you. He has your eyes and that blond hair."

"All right. He's fine, just like his mama and daddy."

Topaz smiled as she watched the small rolls that had formed around her waistline disappear into firm hard flesh. She worked hard to get her figure back. Once her doctor had given her the go-ahead, she was in aerobics class. She lifted weights, ran, and swam laps. She went to the spa every morning, leaving the baby with her grandmother in Baltimore. Chris loved Grand Mama and she never had to feel guilty about leaving him there.

"I want to go to California, Germain," Topaz announced over dinner one evening. They were watching *Coming to America* and eating Chinese food in the family room.

"Why?"

"To work on my singing. I want to sing, remember?"

"I know. Have you talked to anyone here?"

"You can't get a record deal in Baltimore. You have to go to Los Angeles," she wailed.

"I thought you were going to take a music class at Howard?"

"That's a waste of time," she snapped. "I'm ready to sing, not learn about singing. I won't stay long, Germain, just a couple of months. I can stay with my aunty."

"You have an aunt out there?"

"Yes, one of my mother's older sisters."

"You really want to go?" He gazed into her tawny eyes.

"Yes."

"What are you going to do with Chris? Take him, too?"

"Oh, no. I'd leave him here. Grand Mama said she'd keep him as much as you like."

"I would be able to stay home nights and study if you were away."

"Please, baby, please?" She searched his pensive face. "I won't go if you don't want me to," she added softly, looking at him through lowered lashes.

I told her I'd support her with her singing, he reminded himself. I have to let her go. Especially since this is so important to her. Maybe she'll get bored and come home in a week or two. He sat in silence for a long while, thinking. "Okay, you can go," he finally told her, speaking very slowly.

"Oh, thank you, Germain, thank you." She covered his face with kisses.

"You can leave after Labor Day but you have to be back home by Thanksgiving."

"Okay, I will." She was unable to contain her excitement.

"So what happens if you get this record deal? I have three more years of school here in Baltimore. Are you going to move to Los Angeles?"

"Oh, Germain, of course not. I can live here and have my career. I just have to go there and get it started."

"Okay, you can go. You know I'm only doing this because I love you."

"I know, baby." She got up and sat in his lap. "And I'll love you forever for letting me go."

"I'm going to miss you, pretty girl," he whispered, saddened by the thought of her leaving him.

"Not half as much as I'll miss you."

■

"You're a fool," Keisha told her the moment she heard the news. "I can't believe that you'd go to California and leave your husband and new baby."

"Oh, Keisha, it's now or never. If I wait too much longer, I'll be old with three kids. Besides, Germain said I could go."

"You have to be the stupidest person on this planet," Keisha finished, not mincing the truth.

"Forget her." Topaz hung up the phone and threw it across the room. She's just jealous because I didn't ask her to go with me.

"You're ruining your life," her mother declared. "Topaz, how could you leave a wonderful man like Germain and your son for even a week? They're your family and you belong at home with them."

"Why does everyone keep talking about Germain and Chris?" she snapped. "What about me? Doesn't anyone care about how I feel anymore?"

"Topaz, you made a commitment to Germain and now you have a baby. That's what comes first. Not your singing career." Her mother was not pleased with her decision to go to California. "But it is your life, and I know you've got to have your way."

"Stop looking at me like that," Topaz whispered, stroking Germain's face. "You're going to make me cry."

He forced a smile and kissed her on the cheek.

Fighting a deluge of tears, she gently embraced Germain, who was holding the baby between them. She could hear an agent over the loudspeaker announcing flights arriving and departing from BWI Airport.

"Delta nonstop to Los Angeles, last call."

She kissed the tip of Germain's nose gently, then ran her slender bejewelled fingers over her son's soft blond locks and kissed him on the cheek, leaving traces of her tangerine lipstick. "Baby, I better go now or I'll miss the plane."

"I know," Germain mumbled. He kissed her one last time and pushed her away. "Go." She started slowly towards the gate, picking up momentum with every step, but she paused before she entered the jet way to wave and blow kisses at Germain and Chris. "Wave good-bye to Mommy," Germain whispered to Chris, holding up the baby for Topaz to see.

Topaz found a tissue and dabbed at the tears that had collected on her cheeks. Everything's going to be fine, she assured herself. Just fine. If nothing happens by Thanksgiving, I'm coming back home and I'll forget about singing forever. She cried herself to sleep in her business-class seat, never opening her eyes until she arrived in L.A.

Lena Beaubien, her mother's oldest sister, was striking. Topaz spotted her at the gate. Lena's cinnamon skin had been tanned copper by the Southern California sun. She has the family's runway-model looks but not as much savoir faire as my sophisticated mother, Topaz noted, sizing her aunt up quickly.

"Topaz, look at you," Lena cried. "You're so tall and so pretty." She hugged and kissed her niece. "And you look just like your father."

"I do?" she questioned, raising an eyebrow of interest. "What did my father look like?"

"Fine." They stepped onto the people mover in the terminal at LAX. "Too fine for his own good. I told your mother to leave him alone."

"But what did he look like?" Topaz demanded. "What was he like?"

"He was tall with your same blond hair and coloring . . . Gosh, your hair is beautiful." Her aunt ran a hand through her tawny mane. "Just like those white girls."

"Aunty," Topaz protested. "Tell me about my father."

"Your mother's never told you about him or showed you a picture?"

"No."

Lena shook her head. "Get a skycap to help you with your luggage. I'll get the car. It's a white BMW."

Once they were in the car, Topaz prompted her aunt. "Finish telling me about my father, please."

"Greg Villanueva. He was black, Swedish, and Brazilian . . . absolutely gorgeous. He was attending Howard. His family lived in New York City." Topaz gazed in silence out the window at all the cars on the 405 Freeway, waiting to hear more.

"The girls were after him like bees after honey. He was one pretty man. Anyway, your mother, with her fine, stuck-up self, wouldn't give him the time of day."

"She wouldn't?" Topaz laughed. "So what happened?"

"He blew her mind. She was only sixteen and he was a senior in college, so he was five years older. She'd follow me and your aunty Lynn to parties at Howard. She knew how to fix herself up to look older. So he introduces himself to her one night at an Alpha Kappa Alpha dance and practically loses his mind over her." My mother sounds a lot like me, Topaz realized. "She finally went out on a date with him and that was it. Girlfriend got her first taste and lost her mind."

Topaz laughed until she cried.

"Then you turn up, and your daddy . . . I don't know. He wasn't a very strong person. His family felt your mother wasn't good enough for him so he wimped out on her and went to Harvard for law school. She kept hoping he'd ask her to marry him after he finished school, but she never heard another word from him. He broke her heart. I don't think she ever got over him," her aunt finished softly.

"Wow." That could have been me and Germain. His parents could have talked him out of marrying me, Topaz suddenly realized. I wonder if they tried to. Gosh, I never thought about that. I could have been just like Mother, with no man and a baby on my own. She shook her head at the thought of it. Germain loves me, she reminded herself.

"Want to see a picture of my little boy?" she asked, changing the subject. "He'll be seven months in a couple of weeks." She proudly displayed a photo of him attached to her keychain.

"He's gorgeous."

"Thanks. He's fine, just like his mama and his daddy."

"How old are you, Topaz?"

"Twenty."

"And already married with a baby. Child, what are you doing here?"

"I'm only staying for a little while. I want to see what I can do with my singing, and Germain says he has a hard time studying with me around."

"I wonder why." Her aunt laughed.

Topaz smiled. "Where are Nina and Kim?" They pulled into the driveway of a pretty four-bedroom house off Coldwater Canyon in Sherman Oaks.

"Kim's registering for school and Nina works. Kim's twenty-one now. She's in her last year at UCLA. She's getting a degree in finance. She worked for IBM all summer. Nina's here. That's her car there." Lena pulled up behind a shiny, black Pontiac Fiero. "I don't know about that Nina. She's nineteen and she works part-time in Beverly Hills as a secretary for some big public relations firm. She makes pretty nice money, though I wish she'd get her college degree."

Topaz helped her aunt drag the suitcases into the house. She caught sight of a sparkling aquamarine pool in a nice-sized backyard. The redbrick walkway that wound its way through the freshly cut grass was lined with borders of perky, vibrant flowers. Nice place, she noted, admiring the gleaming peach kitchen with greenhouse windows that were filled with flowers. A large television set and a black-and-white plaid sofa directly off the kitchen were inviting. And there were more windows everywhere. Sunlight filled the back of the house.

"You'll be staying in here." Lena took Topaz into a bedroom near the kitchen that had a window with a view of the pool and the backyard. "I hope you don't mind sleeping down here alone."

It's nowhere as big as my bedroom at home, but it'll do for now. Topaz glanced around the peach room that had a double bed and a private bathroom. "Oh, no I don't mind, this is nice."

"Great." Topaz could hear the bass line of a Naughty By Nature song thumping through the ceiling.

"Nina . . ." Lena looked up at the ceiling as she exited the room. "Nina," she yelled, from the foot of the stairs. "Come down here and see Topaz."

"What?" Topaz heard a voice reply.

"Come down here," Lena commanded. Moments later she heard someone running down the stairs. "Go talk to Topaz," she heard her aunt whisper loudly.

"Hi." The voice was friendly yet there was an aura of excitement and sophistication.

Topaz looked up from unpacking and gasped. She's the most beautiful girl I've ever seen. She gave her cousin a thorough looking over. Nina was tall and thin with flawless mocha skin. Her long hair was streaked a lighter golden brown as though the sun had delicately bleached it. Her thin body was extremely toned and her denim shorts and red bustier displayed it nicely. A warm smile lit up her face and her eyes sparkled with mischief.

"Hi." Topaz liked her at once.

"What's up, cuz?" Nina, not shy at all, found a spot for herself on Topaz's bed. "Welcome to Cali."

NINETEEN

GUNTHER UNFOLDED the *Daily Variety* and smiled at the headline on the bottom right side of the paper. "Gunther Lawrence, Majestic Entertainment Golden Boy. New VP of Development cranks out projects with the Midas touch," he continued reading, pleased as punch. He studied the small black-and-white headshot accompanying the brief article that heralded his accomplishments. I'll have to get this article mounted the way I had the piece done from the *Hollywood Reporter*.

His last two projects had done so well financially for the studio that Bob had been promoted to senior vice president of development and Gunther, vice president of production.

"I should have gotten Bob's job," he grumbled when he was first informed of the promotions. "I do all the work and he gets to become senior vice president." But Gunther was actually quite pleased with himself. "Now I'll be able to have my own films made."

He had finished writing *Intrigue*, an excellent, spellbinding, suspense film, some time ago. He pulled it up on the computer and printed a final draft, grinning with pleasure as he sifted through the crisp sheets of paper in the bin of the Hewlett Packard laser printer. He read bits of dialogue from his favorite scenes.

"Vanessa, it's Gunther," he barked into the speaker phone in his office. "I need an appointment with Bob immediately."

"Hey, Gunther, what's up?" She was happy as usual to hear his voice. "Are you going out for lunch?"

Gunther slammed the stack of papers bearing his picture on the floor. Don't answer a question with a question, he wanted to scream. Dang, that heifer gets on my nerves. "I have a meeting at the Bistro," he lied.

"Oh, too bad. Bob wanted you to join him for a meeting with Mr. Z."

Mr. Z? Why didn't she say that in the first place? Witch. "I can cancel my meeting at the Bistro. Where do I meet Bob and Mr. Z?"

"Twelve-thirty at Il Cielo. I'll confirm the reservation."

"Never mind that meeting with Bob. I'll speak to him personally," he informed her and clicked her off the speaker phone. A meeting with Bob and Mr. Z. That's just what I need. Gunther was so excited he rushed down the hall to the big Xerox copier to make additional copies of the script himself. I'll spring this on them at the end. He was already anticipating the look on their faces once he presented them with the script. I've made this studio lots of money. Now it's time for me to have a piece of it.

At Il Cielo, a posh Italian restaurant in Beverly Hills, Gunther left his car with the valet and took a seat at the bar while he waited for his luncheon companions. He glanced at his watch and learned that it was only twelve. He signaled for the bartender.

"Cranberry juice and gin with a slice of lime." Gunther removed his dark glasses and clicked open the shiny gold locks on his black leather briefcase. He slipped his sunglasses into a Calvin Klein case and felt his heart pounding away when his eyes fell across the *Intrigue* scripts inside. He closed the case and drank his cocktail in a series of gulps. That tasted good.

"Linda," he read from the name tag perched near the perky bosom of the pretty, voluptuous blond bartender. "Can I have another one of these?" Gunther looked directly into her eyes and felt his muscles relax almost immediately as a genuine smile worked its way onto his face for once.

"Sure."

He watched her tight skirt move up and expose her thigh as she bent over to fill a clean glass with fresh ice. That alcohol sure kicked in quick, Gunther noted, as he continued watching her prepare his drink. She expertly stuck a wedge of lime on the edge of the glass and set it down in front of him.

"Anything else?" Her voice was cool and crisp.

"Would you like to have dinner?" he heard himself ask. He searched her eyes waiting for a response.

"Dinner?" she repeated.

"Dinner. Anywhere you like, gorgeous," he added softly. He watched her face light up from his sweet talk. I got her already. All you have to do is sweet-talk a female and you can get whatever you want.

"Okay." She spoke slowly as though she wasn't sure.

"Great." Gunther flashed his best smile. "I have a luncheon meeting now." He watched Bob and Mr. Z enter the restaurant together. So Bob drove over with Mr. Z. He focused his attention back on Linda. "Write down your address and I'll stop by for it on my way out. I'm Gunther Lawrence," he finished, still smiling.

"See you later, Gunther." She smiled sweetly. She seemed more sure about him now.

"Bob, Joel." Gunther greeted them crisply, shaking hands firmly and making direct eye contact.

"The man with the golden touch." Joel's smile was genuine and warm.

"Gunther, glad you could make it," Bob declared.

Gunther sat down, spread the crisp white linen napkin over his latest purchase from Maxfield's, and picked up the menu.

"Are you gentlemen ready to order?" a gorgeous brunette inquired.

"I'll have a Bloody Mary," Joel replied. "And the broiled salmon with pasta."

"A glass of red wine and lasagna," Bob ordered.

"Cappellini with fresh tomato and basil," Gunther commanded. He took a sip of his fresh drink. "And bring me another of these."

"Now that the real business has been conducted, I have no pressing business to discuss unless one of you has something." Joel picked up his cocktail. "I just wanted to take you both to lunch." He took a healthy gulp of the tomato juice drink.

"How 'bout those Lakers?" Bob began.

"I have something I'd like to discuss," Gunther interrupted. I have Joel Zwieg's undivided attention in a relaxed setting . . . there's no way I'm going to let Bob sit here and replay a stupid Laker game. He flipped open his briefcase, removed the scripts, and took a big swig of his cranberry cocktail to bolster his confidence. Then he handed them each a script.

"What's this, another million-dollar project?" Joel was hooked already. He flipped open the script.

"Most definitely." Gunther watched Joel's eyes skim the pages.

Bob flipped quickly through the pages and laid the script on the table.

"Is this one of yours, Gunther?"

"It's one of my best." Gunther wondered why Bob had laid the script aside so quickly. "I've got the budget, shooting schedule, and marketing strategy already done." He picked up another package of papers and passed them around. Gunther was silent while the men sifted through the materials.

"This looks impressive, Gunther," Joel finally said. "We can really do this film for five million?"

"Sure." Gunther was already excited. "I'd make sure of that personally."

The waitress arrived with their entrees and the men eagerly laid the scripts aside in anticipation of the exquisite Italian cuisine.

"Who did you have in mind for the director, Gunther?" Bob swirled pasta around his fork with a spoon.

Gunther swallowed a mouthful of pasta and took a sip of his drink. "Me."

"You?" Joel seemed surprised.

"Joel, I studied directing at USC. I was awarded the gold in Drama and the DGA Student Award at the Student Academy Awards two years ago," Gunther boasted.

"What films have you directed?" Joel continued buttering a hard roll but looked genuinely interested.

"I haven't done anything commercial yet except for numerous music videos that have been on MTV. I did that basketball video for Kidd Maxx several months ago."

"You did a video for Kidd Maxx?" Joel sputtered.

Gunther finished off the last of his cappellini before answering. "I sure did. It was really great working with him and Sylk Ross."

"Do you think you could get one of them for this film?" Joel was rapt with attention.

"Not with a budget of five million," Gunther quickly replied. "Those guys are expensive."

"Who did you have in mind?" Bob pushed his empty plate aside.

"Good unknown actors," Gunther informed them. "I'd

rather put the money on the screen instead of into talent. I'll use big names in my next project."

"Tell me about the story, Gunther," Joel prompted. "Where does it take place?"

"It opens on a dark foggy street in Munich," Gunther began, thoroughly overcome by Joel's interest in his project.

"Munich?" Joel seemed confused. "Wait, Gunther, is this a black film?"

"Black? You mean film noir? Oh, no, it's a nineties version of James Bond. Now, the street is dark and there's a flicker of light from an old gas street lamp . . ."

Bob was chuckling. "Gunther, Joel wants to know if the film has black people in it. Is your film about black people?"

Black people? Gunther repeated in his mind. Do I have to write a film about black people because I'm black? "No," he replied slowly as his excitement began to fade.

"Gunther, we're looking for another Spike Lee," Bob informed him. "That was one of the things I wanted to mention today. I want to know if you know of any up-and-coming black directors. I've been hearing about this team of brothers. I believe one's a director and one's a producer and they graduated from Harvard."

"The Hudlin brothers." Gunther struggled to maintain his composure. He was seething. "They did a film called *House Party*." I'd have to scrape them off the walls if I had written something with black people sucking on chicken bones and eating cornbread.

"I heard that film did pretty well at the box office, too," Bob added. It did okay, Gunther remembered. But he was envious because they were more interested in the Hudlin brothers than him.

"Gunther, write us a good black film along the lines of Spike Lee or those Houdini brothers and I just might let you direct it." Joel smiled. He finished the fruit tart he had been eating and tossed his napkin on the dinner table. "Well, I've got some afternoon appointments. Shall we be going, Bob?"

The men stood up and handed Gunther his scripts. He watched them leave the restaurant before he snapped open his briefcase and tossed the scripts back in.

"A black film," he grumbled under his breath. "I'll write

them a black film." He pushed open the restaurant door. But I've still got to find a way to get *Intrigue* made.

He handed the valet the ticket for his car and stared aimlessly at the apartment buildings on Burton Way. I made a date with that bartender, Linda, he suddenly remembered. "Back in a flash," he informed the parking attendant, dashing back into the restaurant.

"Hi," he spoke softly to Linda.

"I thought you changed your mind." She handed him a piece of paper with her phone number.

"No way." He gave her a handsome smile. "I just had a lot on my mind." Gunther read the information over quickly. She lives in West Hollywood, he noted, slipping the paper in his jacket pocket. "Thanks. I'll give you a call."

I've got to chill out. Gunther paced back and forth in front of his desk in the office. I need something to get my mind off these Majestic idiots. The Hudlin brothers . . . I know . . . I'll call that bartender. He invited her to dinner the very same night.

"I'm really a backup singer," Linda explained. They were having drinks at Gladstones in Malibu. "I work at the restaurant when I'm not out on the road on tour."

"That's very interesting." Gunther tried to appear interested. He gazed across the dusky ocean. The sun was just setting and its reflection glowed in the water like a ball of liquid fire. I must have a place near the ocean, he decided, placing another item on his endless list of things to acquire.

Why can't I get into this? he wondered, watching Linda's mouth move. "Excuse me, would you like another drink? I'm about to order one."

"Sure." She polished off a frozen peach daiquiri.

Gunther signaled for the waiter and placed his order. He snatched up the cocktail the moment the waiter sat it on the table and drank half of it in a matter of seconds. I've got to chill out, he told himself, feeling the alcohol relax his body.

"Did you know Linda means beautiful in Spanish?" he rattled off, trying to be charming. "Names can be so revealing."

"Gunther, are you trying to say I'm beautiful?" Linda smiled.

"Yes." His head was spinning. I don't spend enough time around women, he deduced. That's what's going on here.

Linda continued smiling and moved from across the table to sit next to him. "You're sweet." She kissed him gently on his thin lips. "Gunther, why do you work so hard at covering up your real feelings?"

"I do?" He tried to shake the tenderness he felt for this woman he barely knew. I just want sex, he reminded himself, not a commitment.

"Yes, you do." She kissed him again. "Want to go back to my place?"

Now we're talking. Gunther nodded in agreement and quickly paid the check. He felt his knees weaken the moment her fingers intertwined with his as they held hands walking through the restaurant. He glanced at several waiting patrons as the two of them weaved their way through the Thursday night dinner crowd, astonished by their hateful stares. Why are they looking at me like that? He was extremely uncomfortable by their probing glares. Outside, the cool ocean breeze felt good. He locked his arms around Linda and kissed her on the neck, inhaling the scent of her perfume while they waited for the valet to bring the car.

"It's really sad the way people treat you when you date someone from a different race," Linda opened a compact and covered her full lips with red lipstick.

"What?" Gunther helped her into the car. He couldn't resist smiling at the sight of his shiny convertible Beamer with GUNFIRE on the license plates, the top dropped, the beautiful blonde inside, and the breezy night in Malibu. This vision certainly came to pass, he realized, checking off another completed goal from the list of must haves that he kept filed away in his head.

"People immediately hate you when you date outside your race," Linda continued.

So that's why they were looking at me like that. He shifted into first and rolled out of the parking lot onto Pacific Coast Highway.

"I've dated men from various races. If you can't deal with other people's attitudes and what they think of you, forget it."

"Nobody's ever going to dictate who I can or can't see," Gunther declared with a vengeance.

Back at Linda's place they jumped in the sack.

■

"You're an incredible lover, Gunther." Linda walked him to the door of her apartment. "Do you really have to go now?"

"I've got a couple of scripts to read tonight," he lied, kissing her good-bye. "I'll give you a call tomorrow."

"Well, got what I needed." He sighed once he was in the car. It was good, too. I might have to keep Linda around.

His romance with Linda lasted all of three months. They went out several times a week. Linda knew all the industry hot spots. They went to Nicky Blairs, Bar One, Roxbury, and Ava's. She was really great about not wanting to see him all the time. She didn't mind his not calling and whenever he did call she was ready to roll.

It's a perfect relationship, Gunther rationalized, fingering her blond hair. She gives me what I want when I want it, no strings attached, but I've got to let her go. I just can't deal with people staring at us all the time. He glared back at two black women who had given him looks that could kill the moment he walked into Glam Slam with Linda. One of the women stared him down the entire evening. That was the last night he saw Linda.

No more blondes, he reminded himself in Roxbury as he watched a tanned young woman with sun-streaked hair walk by. The noisy restaurant-club-bar located on the Sunset Strip always had a line out front, and it was his favorite hangout because of its star-studded clientele. Gunther became such a regular he never had a problem securing a reservation.

He would sit at the bar in the restaurant for hours watching the rich and famous come and go—Madonna, Eddie Murphy, Norm Nixon, Jasmine Guy—anybody who was anybody had dinner or drinks in Roxbury. Nobody messes over you when you're famous; people practically fall out at your feet and they give you whatever you want, he noted, watching all the women gawk at Denzel. What a life.

He dated several extremely attractive black girls he met in the club. They were all super thin, with long hair and skin the color of golden vanilla wafers. Most of them were aspiring singers, dancers, actresses, and models whose ceaseless adulation of Gunther made him feel like a king. He wined and dined them and treated them like queens until they started making emotional demands on him that he wasn't willing to keep. Besides, those girls aren't good enough for me. They're just a bunch of wanna-bes. The girl of my dreams will definitely be a star.

He was having dinner alone, sipping one of his favorite cranberry-juice-and-gin cocktails when he saw her. She was tall, long-legged, gorgeous, the color of creamy butterscotch, strutting through the restaurant like the Queen of Sheba. He watched male and female heads swivel for a double take. It's Aria, he thought, feeling his blood pressure escalate. Aria Versailles from Paris. I wonder what she's doing in L.A.

Gunther felt time stand still while he watched a waiter seat her and another girl, the color of mocha with long black hair, two tables behind his. Wrong color, he decided, summing up the friend in a glance, focusing his attention on the dazzling black blonde. That's not Aria, he realized, feeling somewhat foolish. He nervously fingered the rim of his glass. Unable to control his body, he found himself turning around again to stare. She's beautiful, he sighed, even more beautiful than Aria.

He switched chairs and sat on the other side of his table so he wouldn't have to turn around to stare. This is great. He smiled. Now she's in perfect view. He watched the two girls for over an hour as they had drinks, dinner, and more drinks. Then he signaled the waiter.

"The ladies having dinner together at that table," Gunther began, cueing the waiter with his eye.

"Ah, yes, gorgeous, aren't they?" The waiter gave the girls a thorough looking over.

"Could you find out what they're drinking?"

"I'll take care of it right away, sir," the man replied, reading Gunther's mind.

"Great." Gunther smiled. It'll only be a matter of seconds before I have her eating out of my hand. He watched the waiter deliver the drinks and the surprised looks appear on their faces. "Good," he whispered, trying to conceal his pleasure. Now it's time for me to go in and make the kill.

He got up from the table, straightened his expensive Maxfield's jacket, and sauntered over to their table. "Good evening, ladies," he began, zooming in on the beauty with the golden mane. "I'm—"

"Oh, please." She laughed, cutting him off. "Thanks for the drinks, but no thank you." The girls, slightly drunk, went into a fit of laughter. Gunther, embarrassed, felt the color quickly drain from his face.

"Topaz, girl, what's wrong with you?" Gunther heard her friend ask as he stood there wishing the floor would just open up and swallow him alive. "He could be the very one to make you a star."

"Not in this lifetime," he heard her reply as his feet began to move him away from their table.

Gunther tossed some cash on his table and headed for the door. I've got to get out of here. He practically jumped down the flight of stairs and made a beeline outside to the valet. "Black women," he muttered. "Always thinking they're so fine."

But she was, his subconscious answered back and he had to smile.

"Topaz," he whispered, driving down Sunset towards his apartment in Brentwood. So that's your name. I'll have the last laugh on this one, Miss Thing.

He glanced at a limousine cruising up Sunset in the opposite direction. When I become a famous director, no girl will ever turn me down again. "But I've got to get my film done," he yelled. "Enough waiting around."

To relieve some of his frustration Gunther started playing golf again. All successful businessmen play golf, he reminded himself. He purchased a set of Ping graphite clubs and spent every Saturday on the course spicing up his game, playing with anyone needing a fourth. When he felt he was good enough, he challenged Bob and Joel and easily beat the pants off them both. He even played an occasional charity game for the various entertainment organizations. You never know who I might meet, he rationalized.

It was a gorgeous day in Laguna Niguel on the Monarch Bay Country Club driving range. The ocean and sky were vibrant and a breeze blowing in off the Pacific tempered the heat of the sun. For miles in any direction, there were acres and acres of flawless green sprinkled with bursts of colorful flowers arranged in intricate designs. Monarch Bay was one of the most beautiful golf courses in Southern California but Gunther barely noticed.

Gunther smacked the ball viciously. I can't believe the crap Joel's funding, he fumed. Why does he keep turning my projects down, he wondered, staring at his bag of clubs with his name monogrammed in gold. I even wrote a black film.

"Gunther Lawrence," he heard over a loudspeaker and headed towards the main desk. He had been waiting for a group needing a fourth. The starter pointed at a group of three older black men.

Gunther was upset. They only assigned me to them because they're black . . . and they probably don't know how to play. He walked over to the men who were laughing and joking. They appeared to be having a really good time. Gunther remained silent while he stood there watching them.

They were all very well dressed. Gunther could tell they had spent time choosing their expensive sportswear. And they're all wearing Rolex watches, he noticed, and diamond rings, gold chains, and bracelets. Nice ones, too, not that big chunky stuff that black people wear in the hood. This might be interesting.

"Would you like to place a small wager on the game?" one of them questioned, giving Gunther a wink. He was the most interesting and the best looking of the three, and he appeared to be the leader. Gunther had already quickly assessed the situation. But then he gasped when he saw the thick wads of money they each had.

"How much?" Gunther asked quietly.

"One hundred dollars," one of the others rattled off without a second thought.

A hundred dollars . . . Gunther quickly multiplied four times one hundred in his head.

"You down?" He cast Gunther an intimidating glare.

Gunther returned the glare as he pulled a crisp one-hundred-dollar bill out of his Louis Vuitton wallet. We'll see how bad you are, old dude, after I kick your behind all over this golf course. "I'm down."

"Word." The good-looking one extended his hand and grinned like a Cheshire cat. "The one with the big mouth is Jay. This is Boo. Reno's my name and money's the game."

TWENTY

"YOUR CONTRACT'S up for renewal and it's time for us to renegotiate, Sylk. It's a disgrace for a player of your caliber to make what you're getting." George's words flowed through the phone like rushing water.

Sean said nothing. He had been at home in his office sorting mail and listening to Ron Kenoly when the telephone rang. He knew basketball was a business, and his current salary and countless endorsements were constantly a topic of discussion. Sean was an extremely wealthy man, but there was no reason to flaunt it.

"You put that team on the map," George continued. "And you've brought the franchise plenty of revenue."

"What kind of figure did you have in mind, George?" Sean fingered the corner of the new *In Touch* magazine. He flipped to an article entitled "Contentment" and smiled. How appropriate.

"There are guys out there making over five million dollars a year. We ought to be able to get you at least that if not more. You're a free agent when this contract expires, which gives you the right to consider other offers, but the Concordes have the right to match any offer you receive."

Five million dollars . . . Wow, just think of all the things I could do with that money. I could definitely live well for the rest of my life and so could my family. I could put more money into my foundation. More money for the Kingdom . . . "George, do what you have to do."

"Sylk Ross, you'll have a new contract for your sixth season when you go to camp in October," George promised.

Oh, no, how will the guys react if George gets me more? Sean suddenly wondered. The team was already freaking out because I was making three million a year. And things were just starting to get better between us. I can't take the silent treatment anymore.

Sean frowned at the thought as he caught sight of the shiny gold championship ring he wore on the ring finger of his right hand. He took it off to examine it. All this fuss over a ring. He sat back in his chair and reran some favorite plays in his head from the playoffs.

That last game in Detroit was great. I scored forty-three points that night. Afterwards, he had gone out for barbecue with Eric and Keisha. They had sat up until three o'clock in the morning laughing and telling jokes.

And I even got Most Valuable Player. The enormous ornate trophy was in the family room at his parents', housed in a glass case with the rest of the family honors—his father's degrees and certificates, the twins' numerous athletic awards, not to mention his own acquisitions.

Things had gotten very close for a while during the playoffs. The Concordes beat the Hornets in the Eastern Conference semifinals four to two and went on to beat the pants off the Phoenix Suns for the championship title.

Those were some great games. That's when everyone started to become friends. He picked up the team photo, which was in a gold and pewter frame, and examined the expressions on their faces. "E-man." He laughed, referring to Eric, who was now in Atlanta coaching a basketball camp for a few weeks and kicking it with Keisha. This was definitely the best year of my career.

Sean picked up a neatly typed schedule that had been faxed over from his agent's office and perused the list of appointments. I've got a basketball clinic in Philly. Cool . . . I'll be able to spend a few weeks at home with Mommy and Daddy. "And then we're going to Aruba," he sang, when he saw the dates slotted in on the schedule for vacation. Right before we ship off to camp again.

I need to call Topaz and see if she can come in from Los Angeles. He clicked on the speaker phone and dialed the number she had left on his service when she first arrived in Los Angeles several weeks ago.

"Hello, stranger." He recognized her voice as soon as she answered the telephone.

"Hi, Sean." She smiled into the phone. Now that I'm in L.A. maybe he can get me some contacts with a record company.

Sean picked up an ink pen and doodled Topaz's name on a

sheet of paper as he spoke. "What are you doing in L.A.? I thought you were in Baltimore helping your mother with her business."

"Well, that's up and going now," Topaz lied. "So she doesn't need me there anymore. I hired a staff to run the business so I could come out here to work on my singing career," she reiterated, hoping he would pick up on her drift, so she wouldn't have to come right out and ask for his help again. But I will if I have to.

"That sounds great, Topaz." He turned to a clean sheet of paper in his notepad and continued doodling. "I was wondering if you would have time to meet me in Aruba for a week?"

"Aruba?" She was startled by his invitation. Her mind quickly flashed to Germain. I can't go. But Aruba. But Germain . . . he'd kill me if he ever found out. But who says he has to find out? As long as I call him, he'll never even know I'm not in L.A. Besides, I'm not in love with Sean, I'm in love with Germain. If I have to give him some in Aruba that's okay. I'll get my record deal and be able to get back home to Germain even sooner.

"Topaz, are you still there?" Sean's voice was soft and sweet.

"Oh, yes. I was just giving your invitation some consideration."

"You don't have to tell me now, think it over. I'm going to Philly to my parents' house. I'll give you that number and you can call me there."

"Oh, that won't be necessary. I've already made up my mind. I'd love to go." She made sure she was extra sweet.

"Cool." Sean relaxed and a handsome smile took over his face. "It'll be nice to have your companionship on such a romantic island."

"I'm really looking forward to it," she continued, still sugary sweet.

"So am I. Oh, I almost forgot to tell you. Keisha and Eric are coming, too."

Keisha! She felt herself grow warm as panic raced throughout her body. Is she still going out with Eric? This thing is becoming serious. I can't go to Aruba with Keisha. What if she tells Germain . . . ?

"Topaz, are you still there?"

"I'm here," she replied quietly, still trying to figure out how she could go to Aruba and avoid Keisha.

"I'm surprised Keisha hasn't already told you about the trip."

"I'm so busy now I hardly have time to talk to Keisha," Topaz lied, since the two of them hadn't spoken since she left Maryland. "She's so in love with Eric now, she doesn't have time for me anymore."

"I know what you mean." Sean laughed. "I hardly ever see Eric and when I do he's with Keisha, just been to see Keisha, or on his way to see Keisha. He's in Atlanta now."

"They've got it bad, huh?" Topaz questioned, wanting to hear more news about her former best friend.

"Yep, but I'm happy for them. They really have something special. True love is hard to find."

"I know." Topaz's mind wandered to Germain and Chris. "It really is."

"All right, then, I'll phone with your reservations."

"Okay." She hung up the phone and cabbage patched. "Record deal and Aruba, here I come. I'll find a way to handle Miss Keisha."

Sean went into his bedroom to pack. He was going to his parents' house and he couldn't wait to get there. He tossed the last two pills from the bottle into his mouth and swallowed them without water. I'll be needing more of those. He picked up the phone and called in a refill for his prescription at the pharmacy. He had no problem getting refills. He just told the doctor they were for his knee. I am in pain, he convinced himself.

Several hours later, he headed for the New Jersey Turnpike to Philly. He dialed his mother on the car phone. "Hi, Mommy. I'm on my way home. What's for dinner?"

"Hi, baby boy. How's Mommy's baby?"

"Ma," Sean wailed, embarrassed by her baby talk but loving every minute of it. "I'm fine. So what did you cook?"

"I barbecued."

"You barbecued?" He was practically drooling at the thought. "Aw, man. I'll be there as fast as I can," he told her as he stepped on the gas. "I'm hungry."

"Drive carefully, baby," she warned him. "Everything and everyone will be here when you get here."

■

Sean grinned as he drove down the street towards his parents' home. Home at last. Everybody's here, too. He located different family members' cars. "Daddy got his Range Rover."

Sean admired the silver grey truck with shiny rims as he pulled up next to it in the driveway. He pulled his Louis Vuitton tote and garment bag from the trunk and headed into the backyard for the kitchen door. He found the family gathered in the family room eating boiled shrimp and drinking strawberry soda pop.

"Hey, everybody," he called out as he entered the house. He left his luggage in the hall by the front stairs. "I can't believe you guys are eating without me."

"Just a few shrimp, baby brother. What's happening?" Kyle jumped up to give him a hug.

"Home." He leaned over and kissed his mother on top of her head. Sean had inherited her shiny black hair, which was braided in a long ponytail, and her flawless chocolate skin. Then, he scooped up his niece, Kyrie, out of his sister-in-law's lap and planted a kiss on the girl's mother at the same time.

"Hi, beautiful," he cooed. Kyrie, a coffee-colored little girl with big black eyes and a smile like her daddy, was almost three. She giggled as Sean tossed her up in the air.

"She's not a basketball." His father gave him a stern glance and took his granddaughter out of Sean's arms. "She's a princess," he smiled. He kissed her on the cheek and handed her back to Sean. "You need a few of these yourself."

"I know, Daddy." Sean buried his head in the little girl's stomach and made her scream with laughter.

"All right, Sean's here. Let's eat," Kirk demanded. He headed towards the fruitwood dining room table that was beautifully set with his mother's finest crystal and china. "I've been waiting all day for this."

"You can always tell when Sean comes home," Kyle teased. "Mommy always gets the good stuff out."

"Nothing's too good for any of my men." Carolyn Ross had set barbecue, various salads, macaroni and cheese, corn on the cob, fresh-baked monkey bread, and sweet potato pie on the table. "Kenny." She looked across the table at her husband, who promptly bowed his head and clasped hands with Sean and Kyle, who were at his left and right.

After dinner, Carolyn pulled out her Scattergories game, and the entire family sat on the floor laughing at the outrageous answers the game yielded.

"Thanks, Mommy," Sean whispered. He was so sleepy he could barely stand, but he bent over to plant a kiss on his mother's cheek. "Thanks for making that wonderful dinner and for having everyone over."

She stroked her son's cheek. "It's not every day that my baby boy comes home."

Sean grinned and sprinted up the stairs to his room. He laughed at the sight of the little full-size bed in comparison to the huge California king in his loft in the city. The old pictures and posters of basketball heroes, Dr. E, Magic Johnson, Kareem, and George Gervin were still tacked up on the walls. "Let every thing that hath breath praise the Lord," he read from an old Sunday School plaque on his dresser.

He peeled off his clothes and jumped into bed, not minding at all that his feet were hanging out of the bed. He lay there thinking about all the fun he'd had with his family that night. "I want a relationship like Mommy and Daddy have," he heard himself whisper and sat up in bed. Now where did that come from? He rearranged his pillow and laid back down. And I want children. But I need a wife. I'm not going to think about this now, he told himself as he fumbled through his tote for his fresh supply of pain pills. He took three with several swigs of water. I wonder if I'm becoming addicted to them. He sat up in his bed at the thought. No, he convinced himself. I can stop anytime I want.

Sean made his way through Queen Beatrix International Airport in Aruba to meet Topaz's incoming American Airlines flight from Miami. With mixed feelings he waited at the gate, watching the calm, blue-green water gently lap the shore. I wonder if this was a good idea, he said to himself for the thousandth time. It's not like we're a real couple or anything. And it's been almost a year since we were in Los Angeles together. He searched the arriving passengers for Topaz.

There she is. He watched her come in from the jet way shaking out her hair and putting on a pair of dark glasses simultaneously. She still looks good, he realized, noticing the way her body curved nicely under a colorful sundress and how the California sun had bronzed her hair and butterscotch complexion to a wonderful burnished gold.

"Hi, Princess Topaz." He brushed his lips lightly over hers.

"Hi, Sean." She was trying to remain cool. Boyfriend is just too fine. I forgot how fine he is. She smiled as she looked him up and down. He was wearing white Bermuda shorts with a pink Izod polo shirt. His chocolate skin glowed from the caressing rays of the island sun. What is it about this man? He is absolutely gorgeous. I'm going to be alone on this island with this man for a week . . . and I haven't had any loving for weeks. I've got to give him some. "It's good to see you."

"I can't believe it's been almost a year since we were in Los Angeles." He fingered a lock of her golden hair.

After she passed through customs, he retrieved her luggage and they headed for the car. Topaz felt her heart leap when she finally caught a glimpse of the placid aquamarine water and white sand, as memories of her honeymoon in Jamaica flooded her heart and her head. I miss Germain terribly, she realized sadly. She followed Sean out to a white Suzuki and felt a lump begin to form in her throat. We had a car like that in Jamaica. She glanced up at Sean, who had loaded her things in the back of the pint-sized truck, as he held the door open for her. I should be at home with my husband. What am I doing here?

Getting a record deal, her subconscious answered. Now fluff up.

"The lovebirds were going to the beach when I left the hotel." Sean laughed. They were driving along a winding coastal highway that would take them back to the Hyatt Regency. Topaz smiled and gazed at the desertlike tropical island, still reminiscing about her trip to Jamaica.

"Topaz." Sean touched her leg gently, arresting her attention. "You were a million miles away."

"I'm sorry. I was just admiring the island." She took off her sunglasses and smiled sweetly. "You really look great, Sean."

"Thank you. You're ever the eternal beauty."

Someone to give me attention. She smiled and settled back against her seat and thoroughly evaluated the island's terrain. I wonder why Sean and Eric wanted to come here. This place is nowhere near as pretty as Jamaica, she concluded, studying the aloe plants, cactus fields, and eerie divi divi trees. But the water is that same aquamarine color like the water in MoBay. Vibrant Windsurfer sails glided across the sea. I can play in the water this time. I was pregnant in Jamaica.

We never talk, Sean realized, taking a sideways glance at Topaz. And when we do, what do we talk about? Maybe she's too taken in by everything to talk right now.

He turned into the hotel drive and pulled to a stop in front of the pink, Spanish-influenced building with its red-tiled roof and arched doorways. Lush vegetation and brilliant floral arrangements beckoned them out of the car.

Sean led Topaz into the hotel lobby, which was lined with palm trees. "I already checked you in." He handed her a hotel room key.

"Thanks." She sighed with relief. Great, I have my own room. Now I don't have to feel like a total dog.

"All of our rooms are together," Sean continued as they got on an elevator. "My room is to the right of yours, and Eric and Keisha's is on the left."

They took the elevator to the penthouse floor. Topaz followed Sean down the hotel corridor. She bristled when she heard familiar female laughter.

"I thought you guys were at the beach," Sean teased when they met Eric and Keisha in the hallway.

"We were but we had to come upstairs for a minute," Eric replied with twinkling eyes.

Sean shook his head and laughed. "Look who's here." He exposed Topaz, who was trying to keep out of sight behind him for as long as she could.

"What's up, lady?" Eric bent over to kiss her on the cheek.

"Hello, Topaz." Keisha's greeting was very formal.

"Hey, girl." Topaz smiled sweetly as she planted a kiss on Keisha's cheek.

"Yo, man, we were just about to order some lunch on the beach, so why don't you two meet us down there?" Eric suggested.

"Word . . ."

"Sean, I'd like to lay down for a while," Topaz interrupted, cutting him off. "I'm tired." She was starting to feel uncomfortable. She could feel Keisha's eyes boring holes through her soul.

"You guys go ahead. I'll come down as soon as I get Topaz in her room."

"All right, G, we'll catch you downstairs." Eric took Keisha by the hand. "Later, Topaz."

Topaz couldn't even look at Keisha as she headed down the hall towards the elevator with Eric. Sean walked her to her room and helped her open the door. "Why don't we get together before dinner? Then we can decide what we want to do this evening."

"Okay," she agreed, and gave him a kiss. "I'll see you later, okay?"

"Cool." He flashed his matinee-idol smile. "Get some rest."

Alone at last. She closed the door after him and inspected the room's colorful tropical decor—vibrant coral, teal, and black draperies and bedspreads. She squealed with delight at the coral bathroom with its glossy black-and-white tiled floor. "Tres art deco," she whispered. She peeked in the drawers, which were laden with toiletries, discovered a blow-dryer attached to the wall, and a television equipped with cable. She was just about to inspect the contents of the minibar when a knock on the door interrupted her escapade.

That must be my luggage, finally. She flung open the door, expecting the bellboy, but was shocked when she saw Keisha.

Keisha, not waiting for an invitation, walked in and closed the door. "Stop trying to avoid me, Topaz. I know you didn't think you could come to Aruba and avoid Sean's best friend and his fiancée." She stood there and glared at Topaz with her hand on her hip.

Fiancée . . . she's really going to marry him. "I wasn't trying to avoid you, Keisha. I'm just a little tired after flying all night."

"Right. Does Germain know you're here?"

Who does she think she's talking to? All in my business. "No. My husband doesn't have to be informed of my every move. Besides, I'm not doing anything wrong." She folded her arms and fixed her amber eyes on Keisha.

"Does Sean know you're married to Germain?" Keisha was livid.

"No."

"And you're not doing anything wrong. So just why are you here? I thought you were in Los Angeles working on your singing career."

"That's why I'm here. I want Sean to help me with my record deal. You know that, Keisha," Topaz wailed.

"I can't believe you, Topaz. I honestly cannot believe you." Keisha was amazed. She stood there shaking her head, astonished by Topaz's revelation. "You will use anybody and anything to get what you want."

"Keisha," Topaz whined. "You won't tell Eric, will you?"

"Me telling Eric? Is that all you're concerned about? You should be concerned about Germain and Chris and this lie you're perpetrating. Sean's my friend, too, and he doesn't deserve to be used like this."

Topaz stood there in silence, allowing Keisha to vent her anger.

"I thought you were my friend. But you're nobody's friend. You're a wanna-be and that's all you'll ever be. Germain's too good for you. And don't ever think you'll get Sean when Germain divorces your two-timing behind because he would never marry a tramp like you." Keisha put her hand on the doorknob and turned around to face Topaz one last time. "And as far as me telling Sean, or for that matter, Germain, I won't, because your lies will catch up with you soon enough, Miss Wanna-Be." She left Topaz's room, slamming the door behind her.

"Witch," Topaz screamed after her. "Don't you ever speak to me like that again." She slammed into the bathroom and cried her eyes out. "I'll show her who's a wanna-be." But her tears couldn't wash away Keisha's stinging words. She always succeeded in making Topaz feel cheap.

"Is Topaz okay?" Sean questioned when Keisha arrived back at the their table on the beach.

"Yes." Keisha tried to conceal her anger. "She said she might come down and join us a little later."

"I'm sorry I spent so much time in my room," Topaz apologized to Sean at the airport in Miami. "Something in Aruba just didn't agree with me." She watched Eric and Keisha head for their flight back to Atlanta.

"That's okay. I had fun anyway. Look, I've got to run if I'm going to make my connection to JFK." He kissed her gently on the lips. "Call me when you get back to L.A." He picked up his Louis Vuitton tote and trotted off towards the escalator.

■

Sean stared out of the window in George's posh executive penthouse office with a panoramic view of the Manhattan skyline. *Buildings, for as far as I can see. And the dirty Hudson River. I've got to get out of New York. I dislike this place more and more every day.* He was waiting for his agent to get off the phone so they could begin their meeting.

"Things might get a little rough when you get to camp next week," George cautioned.

"Why?" Sean questioned, growing concerned. "What's up?"

"We still haven't settled your contract. I got them to go as high as five million a year but that's not enough."

Five million a year, for playing basketball? Wow . . .

"I won't take less than six million." The numbers rolled off George's lips like butter.

"Six million?" Sean finally spoke out.

"Yes." George poured himself a glass of water from the crystal decanter on his desk. "You deserve eight. I've already got my feelers out in case the Concordes drag their feet. The Lakers are willing to pay you that kind of money. And Atlanta will, too. So, they'll give you what I asked for or we'll go elsewhere."

"Okay, George, you're the man. Just hook it up before the season gets underway."

By the time Sean arrived at the Concordes' camp in Virginia Beach, the rumors about his contract negotiations had already started to fly.

"Yo, G, the word's out about your contract," Eric informed him after practice one evening.

"What? How did everyone find out?"

"It was on the news, man."

"On the news? You're kidding?"

"Nope. Everyone wants to know what's up with the Sylkman."

Sean smiled for a minute when he heard Eric use the nickname he first heard the kids call him on the set of the Kidd Maxx video. "I don't even know what's up with the Sylkman at this point, man. My agent's been handling everything. I thought the contract would be finalized by now."

"Well, according to the news, it's not. What's this stuff about the Lakers?"

"George said they're willing to pay what we want." Sean didn't want to go into details because he was uncomfortable about discussing his salary or his contract, even with his best friend.

"I heard that. Go for it, G!"

"This won't change things between us, will it?"

"Naw. I just get tired of hearing the other fellows dissin' you."

"So, we're back to that again. Just when things were starting to turn around."

"Yep." Eric sighed deeply. "You're a good brother and I hate to hear them talk about you. Tell you what, man." A smile lit up Eric's handsome face.

"What?" Sean returned his smile.

"Tell George to add an extra item to your contract. If you leave the Concordes, I have to go with you."

"Word." Sean laughed despite the heaviness in his heart. "And you really should talk to George about handling you. He's a barracuda when it comes to business, but he's straight and above board, you know what I mean?"

"Sean, if you say the dude is straight then I know he's definitely straight."

The next day the Concordes' owner and the general manager flew in from New York to meet with Sean. "Six million is astronomical," the team's owner blurted out as soon as they sat down to dinner.

"I don't think so." Sean was cool. "Shouldn't you discuss this with my agent?"

"Look, son, we wanted to talk to you personally. We gave you a chance with that bum knee of yours when no one else was willing to," the general manager reminded him.

"My bum knee?" Sean fixed his eyes on the general manager.

"We took a chance on you and this is how you repay us?" the man barked, turning a deep shade of red. "By asking for astronomical amounts of money?"

"I won't sit here and listen to this." Sean got up from the table. "Nor will I begin to reiterate the numerous contributions

I've made to this team nor the countless advantages that have been afforded this team since I came here. If you have anything further you can discuss it with my agent."

How dare they? Sean fumed as he walked towards his room at the hotel. My God has blessed me with everything I have and they want to sit there and act like they made me. Bum knee . . . my knee is fine. God healed me.

"George." Sean spoke into the phone from his hotel room. "I know it's late and I'm sorry to disturb you, but things are a little crazy down here."

"What's up, kid?" George asked with concern.

"I just had dinner with the big brass . . . no I didn't have dinner, because I walked out—"

"You mean they're down there?" George's voice rose an octave.

"Yes. And they had the nerve to make reference to, I quote, my bum knee."

"What?" George was practically yelling.

"Yes. And how they took me on when no one else would."

"You get out of there, right now," George commanded.

"What?"

"You leave now."

"Tonight?"

"Yes."

"There aren't any flights out of here to the city now."

"I don't care. You check into another hotel in town and fly back in the morning. And don't tell anyone where you are. I won't have them harassing you like this. And with you not at camp, that'll put more pressure on those jerks to settle this thing for once and for all."

"Okay." Sean was discouraged when he hung up the phone. People are acting like I committed murder and all I ever wanted to do was to play basketball. He began to toss his clothes into his Louis Vuitton carry-all. He picked up the Demerol tabs when the phone rang again. He picked it up, thinking it was George with additional information.

"Dennis Johnson, UPI," a voice boomed through the receiver. "Is it true that you'll be leaving the Concordes to play for the Lakers?"

"Speak to my publicity people," Sean replied with no enthusiasm.

"Have the Concordes agreed to your new contract yet?" Sean heard him ask as he hung up the phone.

By the time Sean returned to New York, the wheels of the press had been running full steam. He saw his smiling face all over newspapers, magazines, and television. He was in the middle of a war. The press made him out as the villain, they said he was greedy and that his phenomenal success had overinflated his ego.

Whatever happened to innocent until proven guilty? Sean wondered as he flipped the channel from yet another unfavorable report.

His contract was finalized by the time the season began. George got him a guaranteed contract for five years at six million a year and loads of extra goodies for all the stress they put him through. "They'll have to pay you that thirty million dollars even if you never play another game." George laughed.

Back in action, his teammates were giving him the silent treatment again, or if they spoke they were always unkind.

"Man, you should've went to play for the Lakers," a teammate growled when he saw Sean stop to sign an autograph at the airport. "This ain't Hollywood."

"Things'll get back to normal now that your contract is settled," Eric encouraged as he and Sean passed through the hotel lobby in Orlando on the way up to their rooms.

"I sure hope so, man." Sean was hopeless. He knew in his heart things would never be the same. "I can't take too much more of this." The pain pills were no longer able to relieve the heaviness in his heart.

"Hi, Sylk, want some company?" A gorgeous girl stood in his path, seeming to appear out of nowhere.

"No, thanks," he replied flatly, walking around her.

"Honeys in the hotel." Eric laughed.

"Later, man. I'm going to do some reading and go to sleep," Sean announced when they reached their rooms. Eric watched his friend walk away disheartened, wishing there was something he could say to cheer him up.

Sean opened the door to his room and was surprised to find

a girl lying in his bed. "Hi, baby," she greeted him lustily, exposing her nude body. He turned right around and headed for Eric's room.

"There's a naked girl in my room, man, call security," Sean informed him with little enthusiasm. He walked into the room, tossed his bags on the floor, and flopped on his friend's bed.

"A naked girl? You lying?" Eric stifled a laugh.

"Yeah, man, all curled up in my bed." The corners of Sean's mouth turned up into a smile.

"Honeys in the hotel," Eric yelled, laughing.

"Man, this is crazy," Sean hollered as Eric fell out laughing on his bed. "Totally insane."

"Yo, G, I wanna be just like you when I grow up," Eric laughed.

It was the third quarter with one minute and twenty-two seconds left on the clock. The Concordes were playing the Orlando Magic. Sean felt perspiration dripping from his hair into his face as he dribbled the ball searching for the open man. He passed it to the small forward who passed it back to him. It's on me, he realized, as he snuck in between Orlando's guards, leaped in the air, and expertly tucked the ball through the net.

"Punk showoff," he heard one of his teammates say just loudly enough for him to hear. The piercing statement broke Sean's concentration. As he landed on his feet, he heard a loud cracking in his left knee and he felt his ankle give away. His body hit the floor with a thud, and he lay there writhing in pain. He tried to get up, but the pain was too severe.

It's my knee again, he realized, and then he closed his eyes and sighed with relief. For the moment, basketball, with all of its pressures, was over.

TWENTY-ONE

"TOPAZ." SHE heard Nina call from outside her door. "Topaz, wake up."

Topaz turned over, stretched and glanced at the clock. "Wow, I can't believe it's three o'clock."

"You decent?" Nina opened the door and came into her room.

"Yes." Topaz rolled over to look at Nina. "Where you been?" She noticed that her cousin was wearing a dress and pantyhose.

"Work." Nina sat on the bed next to Topaz and peeled a banana.

"Work?" Topaz repeated, somewhat surprised. She reached over and broke off a piece of Nina's banana.

"Work. Everyone isn't afforded the luxury of staying out all night partying, sleeping in until three in the afternoon, and traveling to the Caribbean. In the real world we work."

Topaz laughed and fluffed her pillow. "I'm going to be a star, Nina. You know I can't work." She ignored the dirty look her cousin gave her. "Do you know I've never had a job? You know, the kind where you have to get up every day and be there by a certain time."

"I wouldn't work either if I had a husband to take care of me and a famous basketball player for a boyfriend."

"Sylk isn't my boyfriend," Topaz laughed. "We're just friends."

"Yeah, that may be true, but any man that invites you to Aruba for a week wants to be more than your friend. But you should introduce him to me. He's cute."

"Girl, he is too fine." Topaz sat up in bed. "But he's different."

"What do you mean different?"

"I don't know. He just is. He's never asked me to sleep with him."

"What? You're kidding?"

"Nope."

"That's unusual, especially for someone as famous as him. He can get it anytime, anywhere, and from anybody he wants."

"I know. So what are we doing tonight?" Topaz asked, changing the subject.

"I don't know yet. I'm waiting on some phone calls. Darryl said something might be happening at Glam Slam."

"Glam Slam." Topaz grinned. "Bet. I'm ready to get my boogie on. Hey, now." She hopped out of bed to do the cabbage patch. She was too cute in a pair of pink silk pajamas.

"You know what I'm talking about, girl. Mother and Daddy are out on a date tonight. We'll have the place to ourselves and we can really party." Nina's voice and face reeked of mischief.

Nina glanced around Topaz's bedroom. Dresser drawers were open and Victoria's Secret silk panties, jewelry, a medley of T-shirts, belts, and scarves were strewn out of the drawers. Her clothes were piled up on chairs or on the bottom of the closet floor. Half-empty suitcases were sitting open, and a number of dirty glasses and dishes were scattered about.

"This place looks like a disaster area. You better clean up this room before Mother sees it. You don't want her to go off."

"It is pretty bad," Topaz agreed, looking around. "I got so used to Linda, my cleaning lady in Maryland, taking care of everything for me."

"Well, Mother doesn't allow our cleaning lady to do anything to our rooms. She lets her change the linens and do our laundry, but we have to keep our own rooms cleaned. I'm going upstairs to change and check my messages. I'll be back in a few."

Topaz watched Nina close the door as she left the room and then open the door and stick her head back in. "Clean up this room, girl."

Topaz laughed as she gathered up the dirty dishes and carried them into the kitchen. I guess I better clean up a little. She quickly washed the dishes she had brought into the kitchen, ignoring the others that were sitting in the sink and returned to her bedroom.

She felt the floor vibrating under her feet and looked up at the ceiling and smiled. Queen Latifah. Nina's blasting the stereo. She quickly showered and pulled on her favorite pair of Guess jeans. They fit again. She smiled, as she looked into the mirror and admired the way the jeans fit her behind. I'll clean up later, she promised, not even bothering to straighten up her bed or to pick up her dirty towels from the bathroom floor.

She brushed her hair, which had grown thicker and longer since the baby, and pulled on a black beaded bustier. "There." She closed a tube of Glam lipstick and studied her reflection. That'll do for now.

She wandered into the living room to check the mail. "I got a letter from Germain," she squealed. She ripped the envelope open and read the sugary sweet Blue Mountain greeting card and sighed at the sight of his scrawled writing. I miss him. She dropped the rest of the mail on the dining room table.

"I'd send you a card every day if you were my woman," she heard a voice proclaim.

She looked up, surprised to see Khalil, Kim's boyfriend, sitting on the sofa in the family room. Khalil's cute, she thought, admiring his bronzed cinnamon complexion, black straight hair, and dimpled smile. But too young. Besides, he's Kim's boyfriend.

"Hey, Khalil." Her greeting lacked enthusiasm. "How long have you been sitting there?"

"Long enough. Baby, you are too fine." He jumped up from the sofa to stand next to her. Topaz felt a smile turn up the corners of her pouty mouth. "So, baby, how 'bout it?" Khalil asked, grinning and skinning.

"How 'bout what?"

"Be my lady. I'll give you the world. I'd work two jobs for you, baby. I'd pay your rent . . ."

"Khalil," Topaz giggled.

"I'm ready to go now, Khalil," she heard Kim announce in a tone that let her know she had overheard their conversation.

"Hi, Kim." Topaz didn't really care for this cousin.

She eyed the conservative, bourgeois girl. No sense of fashion or style, Topaz thought, noticing Kim's simple white jeans and frilly lace blouse. She had on a pair of Anne Klein sandals, and her hair was combed back off her face. There wasn't a trace of makeup on her café au lait skin. If she styled her hair and put on some makeup, she'd look so much better. How did she and Nina ever wind up as sisters? They're as different as night and day.

"What were you doing with Khalil?" Kim yelled angrily.

"What are you talking about, Kim?"

"I want to know why you were in here grinning at my man." Kim placed a hand on her hip and glared at Topaz.

"Kim—" Khalil began.

"No, Khalil, you stay out of this. This high-yella heifer is in my house." Kim rolled her eyes at Topaz.

"I don't care whose house I'm in, if you call me high-yella again I'll kick your butt all over this house," Topaz admonished, meaning every word of it. "And I am not interested in Khalil, although Khalil is interested in me." Her eyes were topaz daggers. "I'm married, remember?"

"Then why don't you act like it, you little tramp?"

Tramp. Topaz felt something snap inside her, and suddenly she saw streaks of brilliant red. She slapped Kim so hard that her head turned.

"Don't you ever call me a tramp again," Topaz yelled. Kim lit into her and Khalil jumped up and pulled them apart.

"You witch," Kim lashed out. "You ain't all that."

Topaz flashed Kim a look of death as Nina jumped down the stairs. She had changed into jeans and an orange bustier. Her shiny black hair framed her pretty mocha face.

"What are you guys doing down here?" Nina questioned, looking everyone over. She saw Kim's reddened cheek and noticed that Topaz's usually perfect hair was a mess. "Ooh, you guys have been fighting. I'm telling Mother," she declared without a smile on her face.

"Let's go, Khalil," Kim commanded. She headed for the back door as Topaz slammed into her room. Nina watched her sister and date leave before she headed for Topaz's room.

"What happened with you and Kim?" She made herself a spot on the messy bed.

"She thought I was trying to talk to Khalil. He's such a flirt."

"I know. He's always flirting with me, too. He's such a dog. I tried to tell Kim, but you can't tell her anything. She just says, 'I love Khalil.' " Nina mocked her sister's facial expressions and tone.

"Serves her right if she wants to be so stupid. She should have been cursing him out, not me," Topaz replied to Nina's reflection in the mirror as she played with her hair.

"Word," Nina agreed, mocking the body language and tone of a street brother. "Forget them. It's time to party." Nina grinned and pulled a marijuana cigarette from the pocket of her jeans.

"Ooh, Nina." Topaz was alarmed. "Is that a joint?" Her forehead wrinkled into a frown as she stared at the cigarette and then at Nina. "Where'd you get that from, girl?" Nina fell out on the bed, laughing.

"I can't believe how square you are, Topaz. What else do you and Germain do besides make babies?"

Topaz smiled as she paused to think about Nina's question. "That's about it, girlfriend."

"You guys are so square. Try it," Nina commanded, passing her the cigarette.

"No." Topaz shook her head and frowned.

"Here."

Topaz took the cigarette, puffed on it, made a face, and passed it back to Nina. "Nina, you are too bad."

"You love it." Nina gave her an impish grin. "You know, I was thinking. Maybe you should get a job or something." She blew rings of smoke into the air.

"A job?" Topaz repeated. She was insulted.

"A job. You might be able to meet someone who could help you get a record deal or know someone who knows somebody. You know what I mean?"

"That might be true."

"You've got about six weeks left until you have to go back to Maryland. What's up with Sylk? I thought he was going to help you."

"He said I needed a demo. How do I get one?"

"You need some original songs and then you need someone to record you. Then we get them out to the A&R people at the record companies."

"Can you help me get a demo, Nina?" Topaz begged.

"I know a few brothers who write music, but the negroes will want you to give them some booty for a song." She made a face and continued speaking. "I don't know anybody in the record companies yet. I just started my job right before you came. But I'll do what I can to help you. But the first thing we have to do is get you a job." She glanced around Topaz's messy room. "Before Mother sends you back to Baltimore on the next thing smoking."

Topaz frowned at the conservative black skirt and sweater Nina had given her to wear on her interview with the temp agency.

"They'll only send you to entertainment-related companies," Nina had informed her. "That's how I got my job. I was sent there as a temp back in the summer and they created a job for me."

Topaz brushed her hair and braided it into a French braid the way Nina had instructed.

"You can wear it down after you get the job. We don't want them thinking you're coming there just to catch, although you will."

Then she slipped on a pair of black pumps, checked her makeup one last time, and headed into the family room to wait for Nina, who was driving her to the interview. She flipped on the television to catch a few minutes of *Oprah* while she was waiting.

"Hey, girl, you ready?" Nina burst into the house exploding with energy and color.

"I'm as ready as I'll ever be." Topaz smiled at her cousin, who looked as though she had stepped right out of *Harper's* or *Elle*. Nina was dressed in a lime green minidress and black suede boots. Her manicurist had painted her acrylic nails flourescent orange and the combination was striking against her pretty mocha skin.

"Have you ever thought about modeling?" Topaz inquired, once they were in the car. "I was into it for a minute. They want girls who look like you."

"I thought about it once or twice. People are always asking me to model, but that's not me. I like to eat too much and I'm not interested in living in New York City. I'm not sure what I want to do yet, maybe own my own entertainment public relations firm."

That's a lot of work. Topaz remembered the countless hours of time her own mother had invested into her business. She could get paid just for looking pretty. I know I would if I had those looks.

"Okay, girl, here we are." Nina pulled her black Fiero in the underground parking lot of a high rise in Century City. They caught the elevator to the fifth floor.

"I'm Topaz Gradney," she informed the receptionist. She immediately disliked the sterility of the corporate offices.

The receptionist handed Topaz a clipboard of paperwork to fill out and pointed her towards the waiting area where Nina was already sitting, intently reading a *Forbes* magazine.

"This place is too straight for me," Topaz whispered, as she began to fill out the numerous forms. "I didn't know I had to go through all this to get a job."

"Welcome to the real world," Nina whispered back.

"I got hired as a receptionist. That's probably the only thing I could do since I don't type. I just have to answer the ringing phone," Topaz declared after the interview. "My first assignment is with William Morris. I'll be working in the literary department with the writers. I'm so excited." She giggled.

"That's fresh. You never know who you might meet."

But she never met anyone on any of her temporary assignments. Nor on the assignments at the film studio, or at the big star-studded parties where she was a hostess.

"All that those people have on their minds is one thing," a disappointed Topaz informed Nina. "Sex. They're always trying to get me to go to bed with them. I'm not sleeping with those old men." She wrinkled her nose at the thought of it.

"Yuck." Nina laughed. "Girl, next week is Thanksgiving. You're supposed to go home. What are you going to do about Germain?"

"I don't know." Topaz was on the verge of tears. "I miss him like crazy, but I'm not ready to go home. I was thinking about going home for a week and coming back, but if I do, Germain won't let me come back, and then I might not want to come back," she added softly.

"Married people," Nina commented, picking up the ringing phone. "It's for you." She handed Topaz the telephone. "It's the temp agency."

"Oh, good. I've been waiting for them to call me with another assignment." Topaz took the phone and jotted down some information. "Great and thanks a lot." She hung up the phone and screamed. "Nina, there's no way I'm going home now." She shook her head and laughed as a smile lit up her pretty face.

"Why, what happened?" Nina demanded, sensing Topaz's excitement.

"Nina, I just got an indefinite assignment as the receptionist for Music City Records."

"Hi, baby." Topaz cooed sweetly and softly into the phone. She was in the family room, sprawled across the black-and-white plaid sofa, watching *The Fresh Prince of Bel Air* with Nina. The rest of the family was out. "Whatcha doing?"

"I was asleep, baby," Germain yawned into the phone. "Chris just fell asleep and I dozed off, too."

Chris . . . my baby. She allowed her thoughts to wander for a quick second before she pushed them away.

"I was up late studying. How you doin', baby?" Germain yawned again.

"I'm fine, baby. I miss you."

"I miss you, too. When you comin' home?"

"That's what I called to talk to you about," she finally sputtered, pausing to collect her thoughts. How am I ever going to tell him I'm not coming home yet?

"What is it, Topaz?" Germain was wide awake now. She could tell by the brusk tone in his voice that this was not going to be easy.

"Germain, I just got this job with Music City Records. I just know something's going to come out of it."

"Topaz, before you left, we agreed that you'd come home by Thanksgiving."

"I know, baby, but this thing is taking longer than we thought it would. I just got myself in a position where I can meet people."

"What about Chris? You're his mother. You belong at home with him."

"I know, baby, but he's there with his daddy. And I'll be home as soon as I can."

"No, Topaz. Come home now."

"I can't, Germain. Not now."

"Then when?"

"I don't know. Why don't you and Chris come out here for a while. We can stay in a hotel."

"I can't get off work to come out there, and I'm not letting you take my son out there, either. At least I know he's being taken care of by one of his parents when he's here with me."

"He's my son, too," she wailed.

"Then act like it and come home and take care of him."

Topaz hung up the phone and threw it across the room. "He's ruining everything," she cried, breaking into tears. "He makes me sick."

"Are you going home?" Nina asked quietly when the tears subsided.

"No." She shook her head like an impudent child. "It's not fair." She struggled against another deluge of tears. "Why do I have to stay cooped up back there in Maryland? I have a life, too."

"Because you're his wife." Nina fixed her velvety black eyes on Topaz's amber ones.

"I know," Topaz sighed, giving in. "But I can't go now. This is as close as I've ever been to getting a record deal."

"But you haven't even started the job yet."

"True. But if I can get someone to produce my demo, I just know I'll get a deal."

"But what about your marriage? What about Chris?"

"Chris is fine. He's with his daddy. I can't think about Germain right now. I know he loves me. It'll be okay."

Topaz greeted everyone with her prettiest smile the moment they walked through the door. She was the first and last person people saw at Music City Records. She had been working there for more than six months.

She pretended not to notice when she saw men take second and third looks. She wanted them to stare. She spent practically all of her paychecks on clothes, shoes, new makeup, and hair and nail appointments. The new black wool dress from Saks clung perfectly to her finely toned figure. Her burnished silky hair, sparkling like fire, was tinged with streaks of amber gold. Fire-engine-red nails complimented her slender butterscotch fingers, which were bejeweled with diamond rings. Her makeup was impeccable. Topaz was even polite to the women who gave her looks that could kill.

That was Teddy Riley, she realized as he zipped past her for a meeting with LaTrell Sanders, vice president of A&R in the black music division. This is the most exciting thing I've ever done. She smiled at the gorgeous Puerto Rican girl on her way to a meeting with Abe Wykoff. I wonder if she can sing.

She heard the telephone beep and snatched it up by the second tone. "Music City Records," she answered in her best telephone voice.

"Hi, gorgeous lady."

She smiled at the sound of his voice. It was LaTrell Sanders in A&R. "Hi, LaTrell. How are you?" she asked, sugary sweet.

"Just fine, baby. You got any messages for me?"

"No. I put everyone through to Vickie."

"I've got some food coming over from Thai Barbeque. Can I get you anything?"

"Sure, LaTrell." Topaz's Russian Red lips turned up into a smile. "I'll have some beef satay." He always ordered lunch for her, and she knew this was the primary purpose for his call.

"All right, pretty lady. Let me know when everything gets here and I'll send Vickie up with the money."

She hung up the telephone and sat there staring at the pink neon Music City Records sign in the reception area. I wonder if LaTrell would help me. I should ask him, but Nina said to wait until my assignment's done. I've been here six months already. She glanced up to see the delivery boy from the Thai food restaurant push open the smoked-glass doors.

Topaz quickly dialed LaTrell's number. "Vickie? LaTrell's Thai food is here."

Moments later, Vickie, a heavyset black girl with a cheap weave, entered the reception area and paid for the food. "LaTrell said to come on back and have lunch with him if you aren't doing anything." Vickie barely looked at Topaz when she spoke to her.

"Tell him I'll be right there." Topaz didn't care if Vickie liked her or not. She was already in with LaTrell. Vickie glared at her and took the brown paper bag from the Thai restaurant. She's just jealous because LaTrell always buys me lunch, gives me CDs and tickets to concerts, and invites me to all the parties, Topaz reminded herself while she got her purse. And I won't begin to deal with girlfriend's hair.

"I'll be with LaTrell Sanders in A&R if you need anything," she informed her relief person.

She walked through the maze of desks and departments, listening to brief passages of unreleased music or the label's hottest chart topper blasting out of different offices. It's so exciting.

Her eyes fell on a stack of black-and-white glossies of one of the company's hottest R&B singers who had starred in a Broadway musical as a young girl. Topaz walked right by Vickie without bothering to acknowledge her and headed towards LaTrell's office.

"He's on the phone," Vickie barked.

She ignored Vickie and walked into LaTrell's office. He was playing a song over the phone through a special adapter that played the music directly into the telephone line.

"Hey, baby," he yelled over the music. "Help yourself to lunch."

Topaz smiled and helped herself to a plate of Thai fried rice and several skewers of grilled beef and doused them with the accompanying peanut and cucumber sauces. I just love Thai food. She chewed slowly, scrutinizing LaTrell while she ate.

He's not bad-looking and he's a sharp dresser. She gave his expensive tailored shirt and pants her stamp of approval. He's funny, outgoing, and smart. She looked around his office, filled with the latest and best audio and video equipment on the market. A dubbing cassette, CD player, DAT machine, a 27-inch television with *Video Soul* on and the volume off, a broadcast VCR, as well as a VHS, were housed in the entertainment center. The walls were covered with wooden cassette holders overflowing with tapes of new songs from various publishing companies, platinum albums inscribed to LaTrell Sanders from a host of artists, and a stack of master tapes waiting to be returned to the studio. What a great office. Topaz looked out of the big picture window down on Lankershim Boulevard.

"You enjoy your lunch, gorgeous?" LaTrell hung up the phone and gave her his undivided attention.

"Oh, yes. It was delicious. I just love Thai food."

"Great." He smiled. "Here." He handed her several CDs.

"Thanks, LaTrell." Topaz smiled her best smile.

"Well, I gotta make some more phone calls. I was in the studio mixing and when I'm there, things start to pile up over here."

"No problem." Topaz tried to cover the disappointment of not being able to stay longer. "I have to get back to work anyway."

"You know I always love to see that gorgeous face."

He never asks me out. Topaz took a seat back at the receptionist's desk. I wonder why. He must have a girlfriend. But I have to find a way to ask him to help me.

"Music City Records. Yes, this is Topaz Gradney. Oh, hi, Marcia. Today's my last day here? You're kidding. I thought I had two more weeks. The receptionist ended her maternity leave a little early," she repeated. She hung the phone up with little enthusiasm. What am I going to do now? She picked up the phone and dialed LaTrell's extension.

"Vickie. This is Topaz. I need to speak to LaTrell."

"He's gone for the day," Vickie snapped.

"He left already?"

"Yes. He had to rush back over to the studio and he's not coming back." She hung up before Topaz could say another word.

"Witch." Topaz slammed the phone down. Now what am I going to do? She packed up the CDs and cassettes and other promotional items that she had collected during her stay. My assignment is actually over.

It was Friday after six and most everyone had already gone home. She had seen Vickie walk out with her assistant fifteen minutes ago. Topaz grabbed her purse and ran to the black music department. The entire company was virtually silent now, everyone had headed out on time in anticipation of the weekend.

Good. LaTrell's door is open. She tore off a sheet of paper from a Music City Records notepad on Vickie's desk and scribbled a note. "LaTrell, this turned out to be my last day. Thanks for everything. Topaz Gradney." She looked it over carefully, and on second thought decided to add her telephone number.

Her telephone rang late that same night after midnight. She snatched it up on the first ring, thinking it might be Germain.

"Hey, this is LaTrell. How you doin', gorgeous?"

"Fine." Her heart began to race with excitement. She could tell he was calling from his car.

"I left early for the studio but I had to stop back by the office for a tape and found a note from beautiful Topaz."

She cupped a hand over her mouth to keep herself from screaming.

"Would you like to have brunch at Roscoe's tomorrow?"

"Sure." She tried not to sound too anxious. "What time?"

"I've been up all day and night and I want to sleep in late tomorrow. How about I pick you up around two?"

"Two's fine. I'm staying in Sherman Oaks south of the Boulevard." She rattled off the address and street. "I'm having brunch with LaTrell Sanders, the vice president of A&R for Music City Records," she shouted as she hung up the phone.

"You are so fine. I want you to be my lady," he informed her over plates of crispy fried chicken and fluffy waffles swimming in creamy butter and warm maple syrup. "I think you're sweet."

Your lady? I don't know about all that. What about Germain?

Do what you have to do, her subconscious told her.

"Okay," she agreed sugary sweet, smiling into his eyes.

Germain's really been getting on your nerves anyway, her subconscious continued. Just when things are beginning to happen. Later for him.

That's true. He has been getting on my nerves, she thought, agreeing with the voice in her head and not the one in her heart. Besides, I've wanted this all my life.

"LaTrell, did you know that I sing?" she asked coyly, looking up at him through lowered lashes.

"Really?" He was extremely interested. "Can you really sing or are you all studio?"

"I can blow," Topaz bragged. "I just haven't been able to find the right producer to record me yet," she lied.

"Word?" He sat back and looked her over. She had worn a new outfit for their date, navy palazzo pants with gold sandals that she had ordered from the Bloomingdale's catalogue before she left Maryland. Her makeup was flawless and she was radiantly gorgeous.

"I know somebody who could blow you up big," he began, becoming excited.

"Really?" Topaz felt her stomach turning flip-flops.

"Let me see if the brother's in the studio. If so, we'll drop by."

Topaz watched him dial a number on his portable flip phone. Oh, please be there, she silently prayed.

"Jamil? Yo, man, what up? You just got signed to produce three cuts on Verna's next album? Word. Look, man. I want you to see what you can do with my lady." He glanced at Topaz, rubbed her thigh, and smiled. "Man, she's gorgeous and she says she can blow." He snapped the phone closed and tossed some money on the table. "Let's roll, pretty lady."

Chocolate Star

■

Topaz felt herself start to hyperventilate as she walked into Aire L.A. recording studio in Glendale. I'm actually in a recording studio, she wanted to scream. She examined the redbrick walls that were covered with the same platinum records LaTrell had in his office, but there were lots more here, plus autographed photos and posters of Boyz II Men, Portrait, Shanice, Natalie Cole, Dr. Dre, Ice Cube, Chuckii Booker, Phillip Bailey, and countless others. She tingled with excitement while the receptionist rang the studio to let Jamil know she had arrived.

I'm actually going to start recording my first song. She had already spent several weeks with Jamil and LaTrell listening to song after song and they had finally decided on three, a ballad and two up-tempo. LaTrell and Jamil had put up the money for the studio time. She had spent night after night watching Jamil lay down the tracks. He was extremely talented and he played every instrument. Wow, that's Portrait, she realized, taking a quick peek into one of the adjacent studios.

"Hi, Jamil." Topaz greeted him with her prettiest smile. He is such a cutey pie, she told herself for the umpteenth time. Jamil, tall, thin, and muscular, was a gorgeous cocoa brown cutey with a baby face and a boyish smile that revealed a set of dimples that looked like small dents in the sides of his face.

"Hey, Topaz. You sure look good today." He looked up from the box of tape he was carefully labeling with a marker and smiled.

"Thanks." She smiled back. She was only wearing jeans and a sweater with a bustier underneath. It was a beautiful warm day in Los Angeles, but the air conditioning in the studio made her chilly.

"Ready to sing?" He positioned a reel of wide black tape on the 24-track recorder.

"Yes," she replied softly, too overcome by his boyish charm. She had toyed with the idea of sleeping with him for weeks. What is it with me and these chocolate men? She followed him into the vocal booth. Dang, he's fine. She was putty in his hands as he positioned her in front of the microphone. I know what this is, I haven't had any loving for eight months.

"All right, Topaz." Jamil spoke very softly into her ear. "Don't move, just stand here, and blow."

"Okay, Jamil. But I need to ask you a question first."

"What?" he replied, standing a little too close. The chemistry between them was undeniable.

"How do you feel about this?" She clasped her arms around the back of his neck and pulled him into her arms and kissed him. After they had kissed for several minutes, she pulled away to look into his eyes. The passion she saw there was intense.

"I say hold that thought." He smiled as she tenderly wiped away traces of her red lipstick from his face.

"Okay." She resisted the urge to kiss him again. We'd never get that record done.

She spent that night at Jamil's, and lots of nights afterwards. They were inseparable.

"Topaz, come to this session with me for Verna," he suggested one day. "She's a real good singer and this is her first album. It might be good for you two to meet each other."

"Sure. You know I wanna be wherever you are."

Verna was absolutely gorgeous, a black blonde with green eyes, a real beauty queen who could actually sing.

"She ain't all that," Topaz whispered to Jamil, jealous and intimidated by another woman for the first time in her life.

"She can blow, but you'll knock her right off the charts," Jamil promised with a kiss. They were sitting together in front of the control board, and Jamil was allowing her to manipulate several of the hundreds of buttons on the mixing board.

"Jamil, did you write 'Boyfriend'?" she asked an hour into the session.

"Yeah, baby. You like it?"

"I love it. Why didn't you give it to me?" She spoke very sweetly as she gazed into his eyes.

"Because I had already presented it to Verna."

"But she's just recording it. Tell her you placed it with someone else and give it to me. That song's going to be a major hit and I want it on my album."

Jamil looked her over thoughtfully. "Okay," he finally agreed, completely under her spell. "I'll work it out somehow."

"I thought you were LaTrell's girl?" he questioned one morning in bed.

"I was for about a day until I met you." Topaz laughed.

"I gave him back his part of the money for the session, but I can't take your project to Music City now. Tell you what," he continued, sitting up in bed. "Let's talk business for a minute."

"Business? You know I like to talk about anything with you." Topaz fluffed her pillow and lay in his arms.

"I can take your project to any record company in this city. If you sign with my production company, Just Jam, I'll get you a deal and a good one."

"You will?"

"I take fifty percent of what the record company gives me for producing and the rest is yours."

"Fifty percent? You get that much money?" She frowned.

"Don't worry, Topaz, I'll blow you up."

"I trust you, Jamil."

"Okay, but we're going to do this thing right. Business is business. I'll have my attorney do up a contract for us."

Chao Praya on Yucca at Vine near Capitol Records was unusually busy that Wednesday afternoon. The restaurant, with its small cozy tables covered with pink tablecloths, was a favorite place to discuss business and eat great Thai food in Hollywood.

Topaz spread a linen napkin over her crisp red linen pantsuit and sipped ice water, making sure her red lipstick stained only one spot on the glass. She was waiting for Jamil to meet her for lunch. She smiled when she saw him dash into the restaurant. He looked so good. He was wearing a fierce black suit and crisp white shirt.

"Topaz, guess what?" He kissed her and set his black leather briefcase on a chair at the same time.

"What?" Topaz demanded, aroused by his excitement. She had already ordered their lunch and she was eating jumbo spicy prawns.

"I did it."

"Did what?" Topaz concentrated on the dish of sauteed spicy scallops and string beans the waitress had just set in from of them.

"I got you a record deal." He proudly brandished the contract bearing their names. Topaz's mouth dropped open in surprise. She was speechless. "I just inked you a deal with a budget for two hundred and fifty thousand dollars with Populartis Records."

TWENTY-TWO

THEY CHATTERED nonstop all the way to the ninth hole. Gunther, who played with a vengeance, was ahead. "Now that's the way you hit the ball." Gunther smirked. He watched the ball sail through the air and land in good putting distance from the tenth hole. "That's a birdie." I'll show these old-timers how to play golf.

"Check Junior out." Reno laughed. "He thinks he can play some golf."

"I know I can play." Gunther laughed triumphantly. "I'm bad." He eyed the four hundred dollars in cash tucked between the pages of the *Golfers Handbook* in Reno's golf cart while Boo chopped away at the ball on the tee as though he were cutting hay in a field. I'm going to win that kitty, too.

"You're swinging too high, Boo," Gunther offered, focusing on him. "Put the club right on the ball." Gunther shook his head as he watched Boo's ball sail off towards the Pacific Ocean into oblivion.

"At least he hit it." Reno laughed.

"Yeah," Gunther and Jay agreed, laughing.

"Later for all you fools." Boo's feelings were hurt.

Gunther watched with amusement as Boo found another ball and placed it on the tee. Reno and Jay continued snickering. A large grin spread itself across Gunther's face. I haven't had this much fun in a long time.

Gunther replaced the iron in his burgundy monogrammed golf bag and brushed a spot of dirt from his crisp white pants. The pink Izod polo shirt with a tiny alligator over the pocket accentuated his hard-toned biceps. He had purchased a membership to the Sports Club on Sepulveda some time ago when he heard that it was the spot for industry big shots, pro athletes, and beautiful women to work out. Gunther purchased a VIP membership, and from his daily workout sessions with his personal trainer, his body was tuned like a well-oiled machine.

"Say, Junior, you want to get some of this?" Reno motioned to a mirror covered with lines of white powder.

That's cocaine, Gunther realized, watching Boo and Jay sniff lines through a rolled-up hundred-dollar bill. I wonder what it's like.

"Here, man." Boo handed him the rolled up bill.

Gunther accepted the bill and looked at the lines sprinkled across the mirror like railroad tracks. He had seen the drug before at lots of Hollywood parties but had refused to participate, because he didn't want to look like he didn't know what he was doing.

"You never had blow before, man?" Reno eyed Gunther suspiciously.

"Of course I have." Gunther placed the bill over one of the lines and sniffed until it was gone. Wow. He felt the drug rush his head almost immediately. This is great. He sniffed several more lines and passed the bill to Reno who finished up the remaining lines, rubbed a bit on his gums, and snapped the mirror closed. Gunther laughed when he realized that the *Golfers Handbook* housed the cocaine.

"All right, let's get this party started." Reno jumped into the golf cart with Boo and drove off.

"Yahoo," Gunther yelled, laughing as he pressed the pedal to the floor in his cart and sped past the others across the green to the next hole. He felt carefree, like a child again, and he was loving every minute of it.

"So how you livin', Junior?" Reno pulled his putter out of the bag.

"I'm livin' large. Real large."

Reno smiled and carefully putted the ball into the hole. "How you make your money, man?" he asked pointedly, fixing his hazel eyes on Gunther.

"I make films. I produce, direct, and write."

"Word?" Reno eyed him with newfound respect.

"Word." Gunther chipped in the ball and gave Reno a look that said, "I know I'm bad, so what you got to say."

"Yo, we got Steven Spielberg as a fourth, y'all," Reno told the others. "Junior got it goin' on."

Gunther stuck out his chest and grinned while the guys made

a fuss over him. "You know that video with Sylk Ross and Kidd Maxx?" Gunther asked, cool as a cucumber.

"Yeah," the guys chorused.

"I directed that." He was in seventh heaven as he looked into their impressed faces.

"You all right, Junior." Reno sprinkled more lines of cocaine on the mirror. "I thought you was one of them Oreos, fronting like a brother."

"Naw, man." Gunther remembered to say "man" instead of "dude." "I ain't like that."

"Good." Jay sniffed a line of powder. "I can't stand it when black people get a little something goin' for themselves and then they don't want to be black no more."

"Yeah," Boo agreed quickly. "Uncle Toms."

"Word." Gunther sniffed his lines and wiped his nose. "Y'all had me all wrong." He made a special effort to affect the jargon of the neighborhood. "I'm just a regular brother who just kicked your behinds all over this green." He grinned triumphantly when Reno handed him the cash. "I tell you what, drinks in the clubhouse are on me."

"Aw, man. I was gonna give that money to my woman so she could go shopping." Boo stuck out his bottom lip and pouted.

"Boo, there was no way on earth that you could have ever won that kitty, so your cheap behind might as well reach your hand in your pocket and get some cash for your woman before she kicks your butt again." Reno laughed.

Gunther was practically on the ground laughing. "You crazy, man," he told Reno. "You're crazy. But I like you, man, because you make me laugh."

Inside the clubhouse, Gunther gazed out at the royal blue Pacific and sipped his favorite cranberry juice and gin cocktail. This is the life. I spent the day playing golf. I've got money in my pocket and in the bank, and I just made new friends. He glanced at his golf partners who were clowning with the waitress. They're pretty cool dudes to be black.

"Anybody hungry?" Gunther asked, looking around the table. "There's a great seafood restaurant further down the coast in Dana Point." He didn't want the party to end.

"That sounds good, real good, Junior." Reno grinned.

Gunther tossed some bills on the table for the check and the four of them converged in the parking lot to agree on a plan.

"Let's sit in my car." Reno unlocked the door of a well-detailed pearl black 560 SEC Mercedes with chrome rims. "Sit up front with me, Junior."

Reno got bank. Gunther noticed the buttons for the front seat warming device, the built-in car phone, and the Blaupunkt audio system with a CD player. Levert was kicking through the speakers.

"Nice car, man," Gunther looked the car over and sighed. This baby makes my little Beamer look like dog food.

"Thanks, Junior." Reno flipped open the storage compartment between the seats and pulled out a clear plastic bag filled with cocaine.

Dang. Gunther eyed the bag of coke with bulging eyes. These guys are drug dealers. Drug dealers on the golf course in Laguna Niguel? What is the world coming to?

"Here, man." Reno handed him a vial of white powder. "Save that for later. And get some of this now." He handed him a mirror covered with white lines.

Gunther felt his heart skip a beat as he quickly sniffed up two long lines. I really like this stuff. It just chills me right out. I wonder how much it costs.

"Okay, Junior, you lead the way," Reno commanded when they were done with their hits of cocaine. "Where's you car, man?"

"Over there." Gunther pointed out his black BMW.

"Gunfire, huh?" Reno was reading his personalized license plate. "Okay, Gunfire, shoot your behind on down the road to this restaurant." He grinned like a Cheshire cat.

Gunther couldn't help laughing when he heard Jay and Boo in the back in stitches.

"Gunfire," Boo repeated, shaking his head, as he got into the front seat with Reno. "You all right, man."

"What does it stand for?" Reno asked, while Gunther switched off his alarm and remote-entry system.

"It's the name of my film production company," Gunther yelled out the window. "Okay, follow me."

They caravanned down the coast to the Dana Point plaza and parked.

"There are several restaurants here," Gunther informed them, trying to be cool. "There's a little place in the back that makes slamming shrimp scampi."

"That'll work." Reno smacked his lips. "Let's check it out."

The hostess seated them on the patio. Although their table didn't look out on the water, there was a nice breeze from the ocean that made the air almost chilly.

Gunther thought he wasn't hungry, but he found himself practically drooling when the waiter served his broiled scampi, pasta, and fresh steamed vegetables. All of the guys were silent for once as they devoured their seafood dinners.

"Yo, Spielberg, what does it take to make a film?" Reno sucked his teeth and rolled a toothpick around in his mouth.

"A good script and money." Gunther sipped his ice water and fixed his eyes on Reno, waiting to see what he would say next.

"How much money?" Reno fired back, looking dead serious.

Dang, he's acting like he wants to talk business. Gunther looked Reno over quickly before replying.

"Five million dollars could make a very nice film."

"That's all?" Reno was amazed.

"I said a nice film and that's with me handling the money. There are films that have been made for a hundred million dollars, but you don't have to spend that kind of money to make a good film."

"That's deep." Reno chewed on the tip of the toothpick. Gunther watched him kick back in his chair. He seemed to be contemplating the idea. "So, you got any good scripts, man?"

"Yeah, man. I got one called *The Hood.* It's about my life as a kid growing up in the neighborhood."

"Word?" Reno appeared to be more interested by the minute.

"Yeah. It's about me and my two brothers and how we grew up without a mother and how we dealt with the streets, crime, violence, gang bangers . . . life in South Central, and then how things turn out for each of us. You know what I'm talking about?"

"That sounds good, G," Jay piped in.

"I like it, too. Let's make it," Reno suggested without hesitating.

"You serious, man? You want to make my film?"

"Sure, I do. I'll supply the cash and you do your thing. Draw up an agreement between Reno's Enterprises or some madness like that and Gunfire Films. I'll have my attorney write in a couple of things, and once we get everything straight you can open up a bank account in both of our names."

He can't be serious. Where is this dude going to get five million dollars? Rob a bank. "Okay," Gunther heard himself slowly reply.

"All right, man. I'll give you a call on Tuesday to tell you where you need to send the agreement." Reno took Gunther's Majestic Entertainment business card and stuck it in a Louis Vuitton wallet.

Once he was in the car, Gunther took out the card Reno had given him and read off the numbers to Reno's home telephone number. Reno lives somewhere in the Valley near Encino. That's interesting. I figured dude would live in Inglewood or Compton. He beeped his horn twice at Reno and his posse before hitting the freeway for the ninety-minute ride back to L.A. But I've got company, he remembered, patting his pant's pocket. He pulled out the vial of white powder and cranked the volume on a Wynton Marsalis CD.

I just know I'll never hear from Reno again, and if I do he'll always have some flimsy excuse for why he hasn't been able to get the money yet. It was Monday morning and Gunther was in his office. But I'm going to do my part anyway. He flipped through his Rolodex, found the number for his attorney, and dialed him on the speaker phone.

"Joe, I need an agreement for co-production of a motion picture between Gunfire and Reno's Enterprises. Do a fifty-fifty split and fax me a copy of the agreement at home tonight. I'll call you in the morning with an address and any comments I may have."

He hung up the phone and looked at the stack of scripts on his credenza he needed to read and sighed in exasperation. It sure would be nice to get away from this desk and Majestic Entertainment for once and for all.

He took a small hit of cocaine in each nostril and checked his nose to make sure there were no telltale signs of the white powder on his face. I'm running out of stuff, he realized, noticing the vial was a little more than half empty.

"There's a Reno Velasquez—" Beth chirped through the intercom on the telephone.

Velasquez? Gunther clicked Beth off the intercom in mid-sentence and snatched the receiver up to his ear. "Reno, what's happening, man?"

"Spielberg, have your attorney send that agreement to my people in Century City."

Gunther took a yellow Post-it note, and in careful block letters, jotted down the address Reno rattled off. "Okay, man, I'll have it messengered over by the end of the day tomorrow."

"That'll work, Spielberg."

"Reno, man, can you hook me up with some more blow?" Gunther glanced around to be sure no one overheard him even though he was in his office.

"No problem, man. You want to have some dinner tonight?"

"Sure." Gunther smiled into the phone. "What time?"

"Let's hook up around eight. You know that soul food restaurant Aunt Kizzy's in the Marina?"

"Of course, dude," Gunther lied, writing down the name of the restaurant so he could get the address from information. "I love me some soul food."

"I'll meet you there, Spielberg. Later."

I like Reno. He's an okay dude. Gunther kicked back to a more comfortable position in his executive desk chair. He glanced out the double windows of his corner office at the view on Pass Avenue. Am I actually going to make one of my own films?

"Joe Siegel," Beth chirped through the intercom shortly after nine the following morning.

Gunther snapped off the intercom without saying thank you as usual and grabbed the receiver. "Joe."

"I have the signed agreement back. They didn't change anything except the percentages."

"What are they now?" Gunther sucked in his breath.

"Fifty-five, forty-five."

Fifty-five, forty-five. Gunther ran the figures through his head. I can live with that and I'm the boss. "Fine. I'll be right over to sign the agreement and you can messenger it back over to Reno's people this afternoon."

Gunther hung up the phone and glanced at his watch. It was only ten-thirty in the morning. He buzzed Beth on the intercom.

"I have an appointment off the lot, Beth, and then I'm going to lunch. I'll see you this afternoon."

"Bob called while you were on the phone with Joe," Beth informed him as he was on his way out of the office. "He said something about a possible lunch meeting with Mr. Zwieg." She peered at him out of thick eyeglasses, waiting for a response.

Why doesn't she get herself some contacts? "A possible lunch meeting?"

"Yes. They were both off the lot, so I have no way of reaching them for further details, and their assistants had no further information either."

"Well, I've got to go," Gunther snapped. "I've got an appointment and I'm not available for lunch."

Who cares anyway? He sped off the lot, ignoring the security guard who waved. My days at Majestic Entertainment are numbered.

Gunther signed the documents at his attorney's office on Maple Drive in Beverly Hills, and headed over to Mr. Chow's for lunch. He was glad when the host seated him at a table in a darkened corner. He ordered his favorite cranberry juice cocktail and pulled out one of the vials of cocaine that Reno had given him.

"Where have you been all of my life?" he whispered and kissed the bottle. He took several hits and returned the little glass jar to his jacket pocket just as the waiter walked up with his drink. Gunther flipped through the menu and ordered a number of spicy entrees, fried rice, vegetables, and won ton soup. I'll have the rest of it for dinner.

He eyed the brown paper shopping bag holding the remains of his lunch, which could have easily fed five people, tossed the food in the trunk, and let down the top on his car.

It was a gorgeous day in Southern California. The sky was a brilliant blue and the sun lit up the city with a heavenly glow. Gunther felt like he was sitting on top of the world.

His cellular phone rang as soon as he turned on the engine. I wonder if that's Beth about that stupid lunch meeting. He glanced at his watch as he answered the phone. It was only one-thirty. "Yes?"

"Spielberg?"

Gunther smiled the moment he heard Reno's voice. "What's happening, dude?"

"I've got the money." Reno was nonchalant as he continued speaking. "Why don't you swing by and pick me up at the house and we'll go to the bank? I've got refills, too, if you need them."

"Word, dude. What's your address?"

"I'm in Encino. Up in the hills, man. If you get lost just dial me back."

Gunther dialed his office at Majestic. "Beth, Gunther. I won't be coming back in at all today." He hung up the phone before she had a chance to reply. That's all they need to know.

He took Coldwater from Beverly Hills into the Valley, admiring the gorgeous estates on the palm-lined canyon road. Following the directions Reno had given him, he found himself winding up a hill into the Encino estates.

"Dang." He gawked at the fabulous mansions on the street as he searched for Reno's house. "Reno got it going on like that? I must be in the wrong business." He spotted the address he was looking for, pulled up a steep hill to a black gate with a squawk box, and pushed the buzzer.

"Dang." He caught a glimpse of sprawling grounds that were as smooth as fine carpet on the other side of the gate.

"Yes?" It was a female voice.

"It's Gunther Lawrence."

He watched the black gate roll open, then drove to the top of the hill into a circular drive where a fountain gushed streams of water. Reno's Mercedes was sitting in the driveway behind a cerise 500 Mercedes. That must be hers, Gunther theorized, referring to the female voice on the squawk box. He cast an admiring glance at the Ferrari, Rolls Royce Corniche, Range Rover, and classic MG roadster parked in the bays of the four-car garage.

"Dang." He saw Reno descend the stairs leading into the back of the house. He was dressed in white pants and a black-and-white striped polo shirt. His swarthy tanned skin crinkled around his eyes into his temples when he smiled, and a sprinkling of white hair in the thick black curls covering his head gave him that distinguished look.

"What's happening, Spielberg?" Reno grinned like a Cheshire cat.

"Gunfire and Reno's Enterprises. I'm looking forward to working with you, dude."

"Me, too, man. Let's get over to the bank and take care of business first and then we can hang out at the house and have some dinner."

"Word, dude." Gunther followed Reno into the biggest kitchen he had ever seen in his life. Black marble and hardwood floors precisely matched the wooden cabinetry and black granite counters. A series of windows formed a glass wall that looked into the backyard where Gunther saw a sparkling Olympic-sized pool and tennis courts. Dang.

"This is Gloria." Reno introduced a gorgeous young woman, the color of vanilla wafers, somewhere in her late thirties, with the body of life. "Gloria, that's Spielberg, but you can call him Gunther."

"Gunther, the man with the film. I've heard so much about you from Reno."

"Hi." Gunther hoped he would be able to speak. She is fine.

Gloria was wearing exercise clothes and Gunther could see that her lithe body was in excellent shape. Her jet black silky hair was gathered into one braid, and she wore a nice assortment of gold and diamonds.

"See you later, babe." She gave Reno a long passionate kiss, smiled at Gunther, and slinked out of the room.

Dang, Gunther thought for the thousandth time. Reno's living large.

"I've got the money here in cash." Reno snapped open the gold locks on two large expensive leather briefcases.

Gunther's eyes practically popped out of his head when he saw the briefcases were filled with money. "Dang, Reno." His mind was totally blown. "I've never seen that much money in my life."

Reno threw back his head and laughed. "It's the ticket to life, man." He grinned.

"Word, dude."

Reno snapped the briefcases closed, picked up a Motorola cellular flip phone, and checked his beeper. "Let's roll. We'll take my car."

Reno pulled into the City National Bank parking lot in Beverly Hills and parked. He handed Gunther the briefcases full of money. "Okay, Spielberg. Hook us up."

Gunther swaggered into the bank grinning. They had had a few hits of coke on the way over and he was flying. I've got five million dollars in these briefcases to make my film. He stopped at a desk in new accounts.

"I'd like to open up an account," he informed a cute Hispanic girl with long black hair and a nice body. "A business account for five million dollars, and we really need to discuss the particulars of this account behind closed doors." Reno stood there silently while Gunther barked out instructions.

"We can talk in here." The new accounts rep ushered them into an office behind the vault.

Cute girl, Gunther assessed, admiring her figure in the crisp linen pantsuit she was wearing. He took a seat next to Reno in one of the two chairs positioned in front of the desk.

After filling out a series of forms, he placed his John Hancock on the signature card and pushed the card across the desk for Reno to sign.

"This cash is a loan for my film production company." He snapped open the briefcases.

"You're a producer?" When she saw the cash she was extremely interested.

"We're both producers." Gunther was too pleased with himself. "I'm also the director. You'll have to come down to the set once we get everything rolling."

"I'd like that." She sifted through the stacks of hundreds, fifties, and twenties, counting and relabeling them.

Gunther placed a book of temporary checks in his briefcase when the transaction was complete and grinned. I'm actually going to make one of my own films. "Ms. Gutierrez, it's been our pleasure." He shook her hand firmly. "Good afternoon."

"I like the way you take care of business, man," Reno informed him once they were inside the car. "You don't take no stuff, just like those white boys. You're all right, Gunther Lawrence."

Gunther scheduled six weeks of actual shooting time for the film. Principal photography was shot on location, utilizing various sites up and down Crenshaw Boulevard. He hired an excellent crew, and the top black female casting agent in Hollywood brought in the most talented young actors in the business. The news of Gunther's independent theatrical feature spread like wildfire. Everyone wanted to be involved.

Reno was wonderful. He let Gunther run the show. He made his daily thirty-minute visit to the set to observe the filming and to bring Gunther his daily supply of coke. Under Gunther's rigid helm, the film came in on budget and on schedule.

Gunther kicked back in the red velvet seat in Majestic's executive screening room and inspected his freshly manicured nails while Joel and Bob ranted and raved over the finished product.

"You did this all by yourself, Gunther?" Joel asked him for the hundredth time.

"Yep."

"Where'd you get the money, Gunther?" Bob asked pointedly.

"From an investor I met on the golf course in Laguna Niguel."

"Incredible," Joel continued. "I was deeply moved. This is just the thing the studio needs, Gunther."

I know, Gunther replied in his head. I tried to tell you morons that.

"It's commercial, it's slick, very well done. Well directed and well acted. You did a superb job, Gunther."

"Thanks, Joel." Gunther was too cool. "Your opinion really means a lot to me."

Now, I'll really mess with their heads, he laughed to himself, watching the two men whispering. He picked up the can of film the projectionist brought out to him and headed towards the door.

"Gunther, wait," Bob requested, on the verge of panic.

I've got them right where I want them. He turned to face the men again, waiting to see what they would say next.

"Have you arranged a distribution deal yet?" Bob asked.

"I have some people at Universal and Warner Brothers waiting to see it," Gunther lied.

"Look, Gunther." Joel spoke firmly, placing his hand on Gunther's arm. "If you let us do the distribution, I'll make it worth your while. Say a seventy-thirty split?"

"I want forty-five percent," Gunther declared without stuttering.

"Sixty-forty," Joel quipped.

"I want forty-five percent, Joel, and a good advertising budget." Gunther was as cool as ice. He inspected the gold and diamond band on the ring finger of his right hand and watched Joel cast Bob a look.

"All right, Gunther. You got it. Have your attorney call Business Affairs and we'll get everything nailed down on paper," Joel finished.

"Fine." Gunther smiled and shook hands with the men. I told Reno I'd come back with the deal.

"Mind if we hold on to the print?" Bob asked.

"Send me over that distribution agreement first."

"You got it." Joel grinned like a kid in a candy store.

The Carlton Hotel was *the* spot for Americans attending the Cannes Film Festival in the south of France. Gunther, Reno, and Gloria, dressed in white linen suits, stepped out of the limousine and strolled into the Carlton's lobby. A bellboy pushing a cart of Louis Vuitton luggage trailed behind them. The epitome of wealthy American tourists, Gloria glittered in gold and diamonds and Reno reeked fine in a white straw hat. Gunther clicked open his briefcase and handed the desk clerk a Gunfire Films platinum American Express card.

"I can't wait to get into the casino." Reno grinned.

"Yeah, me too, baby." Gloria gazed around the hotel lobby and smiled. "I bet they have some great boutiques here."

"Let's get changed so we can go party," Gunther suggested.

It was a whirlwind weekend on the French Riviera. Crowded tropical beaches with powdery white sand and azure blue water. Beautiful, tanned women in colorful, racy bikinis. Gunther thought his body would explode with passion.

There were more than six thousand journalists attending the festival from all over the world. Screenings and press conferences for *The Hood* were held daily. Gunther handled the press wonderfully. He was witty, charming, and eloquent, and they proclaimed him the "hottest thing going in young black directors" and *The Hood* "a smashing success."

Reno and Gloria went shopping during the day while Gunther handled Gunfire Films business. In the evening, the three of them hit the casinos and attended parties given by various film companies.

The party of parties was given on a yacht by a Japanese film company. The star-studded gala overflowed with champagne, caviar, sushi, and fresh seafood displayed in fabulous ice carvings.

Gunther, flying high on cocaine, was quite the conversationalist. He exuded money, power, and confidence in his black Armani tuxedo and diamond *G* cuff links.

I can't believe this is really happening. In a bathroom beneath the deck, Gunther checked his nose in a mirrored Gucci compact to make sure he had removed all traces of the white powder from his nose. I've never been in a bathroom on a yacht, he realized, admiring the emerald green marble flecked with gold covering the floors and matching counters with a sink inlaid in gold.

"They really laid this out." There were matching green soaps, velvety green towels embellished with a metallic gold lace border, and a vase of fresh white casablanca lilies and white roses.

"Dang." He took another hit of coke in each nostril and stored the vial in his pants pocket.

The Hood is a hit, he reminded himself happily, and then he sighed long and hard. But what will they think of it when it premieres in the States? He stared into space as a barrage of thoughts bombarded his mind.

"Oh, well, I'm not going to worry about that now." He removed the vial of coke from his pocket again. "It's time to party now."

TWENTY-THREE

TOPAZ'S HAND trembled ever so slightly as she inserted the key into the ignition of the shiny red Miata convertible. A smile lit up her face as she shifted into first gear and drove off the Mazda car lot in North Hollywood. It's mine, she wanted to shout from the rooftops. This fine red Miata is all mine.

She took her hands off the steering wheel and thrust them up towards the sky, swaying with the infectious beat of the music blasting through the car's elaborate sound system. She sang and yelled at the top of her lungs with "Poison."

"This car is the bomb," Nina shouted above the music.

"I know." Topaz lowered the volume. "I used part of my advance from the record company to buy it. Jamil said I needed it since I'm going to be in the studio all the time. He had the record company set everything up with the car dealer."

"How much money did you get?"

"Fifty thousand."

"You got fifty thousand dollars?"

"Girl, yes. Well, actually only twenty-five. Jamil got half."

"That's still a lot of money."

"I have to live on it until my album comes out."

"Are you still moving out of our house?"

"I don't think so. Jamil says I'll never be home, so it doesn't really make sense for me to move out. I think he wants me to move in with him."

"Move in? Girl, what about Germain?"

"I haven't made my mind up about what to do with him yet. Germain's not moving out here, and I'm not going back there anytime soon. He won't let Chris come out here, and I wouldn't have the time to spend with Chris if he was here. So . . . I'm probably going to ask him for a divorce," she finished quietly.

"A divorce?"

"Yes, a divorce. I'm going to be a famous singer now. Marriage and babies aren't part of the plan anymore. No one knows that I've been married or that I have a son, and I intend to keep it that way. I have an image to uphold," she explained, trying to convince herself more than Nina.

"But lots of people are married with—"

"Well I'm not going to be," she snapped, cutting Nina off. "And I don't want to talk about it anymore." She ran her hand through her golden mane and focused her attention on the cars in traffic ahead of her. I'm not going to let myself get depressed about this.

"Let's call somebody on the car phone," Nina suggested several minutes later, breaking the ice.

"All right, who?" A smile lit up Topaz's pretty face. She concentrated for several minutes. "I know, call Jamil." She rattled off numbers while Nina punched them in on the handset. The girls grinned at each other once they heard the phone ringing through the speaker.

"Yo," Jamil answered.

"You talk," Topaz whispered. "Mess with his head a little."

"Hello." He spoke slightly louder.

"Hey, baby," Nina whispered sexily, trying not to laugh.

"Who is this?"

"Your baby, your baby," Nina chanted. She cut her eyes at Topaz who had turned red from trying to stifle her laughter.

"Topaz?"

"Topaz? This ain't no Topaz," Nina was using her best homegirl voice. "And you better stop callin' me some other woman's name before I come over there and kick your butt."

Topaz burst into laughter unable to hold back any longer. "Girl, you're crazy. Hi, Jamil," she yelled into the phone. "I hope you know that wasn't me. That was my crazy cousin Nina. We just picked up the car. Thanks for hooking everything up for me. We're going shopping now on Melrose. Okay, talk to you later." Turning to Nina, she said, "Jamil wants to meet you."

"I still can't believe I've never met Jamil after all this time."

"I know. Things happened so fast. He's cute. You'd like him and he has bank, girl."

"Really? I thought you had something going on with Jamil."

"That was just business. We're just good friends. Besides, I'm still married."

"But you're getting a divorce . . ."

"And after I do, Sylk Ross is going to be my man."

"Sylk Ross. Now that's who I want to meet."

"Oh, no. Sylk's mine. I think it would be good for my image to be dating a famous basketball player." She pulled into Fred Segal's parking lot.

"Girl, I've always wanted to come in here and buy anything I wanted," Topaz whispered to Nina in the ladies' shoe department.

"I heard that." Nina picked up a red sequined pump. "These are nice." She took a peek at the price on the bottom of the shoe. "Four hundred and seventy-five dollars?" She replaced the shoe on the shelf. "I don't think so. They're crazy. I can buy a pair of red shoes and glue my own sequins on," Nina whispered to Topaz.

"Oh, Nina. It's only money, and they wouldn't be the same. I'd like to try on these in a size eight." She pointed out several black dress shoes and a pair of thigh-high boots to the sales clerk. "And the red sequined pump in a seven and a half." She gave Nina a wicked grin.

"Girl, these are to die for." Nina paraded up and down the hardwood floors in front of the mirrors in the red pumps, her toned mocha legs enhancing them nicely. "Crazy cool."

"So are these." Topaz posed in front of a full-length mirror in the black thigh-high boots, looking fine and sassy. Both girls were oblivious to repeated stares cast in their direction.

"Girl, those look good on you," Nina informed Topaz, who pranced up and down the floor yet another time.

"Thanks." Topaz slid off the boots. "Those red pumps are too hot."

"I know." Nina slipped them off and returned them to the box. "But I can't afford them."

"Don't worry about it. I'll take the boots and the red pumps," Topaz informed the salesclerk. "My treat."

"You're getting those for me?"

"Yes, big head."

"Ooh, thank you," Nina squealed. "I love you so much." She gave Topaz a hug.

"Me, too." Topaz kissed her cousin's cheek. "Let's go. We've got more shopping to do."

Nina gasped as she watched Topaz count out more than a thousand dollars in cash for their purchases.

"Don't tell Aunty Lena how much those shoes cost," Topaz warned, on the way upstairs to the women's clothing department. "I still owe her money for my phone bill."

"Uh-oh," Nina moaned. "You better pay her before she gets crazy."

"I will," Topaz promised. One of these days . . .

They spent the entire day shopping. They combed through the rest of the boutiques on Melrose, stopping at Johnny Rockets for juicy cheeseburgers and french fries, which gave them the energy they needed to tackle both floors of the Beverly Center.

In Bullocks they purchased every perfume they thought they liked—Jill Sander, Calyx, Volupte, Oscar de la Renta, Poison, Opium, Escada, and Cartier, as well as Borghese facial products, expensive gold costume jewelry with sparkling crystals, ropes and chokers of faux pearls, designer pantyhose in ultra sheer, fishnet, and lace.

From the MAC boutique, they bought tubes of lipstick in various colors with matching nail polish, translucent powders, eye shadows, and blushes. Dozens of silk and satin panties and bras from Victoria's Secret in a rainbow of colors. An assortment of shower gels and bath salts, a wonderful mud body scrub, loofah gloves, and body lotions from H_2O. Oodles of clothes and shoes—anything they thought was cute from Ice, Privilege, and Charles David. There were so many shopping bags, they seemed to be spilling out of the car.

"Topaz, you spent money like water." Back in Topaz's bedroom, the girls sifted through the bags inspecting their purchases.

"I know. We probably spent over five thousand dollars." Topaz was too happy as she sat amidst her loot. "And I'm just getting warmed up."

But her shopping days were curtailed once Jamil laid down all the music tracks for the songs on her album. He had her recording vocals all day and all night. Most days they started around noon and worked until ten or eleven the same night, or they'd start at midnight and work until very early in the morning. When Topaz wasn't recording, she was tied up in meetings with various departments at the record company to prepare for the release of her album.

One of the first things the A&R department did was get her a personal trainer, even though she was in excellent shape. She worked out with the trainer two hours a day, three days a week. He prescribed a rigorous routine that included weights, stair-stepping, and three hundred sit-ups daily. Topaz was ecstatic watching her great body become even more sensational.

Her favorite meetings were with the art department. They were reminiscent of her modeling days. Topaz, Jamil, and the creative director spent meeting after meeting discussing ideas for her image—hair, makeup, and wardrobe. She brought out her old modeling portfolio and the Johns Hopkins binder of pictures from fashion magazines, meticulously sorted by categories, and presented her ideas for her album cover.

"I love your concept," Gil, the head of marketing, informed Topaz when she explained her own ideas of her image, laying out photos and clothing she had purchased. "It's funky elegance."

"That's it exactly." Topaz smiled. "Funky elegance."

Once the concept was determined, Gil hired a stylist to scour the stores in search of clothing, shoes, and accessories for Topaz's photo shoots for the album cover. The record company went all out and hired the famous high-fashion photographer Francesco Scavullo for the shoot since Topaz had been a model. He brought in his own makeup artist, and Janet Zeitoun did her hair. Topaz was delighted to know that Janet had lots of star customers including Janet Jackson, Lionel Richie, and Natalie Cole, and that she worked out of Umberto's in Beverly Hills so she could see her on a regular basis.

The photographs were shot in black and white on the beach, right where the sand and water kissed as the tide came in. It was very chilly the day of the shoot, but Topaz never complained about the cold weather once. She was too excited to feel the cold, and after several large mugs of steaming hot tea spiked with rum and sweetened with honey, she felt like she was on a Caribbean beach.

Her stylist had dressed her in a double-breasted black wool tuxedo jacket with satin lapels and matching cropped skirt, accented by a crystal rhinestone cuff bracelet and earrings. The wind gently tossed her golden hair and she held a black silk top hat.

Her makeup was flawless. She was absolutely gorgeous and the photographs were fabulous. It took Topaz and Gil several weeks of daily meetings before they finally selected the photo for her self-titled album, *Topaz*.

Theron Perry in A&R at Populartis selected the notorious "Boyfriend," for her first single. Topaz spent two weeks with a choreographer learning the latest hip-hop moves that were an integral part of the routines and combinations she would be dancing in her video. The shoot was scheduled at the beach as well. The director, best known for his work with rock videos, set up a runway on Cabrillo Beach in Malibu.

Nina, who had been hired by the record company as Topaz's executive assistant and project manager, officially began her duties the day of the shoot. She scurried back and forth from Topaz's trailer to the set dressed in a pair of baggy teal shorts, black tank top, and Nikes, with a clipboard, pager, and a cellular phone, the epitome of efficiency.

"Nina, wait," Topaz whispered loudly when Nina ushered the makeup artist into her trailer. "Jamil is here and I want you to meet him."

"Now?" Nina brushed a wisp of hair out of her face that had worked itself out of a long braid. "I look tacky."

"No, you don't, come on."

Topaz pulled a reluctant Nina into the inner chamber of her trailer where a small buffet of fresh fruit, finger sandwiches, and sparkling waters were spread out on a table in a comfortable sitting area.

"There he is." She pointed to Jamil, who looked too cute in jeans and a Cross Colours shirt. He was checking out a TLC video. "Jamil, this is Nina." Topaz wanted to scream with laughter as she watched the coolness drain from Jamil's face the moment he laid his eyes on Nina's gorgeous mocha face and body.

"Nina, Jamil." Topaz smiled knowingly as she glanced in the mirror of her makeup table to see the pleased look on Nina's face once she caught a glimpse of Jamil's pretty brown eyes and charming smile.

"Hi," they both said at the same time.

"Pleased to meet you," Jamil almost whispered as he stood to shake Nina's hand.

"Me, too." Nina exhaled slowly, revealing a shy grin.

Topaz continued smiling as she softly hummed the chorus to "Boyfriend," pretending to be very interested in the outfits hanging on a clothes rack.

"I've got to run." Nina checked her beeping pager. "I'll be back in a few."

Topaz watched her dash out of the trailer towards the set before she spoke. "Well?" She grinned at Jamil.

"She's gorgeous." He was breathless.

"I knew you'd like her."

"She was the one on the phone?" Jamil asked, still collecting his thoughts.

"Yes."

"Word." A huge grin found its way onto his face.

Topaz smiled. She was too pleased with her matchmaking. Now I can get on with more important things, she told herself as she slipped on her first outfit. Like getting a divorce from Germain and hooking up with Sylk Ross.

"Jamil thinks you're gorgeous," Topaz informed Nina as she positioned herself at the back of the runway, which she would strut up and down with two male dancers.

"Great." Nina smiled and revealed a half dimple just before the music began. " 'Cause he is too fine."

The finished product premiered on BET's *Video Soul* in April, one week after the single hit the airwaves. The record hit like a plague and DJs across the country couldn't stop talking about "that gorgeous, gorgeous new singer named Topaz who could really belt out a song."

"Nina, Nina, that's really me on the radio," Topaz screamed, catching the first bars of the chorus as she flipped past stations on the car radio. They were driving home after lunch with a reporter in the Marina. "That's really me," she repeated, somewhat surprised by the realization.

Nina pumped up the volume to a deafening level and screamed along with her. "Crazy cool," she yelled over the music. "You go, girl. You sound good." She gave Topaz an admiring glance. "You're going to be so famous."

The record company sent her all over the United States to promote "Boyfriend." Topaz and Nina flew everywhere first class, traveling in limousines, and staying in the best hotels. They went to all the major cities where Topaz did live radio interviews and hosted autograph parties in record stores where people turned out in hordes to meet her. She reveled in all the attention.

"Nina, order me a lobster salad," Topaz commanded, the moment she checked into her suite in the Regency Hotel in Universal City. "And take my things to the laundry for pressing." She tossed several articles of clothing into a pile on Nina's bed. She pretended not to notice the look of death Nina cast in her direction as she went into the bathroom to run a bubble bath.

"Excuse me?" Nina gave her much attitude and placed a hand on her hip. "Slavery was abolished a long time ago, Miss Thing."

"Look, the record company is paying you a lot of money to work for me, so I suggest you do what I tell you or I'll have them hire someone else."

"I don't care who's paying me what, don't you ever speak to me like that again."

Topaz sucked in her breath and opened her mouth to reply.

"You ain't all that," Nina ranted. "I'll kick your butt all over this hotel. I'm not Kim. I will hurt you." She glared at Topaz as though she had two heads and a tail.

Topaz looked into Nina's eyes, blazing with anger, and realized she had pushed things too far. I don't want to get in a fight with her. She sighed unhappily. She's the sister I never had.

"I'm sorry, Nina." Her words were sincere. "I didn't mean to order you around. I just have a lot of things on my mind. I had my attorney Federal Express the divorce papers to Germain today," she confessed sadly, dropping down onto the bed.

"So you actually went through with it?" Nina relaxed and sat on the bed next to her. "How do you feel about it?"

"Awful. He has no idea that I'm filing for a divorce."

"I can't believe you went through with it."

"I can't believe I did, either, but I haven't seen Germain since I came here and that's been almost two years now." She looked up at Nina through lowered lashes and quickly brushed away a tear. She felt like she had lost her best friend in the world.

"And you were only staying three months," Nina recollected softly.

"I know. But look how long it took me to get this far. Germain just doesn't understand and he doesn't want to understand." Topaz jumped up from the bed as the venom found its way back into her voice.

"Maybe you should go home and talk to him."

"When? I don't have time. You know my schedule better than I do, and he absolutely refuses to come here or even meet me somewhere on the road, so I filed irreconcilable differences." She was sad again. "But I have to move on with my life. Besides, it would really hurt my image now for my fans to find out I'm married."

"What about Chris? What are you going to do about him?"

"Leave him with his daddy. He wouldn't even know me anymore." Topaz cut off the water that had been running for her bath. "Look, I can't talk about this anymore now. I've got to get ready for tonight."

"Yeah, cuz." Nina gathered Topaz's laundry. "You're performing for the who's who of radio and records at the Soul Train Awards tonight and you've got to throw down."

"That's right." Topaz smiled.

"Do you want me to order you a drink or something with your salad?"

"No, that's okay." Topaz went back into the bathroom.

"Well, do you want to smoke a joint or something? To get your mind off you know who."

"A joint?" Topaz giggled. "No, that's okay. But a glass of wine might be nice."

"Okay. We'll party later, after the show."

Topaz was as stunning as a high-fashion runway model at the collections in Europe when she mounted the stage in the hotel ballroom dressed in a pair of black Hunza jeweled pants, black stiletto Charles David pumps, a Courreges jacket, and a sexy bra top. Her freshly coifed golden mane framed her waistline and her amber eyes sparkled with excitement as she gazed out into the Shrine Auditorium filled with recoding industry VIPs and stars.

"Boyfriend, you know I'm the one . . ." Topaz sang into the microphone accompanied by tracks minus the lead vocals. She flashed a dazzling smile as she replaced the cordless microphone in its stand and strutted across the stage several times, stalking her prey carefully before she broke into the same hip-hop routines that had been choreographed for her video. The audience shrieked with approval.

"You know I'm the one, you know I'm the one . . ." She was energized by the audience's captivated faces and shouts of encouragement.

"You know I'm the one . . ." she finished breathless, with her arms thrust towards the heavens, more splendid than any finale by the Joffrey Ballet. She heard the room thunder with applause, but she was unable to move as she felt sweat trickle down her body. "I know you didn't think I was going to throw down like that," she whispered huskily and walked off the stage.

She could still hear them shouting and applauding as Nina and several buff security guards whisked her out the door.

"Girl, you were fabulous," Nina told her over and over. "You turned it out."

"Did I?" Back in her hotel room she kicked off her pumps and nervously paced the floor.

"Yes. Everybody was there."

"Really? Like who?"

"Everybody. Girl, I saw Jheryl Busby, Quincy Jones, Eddie Murphy, Al B. Sure, Cuba Gooding Jr., Jam and Lewis, L.A. and Babyface . . ."

"Quincy Jones and Eddie Murphy?" Topaz repeated, extremely impressed. "Wow." She spotted several large floral arrangements in the suite. "Who are those from, Nina?" She pointed at the vases of roses and exotic flowers. Maybe Mother told Germain about tonight and he sent flowers or even better, maybe they're from Sylk Ross.

"Jamil and me. And let's see who else." Nina took the card from the exotic arrangement. "Theron and Populartis Records and LaTrell Sanders from Music City sent the roses."

"That's all?" Topaz tried to cover her disappointment.

"Yes." A knock at the door ended their discussion on flowers.

"You'd better get changed," Nina commanded. "Mother and Daddy said they would come up, and Theron's coming and bringing guests. And who knows who else," Nina rattled off as she headed for the door. "I wonder where Jamil is?"

"There you are," Topaz heard Nina exclaim. "Hi."

Topaz stood there wearing only stretch pants and her bra top, waiting for the two of them to come into view. She smiled when she saw Jamil enter the room wearing a tuxedo. Jamil is so cute. She smiled and lifted her cheek for him to kiss . . . but I gave him to Nina.

"Hey, star." He greeted her warmly, kissing her gently on the cheek. "You were fabulous."

"You know I'm the one . . ." she sang, trying to hold his attention. She watched him quickly zoom in on Nina and run his hands through Nina's shiny black hair while she looked up at him with adoring eyes. Nina looked particularly gorgeous in a short black beaded evening dress.

"You know I was the one," Topaz sang as she disappeared into the bedroom to change.

"Baby, you were sensational," her aunty Lena told her for the thousandth time. "And you look absolutely fabulous."

"Thank you." Topaz was cool as she checked out her reflection in the living room mirror for the umpteenth time. She had chosen a white silk tuxedo jacket and pants to receive her guests in. She smoothed her flowing tresses, burnished by the California sun, with a black gloved hand and took a hearty sip from the goblet of Cristal she was nursing.

"Lisa wanted to be here," Lena continued, "but she couldn't take the time off from work. Just wait until I tell her how fabulous you were. She'll be so pleased."

I'm sure she will. "Excuse me, I need to speak with Nina." She was bored by their babbling. Topaz smiled a plastic smile at her aunt and uncle and set off in search of her cousin. She found Nina engaged in conversation with Theron and several other executives from her record company. "What do you have for us to party with?" she whispered to Nina through gritted teeth.

"You want to party?" Nina whispered back, surprised.

"Yes."

"Crazy cool. Let's go to the bathroom."

"What's that?" Topaz watched Nina slip a small vial of white powder out of her makeup bag once they were in the bathroom.

"Cocaine, silly," Nina giggled. She tapped the white powder onto the marble counter.

"Where did you get that from?"

"Jamil got it for me."

"Jamil takes drugs?"

"No, well, sometimes. But he got it for me. This stuff is expensive."

She watched Nina sniff the powder through a silver music note. "Girl, where did you learn to do this?"

"You are so square," Nina laughed. "Me and my girlfriends used to do coke in high school."

"High school? Didn't you go to some private school in Beverly Hills or something?"

"Bel Air. That was the place."

"Nina. I thought we were going to smoke a joint."

"Well, we certainly can't smoke a joint with Mother, Daddy, and everyone else in the next room. It smells. Besides, cocaine is cool. Everybody in the music business who gets high does coke."

"Are you sure?"

"I thought you wanted to party."

"I do." I've got to do something to get my mind off Germain and Sylk, she decided. Topaz sniffed the lines of white powder through the music note the way she had seen Nina do it and looked at her reflection in the mirror.

"Here's to your big night at the Soul Train Awards, cuz." Nina saluted her with a flute of champagne.

Topaz smiled in response as the drug rushed her body. My big night. She heard Nina's words echo throughout her mind. It's my debutante ball all over again. I'm even wearing white, she realized, checking out her reflection in the mirror, except this time I won. I'm the queen tonight. She was the belle of the ball when she reentered her hotel suite full of guests who had gathered to celebrate her success.

After the awards she hit the road again, doing more interviews and television shows, including *MTV Jams* and *Arsenio*.

"I'm so busy I don't have time to date," she graciously informed Donnie Simpson and Sherry Carter on *Video Soul*.

Topaz had threatened not to do the interview and had an absolute fit only hours before when she realized Germain had changed all of his phone numbers including his pager number, making it virtually impossible for her to get in touch with him. She wanted to have dinner with him while she was in Washington, and now she couldn't even get in contact with him.

"I'd like to get married and have a family one of these days but right now there's no time," she explained to Arthel Neville on *E!* She fingered the diamond baguette Germain had given her, which she still wore on the ring finger of her right hand.

"Why does everyone want to know about my love life?" she complained to Nina after the interview.

Despite the state of her personal life, "Boyfriend" was a huge success. It was nominated for all sorts of music awards. She received an American Music Award and a Grammy for Best New Artist. She also won a Grammy for Best R&B single, Best R&B Female Vocalist, and Jamil even received a Grammy for Producer of the Year.

This is my life now . . . Topaz glanced out the window at the traffic on the 405 Freeway. She was in another limo, headed for the airport once again, to catch another plane to another city. She looked at Nina who was smiling and whispering into the limo's telephone. That has to be Jamil.

They were on their way to London, where she would begin a six-week promotional tour in Europe. She gazed out of the window of the limousine.

Bored, she decided to look at the stack of mail on the seat that she hadn't had a chance to go over. Nina had handed her the stack before they left the house. She picked up several pieces of mail and began to sift through them. She opened an envelope containing a clip of a *Harper's Bazaar* article. The magazine proclaimed her one of the ten most beautiful women in the world. She flipped through the layout quickly. Nice . . .

Next she opened up a statement from her business manager, detailing her earnings for the last month. She smiled at the seven-figure amount that was the bottom line. That's nice, too. There was an article from *Billboard* that her manager had faxed over. *Topaz* had sold more than five million copies since its release one year ago. Real nice. He had also included a synopsis of a script that had been written originally for Diana Ross that one of the studios wanted her to consider and a tentative itinerary for a world tour.

I'll read the script later, she decided, tossing it aside. The last thing she picked up was a nondescript manila envelope with a Baltimore postmark. What's this? She slit the envelope open with her fire-engine-red acrylic nail.

"Dissolution of Marriage, Gradney vs. Gradney," she read. It's the divorce papers. I had forgotten all about them. She had sent them to Germain almost a year ago, and with her busy schedule she had completely forgotten. Germain hadn't returned them and in her heart of hearts she had been expecting him to show up with Chris in Los Angeles or on the road. Then, they would kiss and make up and things would be just like they were before, especially since her career had taken off and she was a superstar now.

I was right to come to California. I always knew I could do this. She looked at Germain's scrawled doctor's signature and felt herself grow numb. All of a sudden, a small part of her, somewhere deep inside, died. She blinked furiously, making a valiant effort to fight back the tears that wanted to flow.

"I never thought you would actually give me a divorce, Germain. I only wanted you to move out here with me," she whispered as the tears streamed out of her eyes. She wiped her eyes quickly with the back of her hand before Nina, who was still on the phone, hung up and demanded to know why she was crying. Germain always did have a knack for ruining my parties.

She felt around in her oversized Chanel bag until her fingers grasped a small glass container. Topaz pulled out the vial of cocaine. She always kept a little on hand to boost her waning energy during a hectic day of appointments. She stared at the container of white powder then glanced up at Nina who was still smiling and whispering in the phone. Topaz unscrewed the lid and took several hits in each nostril. She replaced the lid, stuffed the container back into her bag, and sniffed. There . . .

She felt the drug work itself through her body as she reached into her handbag for her MAC compact. She brushed on translucent powder, reapplied her lipstick, and fluffed her hair just as the limousine pulled into the international terminal at LAX. The driver appeared in moments to help her out of the car. She ignored him completely and strutted into the gift shop to purchase magazines and munchies for the flight while Nina took care of their luggage. Her eyes fell on a copy of *Essence* with her smiling, gorgeous face on the cover.

"Superstar Topaz Black reflects on life at the top," the cover copy read.

Germain doesn't want me anymore. I'm all alone now. She felt a tear slide down her cheek as she stood there staring at the magazine and fumbling in her purse for a tissue.

"May I have your autograph, please?" she heard a young female voice request.

"I have a plane to catch," she replied nastily, pulling on a pair of dark Chanel sunglasses as she carried her magazines to the counter.

How dare he treat me like this. I'm a superstar, with all sorts of guys throwing themselves at me.

"But the one you want doesn't want you," she heard a voice from deep within reply.

I'm just being silly. Now I can concentrate on Sylk Ross . . . But why does it hurt so bad? she asked herself as she walked through the terminal towards the departure gate. She was fighting the urge to cry again.

"Here." She thrust the airport gift shop bag at Nina when she caught up with her at the airline gate. "Where have you been?" Topaz snapped, her amber eyes blazing with anger.

"Checking our luggage. What's wrong with you?"

"Nothing. From now on, I want a security guard with me everywhere I go. I'm a superstar and people should not be able to walk up to me and just start talking to me when I don't wish to be spoken to," Topaz ranted.

"What?" Nina was confused. "What brought this on?"

"People are getting on my nerves and I won't stand for it."

"Topaz, what is your problem?"

"There's no problem. I'm a superstar, Nina, and it's time you and everyone else start acting like it."

TWENTY-FOUR

SEAN SCRAPED a pile of diced scallions and garlic into the hot peanut oil that danced and sputtered off the sides of the wok and peeked at the rice in the steamer to see if it was done.

"Man, that sure smells good." Eric took a seat at the bar in the kitchen where he could watch Sean cook and talk to him at the same time. The black director's chair he sat in had SYLK ROSS embroidered in red on the back. "You know what you doin' huh?"

"Of course, I know what I'm doin'." Sean laughed and tossed a plate of jumbo shrimp in the wok. "Take a look at these." He proudly displayed Chinese pot stickers neatly lined in rows on a serving dish. "Szechwan," he bragged.

"Dang, those look good." Eric reached out to pluck a dumpling from the tray.

"Oh, no." Sean snatched the tray out of his reach. "Those are for company. If I let you get your hands in those, there won't be any left for dinner."

"Man, you actually made those?" Eric was in awe.

"Of course I did." Sean was too pleased with himself. He poured a savory dark duck sauce into the wok along with a dish of chopped carrots and removed the wok from the stove. "I made these, too." He passed a plate of egg rolls in front of Eric.

"Aw, man, you got to let me try one of those."

"You got it, E." Sean laughed and placed several dumplings and a couple of egg rolls on a plate for Eric. Then he poured 7UP into a blender with crushed ice and wine, ran the blender until the mixture was frothy, and poured some into a glass. He pushed the glass across the bar to Eric and waited for his reaction.

"This is good. What is this?" Eric demanded after he tasted the drink.

"Plum wine on the rocks." Sean grinned. "Here." He placed

a small dish with hot oil and sweet and sour sauce for the appetizers on the counter. "Now you're straight."

"Dang, man. I didn't know you could cook like this." Eric eyed the dishes of appetizers as he swallowed his last bite.

"My mother taught me and my brothers how to cook when we were little." Sean tossed sliced beef, onions, and green peppers into the wok for pepper steak. "But I started fooling around with Chinese food while I was around the house off the team."

"So how much longer you gonna be out, man?"

"I don't know, Easy. My doctor wants me to take time and let everything heal thoroughly before I try and play again since I damaged the same knee I busted in college. But he hinted that I should be able to start playing again by the first of the year."

"You look real good, money. How does it feel?"

"Good, man. Real good. I'm still in therapy, but it feels great. Jesus is the Healer. The Lord hooked me up just like He did before. I'm as good as new." Sean paused to dance along with "It's Time," which was blasting on the stereo in the den. "Where's Keisha?" Sean poured the steak into a dish and set it on the back of the stove.

"She should be here any minute. She's getting her hair done."

"I can't believe you let her out of your sight." Sean paused to smile at his friend before preparing mushrooms, broccoli, and scallions for the wok.

"And I can't believe I'm the one who's married now, and you were the one always talking about getting a wife."

"I know, but things happen when they're supposed to. It's not my season yet, man."

"What does that mean?" Eric swiped several carrot sticks from the pile of vegetables Sean was chopping.

"It means that in the great scheme of things, in God's plan for my life, there's a certain time when I'm supposed to get married."

"Word?"

"Word. God has a specific time for everything and if we wait on Him and do things in His timing, that's God's best. Of course, we can do what we want, and that's when things get messed up."

"That's deep." A lightbulb came on in Eric's head. "So you

mean God has a special plan for each of our lives and if we do things His way, that's the best thing for our lives?"

"That's it exactly, man. Except most people are afraid to trust Him. I know I was."

"You were?"

"Yep. I thought He needed help getting me into the NBA. I really messed things up, but the Lord straightened them out."

"So how do you know if you're living in this special plan?"

"That's the million-dollar question, E-man. That's what we all want to know. God requires us to live by faith and He reveals bits and pieces of His plan every day as we talk to Him and read the Word."

"You know, I've been reading the Bible every day now, man, and I'm really starting to understand. Me and Keisha pray together every morning before we leave the house, too."

"You do? That's wonderful, man."

"I like it, too. You know I probably wouldn't be doing any of that stuff if we hadn't been friends."

"Really?" Sean was surprised.

"A lot of people go around preaching all the time, telling people what not to do, but you're all right, man. I've watched you ever since you came to the team. You're down with everybody. You treat everybody the same and you don't be trippin' cause you got juice. Most brothers would be trippin' big time if they did one interview and had one major sponsor. And they'd be ready to commit suicide if they'd hurt themselves the way you did and had to be off the team. And you act like you don't even care, Chef Ming."

"Stop, man, you're makin' it hard for me to live up to all of these wonderful things you're saying about me." Sean laughed.

"Man, you know I'm telling the truth."

"Thanks, E." Sean spoke quietly as he tossed the veggies with a spatula and thought about the painkillers, which were starting to become a way of life. Especially since he had reinjured his knee. Now he had a valid reason for taking them. He wanted to discuss his addiction with Eric but now he couldn't. Not after that dissertation. But he is my best friend. "I'll tell you a secret, man—" Sean started, as he led Eric into the den.

The doorbell interrupted their conversation.

"Hold up, man." Sean pressed the intercom button. "Yo."

"It's me, Keisha," a voice yelled into the intercom. "And your brothers are here too, Sean."

"Cool, everyone's here. We can eat before everything gets cold." He opened the door as Keisha, the twins, Karla, Kyrie, and Kyle's girlfriend stepped out of the elevator. "Yo, yo, yo." Sean grinned, holding the door open. "What up, family?" He swooped Kyrie up into his arms and buried his head in the little girl's stomach, laughing as she screamed with laughter.

"You're all she talked about since we left Philly," Karla stood on her tiptoes to plant a kiss on his smooth chocolate cheek. "Unc Sean. Unc Sean. Unc Sean play baskyball." Karla laughed as she imitated her daughter.

"Really?" He looked at the little girl, kissed her, and grinned a lopsided boyish grin.

"Yes." Kirk sighed with exasperation. "She doesn't get that excited over me and I'm her daddy." He pretended to be jealous.

"That's because she sees your big head every day." Karla laughed.

"Yo, G whipped up some serious Chinese food," Eric informed them once they were all in the house.

"Sean cooked? Oh, no. I thought we were going out to dinner," Kyle teased.

Eric rushed to Sean's defense. "It's all good man. Real good."

"I'll be the judge of that. Where's the chow?" Kirk demanded.

"You'd think they could ask me how I'm doin' first," Sean told the ladies, pretending to be hurt. "No, they all rush in here demanding food. Would you ladies care for a drink and some appetizers?" he asked politely, completely ignoring his brothers and Eric.

"Sure, that's sounds nice, sweetie. Do you need some help with things in the kitchen?" Karla offered.

"No, I—"

"You sit down and rest that leg, babe. Karla and I will handle things in the kitchen." Keisha pushed Sean towards the den. "You guys go do some male bonding."

"I'll help, too." Kyle's girlfriend, Diana, was petite and extremely pretty. She joined the other girls in the kitchen.

"Get him. Invites us to dinner and has all of our women in the kitchen waiting on him," Kyle declared.

"Word. He always has all the women making a fuss over him. You know them stars got it goin' on like that." Eric laughed.

"That's not true." Sean stretched his leg out on a hassock and flipped to a basketball game on the big-screen television.

"Yeah, right . . . Yo, did I ever tell y'all about the night this hoochie was waiting for my boy in his bed with her clothes off?" Eric volunteered.

"You're kidding." Kirk tried to keep a straight face while the others howled with laughter.

"Nope." Eric was in stitches. "You should have seen my boy's face . . ."

"I've got to show the girls how to hook up the drinks," Sean suddenly remembered.

"Naw, G, you stay right there and rest that leg," Eric commanded while the others continued laughing. "I'll hook up the drinks." He returned seconds later with huge crystal glasses of plum wine spritzers. "My girl had already hooked these up." He passed the drinks around to the guys.

"Yo, E-man, how did I let you get away with Keisha?" Sean questioned seriously after he had taken a sip of his drink.

"You didn't let me get away with anything, man. The Lord hooked us up. It was part of His special plan for me."

"Word." Sean grinned.

"You know Topaz introduced me and Keisha. We were the chaperons for all your dates," Eric teased. "What's up with you two, anyway? Girlfriend is too large now. I thought she was supposed to be a model. I didn't know she could sing. Every time I turn on BET she's all over the place."

"You know Topaz?" Kyle demanded. "That's one fine honey."

"Yeah, that's Keisha's girl," Eric continued. "She introduced me to Keisha."

"Who's Keisha's girl?" Keisha came into the den with appetizers for the fellas. She had let her short hair grow out into a blunt asymmetrical pixie cut. The change enhanced her pretty honey brown face, and with her large tasteful bronze jewelry and copper makeup, she was as gorgeous as Nefertiti.

"Topaz," Eric replied.

"Oh." Keisha tried to keep a straight face. "Let's eat. We set the dining room table."

"Who's Topaz?" Kirk asked as they moved the conversation into the dining room.

"Sean's woman," Eric replied.

"Sean, you got somebody serious in your life, man? How come we haven't met her?" Kirk wanted to know.

"Because we're just friends." Sean was very cool about the matter.

The girls had set the black lacquer and oak dining room table with candles and seafoam green placemats and napkins that were the same shade of green as the walls. Ice water sparkled in Baccarat water goblets and the gold chargers holding the shiny black dinner plates highlighted the swirls of gold in the Mikasa place settings. Candlelight cast a warm glow on the room, giving it a perfect intimate setting.

"It looks nice in here." Sean took a seat at the table.

"It was easy to do, honey. You have so many nice things."

"Thanks, Karla. Where's my baby girl?" Sean asked.

"Out like a light," his sister-in-law replied.

The girls brought in the dishes of Chinese food and Kyle blessed the food.

"Sean didn't make this," Keisha teased. "Him and Eric ordered this food from a restaurant and then they dirtied up some dishes in the kitchen."

"He really made it." Eric helped himself to a large helping of Chinese chicken salad.

"He cooks, too. I'm impressed," Diana said. "Sean, why aren't you married yet?"

"Cause he's waiting on Topaz," Eric teased.

"Who's this Topaz girl?" Kirk demanded. "You guys keep talking about her."

"She's a star, man," Kyle explained. "She sings that song, 'Boyfriend.' You really don't know who she is?"

"I may have heard the song once or twice, but this girl doesn't sound like anyone for you, Sean." Kirk's tone was serious.

"Baby, don't start in on Sean," Karla began.

"We're all family here," Kirk continued. "Sean is my little brother and I want him to have the best. He's good-looking, rich, and famous. These girls will do anything to get their hands on him.

You know how people are always trying to be friends with us so they can get next to Sean."

"Kirk!" Karla seemed shocked by his frankness.

"Sean needs someone to be there for him, not some famous singer," Kirk told his wife.

"But how do you know this girl doesn't really love and care for Sean?" Karla protested. "Can't a sister have a career and be down for a brother, too?"

"Of course she can," Kirk replied.

Sean pushed a couple of grains of rice around on his plate with a pair of chopsticks, listening to the others discuss his love life as if he weren't there. But he really didn't mind. I know they only want the best for me. Families, you have to love them. But it was still a constant reminder of the relationship he desired but didn't have. He felt a fresh stab of pain and went into the kitchen where he could take his pain medication in private but could still hear their conversation.

"But this girl ain't the one."

"How do you know, Kirk?" Karla demanded. "How do you know?"

"I don't know," he replied, shaking his head. "But something just doesn't feel right. She's probably self-centered, selfish, and an airhead. And Topaz . . . what kind of name is that?" Keisha went into a fit of laughter.

"But she's gorgeous, man." Kyle cast a sideways glance at Diana.

"I don't care how good she looks. That babe would probably be Sean's worst nightmare."

"What do you think, Keisha?" Eric demanded. "You know her. She's your friend."

"Kirk hit the nail on the head. Topaz doesn't love anyone but herself."

Sean returned to the dining room when the conversation switched to basketball. But he kept thinking of Topaz. I've been trying to get her to come for a visit and she never has time. Kirk's right. I need somebody who's going to be down for me and not because I have money and play basketball. Does a girl like that really exist? He thought about all the girls who were always trying to get next to him because he was Sylk Ross and sighed again. What if I never meet the right person?

■

Several days later, Sean was back in the kitchen baking chocolate chip cookies from scratch. "I'm getting soft. Baking cookies." He laughed as he piled half a dozen cookies on a plate and took them back into the den where he had been reading *This Present Darkness*.

It's so peaceful, he realized. This has been great just being around here doing what I want to do for a change. No press people hassling me, no teammates to be upset with me because they're not being interviewed . . . no more women hanging out in the hotels. He chomped on a cookie still warm from the oven. Almost as good as Mommy's, he thought, chewing on a second. She had faxed him the recipe from his father's office. A ringing telephone interrupted him from his thoughts.

"Sean, hi, it's Topaz. I'm in New York."

"You are?" He wondered why she hadn't phoned before to say she was coming.

"Yes. Let's have dinner tonight. I'll take you out."

"Okay." He smiled. She wants to take me out. That's a change. Maybe Kirk was wrong.

"I'm staying at the Waldorf Astoria. Meet me here at eight and we'll take my limo for the evening."

The phone rang again as soon as he hung up.

"Mr. Ross, I'm Ms. Black's assistant, Nina Beaubien."

"Yes?" Sean replied, wondering what was the purpose of this phone call.

"Ms. Black wanted me to tell you to wear something appropriate for dinner at Tribeca Grill."

"What?" Sean was astonished by her request.

"She'd like you to wear something—"

"I heard you," he replied, cutting her off.

"Is there anything else I can assist you with, Mr. Ross?"

"Yes. Where is Topaz? I'd like to speak to her, please."

"I'm sorry but Ms. Black isn't available right now. Would you care to leave a message?"

"I just spoke with her a few minutes ago. How did she become unavailable so quickly?" He was losing his patience.

"I'm sorry, Mr. Ross, but she's not available. Is there a message?"

"No. Tell her I'll see her at eight. Good-bye." He slammed the phone down. How dare she tell me to dress appropriately? I know how to dress, and just who does she think she is?

He stared at the phone for several minutes and took several deep breaths to calm himself down. I don't know when I've been that angry at someone.

At six o'clock he began dressing for his date. "Dress appropriately," he mumbled to his reflection in the bathroom mirror while he shaved. He splashed water on his flawless chocolate skin and inspected a tiny bump on his jawline. What's that? He dabbed extra toner that had been mixed specially for him by his cosmetologist over the minuscule imperfection in his smooth skin. Time for another facial. "Dress appropriately." He shook his head, still amazed by Topaz's outrageous request.

He opened the door to his huge walk-in closet and walked over to the wall that held his dress pants and jackets and sifted through them. He paused at a new black Armani suit that he had just picked up from his tailor. "That'll work."

He hung the suit on the closet door and walked to another wall of the closet that held countless shirts. He selected a royal blue silk shirt. Then, he pulled out several pairs of black dress shoes before he selected a new pair of black boots and a pair of black silk socks from his sock drawer.

Dress appropriately. He showered quickly and massaged his favorite lotion from Neiman Marcus into his skin. At seven-fifteen he gave himself a once-over in the full-length mirror in his bedroom and carefully inspected the new way the barber had cut his fade.

"I look good." He grinned at his reflection in the mirror and picked up a midi cashmere overcoat.

"Good evening, Mr. Ross." This must be the assistant. He carefully observed the thin mocha girl, conservatively but well dressed in a navy wool skirt and white sailor blouse. She wore very little makeup and her hair was twisted up in a topknot. "I'll let Ms. Black know you're here."

She disappeared behind a door in the lavish hotel suite. Sean glanced around at the room's exquisite furnishings, noticing the vases of ruby red long-stem roses and the large basket of assorted fruit.

"Ms. Black will be with you in a moment. Would you like something to drink?" Nina offered, the epitome of professionalism.

"No, thanks."

Sean glanced at his watch. It was eight-fifteen. He was starting to feel uncomfortable. Moments later he heard a door open and Topaz, looking more glamorous than he had ever remembered, made her grand entrance. She strutted into the room wearing black stretch pants that hugged every curve of her body like a glove. Her black angora sweater was embellished with jet beads and crystal rhinestones and she wore thigh-high black suede boots with spiked heels. Her tawny tresses framed her exquisite butterscotch face like a golden mane. He could see several enormous diamonds sparkling on her slender fingers and on her earlobes, and a fur coat, the color of her hair, dangled over her arms.

"Sean, darling, it's so fabulous to see you." She planted a kiss on his lips.

"Hi, Topaz." He stood to his feet, once again awed by her beauty.

"Oh, darling, we practically match," she exclaimed, referring to his attire. "Don't we make the most perfect couple?" She giggled and handed him her coat so he could help her put it on. "Let's go, darling." She pulled on a pair of leather gloves and took him by the hand. "The car is waiting."

"Good night," Sean called out to Nina as they left the suite, noticing that Topaz said nothing.

"I've been so busy, Sean." They were cruising through Manhattan in a black Lincoln stretch limousine. She chattered on and on about her singing career. "So how do you like my album?"

"I don't really listen to the radio much, but I've seen your video."

"I'll have Nina give you a copy when we get back to the hotel. So, you aren't playing basketball now." She paused to flip her hair out of her eyes. "Will you be off the team much longer?" She fixed her huge amber eyes on him.

She is so fine . . . "I'm in physical therapy until Christmas."

"Oh, so I won't be seeing you play in any basketball games until the New Year. That's a pity. I'll be starting my world tour the first of the year. You'll have to come visit me on the road." She gave him a dazzling smile.

Sean swallowed hard and returned her smile. "We'll see."

When the limo stopped in front of the doorway of Tribeca Grill, Sean hopped out first to help her out of the car.

"Don't ever do that again," she commanded sharply. "I get out first."

"What? Suppose I want to open the door for you myself? That's not allowed?"

"You're sweet, Sean." She stroked his cheek as he held the door open to the restaurant. "But that's what the help is for."

He looked at her like she was crazy as she strutted off ahead of him through the restaurant like the Queen of Sheba. He watched her stop at a table and speak to a lady whom he recognized as a celebrity gossip columnist. Topaz flashed a dazzling smile when he arrived at the table and tucked her arm through his.

"Darling, this is our dinner guest."

"Thanks for telling me," he whispered coarsely as he pulled out Topaz's chair.

Sean sat there the entire night completely bored while she went on and on about her singing career.

"Sylk and I have been dating for years," she informed the writer, cuddling up next to Sean. "I met him here in New York before I began singing, when I was a model. I joined him on the road several times and we even went to Aruba. And now he's going to join me on my world tour as often as he can."

She's telling my business and she's lying. His brother Kirk's words came to mind. *That girl is Sean's worst nightmare.* Just wait until I tell Eric and Keisha about this.

"Sean, darling." Topaz tapped him lightly on his hand. "She wants to know if we're getting married."

Married? "We're just friends."

"Sean hates talking about personal things with the press," Topaz laughed. "But marriage could be a very strong possibility by next year."

"I'm exhausted," she confessed once they were back in the limousine. "Are you spending the night with me?" She looked up at him through lowered lashes as she cuddled into his arms.

"No, I've got to get up very early in the morning," he replied, halfway wishing he could spend the night with her. It would be nice to have someone to just hold me for once.

"Oh, darling, I thought you could spend the night and then we could have some time alone," she pleaded in her little girl's voice, nibbling on his ear.

Dang. Why is life so hard? I have this gorgeous woman begging me to spend the night and I have to go home. I'm only human. He could feel his defense mechanisms wearing down.

"I really have to go home," he heard himself say.

"Oh, darling." She kissed him tenderly. "Don't go."

The limo stopped and Sean heard the driver get out of the car. Saved by the bell. "We're back at the hotel." This time, he waited for the driver to open the door, and then he climbed out of the car behind her.

"You at least have to come up for a drink." She took him by the hand and led him towards the entrance of the hotel.

"No, really, I can't. You know it's past my bedtime. He knew if he went upstairs with her they would wind up in bed. "When are you leaving?"

"First thing in the morning. I only flew in for dinner. Anybody who's anybody has to have dinner with me," she explained, flipping her hair.

"Well, maybe I'll come to L.A. and spend some time with you while I'm not playing ball."

"Will you, really?" She wrapped her arms around him and stood so close he could feel her warm breath on his face.

"We'll see." He kissed her on the cheek. "Goodnight, Princess."

It was only eleven by the time he arrived at home. He tossed his house keys into a vase in the foyer, tossed his jacket over a chair, and went into the kitchen to pour himself a glass of juice. He look at the container of pain pills in the medicine cabinet. "No," he closed the mirrored cabinet firmly. "I have to stop this."

He picked up the phone and hung it up again.

"Better not call E-man now," he chuckled. Him and Keisha might be getting busy. He's not even in town, he realized when he checked the Concordes basketball schedule tacked on a bulletin board by the phone.

He went into the den, flopped down on the grey leather sofa, and stretched his injured leg out on the hassock that usually sat in front of the oversized chair. Sighing, he flipped on the television set, checking every channel on the cable lineup and flipped the set back off. He closed his eyes and sighed unhappily.

I'm tired of being by myself. I wonder what Topaz is doing. He looked at the phone again. I don't want to talk to her. I want to be with her. I wonder what Mommy and Daddy are doing. Probably gettin' busy. He laughed out loud at the thought. Everybody's gettin' busy but me.

He passed through the kitchen and picked up several chocolate chip cookies before he mounted the stairs to the loft where his office was located. He switched on a light and took a seat behind the glass desk in its black metal frame and clicked on his CD player.

There's always work to do. He picked up a stack of letters that George had sent over several days ago. He sifted through the letters requesting him for personal appearances at various fundraisers and benefits or donations from his Smooth as Sylk Foundation.

What's this from *The 700 Club*? He quickly read the letter requesting him to appear on the television show. "I've got to do this."

"God put me in the NBA." Sean spoke with Ben Kinchlow freely. He felt tiny beads of perspiration form around his hairline from the intense heat of the television lights, but he remembered not to wipe his face because of the translucent powder that had been applied to his skin to eliminate any shine.

"I know He did, because after I injured myself in college I didn't even make the draft. I had to try out for the Concordes as a free agent. But I made it and I promised the Lord I would never compromise my righteousness for anything the world had to offer."

He beamed happily while the audience applauded. "I've admired a lot of people. Basketball players like Dr. E, Magic Johnson, Kareem, but my real hero is my father. He taught me how to play basketball and he taught me God's Word. He's shown me what it means to be a husband, a father, and a man of God. Stand up, Daddy."

Sean stood up and, along with the audience, applauded his

father. He smiled proudly as his father, who was sitting in the audience, stood.

"He could have played professional basketball, too, but he knew his purpose was to preach God's Word. That was his passion. When I was a little boy, he told me one of the best ways to find God's plan for my life was to pursue the thing I was most passionate about."

Sean felt a surge of joy well up deep inside of him as he shared his heart with Ben and the rest of the world.

"But you know something Daddy? I realized something while I was doing that interview." He took several sips of ice water.

"What's that, Sean?"

"Basketball is no longer my passion."

"Really?"

"Yes. I guess I've known it for a while, but I wasn't ready to admit it."

"How do you feel about that?"

"I don't know, Daddy. I've played basketball all my life. I don't know what else I'd do if I wasn't playing basketball." He folded his white linen napkin in squares while he spoke.

"You still have that business degree."

"I know, but what am I going to do? Apply for a job with IBM?"

"Now that would be something." His father laughed. "What else do you want to do?"

"I don't know, Daddy. There's not too many things you can do when your name is a household word. The doctor says I can go back to the team now, but I don't know if I want to."

"God has something special for you, Sean. Take some time to listen and hear what He's saying. But take your time, son, and don't let anyone rush you into anything."

Sean nodded in agreement and excused himself from the table. He went into the restroom and dumped the entire bottle of pain pills into the toilet and flushed it. "I don't need you," he whispered to himself. "Because I can do all things . . ."

■

Sean pressed the buzzer marked Johnson on a well-kept brownstone and smiled in anticipation of seeing his best friend.

"What up, E-man?" Sean greeted his friend with a hug. It had been several weeks since Sean's Chinese dinner. "Where's Keisha?"

"Christmas shopping. She made us some lunch before she left." He lifted the lid on a pot on the stove. "Turkey spaghetti."

"Serve it on up, man."

"What's been happening, Sean?" The guys set up trays in front of the television in the living room.

"Lots."

"Word?"

Sean drained his glass of juice and gazed thoughtfully at his friend. "I'm going to sit the rest of the season out."

"What? You're kidding."

"Nope," he replied quietly, waiting to see what Eric would say next.

"Man, you're crazy. You're the juice. This is the prime of your career. What about your fans? What about the team?" Eric yelled wildly.

"What about me?" Sean quietly interjected.

"What do you mean?"

"I'm not happy, man. I haven't been for a long time."

"How could you not be happy?" Eric yelled. "You have everything."

"Some people might see it that way. But from the way I look at things, you're the one with everything."

"What? I have everything? Man, you crazy."

"You're in the NBA and part of the starting lineup. You're getting paid. You have a gorgeous wife who loves you. You just bought a new house, and you have a baby due next summer. Me . . . I can't go anywhere without people bothering me. Every girl I meet wants to meet Sylk Ross not Sean. I'm alone most of the time. My teammates hate me. You're my only real friend. Shall I continue?"

"Naw, man. Dang, Sean. I never looked at it that way. I guess it's not easy being you."

"The price of fame, my friend, the price of fame."

The two sat in silence eating.

"What are you going to do when you're off the team?"

"Figure out what I want to do with the rest of my life. I'm looking for a house in Southern California."

"California?"

"Yeah. I have a real estate agent looking already. I want something near the beach with lots of windows and light, flower gardens, a pool. I'm tired of this dark, dirty city."

"But why California? That's so far away from your family, man."

"I know, but there's just something about California. Maybe it's the palm trees, the Pacific Ocean, the expanse of the city, the weather or the sun." Sean's mind and spirit were already there. "Have you ever noticed how bright the sun shines there?"

"Does Topaz have anything to do with this, man? She's living out there now, isn't she?" A wide grin spread across Eric's handsome face.

"Did I tell you she was here?" Sean asked, as his mind returned to New York City.

"Here? When?"

"You were out of town. We had dinner together with the gossip columnist who has her own magazine. I thought I told you."

"Naw, money, you neglected to fill me in on this one, but wait . . . Keisha did mention that she saw that lady on one of those talk shows and she said you and Topaz were getting married."

"What?" Sean laughed. "She asked Topaz if we were getting married. I told her we were friends."

"Well, Keisha said the woman said you two were getting married. Just what went on while she was here, man?"

"Nothing." Sean laughed.

"Something's up if the girl has you giving up your basketball career and moving to California."

"Topaz has nothing to do with my decision."

"Right. What is it about you and that girl, man? Keisha doesn't have anything nice to say about her and they used to be best friends."

"She's a trip, man. She's really into being a star now. Do you know she even had her assistant who travels with her call me and tell me what to wear to dinner?"

"Word?"

Sean nodded slowly.

"She's out there, Sean."

"I know, but there's something about her, E." Sean's handsome smile lit up his face. He stared into space momentarily and it was obvious that his heart and mind were somewhere else. Then he fixed his eyes on Eric. "The girl is fascinating, E-man . . . and she's fine."

TWENTY-FIVE

"GIVE ME five hot dogs, a couple of large buttered popcorns, and some of those candies." Gunther tapped on the glass concessions counter with his Gucci key chain. "And hurry up with my order. I don't want to miss the beginning of my movie, *The Hood*."

That should be enough junk for me, Reno, and Gloria. Gunther watched the young Asian girl stack the candies and drinks into one cardboard tray and the hot dogs in another. He reached into his pocket and pulled out a wad of bills in a Gucci diamond money clip, peeled off a couple of twenties, and tossed them on the counter.

"I need a receipt." He spoke gruffly to the young girl when she handed him his change. He stuffed the receipt in a pocket, tucked the bills back in his money clip, and beckoned for Reno. "Yo, dude, can you give me a hand?" Gunther grinned. "I got us a few munchies for the flick."

"You sure did." Reno laughed and picked up the red bags of buttered popcorn and the tray of hot dogs. "Gloria likes mustard. What do you want on your hot dog?" he called over his shoulder as he headed in the direction of the condiment table.

"The works. I'll go on in and get our seats." Gunther smiled at the sight of all the people scurrying to find seats and those already seated, chomping popcorn and sipping soft drinks in the half-lit theater. They're all here to see my film. He spotted three seats together, still available in the middle of the theater, and squeezed past several people near the end of the aisle to the middle. Reno and Gloria joined him several minutes later just before the lights went down and the trailers began.

"Check it out, Spielberg." Reno nudged him and pointed as the words A GUNFIRE FILMS PRODUCTION appeared and disappeared on the screen.

"Yay," Gloria called softly.

Gunther felt his adrenaline surge, and he grinned from ear to ear each time he spotted his name in the credits as the writer, producer, and director of the film.

"Spielberg." Reno laughed each time.

"Woof, woof, woof," Gunther barked over the music.

"Shut up already," somebody yelled.

Gunther, floating in seventh heaven, burst into laughter. "It's my dang film, I'll woof whenever I feel like it," he informed the anonymous voice. Gunther remained silent once the action began, nervously shoveling handfuls of popcorn down his throat as he observed the people around him and their reactions to the film. He watched them laugh, cry, stamp, and shout, and at the end they applauded.

"I think they liked it," Gloria declared on the way out of the theater after the last credit had rolled.

"Well, Spielberg, it looks like we've got ourselves a major hit," Reno commented.

Gunther pulled on a pair of Calvin Klein shades as they walked out of the theater. He watched their shiny black limousine immediately pull up to the curb in front of them. This is the life. He climbed into the car behind Reno and dropped onto the seat across from Reno and Gloria so he could ride backwards.

"Ready to go to Vegas and celebrate, dude?" Reno grinned like a Cheshire cat.

"You know it, dude." Gunther was ecstatic. "I can't wait to hit those tables. I feel lucky tonight."

"Check Junior out." Reno laughed. "He thinks he's a high roller. We'll see what you're made of tonight, Spielberg."

Gunther smiled and gazed out the window at the traffic on Lankershim Boulevard as the limo traveled north to Burbank Airport. Reno had chartered a private jet to fly the three of them to Las Vegas.

"I'm glad we decided to go to Vegas instead of giving a premiere party," Gunther announced. "I want to invade Hollywood smoothly and quietly. Next time we'll give a big premiere party crawling with stars."

"Let's have the champagne now, Reno." Gloria, gorgeous as usual, glittered in diamonds and gold. She winked at Gunther as Reno reached into the storage bin for the drinks and pulled out a chilled bottle of Dom Perignon. Reno popped the cork and poured the bubbling liquid into three champagne flutes.

"How 'bout a toast, Spielberg?"

"Okay." Gunther stared into his glass for several minutes.

"Come on, Junior, this stuff will be flat," Reno urged.

"All right, dude, all right. This is a big moment in my life." He closed his eyes for a moment and then raised his glass slowly. "To Gunfire Films, may we produce hundreds of successful films, each one better than the last. To Reno Velasquez, my partner in crime, may we become trillionaires together, and to *The Hood*, my ticket to the good life, the best is yet to come."

"Hey now." Gloria grinned as they clinked glasses.

Reno drank his champagne in a series of gulps and poured himself another. "Let's get this party started." He reached into the black leather pouch he was carrying and pulled out a plastic bag with cocaine, poured a little out on a business card, and passed it around.

This is the life, Gunther contemplated as he took several hits. The ultimate life.

The plane was ready when they arrived at Burbank Airport. The aircraft's maroon-and-gray cabin with seating for eight resembled the interior of a customized van. There was a small refrigerator and a 20-inch color television and VCR in the entertainment center. Gunther spotted a CD player in the stereo cabinet and flipped through the assortment of CDs.

Just the thing we need. He closed the smoked glass door of the entertainment center just as "Whip Appeal" began to play softly. He turned to speak to Reno and saw him and Gloria cuddled up together in a darkened corner of the aircraft. Suddenly he felt lonely. I've got to find myself a girlfriend, he decided. Gloria's not bad for a black girl. She looks good and she lets Reno do what he has to do without bothering him. And then she's always available for him when he wants her around. That's the kind of girl I need, he rationalized. He watched the two of them kissing and whispering like teenagers. Somebody who looks good and does what I tell her.

Once the plane landed, they were whisked away in another limousine to the Mirage hotel in the heart of the Las Vegas strip.

I've never been to Las Vegas, Gunther realized as he gawked at the brightly lit hotel and attraction signs on Las Vegas Boulevard. "Wow, look, the Tropicana." He pointed at the landmark hotel, excited as a child the first time in Disneyland. "And look, there's Caesar's Palace."

"Here's the Mirage." Reno pointed to an exploding volcano and gigantic waterfall in front of the hotel as the limo made a left turn off the boulevard and into the hotel drive.

Minutes later, on the way into the lobby of the hotel, they were strolling through the largest atrium Gunther had ever seen. He almost tripped over his own feet and bumped into Gloria as he gawked at the atrium's lofty palm trees, lush vegetation, and cascading waterfall. I wonder if all that stuff is real. There was a huge crystal-clear fish tank with exotic fish built in the wall behind the reservations desk.

"Dang, this place got it goin' on," Gunther whispered to himself. He stared at the fish in the tank while Reno checked them into their rooms. I've got to have one of those in my house.

"Thanks for checking us in, dude," Gunther told Reno in the elevator on the way up to their penthouse suite. "I was a little spaced out back there."

"That's okay, Junior, I understand." Reno grinned. "Stick with me and I'll show you the world."

After they changed clothes, they went right back downstairs to the casino, too wired and too excited to sleep. Reno led them through the casino. Gunther was enchanted by the ringing bells and the sound of coins falling out of the slot machines.

"Mo money, mo money, mo money." Gunther stuck a couple of quarters in a slot machine and pulled the handle. Quarters spilled out of the machine. "I won, Reno, I won." He found a change bucket to gather up the two hundred quarters.

"You're hot tonight, Spielberg, but that's chump change. Let's see what you can do in the VIP room."

"The VIP room? Now that's the place for me." Gunther strutted behind Reno with his bucket of quarters.

"Good evening, Mr. Velasquez." An attendant greeted them at the entrance.

"They're always polite when you're spending money. So where do you want to try your luck?" Reno asked Gunther.

Gunther scoped the room quickly, noticing the well-dressed Japanese men at the baccarat table and a sampling of other nationalities casually placing bets at the roulette wheel and the blackjack table. Wow, these people are rich. He checked out their expensive clothing and gold and platinum jewelry. And, we're the only black people in here, Gunther realized. I wonder how Reno managed to finagle his way in here.

"What's up, Junior?" Reno was starting to get impatient.

"Oh . . . what are you going to play?"

"I'm a black man. Blackjack's my game." Reno was cool and collected in a custom-tailored black silk shirt and trousers. Gunther watched Reno and Gloria lose several hands each.

"I'm not doing so well, Spielberg. You're the man of the hour. Why don't you give it a shot?"

"No sweat. How much is it?" Gunther sat his quarters down and reached into his pocket for his money clip.

"Ten thousand dollars."

"Ten thousand dollars?" Gunther almost choked on the glass of champagne he was drinking. All of a sudden he was very sober. "Ten thousand dollars?"

"Yeah, Spielberg. It's only money. You want in? I got your back."

Gunther swallowed hard as his mind quickly went to work. If I don't play, Reno will think I'm a wimp and he won't want to hang out with me anymore. But ten thousand dollars . . . I can't afford to lose ten thousand dollars. But then I might win . . . oh, what the heck. "All right, I'm in," he replied slowly.

"Spielberg, hanging with the high rollers." Reno laughed and slapped him on his back. "Go for it, dude."

Gunther felt his blood pressure rise when the dealer revealed his top card as the ace of diamonds. If that's a face card I won. Gunther stared at the card turned facedown underneath the ace. Oh, what the heck, it's only money and tonight's my night. I'm only the hottest thing happening in young black directors. "I'm good," he informed the dealer in a soft voice.

"Way to go, Spielberg," Reno laughed, cheering him on.

Gunther sucked in his breath as the dealer revealed his bottom card.

"Queen of spades. Dealer pays twenty-one."

"You won, Gunther," Gloria squealed.

"Can't go wrong with the black lady." Reno laughed.

"Word, dude, word." Gunther laughed and slapped a high five with Reno. "You know I got it goin' on like that."

They stayed up all night gambling and flew back to Los Angeles the next morning, Gunther ten thousand dollars richer.

Gunther was on the telephone ordering lunch from one of the local delicatessens in Brentwood when call-waiting interrupted his line. Who's that bothering me now and what do they want? I hope that's not Rita bugging me. He glanced at the message pad where he had written down the phone calls from his answering machine. There were at least half a dozen calls from his mother.

"Siskel and Ebert gave it two thumbs up," Beth yelled excitedly into the telephone.

"What?"

"Siskel and Ebert gave it two thumbs up," she repeated slowly and a little more calmly.

"Oh yeah?"

"Yes." Beth was shouting again. "The phone hasn't stopped ringing yet. Everybody wants to talk to you."

"Who wants to talk to me?" Gunther spoke softly as he fought to maintain his cool.

"Let's see. The *Arsenio Hall Show*, *The Tonight Show*, the people from *Oprah* called, UPI, AP, *Essence*, *Ebony*, *Jet*, *People*, Black Entertainment Television, the *Los Angeles Times* . . ."

I did it, Gunther marveled in a world of his own. I actually pulled it off. I'm the stuff. "Do you know what was yesterday's box office?" he asked quickly, cutting her off.

"Oh, yes, Bob called. He wants to speak with you right away. But he said to tell you the film grossed four million yesterday."

Four million! We'll have our budget back by tonight, he realized as he quickly ran the numbers through his head. "Okay, Beth, I'll call you back later." He hung up the phone and danced a jig. "Yahoo," he screamed.

He quickly dialed Reno's number. "We're in the money. We're in the money."

Reno chuckled in the phone. "Way to go, Spielberg. I've been hearing good things on the tube. Did you know that some of the gangs rioted in Westwood? It seems like they couldn't get in the theater or something."

"What? That's awful." Stupid black people. Always messing something up. You can't take them anywhere.

"But that's good, Spielberg, it's controversy and controversy is news."

"I never thought about it like that." Gunther spoke slowly as Reno's words registered in his mind.

"It's all good. It's all good, Spielberg."

Gunther checked the makeup that had been applied to his face once last time in the mirror of his dressing room at the *Arsenio Hall Show*. His face was practically pressed up against the mirror. This stuff isn't bad. It makes my skin look so smooth. But then I look good anyway. He admired the reflection of his latest purchase from Maxfield's before he ducked in the bathroom one last time and took several hits of coke from the vial he was carrying in his pocket.

What was that? He felt a sharp pain shoot through his chest. He exhaled slowly and noticed that the pain was gone. I need to take some time off to relax. I've been working too hard. He heard a knock at the door, but before answering it, he checked his nose quickly for any traces of the white powder. I can't let Arsenio know what I've been in here doing. He put on his Calvin Klein shades and followed a production assistant backstage where he would wait until Arsenio announced him.

"He's the hottest thing going in young black directors, ladies and gentlemen, Gunther Lawrence," the announcer proclaimed.

Gunther felt his chest swell with pride when he heard all the applause and he fought the huge grin that wanted to take over his face. He strolled onto the set, too cool, waved a hand at the audience, shook Arsenio's hand, and took a seat on the infamous black leather sofa. I'm on the *Arsenio Hall Show*, Gunther wanted to shout as the audience continued to applaud. Dang, they really like me. He balled his hand up in a fist and woof-woofed along with the audience.

"I feel great, Arsenio." The smile he had fought so hard took over his face momentarily. "I've worked hard for a long time to get this point and the best is yet to come." Gunther was extremely cocky and arrogant.

■

"It's about business and commerce. It's about working your butt off to get a piece of the American Dream," he explained to Jay Leno. "People are always bellyaching about someone not giving them an opportunity because they're underprivileged. No one ever gave me anything. When I see an opportunity, I take it because no one will ever give you anything. Life is what you make it."

People were intrigued by Gunther's no-nonsense attitude. They admired his cockiness and they just couldn't get enough of him. As *The Hood* grew in success so did Gunther's popularity. He was on Hollywood's A list, which garnered him invitations to film premieres, concerts, star-studded parties, memberships to private clubs, preferred tables in industry restaurants, and courtside tickets to Lakers, Clippers, and Raiders games.

It was the hottest concert in town. TLC, Boyz II Men, Jodeci, and Hammer were appearing at the Forum, and Gunther had tickets and backstage passes. Gunther pulled up to Reno's gated Encino estate and pressed the buzzer on the squawk box.

"Yo," Reno replied.

"It's Spielberg, dude." Gunther watched the black gate slowly roll open. When it stopped, he drove up the hill and parked behind Reno's Mercedes. He found Reno and Gloria in the family room drinking champagne.

"Just getting the party started." Reno grinned like a Cheshire cat.

"Word, dude."

"Gunther, this is my cousin, India. She's visiting from Louisiana." Gloria introduced him to a beautiful girl who was in her early twenties. She had long silky jet black hair like Gloria and the same golden vanilla wafer complexion. But she lacked Gloria's sophistication. Probably because she's from the country, Gunther rationalized. India was dressed in a simple red linen dress with red stockings, red pumps, and red earrings. She's cute, but someone needs to tell her how to dress.

"Hi, Gunther." India's smile revealed a front tooth outlined in gold.

The gold tooth has got to go. "Hi," Gunther replied coolly.

"Get yourself a glass of champagne, G, and let's go in my

office for a minute before the limo gets here," Reno suggested.

Gunther took the glass of champagne Gloria handed him and followed Reno into his wood-paneled office with its fine leather furnishings. Dang, Reno's got an office like this and he's just a drug dealer. I'm a film director. I'm the one who should have an office like this, not a drug dealer. He took a seat on the burgundy leather sofa and Reno offered him a ceramic dish of cocaine.

"Help yourself, G."

Gunther was shocked by the amount of powder in the mauve, jade, and gold Oriental bowl. "Thanks, dude." He sniffed greedily until he felt the inside of his nose turn raw.

"India's nice, huh." Reno took a seat behind his desk and tapped some fish food into the sparkling aquarium in the corner behind the desk.

"Yeah, she seems nice, dude." Gunther was still busy taking hits of coke.

"Good, I'm glad you like her. You know Gloria wasn't the way she is now when we first met. She was a diamond in the rough. But with your Midas touch India will make you a pretty nice companion."

"Okay, dude," Gunther agreed, totally out of his mind.

A light tap at the door interrupted them.

"Come in," Reno commanded.

"Baby, the limo's here," Gloria informed him, speaking very softly.

"Thanks, honey, we'll be right there. Let's go party, dude."

Gunther sat in the limousine, riding backwards next to India, who just smiled and giggled as he nibbled on her ear and kissed her neck.

"You're so beautiful," he whispered, drugged out of his mind. "Spend the night and I'll take you shopping tomorrow."

"Okay." She giggled. "I just love shopping."

"Yo, driver, we've got VIP parking," Gunther yelled. "Here." He rolled down the privacy partition and threw the VIP parking sign at the driver. "Take us to the Forum Club. The stars have arrived," he warbled. He laughed as he grabbed India and gave Reno a wink.

They stopped in the Forum Club for more champagne before they took their fifth-row center seats.

"These are great seats, Gunther," Gloria squealed.

"I know, baby. I know. That's because I'm a star and I deserve the best." Gunther sat there for the entire concert cool as ice, hugged up with India while people continuously acknowledged him and approached him for autographs between shows.

This is the life. He eyed a gorgeous butterscotch-colored girl with long hair and the body of life who approached him for an autograph.

"I just loved your film," she offered sincerely. "I was very moved."

You move me, too, baby. He ogled her voluptuous curves spilling out of her tight black Spandex mini. Dang, she's fine.

After Hammer burned up the stage, Gunther and his entourage made their way through the crowd backstage, but they were halted as Topaz was quickly ushered in first with a phalanx of security guards.

"That was Topaz," he heard people around him whispering loudly. "Topaz was sitting in the audience at Hammer's concert."

Topaz. All of a sudden he was very sober. That's the girl from Roxbury. Who is she that she has to have security guards around her like that?

"Wow, there's Topaz," India practically screamed, once they were backstage. "Do you have a pen, Gunther? I want to ask her for her autograph."

"You'll do no such thing," he whispered sharply.

"But I just love her music. Can't I get her autograph?" she pleaded like a child.

"You're with a star. And stars don't ask other stars for autographs," Gunther snapped. You little gold-tooth heifer. You'll never go anywhere with me again.

So she sings, he mused on the way out to the limo. I'm going to stop at Tower Records on my way home and check this out.

"Gunther, want me to come home with you?" India asked hopefully, once they were back at Reno's house.

"No. I've got some things to do."

"Are we still going shopping?"

"I'll call you." He brushed his lips across hers.

I don't have time to fool around with a nobody like India, he told himself in the car. I'm a star and I have to date stars, not nobodies like India. At Tower Records on Sunset Boulevard, Gunther found a huge display set up in the center of the store with posters of Topaz.

"Dang, she's fine," he exclaimed a little too loudly. He quickly purchased a CD and stuck it in the CD player as soon as he got in the car. "And she can sing. I didn't know she sang that song," he commented out loud when "Boyfriend" came on.

"Miss Topaz." Gunther drove down Sunset towards Brentwood with Topaz's music blasting in the car. He picked up the CD cover and studied it while he was stopped at a red light. We'll be wonderful together. The perfect star couple. I can see us both dodging the paparazzi. A smile graced his cappuccino face. "You'll be all mine, one day. All mine," he informed Topaz's beautiful face on the CD cover. "I'll find a way to get you. Because Gunther Lawrence always gets his way . . ."

TWENTY-SIX

TOPAZ QUICKLY unlocked the door to her penthouse condominium on Wilshire Boulevard. The Blair House was one of the finest highrises on the section of the boulevard known as the Wilshire Corridor, which was nestled between Beverly Hills and Westwood. The corridor was famous for its million-dollar condominiums. Some of the highrises even offered a Rolls Royce with the purchase of a unit.

Who can that be? Topaz tossed her shopping bags on the sofa and rushed into the kitchen to answer the phone. Hardly anyone has my private number, and I just left Nina.

"Hello."

"Hi, Topaz," she heard a male voice speak softly into the phone.

It's Germain, she realized the second she heard his voice. She felt her knees grow weak and took a seat at the Oriental dining room table. She focused on an invisible spot on the brand new mauve carpet she had chosen for the apartment and swallowed hard as her stomach turned flip-flops.

"Yes, Germain." Her tone was cool.

"I hope I'm not disturbing you. Your mother gave me your phone number. I asked her to make this call but she refused."

Oh, no, something must be wrong with Chris. Why else would he call? "What is it, Germain?" she demanded, growing more impatient by the second.

"I can call you back at a more convenient time if you're busy. I know you're a very busy person."

"What is it, Germain?" she yelled in the phone, upset for so many reasons but mostly because he was still able to push her buttons without even trying. Darn you, Germain Gradney.

"Chris has seen you on television. Your mother gave him your

CD and video for Christmas last year and told him you were his mother, and now you're all he talks about."

"He does?" She felt herself relax for the first time during the conversation as a little smile found its way onto her face. Chris, my baby . . .

"Yes. Now he's asking all sorts of questions about you like where you live, and when he found out you lived in California, he started telling me he wants to go there to see his famous mommy and Mickey Mouse."

"Oh, how sweet." Topaz got up from the table to straighten the Kathleen Wilson original on the dining room wall.

"Well, Thanksgiving is next month and we're off from school so I thought we'd come to L.A. Will you be in town then?"

Topaz felt her heart skip a beat. My fans can't know that I have a son. No one even knows that I've ever been married except my family. Topaz had sent her son Christmas and birthday presents through her Grand Mama in Baltimore and had even talked to Chris once or twice when she'd called Grand Mama when he'd been there for the day. But that was before her record was out. I haven't seen Chris since he was six months old and he'll be five in March, she realized. The time has gone by so quickly.

"Topaz, are you there?"

"Yes. I was trying to remember my schedule. Hold on while I get my appointment book." She knew without even checking her schedule that she was basically free until the first of the year. She had to begin rehearsing for her world tour in December. Rehearsals were already scheduled for Third Encore in Burbank. She walked into the den, which had been converted from a second bedroom, and picked up the phone on the antique secretary desk where Nina kept her schedules and correspondence.

"I'll be in town for Thanksgiving."

"Great. Do you have any recommendations for a hotel?"

Hotels? She walked back into the living room. The huge picture windows provided her with a breathtaking view of the city, and she stood in front of the west window gazing in the direction of Santa Monica and the Pacific Ocean.

"Maybe Chris would like to stay here with me?"

"With you?" She smiled when she heard Germain's steady voice crack and tremble.

"Yes." She felt like she finally had the upper hand in the

conversation, for the moment. What a beautiful night. She stood there admiring the gorgeous L.A. sunset. The sun had turned into a ball of orange fire and it cast a wonderful glow over the heavens as it sank below the horizon. "He is my son, too." While she waited for him to respond, she moved to the sofa in the living room to admire the new black sofa with its abstract Oriental design of mauve and pink, part of the set that included a chaise and love seat.

"No one's disputing his parentage. But Chris doesn't know you. He may not feel comfortable staying with you."

How dare he speak to me like that? She wanted to scream as her blood pressure escalated. But he was probably right; Chris might feel uncomfortable. "Well, maybe you should stay here with him. I have an extra bedroom," she added quickly. She stretched out on the chaise and inspected some of the African art pieces she had purchased for the living room. I need more, she decided, while she waited for Germain's response. The ball's back in your court. Now what are you going to do?

"All right. Chris would love it, but are you going to spend time with him, Topaz? I'm not coming out there for you to be on any star trip with my son because if that's what you want to do, we'll stay in a hotel and get together with you for dinner when you have the time."

"What do you mean, star trip?" She was growing angrier by the second.

"I used to be married to you. I know how you were before you were married, so I can only imagine what you're like now that you're famous."

"You may not believe it, Germain, but I love my son very much," Topaz yelled. She was on the verge of tears.

"Well, you certainly have a funny way of showing it. Look, I didn't call you up to get into this. It hardly matters now. You made your choice. I'll call you in a few days with our flight information."

Topaz heard the phone click in her ear. He had hung up without even saying good-bye. "How dare you, Germain Gradney! How dare you talk to me like that! No one talks to me like that." She threw the phone across the room and broke into tears.

Thanksgiving week arrived all too quickly. Topaz paced nervously back and forth while she watched her maid make the final touches on the apartment.

"Nina!" She ran into the den where her cousin was typing on her laptop computer.

"What?" Nina didn't even bother to take her eyes off the screen.

"What time is the limo coming again?" Topaz demanded, her amber eyes blazing.

"They arrive at LAX at three. The limo's already been scheduled. I told them to take a sign that said GRADNEY so Germain would know the driver. Dang . . . How many times are you going to ask me?"

"Sorry. Could you pay Lupe and then come into the bedroom with me? I need your advice on what I should wear." She saw Nina make a face as she walked out of the den and into her split-level master bedroom suite. The queen-size bed, television, and dresser were on a different level from her small sitting room. The sitting room was between the bed and her pink bathroom, with its Jacuzzi bathtub, steam shower, and huge walk-in closet. It and every other closet in the apartment was overflowing with her clothing. She walked into the closet and snapped on the light.

"Nina!" She was frantic. "Where are you?"

"You rang, madam?" Nina walked into the closet and gave Topaz a small curtsy.

"Yes. What should I wear?" She fixed her tawny eyes on her cousin.

"I don't know." Nina sifted through the outfits in the closet. "What do you want to wear?"

"I don't know," Topaz snapped, stamping her foot. "That's why I called you in here."

"Chill out. Take it way down, girlfriend. Here, wear this." She handed Nina a short, black-and-rose paisley print dress that had tiny pleats all around the bodice. "Wear that with some black tights and black boots. That'll be too fresh."

"I'm not wearing that old thing." Topaz snatched the dress from Nina and returned it to the closet. She sifted through the clothes and pulled out a fabulous electric blue alex jersey dress. "What about this?"

"Oh, that's just great. Germain will certainly think you're the perfect mother if you meet him at the door with that on."

"Nina!" She returned the dress to the closet. "I don't know what to do."

"Why are you making such a big deal about this?" Nina made herself comfortable on the floor.

"I'm not making a big deal about this." Topaz sifted through outfit after outfit.

"Yes, you are." Nina inspected a little chip in the side of her nail. "Why don't you just admit you're still in love with him?"

"In love with who?" Topaz stuck her head out of the closet.

"Oh, now she wants to play games. You know good and well who I'm talking about. Your ex, Germain."

"I am not in love with him."

"It's okay if you are." Nina got up to search in the bathroom cabinet for nail polish remover. "I won't tell anyone. Just tell me one thing. Why did you make me wear those stupid clothes when we were in New York and Sylk Ross came to the hotel? You couldn't care less about him."

"I made you wear those clothes in case you decided to make a play for my man, and I do care about Sylk, I'm just not in love with him." Topaz turned on the water in the bathtub.

"Because you're still in love with Germain. Otherwise how could you not be in love with Sylk Ross? He's so fine and he seemed so sweet."

"Nina, does the building clean the skylight?" Topaz changed the subject and pointed to the skylight over the bathtub.

"Yes. Are you going to give Germain some while he's here?" She carefully applied a coat of orange polish to a nail before she looked up and gave her cousin a wicked grin.

"Nina." Topaz sputtered and blushed a thousand shades of red. "I don't believe you said that."

"Oh, please." Nina fell out on the floor laughing. "See, you know you love that man. Why are you tripping?"

Topaz tossed some bath crystals and oils in the water and sat on the floor. "What should I wear, Nina?"

"Why don't you wear what you have on?" Nina pointed to the faded Guess jeans that fit her body like a glove. "They look good on you."

"These old things?" Topaz looked down at the faded jeans that she had carefully ripped in the right places.

"Well, you don't have to wear those, but wear jeans. Be casual." Nina screwed the cap on the bottle of polish and got up from the floor.

"Where are you going?" Topaz was panic-stricken.

"I'm going to hang out in the studio with Jamil and then we're going grocery shopping for Thanksgiving dinner." Nina was already on her way out of the bathroom.

"But I want you to be here when Germain and Chris arrive."

"No way." Nina got her coat from the bedroom. "I'd love to be a fly on the wall when Germain gets here, but you're on your own for this one, cuz."

By three Topaz had finished her bath and dressed. She had made a special trip to the hairdresser early that morning and her hair looked fabulous. She had taken Nina's advice and worn jeans with a black sweater and boots. Now she checked her makeup for the thousandth time in the mirror over the fireplace in the living room as she paced nervously back and forth.

"I'm going to lose my mind or wear a hole in my new carpet." She glanced at the clock in the kitchen and saw that only twenty minutes had passed. Dang . . . I have got to have something to calm my nerves before I completely lose it. Topaz walked into the bathroom and looked in her medicine cabinet, where she found the small stash of cocaine she kept there. She took several hits and immediately felt herself relax. "There, that's better." She went into the den and turned on the television and mindlessly flipped from channel to channel until the telephone rang.

"Ms. Black, there's a Germain Gradney here to see you," the front desk informed her.

"Fine. Send him up." They're here . . . She checked her makeup one last time and prepared for the performance of her life.

Several minutes later she heard her front doorbell ring and she slowly walked over to the door. She put her hand on the brass handle and took a deep breath. Okay, I can do this. She slowly exhaled and opened the door. Standing there in faded jeans and a heavy teal sweater, Germain was finer than she had remembered. She couldn't keep herself from looking into his hazel eyes, and she felt her stomach turn flip-flops as their souls knowingly rejoiced because they were together once again.

"Hi," she finally managed to say.

"Hi, Topaz." His voice was soft and vulnerable. She was more beautiful than he ever remembered and he immediately wanted to hold her, kiss her, and make love to her. He longed to reach out and touch her soft skin and silky hair and reacquaint himself with her scent and her touch.

"Hello, Mother," she heard the voice of a young child say.

Chris . . . She kneeled down to gaze into the little boy's face and gasped as she stared into a pair of amber eyes identical to her own. "Hello, Chris." She stroked his face gently. She felt herself choke up when she saw the blond curly hair, the exact same color as her own, and the same butterscotch complexion.

"This is for you, Mother." Chris handed her a single red rose and smiled Germain's boyish grin.

"Thank you, Chris." Topaz took the rose and gently kissed it before she knelt down and pulled the little boy into her arms. "Come give your mommy a hug." She closed her eyes and tried to fight back the tears that wanted to flow. "You're so handsome." She quickly wiped a tear from her eye.

"Thank you, Mother." He looked at her as he took Germain's hand.

"Come in, come in." She stood up and brushed another tear away. As she showed Germain where to put their things, she realized she was having a hard time making eye contact with him. So she focused on her son instead. "What would you like to do first, Chris?"

"I want to go to Disneyland and see Mickey Mouse."

"It's too late to go to Disneyland today, but I'll take you there on Friday." Chris looked up at Germain to see if he had anything different to say about the matter.

"We'll go on Friday, like your mother said, Son."

"Okay, Daddy."

"Are you hungry? Would you like to go out to dinner?" Topaz racked her brain trying to think of something for them to do.

Chris gave her question a fair amount of consideration. "Well, I am a little hungry. I didn't like the food on the airplane."

"I don't like airplane food, either." Topaz laughed. "Come on, we'll find you something yummy to eat." Down in the garage she headed for her new pearl black 300 CE Mercedes and opened the door.

"What, no limousine?" Germain smirked.

"I only use limos when I'm going to the airport, otherwise I drive myself." She forced herself to make eye contact. "But if you'd like to go in a limo, it won't take long for me to call one."

"No, this is fine." She noticed that there was a little smile on Germain's face.

"Whose little red car is that?" Chris pointed to her Miata parked in front of the Mercedes.

"That's mine, too. It's a Miata."

"That's a nice car." Chris walked over to take a closer look.

"Would you like to ride in the Miata instead, Chris?"

"Oh could we, Mother?" His amber eyes sparkled with excitement.

"Sure we can if your daddy backs the Mercedes out for us." She handed Germain the key and smiled when she felt Chris slide his small hand into hers. She led him over to the car, opened the door, and helped him in.

"Shall we put the top down, too?" She was so pleased that she had found something to talk about with her son.

"Oh, yes, Mother." Germain got in and held Chris on his lap. Topaz pulled out on Wilshire, circled the block, and stopped in front of the building.

"Germain, it might get a little cool. Maybe you'd better go upstairs and get him a heavier jacket." Topaz handed him the key to the apartment. "What would you like for dinner, Chris?" She talked as she watched Germain go inside the building.

"A Happy Meal, please."

"A Happy Meal? Your daddy lets you eat that junk?" She reached into her glove compartment and found an old black baseball cap that said BOBBY and pulled her hair through the back.

"Daddy takes me to McDonald's before I go to school in the morning. And sometimes we go at night."

"Hmmm. Do you like school?"

"Oh, yes. I'm already in kindergarten and I'm only four. I was skipped. I'm going to be a doctor when I grow up just like my daddy and granddaddy."

"You are?" Topaz watched Germain come out of the building. "That's wonderful."

"Chris wants a Happy Meal," she informed Germain, making a face. "I thought we'd go to a restaurant."

"Fine, just go where he can get a burger and some fries." Germain smiled.

She took them to dinner at Larry Parkers in Beverly Hills. Chris was so excited by the music and videos that he could hardly eat. "Look, Mother, that's you." He squealed with delight when her video came on as he stuffed himself with french fries and catsup.

"Shhh." Topaz laughed, but not really caring for the moment if anyone recognized her or not. She was having the best time she'd had in a long time.

"You're really good with him," Germain offered. "And he's having a great time. Thanks, Topaz."

"You don't have to thank me." Topaz felt her stomach turning flip-flops as she looked at Germain's handsome face. "I am his mother."

"I know," Germain replied in a tone that made her melt all over.

She wasn't really hungry but she nibbled on the burger she had ordered. She found herself watching Germain instead. He looked up from his burger and she smiled at him and he smiled back. Dang . . . I can't keep my eyes off him.

After dinner she drove them through Beverly Hills and down Rodeo Drive, pointing out the sights on the way back to the apartment. Chris fell asleep in the car and Germain carried him upstairs to the apartment in his arms.

My son . . . She ran her hand through his blond curls. This is great, we're like a real family. She pulled out the sofa bed for Chris while Germain gave him a bath. She wanted to go in and kiss Chris good night but she didn't want to rush things.

"He's sound asleep already." Germain found her sitting in the living room.

"Would you like a glass of wine or something?" she offered, trying to make conversation. This was the first time the two of them had been alone together without Chris.

"That sounds nice."

She brought two glasses and a bottle of chilled zinfandel into the living room and found Germain looking out of her favorite window at the Los Angeles skyline.

"That's my favorite view." She handed him the glass of wine.

"I really like your place." He spoke softly as he turned to look at Topaz.

"Thanks. I only bought it this summer."

They stood there in silence drinking wine and looking out the window.

"Wow, this is making me so sleepy. It's really been a long day. We left Baltimore very early this morning. I'm going to bed now. I brought some of my medical journals so I could do a little reading. Good night."

She watched him disappear down the corridor and heard the door to the den close. Dang. Why did he have to go to bed now? He never goes to bed this early. She went into her bedroom and flipped on the television. He's right there in the next room reading medical journals and I'm in here all alone. Nina's words flashed through her mind and she laughed. My cousin knows me too well.

She took a quick shower and pulled on a midnight blue silk nightgown that gently caressed her generous curves. I'll have another glass of wine and go to bed, too. She opened the door to the suite and peered out into the hall. There was no light coming from under the door in the den where Germain and Chris were sleeping, so she tiptoed down the hall into the kitchen where she felt someone brush past her.

"Ahhh," she screamed.

"Shhh," she heard Germain command. "It's only me."

"Oh." A hint of a smile found its way onto her face. "I thought you were asleep. What are you doing in here in the dark?"

"I couldn't sleep. Chris kept kicking me so I came to get another glass of wine to help me endure the torture."

"Oh." Topaz giggled.

"What are you doing in here?"

"It's my house," she replied like an impudent child.

"I know that, girl. What did you come in here for?"

"A glass of wine." She opened the refrigerator.

"I knew it." The light from the refrigerator cast just enough light so he could see the silhouette of her body underneath her nightgown. She took out the wine and carefully poured two glasses. As she handed him a glass, she could see he was only wearing the bottoms to a pair of black silk pajamas she had given him for Christmas one year. Neither of them said anything while they stood there sipping the chilled wine in the dark.

"You look so good," she finally heard him say as her heart skipped a beat.

"So do you," she spoke softly. "I've missed you, Germain."

"I've missed you, too." Moments later they were in each other's arms, kissing. "I've missed you so much, baby," he whispered in her ear.

"Me, too," she whispered back. "Shall we christen the kitchen?"

"How about the entire apartment?" Later that night she led him into her bedroom, where they both slept peacefully for the first time in years.

After Topaz and Germain had properly initiated the Jacuzzi bathtub, the three of them had breakfast at Roscoe's. Then Topaz took them shopping at the Beverly Center and on Rodeo Drive in Beverly Hills. They stopped at the condominium long enough to drop off the shopping bags before they went to dinner at the Cheesecake Factory in Marina del Rey and grocery shopping for Thanksgiving dinner.

"You know we don't have to do this." Topaz and Germain stared at the turkeys in the meat department at Mrs. Gooch's. "We can go to my aunty's house for dinner."

"No." Germain nudged his chin a little deeper into her shoulder. "Let's make our own."

"Have you ever cooked a turkey?"

"No." He smiled. "But I'm willing to try."

"Well, you know I haven't. Maybe we should just order dinner from a restaurant," she suggested, looking up at him.

"Nope. We can do this. We'll buy a cookbook." She giggled as she watched him point out a turkey to the butcher.

"What are you laughing at?" Germain grinned as he stuck the turkey in the cart behind Chris.

"Nothing." She tried to stifle a giggle. "This is going to be fun."

"I know." He gave her a kiss. "And you're going to help."

"Okay." Topaz was happier than she had been for a long time.

They found the ingredients for dressing, macaroni and cheese, candied yams, and salad.

"Oh, no." She watched Germain eyeing the collards. "We are not making collard greens."

"All right." He gave the collards a final glance.

"We can always go to Aunty Lena's on Friday and eat leftovers. I know she's making greens."

"That's true." Germain tossed a cookbook in the shopping cart. They purchased pies from Marie Callender's and several bottles of Cristal from the liquor store.

"I guess we have everything." Germain looked in the shopping bags as he pulled them out of the trunk.

"If not, I can always go to the store tomorrow."

"Great. If you carry Chris I'll take the groceries."

"No problem." Topaz picked up the sleeping child. "Your mommy and daddy are trying to wear you out." She kissed him gently on the cheek.

"He's like his daddy," Germain informed her coming out of the guest bathroom. "He wants you to give him his bath tonight."

"He does?" Topaz was surprised.

"Yes. You put him to bed and I'll get the turkey started."

"He's fast asleep." Topaz walked into the kitchen after she had bathed her son and tucked him into bed. "I even sang to him."

"You did?"

"Un-huh." She grinned as she opened a carton of Häagen-Dazs.

"What did you sing?" Germain looked up from the turkey he was stuffing.

"Just a little lullaby I made up."

"Really?" He was shocked. "Sing it to me," he pleaded like a child.

"Okay, I will when we go to bed." Topaz smiled and fed him a spoonful of the chocolate ice cream she was eating.

"Check that out." Germain proudly displayed his stuffed turkey. "How do you turn on the stove, pretty girl?"

"I don't know." She turned several shiny knobs on the appliance. "I've never used it. The turkey looks great, baby."

"You've never used the stove? What have you been doing for food?"

"I eat out or I nuke it."

"Topaz . . ."

"I'm hardly ever here, Germain. I've got some time off right now, that's the only reason I'm in town. So when I come in I've already eaten or I bring something. I don't have time to cook."

"I guess you wouldn't."

It was three o'clock in the morning by the time they finished cooking everything, and they had finished off two bottles of Cristal.

"I'm so sleepy I can't see straight." Topaz laughed as she fell into bed.

"Me, too."

Chris finally woke them around eleven the next morning. "I'm hungry, Daddy." He climbed into bed between them.

"Okay, Chris. Daddy's got some stuff for breakfast in the kitchen. I'll make you some bacon and eggs."

"Okay." Chris was too happy as he snuggled up to Topaz. "Are you going to fix some for Mother, too?"

"Yes, I'll fix some for Mother, too." A huge smile spread across Topaz's face.

Later that afternoon the young Gradney family sat down in the dining room to a candlelight dinner of roast turkey and oyster dressing, mashed potatoes, fresh green beans, candied yams, and macaroni and cheese.

"Everything tastes really good, Germain."

"That's because I can cook, baby," He was too pleased with the dinner he had prepared for his family. They took Chris to see *Home Alone 2* after dinner and stopped by Aunty Lena's on the way home.

"So this is Germain and Chris." Lena gave them both a hug. "You're a good looking man," she told Germain without any reservations. "It's about time you came out here to take care of this wild child. She needs a good man to take care of her and keep the wolves away."

"Aunty Lena." Topaz was embarrassed. Nina pulled her out of the kitchen and into the bathroom where they could talk privately.

"You gave him some, didn't, you?" Nina asked with a wicked grin as Topaz sucked in her breath. "And don't even try to lie to me. It's all over your face. It's all over both your faces. I just want to know when it happened?"

"The first night." Topaz smiled.

"Dang. You didn't waste any time, did you?" Nina laughed.

"I'm going home." Topaz opened the bathroom door.

"I don't blame you. He's fine. If it were me I would have never left the house."

"Nina." Topaz blushed a crimson red. "I can't believe you."

Chris and Germain's vacation in L.A went by entirely too

quickly. On the last night, they ordered in Chinese food and watched videos.

"I noticed you're still wearing your wedding rings." Germain took her slender hand in his.

"I know." Topaz looked down at her hands. "I like them."

"Topaz, I'll be finished at Johns Hopkins by Christmas. I have an offer to do my residency here in Los Angeles at Cedars Sinai, and I've been giving it some serious consideration. We could be a family again."

Germain and Chris living here in L.A. with me as a family . . . but my career . . . I start my world tour in January and if Germain's here, he'll try to talk me out of going. Still me and Germain together again . . .

"You don't have to give me an answer now. Why don't you take some time and think it over?"

"All right." Things had been going well and maybe they could work something out.

Rather than hire a limo, she drove them to the airport for the flight back to Baltimore.

"Good-bye, Mommy." Chris gave her a big hug and a kiss. He looked too adorable with his Mickey Mouse ears on, carrying the stuffed Mickey Mouse that was almost as big as he. "Will you come visit us in Maryland for Christmas?"

"I'll try, baby." She gave her son a bear hug. "Your mommy gets so busy sometimes."

"I won't say good-bye, pretty girl," Germain told her before he got on the plane. "I'll just say see you later." And then he kissed her so passionately, she thought she would melt right there in the airline terminal.

"Good-bye," she whispered as the men in her life disappeared through the jet way.

The apartment seemed empty once they were gone. How could one little week have made such a big impact? And why do I feel so empty inside? I got along just fine before they came.

I know what it is, she told herself several days later when the melancholy refused to lift. It's just a letdown from all the excitement of the holidays. What I need to do is to go out and party and be seen. She sifted through a stack of messages and invitations that had accumulated over the holidays and checked her appointment book. There just has to be somewhere for me to go . . .

TWENTY-SEVEN

"I SAID take me to the backstage entrance," Gunther barked as the limo driver pulled up in front of the Shrine Auditorium. "Can't you understand English?" Gunther glared at the driver who circled the block in order to drop him at the backstage entrance. "I could have been inside by now. You're wasting my time."

"Sorry, Mr. Lawrence."

You certainly are. Gunther watched the handsome young Hispanic in an elegant chauffeur's uniform trot around the car to open the door. Why does this place have to be in the neighborhood? I hate coming down here. Before he entered the backstage door, he glanced across the street at the University of Southern California. My alma mater . . . life certainly has changed a lot since my days here as a film student.

"Good evening, Mr. Lawrence. Welcome to the NAACP Image Awards."

Gunther stared at the young man who had greeted him. Now who's this nobody trying to kiss up? Although Gunther was wearing an extremely dark pair of Ray Bans, he noticed the young man's expensive suit, shirt, and tie. He sighed impatiently while the man flipped through a box of envelopes.

"Your backstage credentials and tickets for the show, Mr. Lawrence." The young man smiled. "I sure hope you win for Best Director. I really enjoyed your film." Gunther ignored the compliment and quickly inspected the contents of the envelope.

"I need three tickets, not two," he snapped. "I specifically requested three tickets when I agreed to be a presenter on the show. Can't you do anything right?" Gunther shouted. He snatched off his glasses and glared at the young man.

"I didn't have anything to do with the distribution of the

tickets, Mr. Lawrence. I'm just assigned to pass them out." He was intimidated by Gunther's ranting.

"Then who is responsible?" Gunther screamed.

"The production coordinator is in the greenroom. She'll be able to assist you with additional tickets." The young man was still polite, despite Gunther's rudeness. "Her name—"

Gunther stormed off towards the greenroom without another word. The room was buzzing with light conversation when he entered. He ignored the other artists and talent who were mingling with their guests, sipping drinks, and munching hors d'oeuvres. *Now who's the production coordinator?* He looked around the room. When he spotted an attractive woman with a clipboard and a walkie-talkie conversing with the gorgeous actress who portrayed a black American princess on the hit comedy show on NBC, he rushed over to her. The women saw Gunther approaching and both smiled warmly.

"Gunther Lawrence." The production coordinator maneuvered the clipboard under her arm and extended her hand. "It's a pleasure to finally meet you. I enjoyed your film. Is there anything I can do to assist you?"

"Yes," he began bruskly. "I needed . . ." Suddenly he lost his train of thought when he saw Topaz enter the room with several security guards. She was absolutely stunning in an emerald green beaded minidress, her blond hair silky straight in a blunt cut. He watched people react to her mesmerizing beauty the way he had. *She has got to be the most beautiful woman I have ever seen.*

"Gunther, you were saying?" the efficient production coordinator prodded, attempting to bring him back into the conversation.

He looked away from her piercing, probing eyes, embarrassed by his apparent loss of words. *What was I saying? Oh yeah . . . tickets.* "Excuse me." Gunther flashed a plastic smile. "I need an additional ticket for the show. There seems to be a mistake," he finished graciously. He saw the emerald bugle beads on Topaz's dress sparkle as she worked the crowded room, pausing to chat with various actors and singers who were also presenters on the awards show.

"I apologize for that oversight, Gunther."

Gunther noticed the production coordinator had an amused

look on her face as she quickly found another ticket and handed it to him.

"Topaz is gorgeous, isn't she?" The young woman nodded in Topaz's direction. "She's been nominated for Best Female Recording Artist."

Gunther watched Topaz pause several feet away from him to chat with a handsome actor whose face would split open if he grinned any wider. They were so close he could hear their conversation.

"Yes, she is gorgeous," Gunther admitted as he regained his composure. Why don't you mind your own business? You nosey heifer . . . He removed a ticket from the envelope and handed her the others. "Could you leave these at the door for Reno Velasquez?"

"Consider it done." She smirked.

I've got to get out of here. Gunther wandered off in search of the men's restroom. He found it, pushed open the door, and sighed with relief when he realized he was alone. I've got to get myself together. He felt himself sweating and noticed that a fine layer of perspiration had formed around his freshly dyed black hairline. He splashed cold water on his face and entered one of the stalls, locked the door, and sat on the commode.

"Dang," he whispered. Am I having an anxiety attack or what? He felt around in the pocket of his jacket until his fingers grasped the coolness of the little glass jar that housed his supply of cocaine. This ought to chill me out. He took several large hits of the drug and felt his body relax as his energy soared. Now I'm ready to face my fans and Ms. Topaz. He took several additional hits to be sure and left the restroom feeling like a new person.

Gunther's head was racing from the coke, so he decided to skip the backstage banter and find his seat in the audience until it was time for him to present the award. He entered the auditorium wearing his dark shades and ignored everyone until he saw Reno and Gloria, the two people who were closer to him than his own family. They were in the front row, and looked extremely handsome in their after-five attire.

"Hey." Gunther grinned, happy to see his friends. "You guys made it."

"Spielberg, the man of the hour," Reno began, pouring out

his usual dosage of flattery. "I wouldn't miss you being crowned Best Director for nothing in the world."

"Word, dude. Check you out." Gunther stood there glazed with excitement and admired Reno's designer tuxedo. "Hey, Gloria." He gave her a small peck on the cheek. "You look fabulous."

"Thanks, baby." Gloria snuggled up closer to Reno. "You look great, too." Gunther did look handsome in a black tux and white silk tuxedo shirt. He had selected a purple cummerbund, and Gucci diamond cuff links sparkled at his wrists.

"There's some big party afterwards at Glam Slam. And—"

"Gunther, Gunther, darling."

He closed his eyes and made a small face as soon as he heard the prim and proper female voice calling his name. "Yes, Rita." His response lacked enthusiasm.

"How are you, darling?"

"Fine, Rita." He sighed with impatience.

"Sweetheart, you haven't returned any of my phone calls." Rita ignored the fact that Gunther was obviously not interested in having a conversation with her.

"I've been busy."

"I know, sweetheart, but you know how Mother loves to hear from you. I just wanted you to know that we're all here rooting for you. Your father and your brothers and sisters. We're all sitting back there together."

My entire family sitting together . . . that's the first time that ever happened. When he turned around, they all waved excitedly, so he threw his hand up to acknowledge them.

"We wanted to take you out to dinner afterwards to celebrate. We're so proud of you, baby."

Of course you are, now that I'm famous. Where were you when I needed a family? he wanted to shout. You didn't want me then because I was always the weird one. I was the strange one. The thought of it tore him up inside. But now that I'm famous you want to hang out and be a family. Well it's too late . . . it's too late.

"I've got plans."

"Well, can't you change them? I made reservations at Mr. Chow's in Beverly Hills. Your father said Chinese was your favorite."

"No." Gunther was almost whispering. "I said I have plans."

"Well, all right, darling." His mother was obviously disappointed. "Maybe we can do it some other time. But everyone is going to be so disappointed."

Tough. What about all the times you disappointed me? "Sorry." He shrugged, not feeling sorry at all.

"Why didn't you go celebrate with the family?" Reno questioned after his mother had returned to her seat.

"Because you're my family." Gunther meant it, too. "And we have plans for a party at Glam Slam." He watched Topaz take a seat in the front row of the center section of seats just as the show began.

Gunther sat there bored stiff while award after award was announced. He watched the prominent young actor who had been cheesing in Topaz's face earlier mount the stage and proceed to give a short dissertation on the importance of African-American film throughout the decades.

"Just give me my award so we can go party," Gunther whispered loudly enough for Reno to hear. "It's not like this is the Oscar."

"This year the Image Award for the Best Director goes to Gunther Lawrence," the clean-cut rapper-turned-actor proclaimed. The auditorium thundered with applause and yells.

It's about time . . . Gunther mounted the stairs to the podium where a gorgeous toffee-colored girl in an evening gown stood holding the trophy. He took it without acknowledging the girl or the actor and stepped up to the microphone.

"I worked real hard for this but then nothing worth having comes easily. I'm glad you enjoyed *The Hood*. The best is yet to come. Peace." Gunther was the epitome of cool. He followed the actor into the wings where he would have to wait until the show was finished.

After several other awards were given to actors and actresses, Gunther watched a very famous quartet of young male singers take the stage and sing a cappella the names of the nominees for Best Female Recording Artist. Gunther could see Topaz from where he was standing in the wings, and he could tell by the way she drummed her nails on the arm of her chair that she was nervous. I can't believe that she would really care if she won this award after she won all those other big awards. Gunther scrutinized her every move.

"The winner is . . ." the quartet sang in perfect pitch as the girls in the audience screamed their heads off. "Topaz."

She stood gracefully, flashed a dazzling smile, and mounted the stage like Miss America as the Shrine thundered with applause and cat whistles. Topaz extended her cheek to be kissed by each of the singers, accepted her plaque, and stood behind the podium as radiant as the Queen of Sheba. The applause and whistles continued.

"Wow," Gunther said aloud. I've definitely got to get with her. We'd make the perfect star couple. She's just the kind of wife I need. She'll make me look good and I'll make her look good and the money we'd have . . . As soon as the last award was presented Gunther charged back into the audience to find Reno and Gloria. "We've got to get to Glam Slam," he yelled.

"Let's get this party started." Reno grinned.

Gunther led them out the backstage entrance to his limousine, ignoring everyone who attempted to speak to him. I hope Topaz is going to Glam Slam. He had watched her leave the auditorium with her assistant and security guards right after she had accepted her award.

Inside the limo, Reno opened a bottle of champagne and poured a glass for each of them as the limo headed downtown for the private party at Prince's nightclub. Gunther gulped his champagne and passed his glass to Reno for a refill.

"Yo, dude, you didn't even give me a chance to make a toast." Reno laughed as he poured the bubbling liquid into the glass.

"Aw, dude, that's okay. Did you see Topaz? Is she gorgeous or what?"

"She sure is. Did you get her number, G?"

"Not yet, but I will after the party." Gunther wasn't lacking confidence. "Now that's the kind of girl I need in my life."

"Do you know her, Gunther?" Gloria poured herself another glass of champagne.

"Not yet, but hopefully she'll be at the party."

"What if she already has a man?" Gloria studied Gunther as she sipped her champagne. "She's very pretty."

"So?" Gunther was immediately on the defense. "What does that have to do with the price of tea in China?" He glared at her from behind his dark shades. How dare that tramp contradict me? "If she does have a boyfriend he'll be history after me."

"Way to go, Spielberg. You tell her. Women are a dime a dozen. You just have to play the game long enough until you get what you want and then you control things."

"What did you say, Reno?" Gloria was somewhat perturbed with his response.

"I believe I was talking to Gunther," Reno shouted at Gloria. "You women are all the same. You just want someone to be good in bed and to buy you things. That's why I don't believe in marriage. Since I'm financing these escapades, when the stuff starts getting old I find myself somebody new."

"Word, dude." Gunther slapped a high five with Reno.

"Miss Topaz is no different from any other woman except she's a rich and famous bimbo. You got what it takes to pull a babe like that, man."

"What about love, Reno? You don't love me?" Gloria was on the verge of tears.

"Aw, Gloria, don't start that love stuff. That's high school and fairy tales. This is the real deal. The only thing I love is my money and you love it, too. You just think you love me. You'd better love your own self." Reno was oblivious to the pain on Gloria's face.

"Yeah, dude. I don't believe in that love stuff either. Nobody's going to be there for you the way you can be there for yourself. Nobody really cares. People want you because you have something they want. They want to be around you because you're famous and have money. That love stuff is a joke. You better look out for yourself because no one else is going to."

"Like I said, man, find out what this Topaz wants and give it to her and then you get what you want . . . a gorgeous babe who's probably a freak in bed."

Gunther and Reno laughed and slapped another high five as the limo pulled to a stop in front of the club.

"Come on, Gloria." Reno pushed her out of the car. "I want to have a good time, so stop that crying. I'm not in the mood for your crap tonight. I came here to party and if you don't get in line with the program there are plenty other women in here who will." Reno was yelling over the music. As if to make his point he ogled a curvaceous waitress carrying a tray of drinks, who was weaving her way through the crowd.

They were ushered to a private room on the second floor away from the dance floor and the loud music. The art deco furnishings and the dimmed lighting coupled with the soft background music gave the room an intimate romantic setting.

Way to go, Prince. Gunther mentally extended his compliments to the club's owner. Guests mingled around a candlelight buffet with a selection of fresh fruit, hot wings, vegetables, salads, and pasta. At the huge mirrored bar, Hollywood's chocolate stars sipped drinks and rehashed the night's events. Gunther searched the room for Topaz and had just about given up all hope of her being there when he spotted her and Nina sitting on a sofa and drinking champagne. He forgot about Reno, who was at the bar chatting with some pretty young thing, and Gloria, who sat at a table alone looking forlorn, and forced himself to march over to the settee where Topaz was sitting.

"Hello." Gunther flashed his best smile and turned on the charm. "I'm Gunther Lawrence and I just wanted to congratulate you on your award tonight. I think you're fabulous."

"Thank you." A dazzling smile lit up her exquisite face. "I really enjoyed your film."

Gunther felt himself relax although his heart was pounding so loudly he knew she could hear it. *So far so good . . . Wow . . . I can't believe I'm actually standing face to face with the girl of my dreams.*

"Would you like to join us?" Topaz asked sweetly. "This is my cousin and assistant, Nina. Nina, this is Gunther, the director of *The Hood*."

"Hi." Nina flashed a Pepsodent smile that revealed perfectly straight teeth.

"It figures that you two would be related, you're the most beautiful women in the room." Gunther stood there admiring them both. *I never thought dark girls were pretty,* he admitted to himself, stealing another glance at Nina. *But she's gorgeous.* "May I have the pleasure of sitting in between you both?"

Topaz giggled as Nina, who was totally unimpressed, moved over. Gunther inched himself in between the girls and smiled.

"Now where were we?" He fixed his eyes on Topaz's amber ones. *I never realized she had light eyes.* Gunther felt his heartbeat escalate again. She is too fine. I've got to get out of here before I say something stupid. "Would you ladies care for something more to drink?"

"I'd like more champagne," Topaz smiled.

"Your every wish is my command." Gunther swallowed hard. "Back in a flash." He found the restroom and sat on the commode. She's gorgeous. She's absolutely gorgeous. He sat there for several minutes holding his head in his hands and thinking. "Okay," he finally whispered. "I can do this." He found his prized vial of white powder and took several hits of the drug. There, now I'm ready for anything. He stopped at the bar for their drinks and was elated when he returned and found Topaz sitting alone. "Your drink, mademoiselle." He handed her the flute of champagne and sat on the sofa next to her, feeling cool, poised, and calm.

"Have you started on your next film yet?" Topaz batted her eyes and smiled.

"Oh yes. I wrote my next film before I wrote *The Hood.* It's a mystery entitled *Intrigue.*"

"That sounds exciting." Topaz was extremely interested in what he was saying.

"Would you like to go out sometime?" he heard himself say.

"I'd love to." Topaz smiled.

She actually said yes, he wanted to shout with joy. He quickly scribbled his number on the back of a business card while she wrote out her number on a page from a Waldorf Astoria notepad.

"I'll give you a call tomorrow," he promised before he went off in search of Reno.

"Nina, Gunther asked me out," Topaz whispered to her cousin. She had found her engrossed in conversation with one of the young men from the quartet who had presented Topaz with the award earlier that evening. "Excuse me," Topaz said to the young singer. "I need to borrow her for a minute."

"What is it? He was just getting ready to ask me out."

"Ooh, I'm telling Jamil. He's not even cute . . . girl, Gunther asked me out."

"So, he's not even cute." Nina was unimpressed.

"But he's famous. Maybe he'll give me a part in his next film."

"Girl, please, you got juice. You don't need him to be in a film."

"I know," Topaz agreed relunctantly. "But it's something to do until Sean gets here." She sighed and flipped her hair out of her eye.

"Sean! What about Germain? Have you given him an answer yet?"

"No." Topaz spoke softly, ignoring Nina's girl-you-stupid face. Germain and Chris had been gone for several weeks now and Topaz hadn't admitted to anyone that she still missed them. This is my life, she concluded, looking around the room of illustrious entertainers. And I honestly don't see Germain and Chris fitting in.

"I thought we'd have dinner at Le Dome." Gunther informed Topaz when he telephoned several days later. "And then we could go dancing."

"That sounds wonderful, Gunther." Topaz was excited because she would be dining at an exclusive restaurant with the hottest director in Hollywood.

"I can't wait to see you, beautiful," Gunther added, at his charming best. He hung up the phone and smiled. "This is going to be fun." He laughed and keyed Rita Flora into his Wizard. "I'd like two dozen long-stem roses in a vase with crystal marbles and the appropriate greenery sent over to Topaz Black. Make it spectacular," he ordered. "I want to make a good impression."

Next he ordered a limo with a special request for several bottles of Cristal. He skimmed his meticulously written notes and checked off several additional items. Seems like everything is set for the perfect evening of romance.

"Dang." He was in awe when the limousine pulled to a stop in front of the exclusive high-rise on Wilshire Boulevard. "This is a fabulous place." He inspected the mirrored lobby with marble floors while the desk clerk phoned Topaz to inform her of his arrival. Gunther glanced at his reflection before he stepped on the elevator and was glad he had purchased the black Armani suit especially for their date. She's going to make me work hard.

He took a deep breath as he pressed the doorbell. Several moments later, Topaz opened it, looking like she had stepped out of the pages of one of the high-fashion magazines. She was wearing a fabulous Bill Whitten red minidress, and her golden hair was straight and flowing.

"Hi, Gunther," she greeted him sweetly. "Shall we?" As she picked up a small red Chanel bag, he cast an admiring glance at what he could see of her apartment. She's definitely a class act.

"Thank you for the roses, Gunther." Topaz smiled as they stepped into the elevator. "They're beautiful." She was being especially sweet.

"Someone as beautiful as yourself deserves nothing but beautiful things."

Topaz smiled at his compliment. He ordered a limo for our date, she realized when she saw the chauffeur holding the door open for them. I love it.

Gunther opened a chilled bottle of Cristal. "I thought we'd have a little champagne on the way."

"This is nice." Topaz eyed him carefully while she sipped her champagne. Nina's right, he's not a cutey pie but he dresses well and he has class. They made small talk until they arrived at the restaurant. Gunther waited patiently in the limo while the driver opened the door and allowed Topaz to step out first. Then he took her slender hand in his and led her into the restaurant.

"I'll have the escargot," Gunther informed the waiter.

"I'll have pasta." Topaz closed her menu and smiled. "So how does it feel to be a famous director?"

"It feels wonderful." Gunther couldn't stop smiling. "I love what I do. My next goal is to secure a three-picture deal with a major studio."

"I'll be starting my world tour the first of the year with lots of dates in Europe and Japan." Topaz nibbled on a salad of exotic greens.

"That's great. I love traveling and Europe's fabulous. I was in Cannes for the film festival and I've been trying to get back for a little R and R."

"I love traveling, too. I especially like Jamaica. It's a beautiful place."

"Well, perhaps I'll take you one day and you can show me around," Gunther added, smooth as silk.

This is great. Topaz watched Gunther place a platinum American Express card on the bill. He has his own money and he's not interested in mine. That's more than I can say about some of those other dogs who expect me to pay for everything and then have sex with them.

Gunther thought he would lose it as he watched her spin around on the dance floor at Roxbury. He noticed everyone watching them the moment they entered the club and he knew they were staring at them now. I love it when they stare.

He's so cool dancing with his shades, she smiled to herself. He doesn't even mind that all these people are staring at me. Germain would probably be freaking out by now because of all the attention I'm getting. Gunther likes all the same things I like, and he's not intimidated by me. This might be worth further investigation.

"I thought we'd take a drive out to Malibu," Gunther mentioned as the limo traveled west on Sunset. "It's such a beautiful night." He opened another bottle of champagne and watched Topaz empty her glass.

"I'd like to own a big house one day with marble floors and a bathroom with a Jacuzzi bathtub so big I could swim in it." She giggled. "I'd have a staff of servants to do everything and a bunch of different cars."

"Yeah. That sounds real nice. I want a mansion. An estate with a gate and a guard in a little booth. I want houses in other parts of the world, too."

"I usually have to go out with security," Topaz offered. "It's getting so I can't go anywhere without them."

"I wouldn't let anyone get near you." Gunther was serious. "I grew up in South Central. I'd hurt somebody if they tried to mess with you."

"You would protect me, Gunther?" Topaz batted her amber eyes and smiled into Gunther's eyes. "I need someone to protect me." She snuggled into his arms, feeling the effects of the champagne. Then she kissed him and was surprised by the amount of passion she felt for him. Talk about whip appeal . . .

Dang. Gunther was starting to feel vulnerable. I have to watch myself or else I'll fall in love with this girl. I can't let anyone have a hold like that on me . . . especially a woman . . . because just when you start to trust them they leave you . . . like Rita.

Moments later the limo pulled off Pacific Coast Highway into a brand new development of townhomes.

"Did I mention I live at the beach?" Gunther asked as they got out of the car.

"No, you didn't." Topaz was already enjoying the sound and smell of the water, and the chilly breeze that gently tossed her hair.

"I haven't lived here very long." He entered the alarm code and opened the front door. The floors in the townhouse were gray marble and bleached hardwood with a color scheme of black, gray, and mauve. The furnishings were high tech, which made the house seem sterile and cold.

"This is absolutely fabulous, Gunther." Topaz squealed with delight when she saw his master bathroom with its black fixtures and huge skylight. "Did you decorate yourself?"

"I worked with an interior designer named Michael Smith. He does a lot of celebrities' homes. I just told him what I wanted. I didn't have time to do it myself."

"Well it's fabulous." Topaz stopped to admire the collection of Ertés in the living room. "Fabulous. It looks like something out of a magazine. Maybe I should let Mr. Smith do something with mine."

"I like your place. It's pretty and elegant, just like you."

He drove her home himself later that night in his charcoal gray Range Rover. Topaz had noticed the 735i with GUNFIRE on the license plates parked next to the Range Rover in the garage. Boyfriend's getting paid.

"Thanks for allowing me the pleasure of your company, Topaz. I really had a nice time." Gunther walked her into the mirrored lobby of her highrise.

"I did too, Gunther. Thanks for taking me out." She kissed him before she dashed into the elevator and waved good-bye.

"I like her," he whispered to himself on the way home. I thought she was going to be one of those stupid, big mouth, bossy babes, but she's nice, she has class, and she has her own money so I don't have to worry about her wanting mine. And most importantly, she's a star . . . like me. He grinned, too pleased with himself.

"So how was your date with Gunther Lawrence, director of *The Hood?*" Nina couldn't help being sarcastic the next day when she came to work. "Did he take you down to South Central and give you a tour of the hood and introduce you to his gang-banging homies?"

"No, it was nice. Surprisingly so."

"Really?" Nina was surprised.

"He picked me up in a limo and took me to Le Dome and Roxbury and then we stopped by his place in Malibu."

"He lives in Malibu?"

"Yes. He has this fabulous townhouse decorated by some famous interior designer, a Range Rover, and a 735i. He loves to travel. He's extremely intelligent. We have a lot of things in common."

"You sound like you might be really interested in this guy."

"He's different. He kind of makes me think of Germain. You know, he's smart and he talks about things that are important in the world, but then he's famous, too, so he understands what it's like to be a celebrity."

"So what about Sylk Ross and Germain?" The telephone rang before Topaz had a chance to respond.

"Someone's coming up with a delivery, Nina. Could you get the door for me?" She went into the kitchen and took juice, fresh fruit, and croissants out of the refrigerator.

"Topaz, look!" Nina ran into the kitchen with a Tiffany gift bag. "It's from Tiffany's."

Topaz took the bag and pulled out a beautifully wrapped box. She looked at Nina with a dazed expression on her face as she carefully untied the bow and slit open the wrapping paper with fire-engine-red nails. She slowly opened the velvet jewelry case and gasped at the sight of the exquisite topaz and diamond tennis bracelet. "Oh, my God!" She stood there and stared at the bracelet in wonderment. "It's fabulous . . ."

"Who's it from?" Nina shouted. "Who's it from?"

Topaz picked up the accompanying gift card and opened it. "Thanks for a wonderful night," she read and looked at Nina.

"Girl, did you give him some?" Nina shouted.

Topaz shook her blond mane and stared at Nina. "No. He was a perfect gentleman."

"Dang. He sent you that and you didn't give him none . . ."

"Girl, I told you he was different," Topaz whispered as her full lips turned up into a smile.

TWENTY-EIGHT

"THIS IS a beautiful place, baby." Carolyn's eyes were glued on the landscape as mother and son zipped down the Ventura Freeway in a limousine. "I see why you wanted to move here."

Sean smiled at the sight of God's magnificent handiwork in creation. The Pacific was an infinite mass of vivid royal blue water in contrast to the cloudless azure sky. The brilliant California sunshine cast a sheen on the lush green countryside, adding warmth to the chilly December day. It was a gorgeous day in Santa Barbara.

"Mommy, you want some juice or something?" Sean pulled out a carton of orange juice from the beverage compartment of the limousine.

"No, thank you, sweetie. I'm too excited to eat." She turned to gaze out the window of the car. "I can't wait to see your place."

"It's incredible, Mommy. Incredible. I'm not even going to try and describe it."

"I know it's wonderful, baby. I just wish you weren't going to be so far from me."

"Mommy, I'll come home so much you'll still think I'm living there, and the family can come here for holidays now."

"I know, baby, I just don't like you being out here in California all alone. You don't have any friends . . ."

"Mommy, stop worrying," Sean commanded gently, cutting her off. "I'll be fine." He planted a kiss on his mother's cheek.

"I know, I'm just going to miss my baby boy."

The limo made a turn off the highway. "We'll be there in just a few more minutes now." They rode in silence for several miles until the limo pulled up to a gated estate.

"We're here." Sean pressed the gate opener from inside the

limo. When the gate had swung open far enough, the car drove up the graveled road onto a circular drive in front of a magnificent two-story house with Spanish architecture.

Sean jumped out of the car and ran around it to open the door for his mother. "Look, Mommy, isn't it wonderful?"

A double-tiered water fountain in front of the house sent streams of water dancing into the air. A walkway to the house and around the grounds was paved in mosaic tile. The lawn needed work and there was only a sprinkling of flowers along the border, but it was obviously a wonderful piece of property, and with a few cosmetic upgrades it would be spectacular.

"Let me open the front door so the driver can take the luggage in," Sean called over his shoulder to his mother. He sprinted the path to the double doors leading into the house. "Just wait until I show you the backyard."

He opened the front door and then he ushered his mother around to the back of the house, which sat directly above the ocean. The house, nestled on a bluff, overlooked a tennis court and swimming pool. A staircase, built into the side of the hill, led down to his own private beach.

"I'm going to build a basketball court over there." He pointed to a plot of grassy land adjacent to the four-car garage. "But until it's ready, I'll just shoot hoops on the tennis court."

"Oh, baby." Carolyn was in awe as she gazed out at the ocean. "This is too wonderful. I wish your father could see this."

"He will. I always take him everywhere anyway. I wanted to bring you this time so you could see where I'd be staying and so we could talk and hang out. Come on, let me show you inside." He gently pulled his mother by the hand. He led her inside the house into a living room with gorgeous mahogany floors and huge floor-to-ceiling windows that flooded the entire downstairs with light. The living room became a sitting room with a fireplace and a deck that ran across the back of the house.

"That's the dining room." He pointed to a space on the other side of a staircase that wound its way upstairs. "And this is the kitchen." Sean tucked his arm through hers and led her into the huge room with a skylight in the ceiling and red Spanish tiles on the floor. The kitchen offered a spectacular view of the Pacific. "You could burn in here, couldn't you, Mommy?" He opened the doors of the Sub-Zero refrigerator built into the wall and the double ovens by the stove. An island in the center of the kitchen contained a grill, small sink, and work space.

"I've never seen anything like this in my life." She was finally able to speak. She looked around the kitchen, totally amazed.

"There's a bedroom in here with a bathroom that I can use as the maid's room if I want." Sean gave her a tour of the maid's quarters. "They call this a service porch and this is the pantry. Come on, I'll show you upstairs."

Like an anxious child, he pulled his mother up the stairs and led her into a huge bedroom with a fireplace, sitting room, and bathroom. "This is the master bedroom." His mother was speechless. He opened four more doors to bedrooms with bathrooms and turned around to face his mother. "Well, this is my house." He sighed, pleased as punch.

"This isn't a house, this is a mansion."

"It's not a mansion, Mommy. It's just a nice-sized house."

"Just a house . . . Sean, what are you going to do with all of this house?"

"Live in it."

"By yourself, baby?"

"Sure, why not?"

"A house like this wasn't meant for just one person. It needs a family. It needs kids to play in it. It—"

"Mommy," Sean protested, cutting her off. "You're depressing me."

"I know it must be hard for you. So many pretty girls and all of them wanting you for so many reasons but not the right ones."

Sean sighed sadly. He tried not to think about the state of his love life. He looked at his mother with the eyes of a child.

"How can you tell when someone really loves you for you, Mommy, and not because you play basketball and have money?"

"It's hard to explain, Sean, but you'll know."

"How?"

"I don't know. You just do. I remember when I met your father. We were in high school, well, he was in high school. I was still in junior high. He was so handsome then and he still is." A smile spread across her beautiful face. "You look a lot like your father did in those days."

"So what happened, Mommy? Did he see you and fall out at your feet?" Sean's matinee-idol smile appeared and lit up his face.

"Your father? Not hardly." She laughed. "He was too cool."

"Daddy was cool?" Sean laughed as he interrupted his mother's stroll down memory lane.

"He was so cool you could have chilled a grape pop on him. He came to my house to play basketball with my older brothers and here I come strolling in from school still in ponytails and your uncle David introduced us. I thought he was the finest thing I ever laid eyes on. I never dreamt he'd be remotely interested in me. But when our eyes met, I thought I had died and gone to heaven. It was like the two of us had shared some sort of secret without words."

"Wow. I don't think I've ever felt like that about anybody before. Not even Rhonda . . . well, if I did, I don't remember it."

"You'd remember. In fact, you could never forget it. Some people call it love at first sight and it's very, very special. Most people never wait for that one special person. They get married because she looks good or he buys me nice things or she's good in bed. They don't marry for love and that's why it doesn't last. What kind of girl are you looking for, honey?"

They were sitting in front of the fireplace eating Chinese food that had been delivered from a local restaurant. Sean got up to toss another log on the fire.

"She has to be pretty . . ."

"Sean!" His mother was surprised.

"I'm not saying that's the most important thing, but it's important to me. I'm just being honest. I like beautiful women."

"All right, Sean, go ahead. God knows your heart."

"She has to be fun, with lots of personality, and make me laugh. Somebody I can talk to and somebody who can talk to me. Somebody I can be friends with, so we can do things together, but not somebody who wants to run the street and party all the time." His mother nodded, urging him to continue. "She has to be a Christian, but real . . . with the love of God in her heart and in her soul . . . not someone who goes around quoting Scripture all the time but doesn't know God."

"Interesting. Does she have to have money?"

"No, but she has to have a life. I'm real busy sometimes and I don't want someone sitting around with nothing to do, waiting for me to come home, or going out shopping every day. I heard a lot of the guys on the team talk about their girlfriends and wives and a lot of them fool around while their men are out of town."

"Really?" She was astonished.

"Yes."

"Why am I surprised? This world is crazy."

"I know, Mommy, and I've seen a lot of crazy stuff, but the more I see, the more it helps me to realize what I don't want."

"You'll be fine, Sean. Just as long as you don't settle for anything short of what you've prayed for."

"Okay . . . Mommy, I sure need lots of furniture." He looked around the empty room. "And we sure have lots of work to do. Are you sure you don't want me to hire a decorator and we go check into the Biltmore and chill?"

"Baby, no . . . I love doing interior design. I'm going to have a good time with this. I did some research before I left Philly and there's a place in Los Angeles we need to check out called the Pacific Design Center."

"Okay." Sean took the pad his mother handed him. It had the address written on it. "What about people to do the work?"

"Your father gave me some names of some different pastors he knows out here. I'm sure they have contractors in their congregations. I'm sure they also have some nice young ladies for you to meet, too."

"Mother, we're working on the house now, not my love life."

"Who's working on your love life? I just cast all my care on the Lord."

It was the first of the year before Carolyn Ross decided her work was complete. The renovations were well underway and she had left explicit final instructions for the contractors still working on the grounds.

She nodded approvingly at the sight of the freshly painted mauve walls against the wood trim and doors in the living room with the new Italian furniture they had selected. The hardwood floors gleamed from refinishing, and colorful Chinese wool rugs were strategically placed throughout the house. A huge crystal teardrop chandelier was suspended in the foyer and a smaller chandelier hung over a dining room table that seated twelve.

"Are you sure you don't want me to stay a little longer?" Carolyn asked Sean for the hundredth time while they were waiting at the airport.

"No, Mommy. You've been here long enough." Sean forced the words although he really wished his mother could stay forever. "Daddy misses you and I know you miss him, too."

"Okay." She looked at her son with tears in her eyes. They were at the American Airlines gate waiting for her flight to Philadelphia. "I love you, baby." Tears streamed out of her eyes and down her cheeks.

Sean swallowed hard. He was getting a little choked up himself. "Mommy, don't cry. I'll be fine."

"I know you will. I'm just going to miss my baby boy." She smiled and wiped her eyes.

"I love you, Mommy." He bent down and held his mother tightly. She reached up and gently stroked the side of his face. "Go buy some art for those walls of yours."

"What?" He laughed, surprised by the abrupt change in their conversation.

"Go buy some art for those walls, boy," she commanded with a grin.

"All right, Mommy, I will. Traveling mercies . . ." He waved as she disappeared through the tunnel. He watched her plane depart before he headed out to the red Range Rover that he had purchased for the long drives between Santa Barbara and Los Angeles.

"Buy some art." He laughed as he popped in a cassette and cranked the volume. "Mommy's too much."

The Pacific was an abyss of cold, wetness, and gray that January afternoon. Topaz was on her way to visit Sean. It's cold up here, she realized, as she flipped the heat on in the Mercedes. The news came on and she quickly punched the preset buttons and changed the station to *The Beat*.

"Hey." She cranked up the volume when she heard "Love's Taken Over." "My girl, Chante Moore. Sing, girl." Topaz sang along for the rest of the song. Then she gazed up at the sunless sky and wondered if it might rain. "He lives too far," she complained out loud. Why couldn't this man live in Malibu or Santa Monica if he wanted to live at the beach? she wondered for the thousandth time. Talk about the boonies . . .

Sean snapped off his Dictaphone and paused to stare out the window of his office into the backyard at the ocean. The water's not the same without the sun, but it's still nice. I love living by the ocean. He stared at the point where the water and the horizon met and wondered how they seemed to touch but never did.

The front gate buzzer sounded, summoning him back into the present. That should be Topaz. He heard his housekeeper, Dora, quickly tap across the wooden floors to answer the front door. The middle-aged Salvadorian woman lived on the premises with her husband, Eduardo.

"Hi, Topaz." He was in the family room in a matter of seconds, planting a kiss firmly on her cheek before he grabbed her coat and hung it in a closet near the door.

"Sean," she sang, beckoning him seductively and kissing him on the mouth. "Now that's the way you say hello."

He grinned, amused by her boldness. "So how've you been?" He took a seat on the couch next to her. "You're looking fabulous, as always."

"Thanks. You look good, too."

"Come on." He jumped up and pulled her to her feet, flashing his trademark matinee-idol smile. "Let me show you around the house."

"Okay." His smile made her feel warm and alive. Brother man is too fine. She followed him throughout the tastefully decorated house. It makes you feel like you could stay here forever, but it's so simple. I'd lay this house out. She mentally redecorated. Put some marble over these hardwood floors . . . although he does have some nice antique pieces. "Your house is very nice," she informed him at the end of the tour.

"Thanks. My mother hooked everything up for me, the wallpapers and paints and stuff. We had so much fun doing it."

Oh, you and Mommy decorating the house, how sweet. "You'll have to come see my place, Sean. Nina and I did everything. It was so much fun. All the shopping. I just love shopping. No matter what I'm buying."

"It is fun. Especially when you have money to buy things that most people can't afford simply because they aren't necessary. My mother collects all kinds of stuff. She calls it good junk and she's got me buying it, too." He waved at a collection of black memorabilia housed in a curio cabinet.

"Oh." Topaz, not really interested, turned away before he went on about the junk in the cabinet. "So you're sitting out the rest of the basketball season?"

"Yeah," he agreed slowly, apprehensive of her question.

"Why?" she demanded, fixing her amber eyes on him.

"I'm just kind of full of basketball. It's kind of like candy and I've had enough for a while."

"So what are you going to do?"

"I don't know. Relax, work on my house, do some personal appearances for my foundation, come visit you on tour . . ." He smiled.

"Oh." She was too flattered. "You'd come out on the road with me?"

"Sure. It might be fun hanging out with a singing superstar . . ."

"It'll be fun. I'll make sure of that."

"How about a movie?"

"Movie? I don't know when I went to the movies last." Topaz tried to remember the last movie she had seen.

"You want to change or something? Eduardo took your things up to your room."

My room. She looked down at her jeans and wondered if her room was his room. "Yes, I'd like to change." She followed Sean upstairs to one of the spare bedrooms, which was decorated in Laura Ashley wallpaper with a matching comforter and drapes. It also had a television and boom box with a selection of CDs. Classical music . . . yuck. She tossed the CDs in a drawer. Where's "Rump Shaker"? She fished through her box of CDs.

She made her grand entrance into the family room forty-five minutes later, dressed to kill in her newest Donna Karan dress. She was shocked to find Sean in a pair of black sweats and his Nikes.

"I thought we were going to the movies," she snapped. His casual clothing turned her off.

"We are. You look fabulous, but if you want to put on jeans or something I'll understand."

"No, this is fine." You're the one who needs to change, she wanted to tell him.

"You like Mexican food?"

"Sure."

"There's a place by the movies that makes great burritos."

Gunther took me to Le Dome. What is this rat hole? she wondered when he pulled up in front of a white storefront taco stand on the side of the road.

"Come on." Sean opened the door and pulled her out of the car. "What would you like?" He wrapped his long arm around her waist and squeezed her tightly. The menu was a white bulletin board with the selections spelled out in little black stick-on letters.

"A diet Coke." She was too annoyed. How dare he bring me to this tacky little place! She looked around at the neat room with its linoleum floor and a half-dozen or so small tables with red and white plaid oilcloths and red-glass candles.

"A diet Coke? You've got to have a burrito. They're the best. See, they have shrimp tacos. The beans are really good and the chicken burrito is the bomb."

"I said I'll have a diet Coke." She took a seat at a table near the window. It was pitch black outdoors and she could hear the ocean.

"Okay . . ." He placed their order and took a seat across from Topaz and gazed into her eyes. "You are so beautiful."

"Thanks." We're in the middle of nowhere eating Mexican food in some greasy spoon. I don't believe this. The cashier called out their number and Sean went for the tray of food.

I'm bored. Topaz sipped her diet Coke and sniffed hungrily when she caught a whiff of Sean's chicken burrito, Spanish rice, and savory pinto beans topped with melted Monterey jack cheese and green onions. "That smells good," she finally had to admit.

"Here, have some of mine. It's a lot of food." He made her a small plate, which she devoured in a matter of seconds.

"That was the best Mexican food I ever had," she confessed on the way to the movies. But I can't see why he'd take me to eat somewhere like that. They have expensive restaurants out here. He's a big star and he lives so simply. Well, at least he has this Range Rover.

They saw *Scent of a Woman*. Not a single person recognized either of them, or if someone did, no one bothered them to say anything.

"I just love it here. I can go out to dinner and to the movies without being recognized. And so did you. Isn't that wonderful?"

"Yes," she agreed halfheartedly, perturbed because no one had recognized them at all.

Back at the house Sean tossed more wood on the embers that were still glowing in the fireplace in the family room. The sound of the ocean and the black cloudless sky made the room too romantic.

"Sean, do you realize we've known each other almost five years now and you've never asked me to have sex with you?" She finally had to say something after Sean hadn't tried anything with her in the darkened room.

"I know," he spoke softly. "And it's not that I'm not attracted to you. I'm very attracted to you."

"Then what is it?"

"I don't believe in sex before marriage."

"But you've had sex before, right?"

"No."

"What?" she screamed. "You mean you've never done it?"

"No," he replied quietly.

"You mean you've never made love to a girl?"

"No."

Topaz was stunned. This has got to be the finest man I have ever laid eyes on, and he's never had sex. He has absolutely no desire to be with me. He's lying . . . he has to be. I wonder if he's gay . . .

"How would you know if you liked being with that person if you never had sex with them?"

"People ask me that all the time." Sean laughed. "It comes down to trust. I believe in God and I'm trusting Him to bring the right person into my life. And if I can trust Him to bring the right person, I know I'll enjoy making love to her."

"Huh?" Topaz was totally confused. I can understand him believing in God, but trusting God with your sex life . . . that's a bit too much. He's crazy. She looked at Sean like she had never seen him before. He's weird. "So you're trusting God to hook up your sex life?"

"Exactly." He gave her a smile so sweet he could melt butter.

"So you don't want me?" she asked in disbelief, climbing into his lap.

"Not unless you're my wife." Why is she making this so hard for me?

"So, are you asking me to marry you?" Topaz gazed up at him through lowered lashes.

Me and Topaz married . . . I don't know . . . but then it might be nice . . .

That girl will turn out to be your worse nightmare. He could hear Kirk's words echoing in his mind.

"I want a wife, Topaz. And I have thought about what our lives would be like if we were married. That's one of the reasons I came to Southern California. I wanted us to take the time to get to know each other and see if marriage is a possibility."

"Okay, Sean." Topaz was pacified for the moment because he had admitted that he was interested in marrying her.

They talked a while longer and then Sean escorted Topaz to her room.

I wonder if I should tell him about Germain. It's obvious that Keisha hasn't blabbed my business yet. Imagine me and Sean married, she thought as she lay in bed alone, listening to the ocean. I sure could teach the brother a thing or two. She laughed to herself. I'd turn him out.

The sun shining on the Pacific made all the difference in the world for the drive back to L.A. The rippling water still looked cold, but now the ocean was blue and glistening from the late afternoon sun rays.

"Hey, Nina." Topaz shouted over the music into the speaker of her car phone. "What up?"

"Nothing much. I'm just chilling. So how was your big weekend with Sylk Ross?"

"Nina, he's a virgin." Topaz picked up the phone and spoke directly into it.

"What?" her cousin screamed. "Get out of here. Oh, how romantic . . ."

"Romantic? How is that fine man being a virgin romantic?"

"It is. He's never been with anyone. Think how special it would be the first time you're together . . . you'd be his one and only . . . ohhh. How sweet. I wonder if he thinks you're a virgin," she laughed.

"Nina, you're crazy. He can't think I'm a virgin . . ."

"Why? Did you try to jump his bones or something, Miss She's Gotta Have It?"

"Nina . . ."

"You did." Nina screamed with laughter. "I know you did."

"You know, I thought he was gay," Topaz confessed with a laugh.

"Gay?" Nina laughed her head off. "You can look at that man and tell he's not gay."

"But he's still weird, Nina. All we did was go to the movies and talk. You know, chill-out stuff. He made me dinner last night."

"That sounds nice. That's the kind of stuff me and Jamil do."

"Well, you know I like to go out, girl. He's coming down next week and we're going out on the town. He's going to the American Music Awards with me."

I don't know about this . . . Sean tossed his Louis Vuitton overnight pieces in the back of the Range Rover. Topaz seems so different.

"Maybe you never really knew her at all," he heard a voice say.

He paused to think for a moment. All she ever talks about is shopping, partying, where she's been or going, and her tour. She's not interested in any of the things I'm interested in and she keeps harping on me playing basketball again. She's not the person I met four years ago, he finally admitted. I thought she was nice. Maybe I'll never meet someone I can be friends with and be attracted to . . .

He was in Los Angeles with Topaz for a week. I feel like I'm in some fancy department store and I can't touch anything, he realized the moment he stepped into her penthouse apartment with its pastel colors and marble floors. It seems so cold. There's no warmth. Despite his reluctance to go out, he attended the American Music Awards with her and subjected himself to everyone's constant questioning.

"When are you going to play basketball again?" they demanded over and over.

"I don't know," Sean answered kindly with a smile.

"He'll be back real soon," Topaz promised despite the looks

he gave her. "You'll be playing real soon, baby," she told him repeatedly. "You have to make lots of money so we can buy a mansion in Beverly Hills and get you out of Santa Barbara."

She never listens to a thing I say. He parked the Range Rover in the church parking lot and glanced at Topaz before he walked around to open her door. She seemed totally out of it.

"How can two walk together except they be agreed?" he heard ever so clearly as they walked in the church.

The House of the Lord, Sean reflected, feeling peaceful at once. It feels good to be in church . . . especially after that escapade with those pain killers.

"Sean, is it time to go yet?" she whispered halfway through the message.

"Huh?" He was really into what the preacher was saying.

"Is it time to go?" she whispered loudly.

"Not yet. Soon." I hope she's listening. He watched her close her eyes and sit so still he wondered if she was asleep. Sean remembered his father telling him, when he was a teenager and he'd brought his unsaved friends to church, that the Holy Spirit would still be at work long after the service was over.

"So what did you think?" They were having lunch at Coley's Kitchen in Beverly Hills.

"It was okay." Topaz polished off the curried goat, jerk chicken, and plantain from the Jamaican brunch buffet.

"So you didn't mind being in church?"

"Oh, no," she replied, sugary sweet. "I don't mind going to church. But if we have to go to church, why can't we go to that church on Crenshaw where all the other stars go?"

The church where all the other stars go. Sean dropped his fork into his plate. All of a sudden, he was no longer hungry. I've had enough of this girl. And to think I wanted to marry her . . . I would have made a huge mistake. Thank you, Lord.

They left the restaurant in silence and drove over to a nearby gallery. I really ought to take her straight home before I say something I'll regret, but I'll drop her off after this.

The gallery was featuring a mixed media exhibit with contemporary African-American artists. Mommy told me to buy something for the walls, he remembered.

"I'm bored, Sean," Topaz informed him, after she had glanced at all the paintings in a matter of seconds. "I don't see what you see in that stuff. Me, I need something I can understand that doesn't need any interpretation."

"That's why you're you and I'm me," he replied, making an effort to be kind.

"Let's get out of here and go shopping or something. We've been doing what you wanted all morning, now it's my turn."

"I want to see if there's anything here that would go in my house. Why don't you look around to see if there's something you'd like for your apartment?"

"All right. But then I'll be ready to go." She wandered off to another part of the exhibit to look at some sculpture.

Good riddance. Sean sighed as he watched her walk away. Maybe I can have some peace now. He walked up and down the aisles of the exhibit, intently studying each painting. What a fabulous sense of color, he marveled, stopping to enjoy an abstract with vivid colors. It looks like the ocean, he finally decided. He looked further. There's something very peaceful about it, too. There's a whole series of them. He noticed the title cards under his favorite pieces, *Love*, *Peace*, and *Joy*. This is great. I'm going to buy one. But which one? He stood there, so engrossed in his thoughts that he didn't hear her at first.

"What does that painting say to you?" she asked politely.

"It says peace," Sean replied, without taking his eyes off the painting. "It says peace, and I like it so much I'm going to buy it."

"Wonderful," she exclaimed. "This is the fifth one I've sold today."

"Huh?" He spun around quickly, thinking he had been talking to Topaz. When he looked into the smiling black almond-shaped eyes of a beautiful young woman, he felt a tingling sensation—one he had never felt before—permeate his lean, muscular body. She was a slender, caramel-colored girl with long, curly black hair that fell to one side of her face. She was dressed in a tuxedo jacket, a pair of funky blue jeans that were hand-painted with Oriental hieroglyphics and embellished with rhinestones, and a pair of black spike heels. She was obviously Asian and black. She extended a hand and smiled.

"Hi. I'm Jade Kimura, the artist."

TWENTY-NINE

"IS THIS Topaz, the most beautiful woman in the world?"

Topaz smiled the moment she heard Gunther's voice on the telephone. "Yes."

"Is this the internationally renowned recording star with a platinum album and four number-one singles?"

"Yes." Topaz giggled.

"Oh, well, then I've got the wrong number. Sorry," he mumbled and hung up the phone.

"Gunther!" Topaz yelled into the phone. "Gunther . . . I can't believe him." She sighed with exasperation and hung up the phone. She had just flown in from Munich the night before and had two weeks off before she was off to Tokyo. She looked at the suitcases of clothes that needed to go the cleaners and the pile of dirty laundry and made a face.

"I'll deal with that later." It's summertime anyway, she rationalized. She rummaged through drawers of sportswear until she found something she wanted to wear. The front doorbell arrested her thoughts. Who's that? She tiptoed to the door to look out of the peephole. No one knows I'm home. "Gunther," she squealed, opening the door.

"Hi, beautiful." He handed her a huge bouquet of long-stem red roses. "Welcome home."

"You silly." She laughed and took the roses. "You act like you didn't fly home from Germany with me last night."

"I know." He grinned. "I just wanted to welcome you home officially."

She reached up to kiss him and discovered he was holding something else behind his back.

"What else are you hiding, Gunther Lawrence?" Her face was as excited as a child's on Christmas morning.

Gunther laughed and handed her a container of luscious strawberries dipped in chocolate.

"You are just too wonderful. I love these." She popped a huge strawberry into her mouth. "They're my absolute favorite."

"I know. I got you another one of your favorite things, too." He revealed a chilled bottle of Cristal.

Gunther's the most exciting man I've ever known. Topaz smiled. He followed her into the kitchen, where she poured the champagne into Baccarat flutes. The coolness of the salmon marble tile on the kitchen floor felt good under her feet.

"Here, baby." She held one of the strawberries up to his lips for him to bite. "Have one."

Gunther bit into the strawberry. Things are going just as I planned. "Do you have plans for dinner?" he asked while they sipped champagne.

She shook her blond mane in response. I wonder what he's up to now. He's always surprising me. She glanced at the topaz-and-diamond bracelet that she never removed from her wrist and touched one of the matching pendant earrings she was wearing. Gunther had given her several other pieces of jewelry, including the topaz-and-diamond ring on her pinky and an ankle bracelet, all sent over beautifully wrapped from Tiffany or Van Cleef and Arpel on Rodeo Drive in Beverly Hills.

"Great. I thought we'd stay in for dinner."

"Stay in?" Now this certainly is a surprise. We never stay in and we never order out.

"Stay in," he repeated firmly. "Why don't you go get yourself looking fabulous while I arrange everything?" he suggested with a mischievous grin.

"All right," she replied with a kiss. I wonder what he's up to. She was unable to suppress the huge smile that found its way onto her face. He was acting all secretive like this when he took me to Cancún. She sang the chorus to "I Love the Way You Love Me" on the way into the bathroom.

When Gunther heard her start her bath water he picked up the phone and ordered dinner from Monty's in Westwood. He placed the roses in a large clear vase with black crystal marbles in the center of the dining room table, and set the table with Topaz's best crystal and china. He found candles and placed them on the table. She really has nice things, he noticed as he arranged everything perfectly.

He went back into the kitchen and smiled when he heard her singing, poured himself more champagne, and carried the bottle into the bathroom to refill her glass.

"Hi, baby, I missed you." She squealed delightedly the moment he came into the room.

He blew her a kiss in reply. You're not going to get me saying things I'm not ready to say. "I brought you more champagne, darling." He sat on the side of the tub and filled her glass.

"Thanks, babe. That was so sweet of you." She took a long sip from her glass. "Ooh, that tastes so good. Why don't you get in here with me?"

"I can't, sweetheart. I've got some things happening in the other room. But I'll take you up on your offer a little later."

"All right," she agreed with a smile. He stood up and poured the rest of the champagne into her bath water. "Gunther, what are you doing?" she squealed.

"I want nothing but the best for my lady. So, darling, go ahead and bathe in the bubbly." He stood there enjoying the amazed look on her face. Then he stuck his hand inside the tub of swirling, bubbling water. "Girl, you're so fine I could drink your bath water."

She was speechless as he walked out of the bathroom. What do you say to something like that?

Gunther ran outside on the balcony and laughed his head off. Girl, you're so fine I could drink your bath water . . . how horrible. I can't believe she fell for that tired line. "Gag me with a spoon," he whispered as he dashed back into the living room to answer the phone.

"The food's here, Topaz," he yelled towards the back. "Are you looking fabulous yet?"

"Yes." She rushed out of the room in a tiny black crepe dress by Tadashi, adorned with her topaz and diamond jewelry.

"You look exquisite, darling." Gunther gave her a little peck on the cheek. He looked her up and down as though she was under a magnifying glass and she secretly wondered if she really did look okay. She looked down at her bare tanned legs. Maybe I should have put on a pair of pantyhose.

"Come, darling." He took her by the hand and led her to the dining room table, where the candles flickered gently and cast a soft romantic glow in the darkened room. "Sit," he commanded, pulling out her chair. The doorbell sounded moments later and Gunther rushed to open the door.

"What?" Topaz exclaimed as a waiter wheeled in a small serving cart filled with numerous covered dishes.

"Dinner is served." Gunther took a seat at the opposite end of the dining room table. "Just serve us a bit of everything and leave the food on the table," he instructed the waiter. They sat there in silence while the waiter served them Roquefort salad, shrimp cocktail, and cilantro oysters.

"Gunther, this is wonderful." Topaz was ecstatic. "Everything's so delicious." Next, the waiter served a feast of porterhouse steaks, shrimp scampi, broiled Australian lobster tails, colossal baked potatoes, and steak-cut french fries.

"Is everything hot?" Gunther barked.

"Yes, sir, very hot," the elderly Hispanic replied.

"The food's delicious, Gunther." Topaz dipped a piece of lobster into a cup of melted drawn butter. "Absolutely delicious."

Gunther handed the waiter a twenty-dollar bill as he wheeled his cart out of the door.

"Everything's fabulous, Gunther. Only I'm starting to get a little full. There's so much food."

"I know," he agreed, looking at all the food. "I was hungry when I ordered dinner."

"Gunther, move those roses so I can see your face," Topaz demanded. "I can't see you."

"No, precious. They're perfect there. They give the room so much ambience. I don't want to disturb the mood."

"But I can't see you," Topaz complained.

"Do you know what we're celebrating?" Gunther asked, changing the subject.

"No, I didn't know we were celebrating." Topaz tried to catch a glimpse of his face through the spaces between the roses.

"This is our sixth-month anniversary. We've been dating six months now."

"Happy anniversary, darling." Topaz rose from her seat and sat in his lap.

"Topaz, darling," Gunther protested, trying to avoid her kisses so he could finish dinner.

"Yes?" she cooed.

"Nothing." He felt himself giving in to her womanly wiles. Okay, you win this time. He was slightly annoyed at himself because he had succumbed to her charms so quickly. But don't think you'll always be able to control me like this.

It's not like it used to be with Germain, Topaz reflected. She sat up in bed after their lovemaking and watched Gunther sleep. Germain was so tender and Gunther always seems like he's fighting me. She smiled at the new diamond bracelet he had given her to celebrate their anniversary and kissed him gently on the nose. Oh, well, two different men . . . two different lovers.

Topaz rubbed herself down with tanning oil and squinted at the hot July sun. She was in Malibu on the private beach adjacent to Gunther's townhouse. It is so hot today. She poured herself a glass of champagne from the chilled bottle on ice in the cooler and glanced at Nina and Jamil, who were curled up on a blanket on the sand under a colorful beach umbrella several feet away. She had heard them laughing and whispering for the last hour. Out of the corner of her eye she saw Gunther busily typing on his laptop computer. I can't believe he's out here working on a Saturday afternoon, she frowned.

"What's so funny, you two?" Topaz got up and made a spot for herself on their blanket.

"Nothing." Nina giggled and glanced at Jamil, who looked like the cat that had swallowed the canary.

"Yes, there is."

"Jamil, could you get me some more champagne, please?" Nina asked.

"No, you've had too much already," he replied firmly. "Topaz, she's over here baggin' on Gunther."

"I am not. I just said he was a nerd." She fell out on the blanket in a fit of giggles.

"Nina, stop talking about my man," Topaz demanded as she tried not to smile.

"Look at him." Nina glanced in Gunther's direction. "Sitting out here with his computer. He's so tired and he thinks he's the stuff. In a minute he'll be over here saying, word, dude," she finished, imitating Gunther's nasally speech.

"I'll take her home right now," Jamil laughed apologetically while Nina lay out on the blanket and laughed until she cried.

"What's happening, dudes?" Gunther joined the group and Nina howled with laughter. "I just finished the treatment for my new script."

Gunther was all smiles as he focused on Topaz. "Don't you think it's about time we started getting ready for the Natalie Cole concert at the Bowl, darling?" he questioned, playing with a lock of her hair.

Nina buried her face in the blanket to conceal her laughter and Jamil choked on the soda he was drinking. Topaz looked for something to focus on over the ocean before she burst into laughter. Gunther could be a trip sometimes. "He just acts that way because he went to school with all those white people," she had explained to Nina.

"What's wrong with her?" Gunther asked, pointing to Nina.

"Nothing, babe. Could you go in the house and get more champagne? Nina just finished the bottle."

"Of course, my pet." Gunther started towards the house for the water.

"Of course, my pet," Jamil repeated and fell out on the blanket next to Nina and howled.

"He thinks he's a character out of *Dynasty* or something." Nina sat up and wiped her eyes.

"Go home," Topaz commanded, pretending to be mad as she tossed a handful of sand on them.

"Shall we, my pet?" Jamil asked, enunciating every syllable as he spoke. He extended a hand to Nina.

"Oh, darling, let's skedaddle. Bitsy's waiting." Nina spoke in a perfect English accent as she sprinted across the beach.

"Later, star." Jamil planted a kiss on Topaz's cheek.

"Darling, don't dawdle," Nina scolded Jamil. "Ta ta, cousin." She waved good-bye to Topaz.

Topaz watched them drive off in Jamil's convertible Mercedes, then followed Gunther to the house. "Sick. The girl is sick."

"What are you wearing to the Bowl?" Gunther asked once they were in the house.

"This." Topaz held up a simple but elegant black lace dress.

"That?" he questioned, making a face. "Do you always have to wear black?" he complained.

"I like black," Topaz protested. "And it looks good on me."

"It's so morbid," Gunther said with disgust. "But if that's all you have to wear, it will have to do. The limo will be here any minute. I'll have to take you shopping and pick out some more suitable things for you."

Germain always liked the things I wore, she reflected. But Gunther does have excellent taste. Maybe he's right.

"These are fabulous seats, Gunther." The usher seated them in box seats right down front at the Hollywood Bowl.

"I know. But it's nothing but the best for my lady. Kiss me," he demanded roughly, grabbing her face and pressing his lips to hers.

Topaz felt no passion for him whatsoever. Stupid. She glared at him as she took out her compact. Messed up my makeup.

Moments later, a waiter brought them a picnic basket dinner that Gunther had ordered with barbecued chicken, an assortment of salads, and a selection of cheese, crackers, and fruit.

"Is there anything else I can get you, Topaz?" Gunther asked graciously as a waiter filled their glasses with champagne.

"No, Gunther, you thought of everything as usual." Topaz smiled. They had both sneaked a few hits of coke during dinner and now she was ready to party.

Natalie closed the show with "Unforgettable" and the music was still in her head. She sang the words to Gunther after the concert as they walked out front to the car. Inside the limo, they snorted more coke and drank more champagne. Topaz continued singing "Unforgettable." Gunther joined in, singing off-key, and Topaz laughed her head off.

"Babe, stick to film directing and leave the singing to me."

"All right, dude. You ready to get this party started?"

"Word, dude, let's get this party started." Topaz sat in his lap and imitated his flip way of speaking.

"Yahoo," Gunther yelled. "To the airport."

"You were serious about the airport," she commented when she heard the airplanes flying overhead as the limo drove down Century Boulevard to LAX.

"Of course I was."

"Are we going somewhere?" Topaz asked as they walked through the airport.

"You ask too many questions." Minutes later, they boarded a small private jet.

"Gunther, this is a private plane!" Topaz squealed. She was so excited she ran from window to window. "I've never been on a private jet!" Her amber eyes sparkled with excitement.

"Stick with me, lady, and I'll show you the world," Gunther barked.

"Where are we going, Gunther?" Topaz pleaded as the aircraft taxied down the runway. "Won't you please tell me?"

"Nope, it's a surprise." He helped her fasten her seat belt. "You'll just have to wait until we get there."

Fifteen hours later she found out when the pilot announced they would be landing in Paris, France.

"Paris, France!" Topaz shouted. "Gunther, you brought me to Paris?"

"Yes, darling," he replied with a kiss.

"Ooh. You wonderful, wonderful man!" She covered his face with delicate little kisses. Germain would have never done anything like this.

There was a limousine waiting to take them to the George V, a haven for movie moguls and international tycoons. The limo waited while they checked in and showered and then sped them off for a day of sightseeing in the City of Lights. Topaz was speechless as the car traveled down the city's famed Champs Élyseés, which was lined with trees, shops, cafes, and cinemas.

"I can't believe I'm really in Paris. When I came here on tour we were in and out so quickly, I didn't get a chance to see much of anything."

"I came here for several weeks when I was in high school," Gunther bragged. "We stayed in a little hotel on the Left Bank and attended classes at the Sorbonne. I met the most beautiful girl. She looked a lot like you. She was from Rio."

"That's funny, some of my father's people are from Rio. She could be my cousin." Why is he telling me about other women?

"Look, the Arc de Triomphe," Gunther rattled off with a perfect French accent. They stopped and took an elevator to the top for a magnificent view of the city. Next, they went to the Louvre and then to the Left Bank for a late lunch in the Latin Quarter. They ended the afternoon at the Eiffel Tower.

"I'm sleepy, Gunther," Topaz mumbled. She was curled up in the limousine next to him.

"Okay, darling. I'll have the car drop you off at the hotel so you can take a nap while I pick up a few things for us."

"All right," she agreed, yawning. She climbed into the four-poster at the hotel and slept until Gunther returned with shopping bags.

"I bought you things to wear for dinner." He removed the garment bag to reveal a fabulous white Kenzo suit on a hanger.

"Gunther, it's gorgeous!" Topaz jumped out of the bed to touch the crisp white linen. It wasn't her normal trendy look, but it was very elegant and sophisticated.

"I have excellent taste." Gunther handed her a pair of Charles Jourdan sandals and an Hermes bag. "You'll look like a million dollars in this outfit."

"Did you get anything for yourself?"

"I got a Kenzo suit, too." He showed her a cream-colored linen suit and an ivory silk shirt.

"That's going to look so fabulous on you, babe," Topaz cooed as she massaged his shoulders. "Are we going somewhere special for dinner tonight?"

"You ask too many questions." He laughed.

After a late dinner at Maxim's, they stopped by Regine's and danced until the wee hours.

"Gunther Lawrence, I love you." They were on the way back to the hotel in the limousine. "You are the most fabulous, the most wonderful man I have ever known."

Gunther smiled and pulled her hair out of its chignon. "The best is yet to come," he whispered softly in her ear.

The next day after breakfast in bed, they were off for a shopping spree at the designer boutiques—Chanel, Saint Laurent, Chloe, Christian Dior, Hermes, Givenchy. Gunther chose everything and charged endlessly on his platinum American Express card. In the Baccarat shop, they ordered crystal trimmed in eighteen-karat gold. Then they had to purchase several pieces of the newest Louis Vuitton accessories and suitcases to take everything home.

Topaz was like a kid in a toy store with her new wardrobe of elegant French designer clothing. She spread everything on the bed and sat there gazing at her new clothing, shoes, and accessories.

"Well, are you going to wear it or watch it?" Gunther laughed when he came out of the shower and found her still sitting there.

"I'm going to wear it, silly."

"Wear something very special, darling. Because tonight's a very special night."

"All right, darling." She kissed the back of his neck. "I'll look so fabulous you'll go crazy." She chose a gold Chanel dress and sandals and wore her hair down with her favorite copper makeup.

"You look exceptionally beautiful tonight," Gunther told her as they left the hotel. He was oblivious for once to all the stares from guests in the hotel as he ushered her out to the car.

Topaz was too impressed when Gunther ordered their dinner of caviar, seafood, pressed duck, and truffles at Lasserre in perfect French. "I didn't know you could speak French like that." Topaz caught a glimpse of her reflection in the gold rim of her dinner plate.

"I learned it in high school." Gunther sampled the champagne the waiter poured into his glass. He nodded his approval and watched the waiter fill their crystal flutes with bubbly.

"Gunther, look!" The ceiling had just opened up over them, revealing a starry Parisian sky. "How romantic." She gazed up into the moonlit night as the candlelight from the table cast a wonderful luminous glow on her beaming face.

"I don't know when you've looked more beautiful," Gunther admitted sincerely. "There's something I want to ask you, Topaz."

"What's that?" She noticed the serious tone in his voice and focused her attention back on him.

How do I say it? he asked himself quickly. I had this all planned and now I don't know what to say. "Will you marry me?" He spoke barely above a whisper.

"I'm sorry, Gunther, what did you say?" Topaz was watching the roof again as it slowly closed.

"I said, will you marry me?" he repeated a little louder.

Gunther watched her face register the shock from his question as she sat there stunned.

"You want me to marry you?" she repeated. Her mind raced with thoughts of Germain and Chris. I'll be closing the door on that part of my life forever.

"This is for you," he continued, speaking ever so softly. He opened a red velvet jewelry case and exposed a magnificent eight-karat diamond ring, brilliantly cut, that reflected the rays of flickering candlelight. Topaz stared at the ring in disbelief. Is this really happening to me? I'm not sure about this . . .

Her mind raced like crazy. She recalled the afternoon in Malibu when Nina and Jamil called him a nerd at the beach. But that seemed like eons ago after their whirlwind, crazy weekend in France. She took the magnificent diamond ring out of its case and thought about the one-karat diamond ring in her jewelry box in L.A. that Germain had given her on their wedding day. That was a Cracker Jack ring compared to this Rock of Gibraltar. Still marriage is more than just a ring . . .

She's going to say no, he realized. She's taking too long. I thought after all the wining and dining she'd just fly into my arms. Topaz looked into Gunther's face. His eyes were patient and vulnerable as he waited for her response. She looked at the ring. Gunther's given me the life I've always dreamed of. He understands me and he's an entertainer, too. This is your life now, she reminded herself.

"Yes, Gunther Lawrence." She gave him a dazzling smile and handed him the ring so he could place it on her finger. "I'd love to be your wife."

The wedding was scheduled one week before Christmas. In between listening to songs for her next album and finishing up the last of her tour dates, Topaz compiled a guest list of the who's who in Hollywood and sent out the invitations. The press had a field day. News of the Black-Lawrence engagement was the talk of the town and everyone wanted interviews. Topaz's publicity people were ecstatic because the news of her marrying Hollywood's hottest young black director put the famous couple on the cover of *People*, *Ebony*, *Essence*, and *Jet*, and there were feature layouts in countless other magazines. *Entertainment Tonight* heralded the news as well.

"Who's that man with my mother?" Chris demanded while he and Germain were watching television one night.

"That's your mother's fiancé," Germain replied quietly.

"What's a fancy, Daddy?"

"A fiancé," Germain corrected. "That's the man your mother is going to marry."

"How can she marry him and marry us, too?"

"She can't, baby. She's not going to marry us. She's marrying him," Germain tried to explain calmly. But he was angry. *She could have at least told me she was going to do this so my son wouldn't have to learn about his mother's life from the television. And she could have told me she didn't want me, either. Heifer . . .*

"My mother is making me very sad." Chris climbed into Germain's lap. "How come she doesn't want us?"

"I don't know, Chris." Germain stroked his son's golden curls. "Maybe because we're not famous enough. She's making me very sad, too." He sighed. *I thought we'd be a family again after last Thanksgiving.* Germain glanced at the letter he had received only days ago from the world's foremost school of cosmetic surgery in Stockholm, Sweden. He had been accepted into the program last year but had declined the invitation because he had thought he would be getting back together with Topaz. Now the school was writing again to inform him of an available space in the fall class. This school was much more advanced than those in the U.S. *Chances like this don't come around often,* he told himself, looking at the letter. *I thought she would have grown up and gotten this show business thing out of her system by now, but she's just getting in deeper. Well, she made her choice and she's doing exactly what she wants, so now it's about time for me to do what I want to do.* He looked at the little boy sleeping in his arms and carried him into his room and put him in bed.

"We're going to Sweden, Chris." Germain spoke softly to his sleeping son. "We'll have ourselves a new life over there."

■

In a two-bedroom suite overlooking the ocean at the Ritz Carlton in Laguna Niguel, Topaz sat in front of the dressing table. She was wearing a white silk teddy. Her face wore a slightly dazed expression. All around her people scurried back and forth making last-minute preparations for her wedding, which was scheduled to take place in less than an hour.

"Baby, I don't like the way that makeup artist did your face," her mother complained. She rubbed a finger along Topaz's cheekbone to blend the blush into her daughter's creamy butterscotch skin.

"Mother, would you leave my face alone?" Topaz snapped. "That makeup artist gets paid lots of money to do makeup for the stars." A hairdresser fussed over her hair with a curling iron and hair spray.

"I was only trying to help." Lisa's feelings were obviously hurt.

Topaz glanced at her mother and her sisters, Lena and Lynn, and noticed how beautiful they were. Cinnamon, copper, and caramel women with runway model looks. My mother is the most elegant of them all. She watched the woman pluck off a bunch of grapes from a large tray of fruit and eat them ever so daintily.

Topaz could see her cousin Kim glaring at her in the mirror and Nina, her maid of honor, who was too gorgeous in the straight black gown that clung gently to her body, trying to be the gracious hostess. This place is a madhouse, she realized as her little cousin Amber, her flower girl, socked her older brother, Anthony, in the mouth. Topaz giggled softly. Aunty Lynn said she has my temperament. She admired the pretty cocoa-brown child with Shirley Temple curls wearing a black-and-pink taffeta dress.

It wasn't this crazy when I married Germain . . . Germain . . . I didn't even tell him I was getting married. Grand Mama said he and Chris had left Baltimore without a word and no one knows how to get in touch with them.

When is this heifer going to be finished with my hair? The heat from the curling iron was a little too close to her ear. If she burns me, I swear I'll kick her butt. Keisha was here last time. She was my maid of honor. I hear she has a little girl now, Kendra, and she didn't even bother to tell me. That cow . . .

"Honey, don't you think it's time you put on your dress now?

Mother will help you. I just know you're going to look so gorgeous."

"Ouch," Topaz yelled as the curling iron touched the tip of her ear. "That's it," she screamed. "Everybody out."

"What?" Lisa couldn't believe what she was hearing.

"I said everybody get out," Topaz yelled at the top of her lungs, enunciating every word. "Go downstairs, go somewhere . . . just get out." She watched her family file out of the room in silence, surprised by her rude outburst. "Nina, not you. I need you to stay, please," she pleaded.

"What's wrong, Topaz?" Nina stroked a lock of her cousin's blond hair. "Got the prewedding jitters?"

"Yes." Topaz played with her hair in the mirror. "Could you find my purse, please?"

"Sure, babe." Nina searched around the suite until she found the Chanel backpack and handed it to Topaz. "Whatcha looking for?" She watched Topaz feel around in the backpack.

"This." Topaz exposed a vial of cocaine in her palm.

"Girl, on your wedding day?" Nina was shocked.

"Why not on my wedding day?" Topaz dumped the powder out on the marble countertop. "I've got to make it down that aisle somehow." She sniffed line after line through a dollar bill.

"Girl, if you keep going at that stuff like that, you'll be flying down that aisle." Nina laughed.

"Come on, Nina, this is the happiest day of my life. Let's party." She handed her the dollar bill.

"Look, Topaz, if you don't want to marry the nerd, I'll go down there and call it off right now." Nina wiped the smile from her face and tried to be serious.

"You fool." Topaz laughed and gave Nina a hug. "Stop calling him a nerd. I love Gunther. It's just not like it was with Germain and I've got to accept that."

"How can it be like Germain? He's not Germain."

Several minutes later they both stood admiring Topaz in the one-hundred-thousand-dollar antique lace wedding gown that had been designed for her by Bill Whitten.

"You look bee-yew-tah-full." Nina arranged the antique lace veil with its diamond tiara over her face. "Just like a storybook princess."

"Thanks, babe."

"I can't wait until me and Jamil get married now."

"Are you and Jamil getting married?" Topaz asked excitedly.

"We talk about it sometimes. But that's all it is right now, talk."

"Well it's time to stroll, girl. Let's go."

Topaz felt her mind racing as she repeated her vows. Gunther looks so handsome in his suit. Why do I keep thinking about Germain? she asked herself as the minister pronounced them man and wife.

I did it, Gunther wanted to shout from the rafters. I actually got her to marry me. I knew I could do it. Well, one more goal achieved, he thought as he smiled for the camera. Now I can get on with the rest of my life.

Ebony proclaimed the Black-Lawrence wedding the media and social event of the year. Lots of photos of Hollywood's finest chocolate stars were included in the spread. "The guests feasted on lobster and filet mignon, and Cristal flowed endlessly. The newlyweds honeymooned on a private chartered yacht in the South of France," the magazine reported.

THIRTY

SEAN STARED in disbelief at the huge bowl of Cajun jambalaya pasta that the waitress had just set in front of him. "That's a lot of food," he exclaimed. The dish practically overflowed with chicken, shrimp, and assorted pastas, all tossed in a spicy sauce. "But it smells so good. Are you sure you won't have some?" he pleaded, looking into Jade's smiling almond eyes.

"Well, maybe just a little." She laughed. "It is a lot of food, but I'm sure a big guy like you can handle this little dish of pasta." She smiled as she spooned noodles and shrimp onto her plate.

"Is that all you're eating?" He nodded at the huge Caesar salad in front of her. Those eyes . . . he looked away so he wouldn't stare. She's beautiful. Sean found himself drawn to her eyes again as they began to eat.

"Excuse me." Sean dropped his fork into his plate. "I have to ask you something and please don't think I'm rude. Are you Asian or something? Because you have the most incredible eyes and you just look, I don't know. You're very pretty."

She blushed before she burst into laughter. "My father's Japanese and my mother's Jamaican."

"That's an interesting combination. How did they hook up?"

"Well, they're both artists and they fell in love while they were attending school at the California Institute of the Arts. My father's a graphic artist. He has a design firm and my mother was a dancer. She performed with the Dance Theater of Harlem for a while, but now she just teaches."

"So you got the painting from your father?"

"Yes." She nodded, chewing a mouthful of romaine lettuce. "I danced, too, until my painting really took off."

"I think your work is fantastic. You have such a wonderful use of color."

"Thank you. I sure hope you like my work, since you bought three of my paintings." She laughed. "My parents exposed me to the arts when I was a child. I lived in Japan when I was a little girl. My father started his business there and now he has branches in San Francisco and New York."

"Wow. So you speak Japanese, too?"

"Yes." Jade rattled off a phrase in fluent Japanese.

"What did you just say?"

"I said enough about me. What do you do?" She focused her fascinating eyes on Sean, as he burst into laughter.

"I play basketball." This is so great, he wanted to scream. She doesn't know who I am.

"You play basketball? What's so funny about that?"

Sean grinned and shook his head. "I play for the Concordes."

"Oh?" She was obviously confused. "I still don't see why that's so funny."

"I love it." Sean laughed. "Now I don't want you to take what I'm going to say the wrong way, but you don't know who I am?"

"Should I?" she asked politely.

"No. There's no reason why you should. It's just that most people do. I'm Sylk Ross."

"Sylk Ross? Oh, my goodness!" She clasped her hands to her face. "How could I not know who you are. Your face is everywhere. Oh, I'm so embarrassed. You told me your name was Sean," she scolded softly.

Sean was still laughing. "Sean is my name. But only my family and friends call me Sean, everyone else calls me Sylk." He was enjoying the surprised look on her pretty face.

"So, I'm a friend?" Jade asked coyly.

"I sure hope you will be."

She smiled in response. Good. I like that.

The huge slice of cheesecake topped with large strawberries and sauce caught Sean's eye. "Hey, that looks good. I see why they call this place the Cheesecake Factory." He picked up a fork. "May I?"

"I'd be afraid to tell you no, the way you're holding that fork." Jade laughed, and pushed the plate towards him. "I noticed you ate all that pasta, too. You like to eat."

"You found me out," he confessed, with a smile. "I love to eat."

"Me, too. I always come here whenever I'm in Los Angeles."

"You're not from here?"

"No. I work out of a small gallery in Atlanta. When I graduated from Spelman, I just stayed in Atlanta."

"So how'd you like going to an all-black school?"

"I loved it. Especially after two years of college in Japan. I loved that, too, but I was ready to come back to the States."

"Wow, you went to school in Japan! That's amazing. I thought about going to a black college but I went to U Penn so I could be near my family in Philly."

"You went to U Penn?" Now it was her turn to be shocked.

"Yes. Is there something wrong with that?"

"No, I just didn't think basketball players went to U Penn, just brains. Do you know how hard it is to get in there?"

"Are you saying that basketball players can't be brains?" Sean asked with a boyish grin.

"Well, I, you know what I mean. Jocks aren't known for their brains, they're athletes."

"Lord, help us Jesus," Sean mumbled teasingly. "The girl just called me stupid."

"No, I didn't. Sean! Stop putting words in my mouth," she chided.

"I love it." Sean laughed. "I love it. Ms. Kimura, I'm going to destroy every stereotype you ever had about jocks."

"Oh?" She sipped a glass of ice water. "What did you study?"

"Finance, and I graduated with a 3.5 G.P.A."

"Dang . . ." She pretended to gather her things. "You just broke my face. I'm going home."

"Oh, no, please don't. I've been having so much fun talking with you."

"I've really enjoyed talking with you, too." She smiled shyly.

They pulled up in front of the Bel Age Hotel where she was staying. "So when do I see you again, Ms. Kimura? Am I going to have to come all the way to Atlanta?"

"I won't be in Atlanta for a while. From here I'm going up to San Francisco to spend a few days with my parents, then to New

York, Paris, Tokyo, and the Virgin Islands. My work is being shown around the world as part of this traveling exhibit, and where it goes I have to go."

"So how long will all that take?"

"I'll have some time off in about six weeks, and I was going to treat myself to a little vacation. I could spend some time in Los Angeles."

"That would be great. I have a house in Santa Barbara. You could come and hang out or I could get you a room at the Biltmore. It's up to you."

"All right," she agreed softly. "We'll see."

"Here." He handed her a piece of paper. "These are my numbers at the house. You can call me collect whenever you like from anywhere. I'd call you, but you'll be traveling," he finished, looking like a little boy.

"I'll fax you an itinerary." She smiled, not wanting to get out of the car.

"Good night, Jade Kimura." He leaned over and kissed her on the cheek before he got out of the car to open the door for her. Sean watched her walk into the hotel before he drove off.

"Yes," he exclaimed loudly. He cranked the volume on a CD of Motown oldies but goodies and sang along to "My Girl" at the top of his lungs, inserting Jade's name as often as he could. This was a great day, he reflected. I went to church, met the most incredible woman, and got some fine paintings . . .

"Wait, Mommy told me to buy art. That's deep." He picked up the car phone and dialed his parents' number and glanced at the clock. It's one in the morning. Oh, well . . .

"Hello," his father answered sleepily.

"Hi, Daddy. I need to speak to Mommy," Sean demanded.

"Is something wrong, son?"

"Oh, no, I just need to speak to Mommy."

"Hi, baby," his mother answered yawning.

"Mommy, guess what? Remember you told me right before you got on the plane to go buy some art for the walls?"

"Yes."

"Well, I did."

"Sean, did you call here at one in the morning to tell me you bought some paintings?" she scolded. She was wide awake now.

"No, Mommy." He laughed. "Well, yes. I bought the paintings and I met the most incredible young lady."

"You met somebody?" His mother's voice brightened.

"Yes. She's an artist. She painted the pictures I bought. And she's gorgeous. She's Jamaican and Japanese."

"Really?"

"And, Mommy, she didn't know who I was," he finished happily.

"Kenny, Sean's getting married," he heard his mother tell his father.

"Mommy," he protested. "I didn't say all that. I just met her today."

"What's her name, baby?"

"Jade," he replied softly. "Jade Kimura."

Sean and Jade talked on the phone several times a week while she was traveling. On other days she sent him cards that she had made herself with poems she'd written and embellished with Japanese watercolor sketches. Sometimes he'd find himself waiting for her calls or checking the mailbox for one of her cards. It scared him, the way he found himself needing her and the way her love gently pulled on his heartstrings.

It seemed like eons before she returned to L.A. Sean thought he would explode in a million pieces before the Virgin Airlines flight from Paris landed and taxied in to the jet way. She's here, he wanted to shout from the rafters. She's actually here. He clutched the huge bouquet of long-stem white roses behind his back as passengers began to pour into the terminal.

There she is. Her black hair was braided and the shiny black bangs cut above her eyebrows only enhanced her almond eyes. The black catsuit she wore nicely enhanced her dancer's body and was set off with a cranberry red jacket and boots. When she finally saw Sean her eyes and mouth crinkled up into a radiant smile.

"Hi, Sean." She flew into his arms.

"Hi, Jade." Sean kissed her gently on the lips. "These are for you." He handed her the bouquet of roses.

"Thanks, Sean." She smiled into his eyes. "I was wondering how long it would take you to do that." She buried her face in the roses and sniffed.

"Do what?"

"Kiss me." She smiled.

"I'll do it again if you like." He grinned, pausing to kiss her in the airport, not minding at all if anybody was watching.

They retrieved her luggage and chatted nonstop all the way to the Santa Barbara Biltmore, where they checked her into her room before continuing on to Sean's house.

"You live here?" Jade squealed as they waited for the gate to open so they could drive onto the estate.

"Yes." Sean laughed, enjoying the pleased look on her face.

"Oh, this is too serious." She jumped out of the Range Rover before he had a chance to open the door. "You have the ocean in your backyard. Oh, I'm going to have to paint a picture of this."

"A picture of what?" he asked excitedly as he escorted her into the house.

"A picture of your house, the ocean . . . you'll see. Oh, I like where you hung these." She pointed to the paintings hanging in the living room. "You need something over the fireplace."

"I do?" Sean loved the way she seemed to fit right into his space.

"Yes. I'll paint the picture large enough so you can hang it there." She pointed to the empty space over the fireplace in the living room. "Oh, I'm sorry." She clasped a hand to her face. "I'm telling you where to hang stuff. I'll just paint it and you can hang it wherever you like."

"Jade Kimura, you can hang your pictures wherever you like in this house." Sean took her into his arms so he could kiss her again.

"All right," she agreed happily.

She stayed for ten days. Sean left her the Range Rover at night so she could drive over early in the morning from the hotel. He'd awaken and find her painting at her easel, which she'd set up in the front yard or in the back, on a grassy knoll that overlooked the beach. She also made his breakfast herself every morning. She'd prepare scrambled eggs, bacon, fried potatoes, homemade waffles, French toast, and grits, and plenty of fresh fruit and juices.

"You're going to spoil me, Jade." He carried his food outside on a tray so he could watch her paint.

"Good. You're a sweetie and you deserve spoiling."

They'd sit there for hours enjoying the beach and talking or Sean would read a book and just quietly watch her paint.

"I'm going to miss you," he whispered in her ear at the airport.

"Not even half as much as I'll miss you," she whispered back as she kissed him good-bye.

It was mid-June and the basketball season had ended. The playoffs were over.

"Sylk, the Concordes are waiting for your decision," George barked into the phone. "They want to know if you're coming back. Look, I know you've got yourself all set up in that house in Santa Barbara, so if you want I can talk to the Lakers. They still want you badly."

"I haven't made my mind up yet, George."

"You haven't? How's the knee?"

"My knee's fine. Sean rubbed his knee as he spoke. "I've been working with a personal trainer since March and I run five miles every day on the beach."

"Well, you sound like you're in excellent shape, so what's the problem?"

"There's no problem, George." Sean smiled at the magnificent painting of the house and the beach that Jade had painted for the living room. "I've just been having such a good time that I don't know if I want all that stress back in my life."

"Are you thinking about retiring, Sylk?"

"Yes." He had finally said it.

"You've had some great times in basketball. Can you honestly put all of that aside? You're twenty-nine, but you still have several good years left."

"I know, George. I'd be throwing in the towel a little early. But let me pray about it and I'll get back to you." Sean said good-bye to George, then dialed his father at the church. "You got a few minutes to talk, Daddy?"

"Sure, son, what's up?"

"George called. They want to know what I'm doing. He even mentioned working out something with the Lakers. I think I'm ready to throw the towel in. What do you think?"

"I don't know, Sean. What do you think?"

"Well, I'm happy, Daddy. I'm really enjoying the house in California. I'm really at peace and I'm content. I have a wonderful lady in my life."

"She is wonderful, Sean. Your mother hasn't stopped talking about her since you guys were here for Easter. Have you been thinking about marriage?"

"Yeah, Daddy. Especially with Jade living in Atlanta. Long-distance relationships are hard."

"Well, you're financially set for the rest of your life, so it's not like you have to play anymore. You've handled your money well."

"I know, Daddy, but I'm just wondering if I'd miss basketball once I give it up for good. Even though I'm not playing right now, that's my choice."

"You're going to have to trust the Lord for the answer, Sean. Wait on Him and He'll direct your path."

"I know, Daddy. Thanks for listening."

Sean sat outside on the deck watching the tide, which was still way out from the shore. I'm happy for the first time in months, he realized. But it wasn't basketball that made me happy, though, it was love. Sure, I have this fine house, nice things, but these things didn't make me happy. To be honest, I was a little lonely when I first moved here.

What's made me truly happy is my relationship with You, Lord, and Jade. Look at my family, Mommy and Daddy, Kirk and Kyle. We've always been rich, rich in our love for God and each other. I've always been blessed, even before basketball. I know the answer . . .

Sean walked into the living room to phone George. He had made up his mind.

THIRTY-ONE

TOPAZ STOPPED her black Range Rover in front of a massive black-gated estate and looked at Nina to see her reaction. There was no sight of a house. Even peering through the gate revealed only a gleaming white driveway and sprawling grounds with grass that was green and thick like plush carpeting.

"Where are we?" Nina squinted as she looked out of the car window at the gate.

"In Bel Air, on Somera Road," Topaz informed her. "Remember the entertainer's paradise listing? Seven bedrooms, seven baths?"

"I don't know." Nina frowned.

"Nina."

"You guys have looked at a zillion houses. How do you expect me to remember them all?" she snapped.

"Dang, girl. Don't be so touchy. Jamil been holding out on you or something? Because you sure are cranky these days." Topaz laughed.

"Everything's fine with Jamil, I'm just tired, that's all." Nina sighed. "Between being in the studio with you and then with Jamil, I'm going crazy. Come on, Fresh Princess of Bel Air, let's check out your crib."

"Okay. I can't wait for you to see everything. Of course, you know Gunther and I are doing major renovations."

"Of course, I know you and Gunther are doing major renovations," Nina mimicked. "A plain old mansion in Bel Air isn't good enough for the Lawrences. Knowing you guys, it'll probably have a landing strip in the backyard for your Learjet and an eighteen-hole golf course for that nerdy husband of yours."

Topaz burst into laughter as she pointed the clicker at the gate and watched it slowly roll back. "Drum rolls, drum rolls," she demanded as she slowly drove up the white granite driveway, which was lined with lofty shrubbery.

A flat, wide staircase carved out of stone led up to a huge gleaming white stucco house with a red tile roof. The house sat at the top of the hill proudly screaming "I'm all that," while sprawling grounds trimmed with a medley of colorful flowers and carved shrubbery rolled across the estate. Eucalyptus and palm trees stood at attention on all sides of the two-story Spanish-influenced house. The driveway ran parallel to a tennis court and smack into a basketball court and a six-car garage. A dampened redbrick path wound its way through freshly watered flower gardens and parted charmingly before a fountain and goldfish pond.

It seemed like miles to the back of the house, where another staircase, also carved out of stone, led down to a sparkling black rock pool surrounded by tropical foliage. A small footbridge led past a gushing waterfall that cascaded down three tiers of smaller pools into one big one.

Topaz stopped the Range Rover by the side of a veranda, cut the motor off, and jumped down out of the car. "Come on. I'll show you inside."

"This is nice, cuz. Is it really yours?"

"Yes," Topaz squealed, brandishing a fancy gold key on a Chanel keyholder. "I even bought a new keychain for it."

They followed a path to a redbrick porch framed with white columns and arches that faced the pool. "We'll have breakfast out here sometimes. Or a romantic candlelight dinner."

"With Gunther, please . . ."

Topaz laughed at Nina's expression and walked into a huge kitchen that was tiled in black and white squares of marble. The shiny black appliances and black granite countertops glistened. Gleaming mahogany cabinets matched the hardwood floors in the family room and breakfast nook.

"The kitchen."

"Oh, like you're going to magically turn into Suzy Homemaker now that you have this fabulous kitchen. Does your new husband know that you burn water?"

"We're going to have a full-time chef, smarty pants. Gunther already hired him. He cooks Indian, Szechwan, Thai, and a few Italian dishes."

"No soul food?"

"No. Gunther hates soul food. We're also hiring two live-in maids and a houseboy, and we're going to have guards on the premises twenty-four hours a day. We're installing a security room that will have monitors showing all key points on the grounds and a guard who'll just sit in there and watch the monitors and the alarm panel. The office will be in there." Topaz pointed to a large room down a hall at the end of the house.

The kitchen was actually the dividing point between the east and west wings of the house. The living room, dining room, library, and screening room were in the east wing with the master bedroom suite and two spare bedrooms upstairs. The west wing contained the maids' quarters, the office, and four additional bedrooms. Gleaming mahogany floors covered the entire house.

"So what renovations are you going to make?" Nina asked after the grand tour.

"We're going to add an additional bath in the master bedroom so we can have his-and-her baths. The new one will be mine. It's going to be so fine . . . pink marble, the actual stone, not tile. The sinks are handpainted with swans and lilies, and the faucets are handpainted, too, and trimmed in gold. The toilet is carved out of marble with a gold lid. The lid is real ornate. It looks like a giant seashell." Topaz's amber eyes sparkled with excitement.

"A gold toilet seat in your own bathroom? Sounds crazy cool, cuz." Nina laughed. "I just have one problem."

"What's that?" Topaz opened and closed door after door.

"I just have a hard time putting that nerdy Gunther into the scene. He ruins the whole thing."

"Nina! Stop talking about Gunther." Topaz laughed.

"You're really in love with him, aren't you?" Nina looked at Topaz as though she were seeing her for the very first time.

"Yes. He's my husband. Gunther's very lovable in his own special way." She rubbed at a spot on the black marble kitchen counter.

"Hmmm." Nina grunted. "You really love him and all this time I thought you were hanging out with him because he does nice things for you."

"My point exactly. How could you not love someone who does nice things for you. I'm adding a recording studio under the house. A gym and sauna in the pool house, and . . . come with me." Topaz led Nina to the front of the house into a vestibule with a towering domed ceiling. "We're going to take out all these walls and the ceiling of this room and replace them with glass and make this an atrium. We're putting in a black marble floor and a waterfall that will run into a little flowing stream with exotic Japanese fish and lots of tropical plants like a minijungle."

"A jungle in the house? Now that I have to see." Nina studied the white walls and columns in the entryway. "Maybe you guys could even play sound effects through the intercom system," she grinned impishly.

"White pinewood floors," Gunther instructed Beth. "And get some pine furniture with teal green, coral, and mauve cushions. I want a relaxed environment . . . you know, that Southwestern look."

Beth nodded as she busily scribbled notes on a Gunfire Films memo pad. Gunther and Beth were inspecting the bungalow that would house Gunfire Films now that Gunther had signed a three-picture production deal with Majestic Entertainment. In addition to Gunther's office and private bath there were two additional offices, a common bathroom, a conference room, and a kitchen complete with dishwasher.

"Leave me," Gunther growled, waving Beth out of the office. "But I want to see some samples of the upholstery fabric before you make any final decisions on anything," he yelled after her. He closed the door to his office behind Beth before he went into his private bath and carefully closed the door.

Gunther poured the contents of an entire vial of cocaine onto the counter by the sink and sniffed the powder in a matter of minutes. He ran his moistened fingertip along the counter for any missed particles. It takes more of this stuff to get me going now than it did at first. But that's okay. My boy Reno keeps me supplied and there's plenty more where that came from. He stuck the empty bottle in his pants pocket and returned to his office. A folding chair was set up beside a card table that held his laptop computer, his briefcase, and his yellow legal pad of carefully written notes.

"Beth, have them get the phones on, now," he yelled as he

flipped open his cellular phone and dialed Reno's number. "Reno, what's happening, dude?" Gunther grinned into the phone. "I've got great news."

"What's up, Spielberg?"

"I'm in Gunfire's new bungalow that was included in the deal. Is there anything you'd like in particular for your office?"

"Naw, dude, hook it up any way you like. Just get me a big television and a VCR so I can kick back whenever I come by." Reno laughed.

"Word, dude. We need to celebrate. Let's go down to the Caymans for the weekend and play some golf while the ladies shop and hang out at the beach."

"That sounds like a party. Let's go down Thursday night."

"That'll work." Gunther pulled up his schedule on the computer screen while he talked. "I need to have a drink with a man about some offshore investments and that'll give them some time to get things in order around here." He frowned at the furnitureless office. "It'll also be a great time for Topaz and Gloria to spend some time together."

"I'll hook up the jet and you take care of the hotel, Spielberg."

"Word, dude." Gunther sighed happily and hung up the phone. This will be great. Topaz needs some new friends besides that stuck-up cousin of hers. She acts like she's the star. I don't care if they are related, Topaz doesn't need to be seen hanging around the help.

A few hours later, Gunther pulled his 735i next to the Range Rover at the house in Bel Air. Topaz and Nina were sitting on the veranda eating Japanese food with chopsticks.

"Hi, baby," Topaz cooed. "Have some?" She held a piece of shrimp tempura between her chopsticks up to his lips.

"Hi, darling. We're traveling with friends to the Caymans on Thursday," he informed her, crunching the shrimp hungrily.

"The Cayman Islands? You and Jamil want to come, too?" Topaz suggested to Nina with a mischievous grin.

"Darling, I've already made plans for us with another couple," Gunther protested, glaring at Nina.

"Who?"

"My business partner, Reno, and Gloria," he replied quickly.

"I don't know those people and you know how I hate to be around people I don't know, so Nina has to come." She flipped her hair and picked up a California roll and dunked it in a dish of soy sauce. "Besides, Nina worked very hard on the tour, and now I'm going to have her oversee the renovations of the house. She deserves a little R and R before she gets started."

"All right," Gunther agreed reluctantly. "Just make sure that you two include Gloria and that she has a good time with you."

They arrived on a chartered private jet Thursday night when it was too late to see anything. Topaz could feel the balminess of the sea on her skin as a gentle wind tossed her hair and whispered through the lofty palm trees at Owen Roberts Airport.

Even though it was night, she put on a pair of Chanel sunglasses so she wouldn't have to deal with Gloria staring at her any longer. She grabbed Nina by the arm and whispered loudly in her ear.

"I can't believe she kept watching me for the entire flight. Every time I glanced up she was staring at me, Nina. Why did Gunther have to bring them?"

"I know. I don't like them," Nina whispered back. "Jamil said Reno is a drug dealer."

"A drug dealer?" Topaz giggled. "That's Gunther's business partner. He's not a drug dealer. Jamil." She beckoned him. Jamil smirked, almost laughed, as he strolled not too far away from the girls, heading for the limousine. "You think Reno is a drug dealer?" Topaz was amused.

"Of course. Look at him, can't you tell?" He laughed.

"No," the girls replied simultaneously.

"That's because y'all are a couple of Valley Girls who don't know nothin' about the hood. He's an O.G. from way back. I bet he's smoked plenty of brothers in his lifetime."

"Get outta here." Topaz wondered if she should believe Jamil's analysis of Reno.

"Where's the limousine?" she heard Gunther scream. She looked up to see him ranting at an attendant in the airport.

"I don't know what limousine you're referring to, sir," the uniformed attendant replied politely. "Shall I hire a taxi?"

"A taxi? A taxi?" Gunther screamed. The veins and blood

vessels bulged in his head. "I don't ride in taxis. Do you know who I am?"

"Darling, calm down, please," Topaz pleaded. "And let Nina take care of this. Nina, could you find out what's happening with our transportation before Gunther blows a gasket?"

"Sure." Nina stifled a grin. She spoke with the attendant briefly and handed him five American dollars. "We're going to take a shuttle to the Hyatt Regency. It should be here any minute."

"A shuttle?" Gunther screamed. "I don't take shuttles."

"You will tonight if you want to get to the hotel," Nina said, with a straight face. Gunther opened his mouth to speak and closed it as Reno howled with laughter.

"Baby girl told you, Spielberg, didn't she? That's the first time I ever saw him speechless. You go, girl." Reno continued laughing while the shuttle driver piled their luggage in the shuttle.

"I told you not to bring her," Gunther whispered in Topaz's ear through gritted teeth. "She's ruining everything."

"And I told you I don't like being around people I don't know." Topaz glared back. "That Gloria person stared at me all the way down here on the plane. So don't you say one word about Nina."

It was a silent party that checked into the Hyatt Regency. Topaz was so tired she took very little notice of the penthouse suite with its marble entrance and oversized marble tub. Or the French doors that looked out over the midnight blue swirling mass of water that was the Caribbean Sea.

She opened the doors and a cool tranquil breeze zapped the last bit of her energy as she climbed into bed. She could hear Gunther in the bathroom snorting cocaine. He's going to come in here and want me to give him some and I don't feel like being bothered, she thought, before she fell asleep.

A sea breeze awakened Topaz. The room was already flooded with sunlight and she opened her eyes to see cool aquamarine blue walls and vases of white fresh-cut tropical flowers.

"Gunther," she called softly. She tiptoed to the bathroom, wondering if he had overdosed on cocaine last night, but he wasn't there. She tiptoed into the living room and found a large pitcher of fresh-squeezed orange juice, fresh fruit, and a plate of croissants. Next to the plate a note scribbled in Gunther's sprawling handwriting informed her that he had gone to play golf. He had also left her five hundred dollars in Cayman money in case she wanted to go shopping. She bit off a big chunk of the flaky, buttery roll as the telephone rang.

"Let's order room service," Nina suggested. "Jamil went to play golf with Reno and Gunther."

"Golf? Does Jamil know how to play?"

"Nope. He said O.G. was going to teach him." Nina laughed. "Those guys were down at the buffet and on their way by seven this morning. He left me money for shopping, too."

"Five hundred Cayman dollars?" Topaz giggled.

"Yes," she laughed. "How did you know?"

"Gunther left me the same thing."

"Men." Nina laughed.

"Where they at anyway?"

"On the golf course."

"Word." Topaz laughed.

"I wonder what that Gloria person is doing." Topaz and Nina sat on the terrace in her suite overlooking the ocean. The girls watched a waiter serve conch fritters, scrambled eggs, bacon, Belgian waffles, and toast on fine china.

"Maybe we should have invited her to have breakfast with us." Nina swirled a bit of her waffle through strawberry syrup and whipped cream.

"No. You can see if she wants to go shopping, but I don't want to see her beady black eyes until then."

"There's a Jeep for us downstairs," Nina informed Topaz on the way down to the lobby.

"Great. You drive and the gangster lady can sit in the back." Gloria, clad in cut-off jeans and an orange bikini, was waiting for them in the lobby when they arrived downstairs. Her jet black hair was shining and wet, as though she had just been swimming.

"The beach is dope." Gloria followed them out of the hotel over to the cherry red Wrangler Jeep in the parking lot. "I had breakfast out there."

"Nina, what kind of shops did you say were on the island?" Topaz asked sweetly, ignoring Gloria and her comments about the beach.

"Well, Princess, there are some jewelry stores that sell black coral, which is supposedly to die for. And then there are rings and things made out of coins found in the sea from sunken treasure chests. Some artwork that might be nice to look at for the mansion, and clothes," Nina reported efficiently.

"Skip the artwork, let's check out the jewelry and the clothes," Topaz commanded.

"You down, Gloria?" Nina questioned in her streetwise voice as she pulled out on the road.

"Sure," Gloria replied flatly.

"Nina, you're driving on the wrong side of the road," Topaz screamed as an oncoming vehicle swerved to avoid hitting them.

"I am not." With that she stuck a Salt-N-Pepa cassette in the tape deck.

"You are if you're going to drive in the Caribbean." Topaz screamed with laughter over the music. She heard Gloria laughing softly in the back.

"All right, all right," Nina laughed.

They drove into town and scoured the shops, purchasing jewelry, clothing, and souvenirs.

"I'm hungry," Topaz said after several hours of shopping. "Let's eat."

"Yeah, let's eat in town," Gloria suggested.

"No. Let's go back to the hotel and eat at the beach and get ripped," Topaz countered.

"Cool," Nina agreed. "Let's go."

"I'm going to stay in town a little while longer and eat here," Gloria decided. "You two go on back."

"Ask her how she's going to get back." Topaz spoke to Nina instead of Gloria.

"I'll take a taxi," Gloria informed them coolly.

"Are you going to be okay?" Nina asked out of concern.

"Come on, Nina, let's go," Topaz urged. "She'll be fine."

The girls dropped off their purchases in the hotel room and changed into their suits and hit the beachfront cafe.

"Bring us two of those tropical rum punches," Nina demanded as soon as the waiter approached the table. "And have two more waiting in the wings."

They chose the buffet featuring turtle soup, fried plantain, oxtail stew, black-peppercorn fettuccine with conch in clam sauce, soft-shell crab, baked grouper with onions, peppers, and tomatoes, fresh salads, and desserts.

"Turtle soup?" Topaz read, wrinkling her nose. "I don't think so."

"I'm going to try it." Nina nodded for the attendant to dish her up a bowl.

"Ugh." Topaz made a face at the bowl of soup when they were back at the table. "I don't hang out with people who eat turtle soup."

"Don't be so close-minded," Nina scolded. She sipped a spoonful of the savory broth. "You should try it. It's good."

"Nope, that's okay." Topaz slurped pasta with clam sauce. "Now this is good. Did you notice all those banks in town?"

"Yeah. This place is a haven for investment opportunities. People come down here just to set up trusts and companies."

"Really?" Topaz raised an eyebrow of interest as she cut into a piece of key lime pie. "How do you know all this stuff, girl?"

"Because I read. Let's go jet skiing," Nina suggested when they were done eating. She watched the colorful water toys skirt across the sea with an eager fascination. "It looks like so much fun."

"Okay." Topaz tossed aside the copy of *Vibe* she had picked up to read. "I wanted to go jet skiing when I went to Jamaica, but I couldn't because I was pregnant with Chris. Let's go."

Topaz watched the attendant fasten her life vest. "I don't know about this, Nina. Am I going to drown?"

"No, silly." Nina revved the motor on her jet ski. "Let's rock 'n' roll." Nina screamed as she lurched out over the clear emerald green sea. "I can see the bottom," she yelled to Topaz who was skimming the water behind her.

The landscape was a splendid contrast of three colors—emerald water framed by a teal sky and white powdery beaches. It was almost surreal, paradise. The girls screamed with laughter as they skirted up and down Seven Mile Beach for two hours on the jet skis.

"I don't know when I've had this much fun," Topaz declared after it was over.

Nina agreed. "Let's go again tomorrow. Girl, you are so dark. You're as dark as me." Nina laughed. She held her arm next to Topaz's. "You look so gorgeous."

"Am I really your color?" Topaz fished her compact out of a big straw beachbag.

"Yes. And you look fabulous."

"Ooh. I've always wanted to be chocolate. This is great."

When the guys returned from golfing, the six of them had an uncomfortably quiet dinner at a very exquisite restaurant in an old plantation house. Soft piano music tinkled in the background as they sat down to entrees of marinated conch, escargot, Cayman lobster, fondue bourguignonne, and chateaubriand. The meal was served on a veranda that overlooked the Cayman seashore. The water had deepened into royal blue without the sun to illumine it. Topaz looked exquisite in a stark white tank dress and black coral jewelry. The dress set off her tropical tan beautifully and her curly blond tresses sparkled with natural streaks of copper and bronze.

"Why did you stay in the sun so long?" Gunther demanded over dinner.

Topaz could tell he was wired from cocaine and he was already on his fourth gin-and-cranberry-juice cocktail. "What did you say?"

"You're too dark. You're . . . you're black. I married you because you were light. If I wanted a dark girl I would have married your cousin," he finished nastily.

"What?" Topaz let her fork drop into her plate.

"You heard me, you're black."

"Look, you South Central gang-banging lowlife. I'll stay in the sun until I'm black, burnt, and crispy if I want. How dare you?" she yelled and stood up from the table. "Don't you ever speak to me that way again." She tossed her napkin onto her plate and walked towards the lobby until she felt Gunther grab and twist her arm.

"You're making a scene," he whispered through gritted teeth.

"You're hurting me," she squealed, trying to be cool as tears squeezed out of her eyes.

"I'll do more than just that if I want to, ho," he threatened, pushing her into the elevator.

"Ho?" she screamed in the elevator. "Who you callin' a ho, you pitiful example of a man? You wouldn't know a ho if she slapped you in your face, because if you did, you'd know how to get busy and not give me that weak, tired nookie that's totally whacked." Topaz glared at him, her amber eyes blazing with anger. "I have to fake it every time you touch me."

"Witch. I'll kick your butt for that." Gunther slapped her hard across the face and ripped the white tank dress from her body as he pushed her into their penthouse suite.

"Don't you ever touch me again." Topaz was livid. She stood there in her black satin Victoria's Secret bra and panties screaming.

"I'll touch you as much I like, you whore," Gunther yelled. "I own you now." He yanked the necklace from her neck and threw it across the room. "I own you, lock, stock, and barrel, and I'll touch you whenever I like and as much as I like." He pushed her into the bedroom and onto the bed.

He's going to kill me. Topaz was suddenly terrified, and she crawled across the bed to get away from him.

"Don't run from me," he commanded, unzipping his fly.

"No, Gunther, no," she screamed. "Don't do this. You're drunk."

"You're the one who said you had to fake it. I'll bet you scream now, ho."

Gunther raped her over and over until his rage subsided. At last he felt relieved and free from frustration for the first time in his life when he climbed off her. He barely noticed she was crying as he headed for the bathroom for more cocaine.

"I hate you," she whispered when he came back out of the bathroom and sat on the bed.

"Good," he replied flatly. " 'Cause I hate me, too."

When Topaz awakened the next morning, he was gone. She stepped out onto the balcony, which was flooded with sunlight, and gazed at the tranquil turquoise water. Topaz felt nothing whatsoever for the newness of the day.

She found her purse on the floor behind the bed, picked it up, and wandered into the bathroom. Her topaz-and-diamond ring and her eight-karat diamond wedding ring were on the counter. She shoved them off the counter into the trash can.

Topaz found the glass vial in her purse and spilled the white powder onto the sink. She sniffed and sniffed, but it didn't do anything to ease the stab of intense pain that enveloped her insides. When she glanced at the clock and noticed it was almost noon, she picked up the phone.

"Fruit punch," she ordered. "Two of them and a cheeseburger." She let the receiver drop onto the floor. "Forget it. I'm going home." She stepped into her jeans and grabbed her purse.

From a carpeted bluff of green at the twelfth hole, Gunther gazed at the emerald green sea. He could smell the salt air and the tropical flowers in bloom on the hillside and he smiled. It's a wonderful day. He found the appropriate iron and placed a ball on the tee.

"Man, this deal with Majestic is what I've been dreaming of since college," he informed Reno. "We got it made. Oh, and I straightened out things with Topaz about Gloria."

"Great." Reno concentrated on his shot. "You got to know how to talk to a woman, keep 'em in line."

"Word, dude."

Reno hit the ball beautifully. It sailed across the vivid blue sky.

"Yo, dude, I ran out of the white girl. Can you hook me up?"

"Spielberg, did you know you're putting a thousand dollars worth of that stuff up your nose every day now?"

"Really?"

"You got a serious habit, man." For once, he wasn't smiling.

"I've just been under a little stress lately with the details of the production deal and adjusting to the marriage. I'll be okay."

"I understand. Man, that Topaz seems like she can be a trip, but she sure is fine."

"She is, isn't she?" Gunther was proud because Reno thought his wife was fine.

"Speaking of the production deal, I'll have another five million for you on Monday and I'll put another five in your hands a couple of days later."

"Five million?" Gunther laughed. "Reno, I don't need any of your money this time. The studio's going to handle all of that."

"That's all good, man, but I got ten million for you to take care of for me." Reno gathered up his clubs and placed them into the golf cart.

"Reno, the studio's accounting department pays all the bills for the production. I don't have anything to do with that."

They drove off in the golf cart across the sprawling green to the next hole.

"Look, Gunther, just spare me the details and hook it up."

"Look, Reno, you don't understand—"

"No, Gunther, you're the one who doesn't understand," Reno snapped, cutting him off. "I don't care what you do or how you do it, just take care of it."

"But how am I going to explain this to accounting? Reno, I can't do this."

"Oh, yes, you can and you will."

"But how?" Gunther was exasperated.

"I don't know. That's your problem, not mine. I've made quite a big investment in you."

"I paid back your initial investment with interest and fifty-five percent of the profits," Gunther barked back.

"Yo, G, that's all good, but from the way I see things, I haven't even begun to reap my profits. You got a thousand-dollar-a-day drug habit, Junior." Reno found a golf ball and set it on the tee. "You're a genius. You'll figure it out, Spielberg . . . that is, if you want to keep on living."

Gunther felt pain grip his chest as he watched Reno prepare for his shot. He just told me he'd kill me if I don't do what he wants me to do. He watched Reno hit the ball, and it was a beauty, landing within inches of the hole.

"A birdie," Reno shouted. "This must be my lucky day." He grinned like a Cheshire cat. "I'm finally beating Gunther Lawrence at his own game."

THIRTY-TWO

JADE DANCED happily to the steel drumbeat of Bahamian music at the Goombay Summer Festival held on the waterfront in downtown Nassau. She fit right into the colorful exotic climate with its spicy island dishes, funky pulsating rhythms, tranquil waters, and gentle breezes.

The Caribbean exemplifies her most endearing characteristics, Sean realized. He couldn't help but admire the vibrant African print she was wearing against her caramel coloring and black almond eyes. "You should always live here." He laughed.

"You know I'm just an island girl." She laughed, applauding the band.

Keisha looked at Sean and smiled. "You guys look so happy. And you're just about to explode, Sylkman."

"I know." He looked at Jade. "God is too good."

"Isn't He? Sean, I know Topaz was my friend but I'm glad you didn't get involved with her."

"Why?" He watched Jade and Eric dancing.

"She would have broken your heart. Topaz is in love with the father of her baby and she's too stupid to realize it."

"Baby? She has a baby? I never knew that."

"They were married when she was nineteen."

"Married? Get outta here."

"She swore me to secrecy," Keisha continued. "I wanted to tell you. But I knew God was watching out for you and that relationship would eventually fizzle out."

"It sure did, thank God. Wow, she was married . . . Keisha, she never told me. She was a beautiful woman but she wasn't right for me. And she would have never broken my heart," he declared reflectively. "Because I wasn't in love with her. I know that now."

But Jade could, he admitted to himself. Now how did I go there? Sean wondered.

"I'm so glad you guys had a chance to come down to hang out before the wedding," Sean said to Eric, who had joined Keisha.

"Man, I wouldn't have missed your wedding day for anything in the world," Eric smiled.

Sean jumped behind the wheel of the doorless white convertible Jeep and headed towards Cable Beach. The road wrapped around the island, taking them past the placid emerald blue sea with sandy beaches like powdered sugar.

"It's so pretty it takes your breath away," Jade remarked. "I'll have to paint it."

"She can paint anything, man." Sean turned around to look at his friend, who was riding in back with Keisha. "She just looks at it and reproduces it on paper . . . colors, details . . . everything. She's bad."

"My soon-to-be husband is my biggest fan." Jade laughed. "My paintings are all over his house. I've brainwashed him."

"Her paintings are in lots of people's houses. Her schedule is so full that this was the first available opening she had to marry me," Sean teased.

"That's not true." Jade laughed.

"You got the brother waiting, girl." Keisha laughed. "What's your secret?"

"The paintings. He stares at them all the time." The girls laughed as a doorman helped them out of the car. "You see, it worked." Jade planted a kiss on Sean's smiling cheek.

"You better start kissing me," Sean demanded. "Selling all those wolf tickets."

"You know I got it just as bad as you." She giggled. "That's what makes it so much fun."

Later that evening, the entire Ross family, attired in evening finery, gathered to sip fruit punch under the stars in the hotel's Romanesque courtyard. Jade and Sean would be married in the courtyard on Saturday. Water danced and flowed through a fountain while a permanent audience of Greek goddess statues observed the family's laughter and gaiety that peppered the warm September night air.

"I think everyone's here." Sean had taken a quick head count as he initialed the tab for their drinks.

"Unc Sean, Unc Sean." Kyrie squealed delightedly, looking too precious in a colorful island outfit with her hair brushed into a bun.

Sean picked up the little girl. "Hi, baby, you ready to go to dinner?"

"Yes. And I'm going to sit next to you."

"See, the more things change, the more they remain the same. I tell you all the time, E, you basketball stars got it goin' on when it comes to the ladies," Kirk stated with teasing eyes. "Do you hear my daughter?"

"Man, I ain't never had it goin' on like Money," Eric replied, trying hard to be serious. "Did I tell y'all about the time this girl passed out because G came to pick her up for a date?"

"Naw, man." Kyle laughed. "What happened?"

"You guys stop teasing Sean." Keisha laughed.

"See, man, he's even got your woman taking up for him." Kirk laughed.

"That's all in the past. He's getting married now," Keisha admonished with a warning glance at Eric.

"So, if Sean thinks he's going to get special treatment because he's getting married he can forget it." Kirk laughed. "Doggin' Sean is a family ritual, Jade."

"Yeah, and if she don't like it we'll dog her out, too," Kyle added.

"I'm sorry, Jade, but they were already here when I came into the family. I inherited them." Sean laughed.

"That's okay. I can handle them." Jade smiled and made a face at the twins. "I just want to know about this girl who passed out at your feet."

"Don't believe them. My brothers bring out the worst in Eric. He gets around them and starts telling all these fantastic stories about me."

"Well, are they true?" Jade asked.

"Partly." Sean laughed. "But Eric just overexaggerates."

They headed for the cars once everyone finished their drinks, caravanning to Sun And . . . for dinner. Kirk and Karla doubled with Sean and Jade, and Eric, Keisha, and Kyle followed in another Jeep. Sean's father and mother brought up the rear in a BMW with the little girls.

The family walked over a drawbridge to the restaurant where both little girls had to be lifted up so they could see the water underneath. The renovated home nestled on a cliff was now a popular restaurant known for serving some of the island's best food. The unanimous choice of the group was platters of fried seafood with an assortment of scrumptious sauces and more tropical fruit punch. The meal was topped off with Belgian chocolate souffle.

"Everything was so good. I think I ate too much." Eric groaned.

"Good, now you can dance the night away." Sean autographed a picture for the owner of the restaurant and signed napkins and matchbooks for several other patrons.

"Dancing . . . I'm ready to sleep, man."

"No way. I've been waiting all evening to see Mr. Soul Train and Ms. Dancing Machine throw down."

"All right, man, but only because you're getting married." Eric yawned. But he came to life as soon as he heard the music, a combination of calypso and American dance hits, sounding too good when he walked onto the floating discotheque, where the young people danced until the early in the morning. Mr. and Mrs. Ross had returned to the hotel with the little girls after dinner.

The next morning, after the family had breakfast in the hotel's dining room, everyone went shopping in Straw Market for souvenirs—purses, baskets, mats, slippers, jewelry, dolls, and wood carvings. Bay Street offered an intriguing selection of international pleasures—British woolens, Swiss clocks, European and Bahamian fashions, watches, jewelry, leather, china, and perfume.

After visiting almost every shop, Sean was hungry. "Enough shopping, let's go have some real Bahamian food."

The entire group squeezed into a tiny restaurant where they chatted endlessly about all of their purchases and ordered dishes of conch—cracked, steamed, and fried, fritters, salad, and stew, fried plantain, rice 'n' peas, and grouper. After lunch everyone split up to explore the island on their own. There were so many things to do—snorkeling and scuba diving, water skiing, deep sea fishing, tennis, golf, horseback riding, or just chilling at the beach with an icy tropical drink and a good book.

Saturday arrived much too quickly. The wedding was held in the hotel's Roman courtyard at twilight. Twinkling stars rejoiced in beams of feathery silver moonlight, and white tapers in antique candelabras softly lit the Roman arches. The reflections from the flickering flames danced joyfully on the crystal vases of long-stem white roses that had been placed on either side of the largest arch. Elongated shadows swayed to the sound of the sea, gently tossed by a whispering wind, white Casablancas sailed aimlessly in the trickling fountain, and Earl Klugh's sparkling acoustic guitar played softly in the background.

Nothing disturbed the natural outdoor setting except a dozen Queen Anne chairs that had been set out under a royal blue moonlit sky. The Rosses, Kimuras, and Greek goddess statues patiently waited for the nuptials to commence. It was an outdoor palace under the heavens and the presence of the Lord permeated the atmosphere as well the hearts of His lovers.

Sean, dressed in a black Armani tux, never looked handsomer. His chocolate skin glowed with happiness. He stood in between Eric, his best man, and his father, who would be officiating the service. The guests were glamorous in after-five attire.

I've been waiting for this day all my life . . . Sean was miles away in his own thoughts until he heard the first strands of "Clair de Lune." It was time to begin. He watched Kyrie and Kendra in coral silk taffeta dresses sprinkle white rose petals across the Roman tiles that led up to the candlelit arch where he and Jade would vow to be one.

Jade's mother came into view when she stepped out of an unlit arch in the rear of the courtyard wearing a coral evening gown and carrying a bouquet of long-stem peach roses. She was the color of Hershey's cocoa with beautiful, strong, chiseled features. Sean watched her stroll gracefully to the elegant piano solo, joining his niece and goddaughter on his right.

A classical version of "Holy, Holy, Holy" filled the heavens and he felt his adrenaline surge and his blood pressure escalate. Where's Jade? His eyes searched the darkness for her. I can't wait to see her. A blaze of candlelight filled a rear arch and suddenly she was standing there in all of her glory.

He could hear everyone gasp softly as they laid eyes on her. She was absolutely stunning in a traditional Japanese wedding kimono. The doves on the white silk brocade and silk satin robe were delicately outlined in minute crystal rhinestones. The bird's feet and eyes were embroidered in metallic gold silk thread. Her hair was done up in a French roll under a white silk cap, and she carried a bouquet of white roses. She glided across the courtyard, a queen made ready for her king, with her arm lightly touching the tuxedo sleeve of her aristocratic Japanese father, who escorted her across the rose-strewn cobblestones to Sean.

"Hi, baby," she whispered with a smile.

She is so beautiful . . . Sean opened his mouth to speak and discovered a huge lump had lodged itself in his throat. Where did that come from? he wondered, swallowing hard. When he felt Jade take his hand, he smiled as his father began to speak about the virtues of marriage.

After they exchanged identical diamond and platinum bands, which Jade had designed especially for them, Pastor Ross spoke a blessing over them.

"I now pronounce you husband and wife," his father declared happily. Sean grabbed Jade and kissed her until he thought he wouldn't be able to breathe, long before his father informed him that he could kiss the bride. "Son, you may now kiss your bride," his father laughed.

"He already did," Kyle yelled out.

"All right, I'll do it again." He laughed, kissing Jade.

"See, that's what happens when you wait until you're thirty before you get some," he heard Kirk remark.

"I'll get you for that, man." Sean laughed, pointing at his brother. "I heard you."

"Everybody heard Kirk," his mother scolded, while the others laughed and jumped up to kiss the bride and groom.

A brilliant piano concerto filled the room in celebration of the marriage of Sean and Jade Ross. After lots of pictures, the newlyweds were ushered to an outdoor terrace overlooking the sea where a magnificent table was set for dinner. Gold-rimmed china and sparkling crystal were set on crisp linen. White Casablancas floated in crystal water candles, and a crystal urn of white roses was the centerpiece. Queen Anne chairs were placed around the table.

"It looks like a dinner table in a palace." Sean's mother laughed as her husband helped her into a chair.

There was a baby grand on the terrace and a rhapsody floated up into the Bahamian night air.

"This is the most romantic date I've ever had," Jade whispered in Sean's ear. "And I can go home and make passionate love after this date for the rest of my life." She grinned mischievously.

"I can't wait to make love to you." Sean grinned. "We can finally do it legally," he finished with a kiss.

Sean and Jade were oblivious to the waiters serving them scallops in brandy, conch salad, steamed shrimp, blackened Bahamian lobster tail, rice 'n' peas, and an assortment of other island delicacies.

"Let's go now," Sean whispered. "I'm not hungry."

"I'm not either, but we have to cut the cake first," Jade whispered back.

"That's right." Sean chewed a scallop and eyed the three-layer cake displayed on a candlelit dessert table. It was frosted with hundreds of paper-thin buttercream rose petals and tiny pearls, much too pretty to eat.

An opening in Jade's wedding robe caught Sean's attention. "I can't wait to see what you have on under that."

"Want to see now?" she teased.

"Nope, that's teasing. Just let me keep imagining what you have on until I can see for myself." He laughed softly.

"Lovebirds," Kirk called out from the opposite side of the table. "Don't think about cutting out of here before I get my boogie on. You waited this long."

"That's right, G," Eric quickly agreed. "We'd better toast them now before they try to leave." Tuxedoed waiters poured sparkling apple cider into everyone's champagne flutes.

"To the best friend in the world," Eric began, extending his glass towards the heavens. "Who taught me the real meaning of life. May you and Jade be eternally happy and blessed."

"Amen," everyone agreed softly as their crystal flutes tapped in approval.

It was hours later before they were finally alone.

"I'm so tired." Sean laughed as he held Jade in his arms on the balcony of a penthouse suite overlooking the seascape.

"I know. I never danced so hard in my life." Jade laughed.

"Now I can finally see what you have on under there." He

removed the kimono and smiled the moment his eyes feasted on her lithe dancer's body scantily clad in a white satin teddy.

"You like?" She smiled shyly.

"I like." He grinned. He pulled the pins out of her silky black hair and watched it fall softly around her face and onto her shoulders. Then he took her face in his hands and gazed into her eyes. "You are so beautiful," he whispered as he kissed the inside of her ear.

I love you so much, Jade thought as he began to kiss her gently all over. She gazed into his eyes. They were so loving . . . tender . . . full of passion. She kissed his face softly. Please God, let him always love me this way . . . Together, they lay quietly in the dark . . . their souls and bodies wanted to play.

"I love you, baby," Sean whispered against the lull of the sea.

"I love you, too," Jade whispered back. Their souls . . . now together . . . dancing . . . in paradise.

"We're going to miss our flight if you don't leave me alone." Jade laughed as she climbed out of the shower and out of Sean's reach. They sat on the terrace in their bathrobes grinning at each other and drinking island dew.

"That's okay." Sean laughed. "We can always catch another one later."

They finally arrived in Exuma, one of the smaller Family Islands in the Bahamas, late that same night. They rented a Jeep at the airport and drove out a dark two-lane road past wild cotton and breadfruit trees to the two-bedroom villa Sean had rented for their honeymoon. He could hear the gulf air whispering through lofty palms as he unloaded Jade's easel and paintbox from their Jeep.

"You actually think I'm going to let you paint." He laughed, setting the items down near the back door of the villa.

"Of course, you are. You love me. Besides, I'll be working on your wedding present." She winked.

"I don't know, Jade," he began, taking her into his arms. "I was planning to get some paintings down here for the house."

"That's all good, baby, because what I'm making won't go on the walls in the house," she replied saucily.

"I hear you." He opened the refrigerator. It was filled with an assortment of fresh-squeezed juices and fruit. There was also a platter of barbecued chicken and a fresh conch salad. He had hired an islander to cook their meals, and he was happy to see that she had already been at work.

The villa was equipped with satellite television in the living room, but they ignored it and instead strolled outside on the terrace of their upstairs bedroom, which overlooked a sparkling blue-green pool, the bay, and the harbor. The closest telephone was several miles away in a telephone station. They lit a single candle on the terrace and sat there watching glimmering lights on yachts docked in the harbor, eating chicken, salad, and fruit in the dark.

"I'm never going to want to leave here," Jade whispered in bed. She lay in Sean's arms, watching the ceiling fan above them gently spin.

"Me neither," Sean replied truthfully, wondering if he could ever love Jade more than he already did.

They were up with the sun, and had boiled fish, guava duff, and johnnycake for breakfast. They were going to Inagua for the day to visit one of the islands' national parks and they had to get an early start. They would have to fly back to Nassau first for the flight to Inagua, where they would take a taxi to the park.

"Isn't it the most wonderful thing you've ever seen?" Jade exclaimed.

Awed by the beauty around them, they watched as thousands of brilliant pink flamingoes in a burst of color soared across a vivid electric blue sky. Jade quickly sketched several of the long-legged birds with a hot pink watercolor marker on her sketch pad. It was a perfect picture already after several deft strokes. She snapped photograph after photograph of flamingoes, flaming orange-and-red parrots, cormorants, and herons.

"I'm going to make a scrapbook of our honeymoon," she explained over lunch with twinkling eyes. "Only this isn't going to be just any scrapbook."

He found the picture of the pink flamingoes she had sketched at the park with a note written on the back of it in his Bible that night. He had finally managed to pull himself away from her for a moment and stepped out onto the villa's terrace.

"I love you because I see love in your eyes," it said. He smiled and returned it to a private place between the pages of his favorite book so he could look at it every day.

They stayed on the island for several weeks, making love throughout the day and just chilling at the beach. That was all they wanted to do. It was so easy to relax with the island's simple, quiet life. Pastel clapboard houses amidst brilliantly colored vegetation, pineapple trees, and beaches with pink sand created a romantic backdrop.

"I'm going to miss her." Sean laughed, referring to their Bahamian cook, Lenora, who kept them satisfied with fresh fish, rice 'n' peas, conch, baked chicken, and Bahamian potato salad.

"Maybe we should take her back with us," Jade suggested.

"Not." Sean laughed. " 'Cause I'd get as big as a house."

Dora, the housekeeper, had the front door open before Sean and Jade were out of the car when the limousine pulled into his gated ocean estate in Santa Barbara. Eduardo, her husband, helped the limo driver carry suitcases, shopping bags, and boxes, all bulging with precious mementos from their honeymoon, into the house.

"Hi, Dora and Eduardo. How've you been?" Sean called happily, as he scooped Jade up in his arms. "Should I dunk you in the ocean first or carry you into the house?"

"You better carry me over the threshold, you big jock." She laughed.

"Looks like the ocean to me." He laughed, carrying her towards the back of the house.

"Oh, no," she screamed. "I take it all back."

"You better," he chided softly. He sat her down gently in the living room by the fireplace in front of her painting of the beach and smiled. "Welcome home, Mrs. Ross."

THIRTY-THREE

HE WAS using cocaine all the time now, and he was unable to sleep. Gunther was so stressed he was a walking time bomb, and the coke did little to calm the tempest of guilt and fear eating away inside of him.

How am I going to launder Reno's ten million dollars? He checked his nose in the mirror of his private bathroom at the Gunfire Films production bungalow and stuck the empty vial in a shoebox in the back of his desk drawer.

The bamboo furniture with cantaloupe cushions, potted palms, ficus trees, and blond wood floors made his office cheery and reminiscent of an island cottage, but as far as Gunther was concerned he could have been in an igloo at the North Pole.

He flipped through pages of meticulously written notes on his yellow legal pad and sighed. He had done extensive research into offshore banking. The prospects for moving large sums of money to the Bahamas and the Cayman Islands were favorable. He had had drinks with a gentleman while he was in the Caymans who wanted to help him set up a Gunfire Films corporation in the islands.

I can have all of my future earnings in filmmaking deposited into a bank there and not have to pay all these high U.S. taxes, he realized. It just has to work . . .

He glanced at his watch and tossed his notepad and several vials of coke into a secret compartment in his briefcase. He hadn't seen or spoken to Reno or Topaz since he returned from the islands a week ago.

I can't believe it, he thought, shaking his head. I changed all the numbers in the house the day after I returned from the Caribbean and Reno phoned me on my private line the same night.

"Don't ever think you can hide from me, Gunther," Reno had growled nastily over the phone. "I can always find you, and if you try to mess with me I'll kill you."

He'd do it, too, Gunther realized sadly. I don't want to die. I've worked too hard to get to this point. My life is just beginning. And Topaz . . . He hated himself more every time he thought about what he had done to her in the islands. It was supposed to be a celebration and it turned into the weekend from hell.

"The limo's here to take you to LAX, Mr. Lawrence," a female voice chirped through the telephone intercom, interrupting his thoughts.

"I'll be right there," he responded with little enthusiasm. He tossed an American Airlines ticket into his briefcase, snapped the case closed, and picked up his Louis Vuitton garment bag and tote. A suit and a couple of shirts were the sole contents in the nearly empty garment bag and ten million dollars in cash was stashed in the tote. He would arrive in the Caymans later that night, spend the following day setting up the corporation, and fly back to Los Angeles Sunday morning.

Now if this thing just works. Unable to think about anything else, Gunther ran the details of the transaction through his mind. I form a corporation, invest the ten million in foreign securities until the picture is complete, and then I write Reno a check from the account and give him his ten million back with interest, all clean and legal. What could possibly go wrong? Heck, I even stand to make a little something on this arrangement myself. If those securities make a killing, I'll take Reno's ten million out of my own money and live off the interest from the Caribbean investment. No, wait . . . I don't have ten million yet, but I should have about eight or nine by now. Gunther checked some figures stored away in his Wizard. That means I'd have to use some of Topaz's money and she'd never go for that. I could borrow two million from the bank, if it came to that. Reno's right, I am a genius. And I'm glad we came to an understanding. I don't owe him anything else and I'll pay him for my drugs. Heck, when I get things straight I'm going to stop this, and if I do buy drugs, they won't be from Reno.

Gunther smiled and felt himself relax slightly for the first time in a week. Everything's going to be just fine. He settled back into the limo with a beer and several lines of coke. But what am I going to do about Topaz, he asked himself on the plane. His pretty blond flight attendant had already served him several of his favorite gin-and-cranberry-juice cocktails but his mind just refused to chill.

At home, he had been camping out in a spare bedroom in the west wing and was able to avoid Topaz completely because the house was so big and their schedules so diverse. He didn't come home until very late and by that time, she was in her room sleeping or watching television. He hadn't been able to sleep anyway. He couldn't write, so he stayed up until four in the morning doing coke and playing video games on his Sega Genesis.

What should I say to her? I never thought I would miss her, but I do. I guess I could start with I'm sorry. He picked up the Airphone and dialed her private number. He could tell by the way the phone clicked when she answered that she was talking on the other line.

"Hello," she answered flatly.

"Hi. We need to talk," he began slowly, hoping she would say something to help him along. But he had no right to expect that from her. Topaz remained silent, waiting to see what he would say next. "I'm sorry," Gunther finally mumbled. Still no response. Dang, she could say something, curse me out, yell, or scream. "I'm sorry for the things I said and did . . . Topaz, are you still on the phone?"

"I'm here," she finally replied with very little enthusiasm. "So, you're sorry . . ."

"I've been under a lot of stress lately and I guess I let the drugs get out of hand. I'm going to stop," he admitted, really meaning it. "I'll even check into one of those rehab centers if I have to."

"Hold on," she demanded coldly and clicked the telephone over to the other line to speak to Nina. "Nina, are you still there?"

"Yeah, girl."

"That's Gunther on the other line saying he's sorry and talking about how he's going to stop doing coke and check into a rehab center."

"What?" Nina squealed.

"Yeah."

"So what you gonna do, girl? You said you were kicking brother man to the curb. Are you gonna tell him about the baby?"

"I don't know."

"And you still haven't told me what went on down there. I come back from breakfast and find out you've checked out. What happened?"

"I'll call you back," she lied, unable to tell anyone how Gunther had raped her. "Let me get him off the phone." She clicked back over to Gunther. "So, why are you telling me all this, Gunther? What do you want?"

"I want to be your husband again and I want you to be my wife," he mumbled into the phone.

She felt her growing abdomen. She was already four months pregnant. She knew she was pregnant when she married Gunther. Her mind raced back over the circumstances that had made her decide to keep the baby and not tell Gunther. I don't want him to marry me because I'm pregnant. I already did that once. I want him to marry me for me, not because I'm pregnant. Why can't these babies get made after I'm married and not before? I always use protection.

She had considered having an abortion, but dismissed the idea entirely because she believed life began when the baby was conceived. I've done enough wrong things in my life, she had decided, thinking about the son and husband Gunther never knew about. I'm not about to start killing babies.

Gunther sat there in silence waiting for her to say something.

"Okay," she finally spoke softly. "I'll give it some thought." We've both been wrong and now there's a baby to consider, she told herself, something I never did with Chris.

"Okay," he mumbled. "I'm on my way out of town on business. I'll be back on Sunday. Maybe we can have dinner or something."

Topaz hung up the phone and glanced at her reflection in the mirror in the bathroom. I look terrible, she realized, and began to brush her hair. Her amber eyes lacked their fire and there were dark smudges underneath her eyes from lack of sleep. She splashed cold water on her face and tried not to look at the vial of coke in her makeup drawer. She had broken down and done some the day of her wedding. I don't want to hurt the baby, but I sure could use a few hits now.

■

Gunther arrived back in Los Angeles early Sunday afternoon. He had invested Reno's ten million in oil securities in the Middle East and he stood to make a killing. I feel a lot better now. And I'm going to get paid. Now all I have to do is work things out with Topaz. Back in his room in the west wing he looked at her rings, bracelets, and earrings, which he had recovered from the trash can in the hotel bathroom.

"I still can't believe she threw away over three-hundred-thousand dollars' worth of jewelry," he muttered, sorting through the jewels and remembering exactly when he had given her each piece. I want to give her something, but I don't know what I could give her that would be special.

He showered leisurely and changed into a pair of crisp white tennis shorts and a teal Izod T-shirt, still mustering up the courage to talk to her. "This is it," he told himself, taking one last glance in the mirror. He strolled downstairs into the kitchen but she wasn't there.

"La señora esta en su cuarto," the maid informed him, gesturing to inform him that she was in the master suite.

"Gracias," he mumbled softly and sprinted up the stairs to the second floor. He walked into the bedroom they had yet to share and found her brushing her hair. "Hi," he mumbled.

"Hello."

She had been expecting him. She knew she looked too good in the black bell bottoms and white chiffon romance blouse she was wearing. She put the hairbrush down on her dressing table and tied a black velvet choker around her long slender neck.

"You look nice."

"So, where do you want to have dinner?" she demanded, bored with his small talk.

"I thought we could go to Mr. Chow's. We can talk and I know you like Chinese."

They took his Range Rover and drove in silence to the restaurant.

"I'm pregnant, Gunther," she informed him as soon as they were seated.

"You are?" He was shocked. He felt his nerves tense up, but he refused to order a drink.

"Yes. I'm just four months. The baby's due around the first of June," she informed him with very little enthusiasm. "I didn't tell you sooner because I was thinking about getting an abortion," she lied.

"You aren't going to, are you?" Gunther asked, trying to remain calm.

He seems like he really cares, Topaz noticed. "No, I told you the baby was due in June."

"Oh, yeah." He felt a little smile ease its way onto his face. I'm going to be a father. "So what about us?"

"What do you mean, what about us?" she asked to purposely work his nerves. She knew what he wanted to know.

"Do you want a divorce or what?" There, I finally said the dreaded *D* word, so things can only get better now. I hate not knowing.

"We haven't even been married a month yet and here we are talking about a divorce," Topaz declared with very little emotion. "I'm not going to divorce you, Gunther . . ."

"Oh, sweetheart, thank you so much for giving me another chance. I swear I'll make it up to you and I'll—"

"Gunther," Topaz snapped. "Would you let me finish?" She was surprised to see tears in his eyes. "I'm not going to divorce you as long as you agree to what I want."

"What do you want?" He fixed his eyes on her amber ones, thinking she probably wanted him to buy her new jewels and baubles. He picked up a sizzling shrimp with his chopsticks, ready to eat for the first time in days.

"You sleep in the west wing of the house. I don't want you in my bed," she informed him icily, her eyes topaz daggers. "I don't know if I'll ever want you in my bed. If we're in public I'll be sweet and loving and I expect you to be the same. And when we're behind closed doors, I don't care what you do, just stay away from me and stay out of the east wing."

"But what kind of marriage is that?" he protested.

"The marriage you created."

Turquoise Black Lawrence entered the world on the second Sunday in the month of June.

"She has blond hair," Nina screamed in the delivery room. "Oh, she looks just like you, Topaz, funny eyes, high yellow, and all." She laughed.

Topaz smiled at the sight of the butterscotch baby with a head full of copper hair. "She's beautiful," she exclaimed softly, rubbing the baby's tiny hand between her thumb and forefinger. And she looks nothing like her father, she realized.

"I bet you looked that way when you were born, Topaz," Nina remarked. She cooed softly to the baby. "Hi, pretty little cousin. Your mommy doesn't have any sisters so I'll be your aunty." Turquoise stretched her little mouth into a big yawn as if to say "whatever."

"Look, Topaz, she even has those lips of yours. It's amazing. She doesn't look anything like her nerdy drug addict father at all."

Topaz dropped off to sleep and awakened hours later to find her private room in Cedars Sinai filled with countless floral arrangements. Gunther sat quietly in the corner, next to a huge arrangement of shiny red anthuriums and Oriental lilies. She heard him say hi and tried to focus her eyes on him.

"I saw the baby. She's beautiful." Gunther smiled.

Topaz closed her eyes and rolled over so that her back faced him. I'm not angry anymore, she realized. I just don't care.

She hired a full-time nanny to look after Turquoise. The nursery was on the upper corridor that connected the wings of the house, so it was considered neutral territory for the Lawrences. Topaz stopped in the nursery one night after a day of recording in the studio and found Gunther holding the baby.

"I'm surprised to see you here," she stuttered. "I thought you were on the set."

"We finished early so I came home to see my little girl." He smiled. "Isn't she exquisite?"

Topaz glanced at her baby daughter and smiled. She was exquisite. Her butterscotch coloring had deepened into a golden brown like taffy cookies. Me with a tan, Topaz decided. Her golden eyes were flecked with green and brown, and her silky hair was the color of sparkling apple cider.

"How's Mommy's pretty baby?" Topaz cooed in baby talk. She ran her slender manicured fingers softly across Turquoise's cheek. She caught a whiff of Gunther's Boucheron fragrance as she stood up and felt herself ignite with desire. Now where did that come from? They had been sleeping in separate rooms for almost a year.

The nanny came in and handed Gunther the baby's bottle. Topaz watched him slide the nipple into her little mouth and watch the baby drink. He looks like he knows what's he's doing. He tossed a clean diaper over his shirt and held the baby over his shoulder to burp her.

"You did a big one." Gunther cuddled Turquoise in his arms so she could drink more of the bottle.

"Do you come in here a lot?"

"Every day. If I don't get a chance to feed her, I always stop by for a chat with my beautiful daughter." He cooed softly and nibbled on the baby's cheek.

"Oh, that's nice . . . well, good night." He listened to her shoes tap down the hall towards the east wing.

He spends more time with her than I do, she realized, feeling guilty. Well, I'm glad he spends time with her, she convinced herself, running water into her new pink marble bathtub. Because I don't have time right now.

She climbed into the tub and felt her body relax in the swirling scented water. "This is nice," she whispered out loud. She closed her eyes and all of a sudden she found herself thinking about Gunther and sat up straight in the tub. Now why would I think about him? she wondered as she adjusted her bath pillow. I know . . . she smiled to herself, I haven't had any for a year? Wow! She was amazed herself.

She lay there thinking about what it would be like to be with Gunther and realized she wasn't repulsed. But he hasn't asked me for some the entire time, she reminded herself. Then, I did tell him if he wanted to continue being married to me that he wasn't getting any.

"I wonder what he's been doing for sex?" she asked herself out loud. He's always home when I get here and I know he isn't sneaking women into the house.

The security guards at the house were all sweet on Topaz and they kept her informed of Gunther's every move once he was on the premises. And when he's not here, he's always busy working on the film as far as I know. *Intrigue* had just commenced principle photography.

He's not going to come to me, she finally decided. If I want action, I'm going to have to make it happen. Topaz climbed out of the tub and laughed. I'm going to seduce Gunther Lawrence, she decided. She picked up the phone and dialed his room. "Gunther, have you had dinner?" she asked sweetly.

"Not yet." He was surprised to hear her voice on the phone.

"Great. Niko's making Thai and Inez is serving me in my sitting room. I'm sure there's enough for two," she continued, overly sweet. "Would you like to have dinner with me?"

"In your room?" he asked, to be sure that he had heard what he thought he heard.

"Yes."

"Sure. What time should I come?"

"I just got out of the tub. Say, thirty minutes?"

"Okay." He was ecstatic. "Should I bring anything?"

"No, not that I can think of. If so, I can always have Inez bring it up from the kitchen."

Gunther hung up the phone and shouted. The first steps towards a reconciliation, he marveled. I didn't think this would ever happen.

He showered and changed into a pair of turquoise tennis shorts and a white polo shirt. He still did his daily workouts in the gym and the muscles rippled in his hard cappuccino body as he strolled down the hall towards the east wing. He tapped softly on the door. "I feel like I'm on a date in my own house," he whispered.

"Hello." Topaz greeted him politely, opening the door.

Gunther swallowed hard and walked into the suite. She's done a fabulous job with the decorating, he noticed. The massive armoire and other antique pieces had come from Mitchell Litt in the Valley. The deep mauve wallpaper trimmed in an ecru lace border and the soft lighting cast from ginger jar lamps made the room extremely romantic.

And Topaz . . . he was trying very hard not to look at her. She's back in excellent shape already, Gunther noticed immediately. You'd never even know she had a baby, he proudly thought, remembering the wives of his crew members who had blown up overnight and stayed that way. She was wearing a pair of caramel jacquard silk lounging pajamas, her hair was pulled up into a ponytail, and her face was free of makeup. She looked like a teenager.

"Hi." He was still standing by the door. He felt awkward and he didn't know what to say. "The room looks great."

"Thanks. Everything turned out really nice. Take a look around if you like. Niko's made pot stickers, chicken with mint leaves and chilies, steamed rice, and a couple of other dishes. Inez is on her way up with the food now."

"Okay." He noticed the table in the sitting room had been laid out with the china and the gold-edged Baccarat crystal they'd purchased in Paris. Gunther saw her sit on the sofa and flip past several of the movie channels as he peeked into her pink marble bathroom.

The slab marble floor was a vortex of pinks, mauves, and rose on ivory. It looked like a creamy strawberry milkshake being whipped in a blender. The dusty rose sunken Roman tub was straight out of Cleopatra's bathroom. Gilded antique mirrors, floral wallpaper, and lots of thick fluffy towels in a spectrum of pinks softened the room's contemporary edge just enough to turn it into a delicately feminine, romantic bathroom.

"Your bathroom is magnificent," he yelled.

"Thanks, take a look at yours."

He walked to the other side of the bedroom and stepped into the "his" bathroom of the master suite. Black and gray marble, sparkling black fixtures, smoked glass, and high-tech lighting embellished with gray and navy towels. He had selected a Jacuzzi shower and it stood there waiting to be used. This is so nice . . . we should be enjoying this together.

"Food's here," he heard Topaz call from the sitting room.

They both sat down at the table and Inez served their plates.

"Enjoy your dinner, Mr. and Mrs. Lawrence," she bid them in perfect unaccented English.

They made polite conversation while they ate.

"Champagne?" Topaz poured herself a glass from the bottle of Cristal that had been chilling in a Baccarat ice bucket.

"Sure." He handed her the flute.

"Let's finish eating in front of the television," Topaz finally suggested, when neither of them could think of anything more to say about the weather. "There's a lot of good stuff coming on."

"Okay. It's been a long time since I just did nothing and watched television." They finally decided on *Breakfast at Tiffany's* on American Movie Classics. "I can't believe you've never seen this," Gunther marveled. "It's an absolutely wonderful film. I saw it when I was little. I used to watch a lot of television when I was little."

"Really? I can't remember what I did when I was a kid. I was probably at my grandmother's playing in her makeup. I was always playing in somebody's makeup." Topaz laughed.

They smiled at each other for the first time in months. She slid her hand over a little closer to his and felt currents of desire sweep through her body. He looks so good in those shorts, she noticed, aching for the touch of his body on her hands. Dang. I thought this was going to be easier.

I want to kiss her so bad, but what if she throws me out? Gunther contemplated. I don't want to rush things. The next thing he knew he was kissing her full bottom lip.

"You can move back in the east wing, if you like," she informed him coolly when she returned from working out with her personal trainer the following morning. She had left Gunther sleeping in her bed.

"Okay," he agreed happily, slipping on his shorts. "I'll have Inez move my things."

The following weeks were some of the happiest times in Gunther's life.

"My life is finally perfect," he realized, feeling the weight of the world lift from his shoulders for the first time in his life. I don't feel like I always have to be reaching after something or obtaining some goal. Everything I could possibly want is right here.

Ever since the night Topaz invited him to her room they were actually talking and working at being friends, and he still rushed home to spend as much time as he could with Turquoise. The film was on schedule and on budget and his investment in the Caymans was growing quite nicely.

He sat down in the family room and flipped on the colossal-sized Mitsubishi television. I love this room. It reflected their two careers perfectly. Topaz's platinum album plaques in black lacquer frames lined the walls, along with photos of the two of them with various celebrities. Her Grammys, the crystal pyramids from the American Music Awards, the Soul Train Awards, Image Awards, Billboard Awards, and his NAACP Image Award and student directing awards from the Academy of Motion Picture Arts and Sciences and the Director's Guild were all housed in a custom-made trophy case. There was a restored Wurlitzer jukebox that played R&B hits from various decades, an old-fashioned ice-cream soda fountain, and a fire-engine-red popcorn cart. A redbrick fireplace added the perfect touch on a chilly night. He sighed and smiled again. Life is too good.

He flipped past channels on the television killing time. Topaz was upstairs changing, and Nina and Jamil were on their way over. He had ordered prints of *Forrest Gump* and *Crooklyn* from the studio for them to watch in the screening room. Niko was making Indian food: tandoori chicken, curried shrimp, saffron rice, and naan. He flipped past CNN and flipped back.

"What's happening in the world today?" he wondered, turning up the volume.

"A coup d'etat in Qatar has the country in turmoil. All of the country's banks and private businesses closed their doors early today when revolutionists seized all of the country's assets . . ."

"What?" he screamed. "Reno's money is in one of their banks in the Caymans."

"This change of events ushers in a new regime for the tiny country of Qatar," the newscaster continued.

"They can't do this," Gunther yelled at the television. "Those crazy Arabs. They just can't take people's money like that. They're filthy rich already," he screamed.

"What are you yelling about?" Topaz walked into the room with Nina, Jamil, and the baby. "Everybody's here and Turquoise wants to say good night to her daddy."

Gunther was already picking up the phone. "I can't talk right now," he mumbled. Maybe this won't affect the bank in the Caymans. Maybe I can get down there tonight and get my money out of there . . .

"Gunther, what are you doing?" Topaz demanded. "Dinner's ready and we want to eat."

"I said not now," he screamed even louder, as he pushed past them to leave the room. His eyes were crazed and he looked like a mad man.

"Gunther, what's your problem?" Topaz yelled after him.

"Living," Nina replied under her breath.

Topaz glared at Nina before she left the room to follow him upstairs. "Go ahead and start dinner without me," she yelled over her shoulder. "I'll be back in a minute."

When she reached their bedroom it was a mess. Clothing, shoes, books, suitcases were strewn everywhere. Gunther was nervously pacing back and forth.

"What are you doing?"

"Waiting on a phone call." He continued pacing.

"What are you doing with those suitcases? Are you going somewhere?" she demanded.

"Yes, I have to go out of town on business."

"Tonight?"

"Yes, tonight."

"Why?"

To get my fifteen million dollars. He fought the urge to scream at her. It isn't her fault that there was political unrest in the Middle East. "Something urgent just came up and I don't have time to explain now," he replied slowly, trying to restrain his fury.

He flew down to the Caymans the same night. When he reached the Bank of Qatar the following morning, Gunther found its doors closed. His financial consultant, Niles Bellingham, offered little hope on the situation.

"Those oil securities were a great investment because you could virtually triple your dollars, but at the same time, the governments in these small Middle Eastern countries tend to be very unstable. But that's the risk you take," he explained to Gunther.

"Why didn't you inform me of these risks up front?"

"Middle Eastern governments have been very stable since the oil embargo in the seventies, but ever since Muammar Gadhafi rose to power, anything's subject to happen. This may be a temporary situation and this new regime could be out within a week. Then again, they may be around forever."

I have to find a way to get Reno's money back. And I can't give him mine. I'd have to borrow and sell everything I've got. All the things I've worked so hard for.

He flew back to Los Angeles the same night drinking gin-and-cranberry-juice cocktails until he was drunk. When he reached the house, he was glad to find that Topaz was out at some party. He rushed up to her bathroom and opened her makeup drawer. She doesn't know that I know she keeps her stash in here. He rifled through the drawer until he found the glass vial of powder.

"Bingo." He rushed to his own bathroom to inhale the drug secretly just in case she came home while he was taking it. I'm only going to do a little to calm my nerves, he rationalized. Just until I figure out a plan.

As the producer on his project he did have the authorization to sign all check request vouchers. I'll just turn in ten million dollars' worth of expenses. Films are always going over budget and with all the prima donnas I've got in this one I can charge these expenses to them. A little here, a little there. It'll all add up. Maybe I can get that cute Hispanic teller who's always flirting with me at the bank to cash all the checks for me.

Carmen Martinez agreed to help. Gunther bought her a black 5.0 convertible and agreed to pay her twenty-five thousand dollars cash when the last check was cashed and deposited. He had already deposited close to five million dollars in a new Gunfire Films account. He was also seeing her on the side and his drug habit had escalated up to a thousand dollars a day again.

I'll stop as soon as I get Reno's money back, he promised himself, as he checked his nose in the bathroom mirror.

"Gunther's back to acting weird again," Topaz informed Nina. "Ever since that night two months ago when he ran out of town when we were watching *Crooklyn*. Things had been going so well."

"What do you think is wrong?" Nina asked with concern.

"I don't know. He's never interested in having sex anymore. Sometimes he even sleeps in the west wing. He says he's working on a new script and he doesn't want to disturb me."

"Yep, sounds like that nerdy husband of yours to me." Nina laughed. "You know how Mr. Dynasty gets when he's on the set. Nothing can compete with his quest for power, not even the fair and lovely Topaz. I don't know who that other fellow was, spending time with the baby and being so attentive to you. I knew he wouldn't be around long."

"You're probably right, Nina. He does start tripping when he gets into his writing and directing mode."

Things were great until the production accountant got nosy.

The budget was way over, so she decided to run a report and analyze the additional expenses. Most of them were for items that were never delivered or used. Some were even for people who were supposedly employed by the production but weren't. Further investigation turned up Gunther as the originator of all the questionable invoices.

Gunther stepped out of his private bathroom in the Gunfire bungalow. He had just done several lines of coke and he was soaring. He heard the buzzer signaling the receptionist that someone was entering the bungalow.

"Good afternoon, Mr. Zwieg," she greeted the visitor.

Mr. Z? What's he doing down here, Gunther wondered, as he rushed to check his nose. He's probably coming to tell me how well he liked that footage I sent over.

"Good afternoon, Gunther." Mr. Zwieg was unusually formal.

"Hi, Mr. Z. What did you think of that footage I sent over?" Gunther asked with a big grin, hoping to loosen him up.

"Gunther, I'm not here to discuss footage," he informed him without a hint of a smile. "It's been brought to my attention that your film is extremely over budget."

"You know how it is when you get those big names in a production." Gunther grinned and skinned. "They want to be picked up in a limousine every day or they want hardwood floors in their trailer instead of berber carpeting or they want you to pick up the tab on a weekend jaunt . . ."

"Gunther, I know all about the stars and their petty habits. Something's been going on, and I've come to you for answers before I turn this entire situation over to the authorities."

The authorities. Gunther felt his blood pressure escalate a thousand degrees and he heard the sound of his heart pounding inside his ears. He knows . . . Gunther swallowed hard and tried to think of something to say.

"There are more than seven million dollars in expenses that can't be explained, and you okayed them. And the checks for these expenses were all cashed by the same person at the same bank," Mr. Zwieg continued. "When the teller who had been cashing the checks was questioned, she claimed she never knew that she was doing anything illegal and that she had cashed all those checks for you."

I never signed my name to any of those checks I cashed; they'll have to prove it first. "I don't know what you're talking about, Mr. Zwieg," Gunther lied cool as ice. "I sure wish I could help you." The sound of his beating heart intensified in his ears.

"All right, Gunther. We're still checking things out with the bank. I'll be in touch," he called over his shoulder as he walked out of the door.

Gunther paced nervously back and forth in front of his desk. They're going to trace everything back to me. That big-mouthed Carmen. Stupid Mexican. I'm going to kill her. "My life . . . it's over," he wailed. "I'm going to jail. Everything that I've worked so hard for . . . gone . . . like that."

He sat down at his desk and pulled out a fresh vial of cocaine. All of a sudden he was angry. "Well, I'm not goin' out like that. I'll think of something. Stupid white people, always tryin' to put a brother in jail."

He was tapping a bit of the powder out of the container onto a business card when he felt a sharp pain, like a knife, being thrust through his chest.

What was that? he wondered, as he sucked in his breath and clutched his hand to his chest in an effort to squelch the pain. He had been having chest pains off and on for several months, but he had continually ignored them. Suddenly his heart felt like it was exploding inside of him and he grabbed the desk. His palms were sweaty and he could feel beads of perspiration dripping from his forehead.

"Oh, my God," he whispered, clutching his hand to his heart. He felt another pain so sharp that it took away his breath. Then everything was silent and still.

His executive assistant, Beth, found him on the floor behind his desk, unconscious. The paramedics rushed him to the hospital where the doctors tried everything, but Gunther Lawrence was pronounced dead shortly after his arrival.

THIRTY-FOUR

"I CAN'T believe Gunther's dead," Topaz whispered through her tears. "He's dead, Nina." She plucked a tissue from a box of pink Puffs and blew her nose.

"I know, honey," Nina replied softly. "But we've got to make the arrangements for the service. And his mother keeps calling."

"Then let her make the arrangements. I can't deal with this," Topaz cried.

"You're his wife, Topaz. You're supposed to make them."

"Well, I can't. I can't," she sobbed into a fresh tissue. "I just want everything to be over, Nina." Topaz sat cross-legged in the middle of the king-size bed she had shared with Gunther for less than six months. She was still wearing her pajamas in the middle of the afternoon. She looked a mess. Her nose and eyes were red from crying.

"I don't care what you do, Nina. I do but I don't." She sniffed. "Just handle everything for me, please."

Nina sat on the bed and watched her cousin open the drawer in her nightstand and pull out a vial of white powder. "What are you doing?" she screamed, jumping up and snatching the drug from her. "Do you want to kill yourself like Gunther, you silly girl?"

"No. Oh, Nina. I'm so sorry he's dead," she cried as the tears streamed out of her eyes.

Nina planted a kiss on top of Topaz's unkempt hair. "I know you are, honey, I know. I can't believe he's dead either. I keep expecting him to walk through the door and say, what's happening, dudes."

Topaz smiled for a moment. "I know, he used to always say that, too. Gunther was so different."

"Wasn't he? He definitely wasn't your everyday brother."

"He wasn't a brother. He was a white boy with a black body. I miss him already, though, with his strange self. These last few months were pretty nice. He changed. He was different. He was so smart. He knew something about everything," Topaz reflected. "Germain was like that, too. Gosh, I wonder how Germain and Chris are."

"Aren't they in Switzerland?"

"Sweden."

"How'd you find that out?" Nina demanded.

"Chris sent a card to the house. I know Germain sent it without a return address on purpose, but it had a Swedish stamp," she declared softly. "I need a fill." Topaz rattled on absentmindedly, inspecting the small space where her acrylic nails had grown away. "My son . . . do you know I think about him every day?"

"Topaz's children. Your son has no mother and now your daughter has no father."

"I know . . ."

"That would make a great movie. *Topaz Children*. The saga of the children of gorgeous singer Topaz Black."

Memorial services for Gunther were held at Forest Lawn in Hollywood Hills on a gray winter day. The pale watery sky made the cemetery look extremely green. Topaz watched the wind gently whip the emerald blades of grass as she followed the gleaming mahogany casket to a plot in the cemetery.

"I can't believe the press is here." Nina glared at the camera crews from various local stations. "Don't they ever quit?"

"I don't want to talk to anybody." Topaz was pale, thin, and gorgeous in the new black Chanel suit she had had sent over from the boutique on Rodeo Drive. Her hair, silky straight, was brushed and tucked under a pillbox hat. It glistened like fire against the black silk cap. Her amber eyes were hidden by a pair of black sunglasses and a sable coat was draped around her shoulders to block the chill in the crisp February air.

She sat in a white folding chair and stared blindly into space while the minister read from the Bible. I'm all alone. A widow at twenty-seven. She studied Gunther's family, his mother, father, sisters, and brothers. I don't even know these people, she realized sadly. Gunther never spent time with them or talked about them, and this is my daughter's family . . .

She saw everybody else stand and stood with them. It was over. She took a last look at the casket that held Gunther's body and broke into tears.

"Bye, Gunther," she whispered as security guards whisked her and Nina down the hill to the waiting limousine.

Back at the house, Nina had arranged for Harold and Belle's to cater a Creole dinner. Guests mingled throughout the west wing with bowls of file gumbo, baked chicken, ham, macaroni and cheese, fried seafood, and huge glasses of Long Island iced tea.

Topaz sat in the game room watching the little children play video games on the Sega Genesis. She drank jelly jars of tea while Gunther's mother played the hostess of life and chatted graciously with the guests.

Gunther's father came over to Topaz. He was accompanied by an extremely attractive blond man with cobalt blue eyes. "Topaz, this is Pete Wingate, a friend of Gunther's from prep school."

He is fine, she concluded, noticing Pete's expensive suit, white silk shirt, and shoes. "Hello, Pete, it's a pleasure to meet you," she offered, extending her hand. "You were a friend of Gunther's?"

"Yes, we were roommates in high school."

"That's nice," she replied, smiling easily.

"I'm sorry to have to meet you on such a sad occasion."

Topaz smiled in response.

"Pete, would you care for something to eat or drink?" asked Gunther's dad.

"An iced tea would be great, Charles."

"I'll get that for you, Pete," Gunther's father offered.

"Thanks, Charles."

"I'm sorry. You must think I'm an awful hostess," Topaz apologized.

"I don't think you're an awful hostess. You've been through a lot. I understand."

"Thanks." Topaz smiled.

"I just can't believe old Gunther married such a beautiful famous singer."

"Thank you." Topaz blushed and wondered if this was a line. "Pete, do you live in Los Angeles?"

"No." He took a seat next to her on the sofa. A waiter brought in fresh jelly jars of Long Island iced tea. "I flew in from New York this morning on the red-eye." Pete took several sips from his jar of iced tea.

"Oh, I see. Are you a director, too?"

"Oh, no." He laughed. "I'm not in show business."

"Then what do you do?" she asked, as a smile warmed her face. I kind of like this guy, she thought, admiring his pretty-boy face.

"I'm just a plain old investment banker," he replied, flashing a dazzling smile.

"Oh."

"I'm going to be in town for a few days. Topaz, would you like to have dinner? You're much too young and far too gorgeous to be sitting around this big old house alone."

He is trying to hit on me, Topaz realized. I've never dated a white guy, but he is fine . . . "Sure, Pete," she agreed smoothly. "Dinner sounds very nice."

Topaz studied her wet body carefully in the gilded full-length antique mirror in her bathroom. I need a lift, she decided, studying her breasts. They're not as high as they used to be but I still look good. She smiled. She finished drying off, lotioned her body, and slipped on black satin Victoria's Secret underwear and a fifteen-dollar pair of panty hose. She noticed the price as she tossed the empty package into the trash can. She picked up the phone and dialed Nina, who was now living in the west wing of the house.

"Nina, are you busy?" She was so happy to have her living in the house. A princess in each wing . . .

"No. What's up?"

"Could you come over so we can talk?"

Nina strolled in several minutes later wearing a pair of paisley red boxers and a Just Jam T-shirt. She was eating an apple and carrying a copy of *Waiting to Exhale*. "What's up?"

"I need to have my boobs done. Got any recommendations?"

"Mmmm, I hear there's this doctor at Cedars Sinai who hooks

up all the stars. You actually want to have yours done?'' Nina questioned with a frown.

''Yes.''

''Why, for Pete Wingate?'' Nina teased.

''Nina, I'm not sleeping with Pete. We're just very good friends,'' Topaz smiled.

''You guys have been an item ever since Gunther kicked the bucket. I can't believe Miss She's Gotta Have It hasn't given up the booty to that fine white boy yet,'' Nina remarked, chomping on a piece of apple.

''Nina, I don't know why you think I'm so wild. You're wilder than me and you're the one who comes up with all those crazy ideas, Miss Beaubien.''

''I am not wild.'' She laughed. ''I just have a vivid imagination. As soon as Jamil asks me, I'm going to marry him and stop working for you. I'm going to take a few writing classes and write some scripts. You're such a wonderful character.''

''What? You can't leave me and you can't write about me either.''

''Yes, I can. You can always get Kim to come work for you. She's been looking for a job. And I am going to write about you, only no one will know it's you.''

''Nina, you know Kim and I can't stand each other. Besides, doesn't she work in finance or something anyway? I can't believe you . . . I hope Jamil never asks you to marry him,'' she pouted. ''And I can't wait to see your movies.'' She slipped on the black St. John knit that hugged her figure gently in all the right places and stood in the mirror admiring herself.

''That dress looks good on you, girl. Petey Wingate might jump the widow Lawrence's bones tonight,'' Nina teased.

''Nina, go to your room and find out about that doctor at Cedars Sinai,'' Topaz demanded as the phone rang. ''Get that for me please, Nina.''

''West wing,'' she barked into the phone.

''Girl, what are you doing?'' Topaz laughed.

''Screening the call,'' she whispered, covering the mouthpiece.

''You know the service only rings through if it's someone I want to talk to. Give me that.'' Topaz snatched the phone and removed one of her gold clip-on Chanel earrings. "It's probably Pete. Hello." She smiled into the phone.

"That husband of yours had ten million dollars of my money and I want it back," she heard a male voice growl into the phone.

"What? Who is this?" Topaz demanded as the smile left her face.

"This is Reno, pretty lady."

"Reno?" Reno? Who's Reno? she wondered. Wait, that drug dealer . . . Gunther owes him ten million dollars? Her mind processed the information quickly.

"Reno, remember the weekend we went to the Caymans and you acted like you were too high and mighty to associate with my woman?"

How could I ever forget that weekend. "What do you want, Reno?"

"Ten million dollars."

"I don't know anything about Gunther owing you ten million dollars, and Gunther's estate has already been settled."

He had left every single thing to her and the baby. She and Turquoise were the beneficiaries of a ten-million-dollar life insurance policy, as well as another fifteen million in cash and assets. That, not to mention her own significant earnings from touring and record sales, made her an extremely wealthy woman.

"I have a contract that says I do," he insisted. "I'll drop it by your house tomorrow."

"There's no need—" she began until she heard the phone click and the monotone sound of the dial tone in her ear.

"What was that about?" Nina demanded anxiously.

"That drug dealer Reno said Gunther owed him ten million dollars and he has a contract."

ABC Messenger Service dropped off the contract around eleven the following morning. Nina faxed it over to the attorney, who called within thirty minutes and said it was legit.

"I wonder if Reno killed Gunther over this money?" Topaz asked out loud.

"He died of a heart attack, Topaz," Nina reminded her. "But your husband's skeletons sure are falling out of the closet."

"I never realized how little I knew about Gunther until he died," Topaz declared sadly.

"He sure was secretive. Did you ever ask him anything about the way he ran his business?"

"No. I had my own money to take care of."

"I heard that, but I would have been curious about the money, honey. Why would Gunther need Reno's money, anyway?"

"Well, I do know Reno put up the financing for Gunther's first film."

"Really?" Nina was in shock. "I never knew that."

"Oh, yes. Gunther thought the world of him. They used to play golf together all the time. Personally, I don't see why he wanted to hang around somebody like that. I never liked him."

"Why didn't Gunther ask Pete for the money? His family owns that bank and they were good friends."

"Pete said Gunther had too much pride to ask him for a loan."

"If he had borrowed that money from Pete, he'd probably be alive now," Nina surmised.

"Have you gone through all of Gunther's papers?" Pete asked when they spoke on the phone later that night.

"Just about . . . Nina still has to go through his desk here at the house."

"If you find anything that looks interesting, let me know. There has to be some record somewhere of what he did with the money."

"Petey says that we should look through Gunther's things for some sort of record of what Gunther did with the money." Topaz started pulling papers out of a desk drawer.

"Are you getting serious about Pete Wingate?" The cousins sifted through various papers.

"I like him and he has asked to marry me." Topaz smiled.

"He did? He's moving awfully fast. I wonder if Mr. Wingate is after the widow's millions," Nina stated coolly, fixing her eyes on Topaz.

"Nina, Pete isn't after my money. He's after my body." Topaz laughed. "And I'm after his. His family owns a bank. Why would he want my money?"

"To put into his family's bank."

"Nina, you don't trust anybody. There's nothing in here." Topaz slammed the drawer back into the desk.

"But look at this." Nina pulled out a rubber-banded stack of envelopes from a shoebox that had been stuck way in the back of the bottom drawer.

"What is it?"

"Statements," Nina whispered coolly. "From the Bank of Qatar in the Cayman Islands."

Topaz opened the envelopes and quickly perused the statements. "This is it," she grinned triumphantly, brandishing the statements. "Gunther opened this account a couple of weeks after our trip to the Caymans with ten million dollars."

"Petey's going to check everything out," Topaz informed Nina, as she hung up the phone. "He said something about some sort of a coup d'etat. I think that's how he said it . . ."

"Coup d'etat. Yes. Go on."

"Well, there was a coup d'etat in the country a year ago but he said I can probably get the money back, including whatever Gunther made off the investment. He said there could be even more money now."

"The widow Lawrence just keeps getting richer." Nina laughed.

Topaz headed east on Sunset Boulevard towards San Vicente in her black 500 convertible Mercedes, on her way to Cedars Sinai Medical Towers for an appointment with the plastic surgeon to the stars. She cranked the volume and sang loudly to "Love Sign." I really like this new song by Prince, the symbol, or whatever his name is.

I'm so happy. She smiled to herself. Petey got Gunther's money back and had that drug dealer paid off and I got another seven and a half million dollars out of the deal. Petey said we should get married and buy houses in Martha's Vineyard and St.

Croix. We sure would have some pretty babies. I might even chill out and stay home and be a banker's wife . . .

"What was that doctor's name?" she asked herself as she entered the lobby of the medical center. She fished through her Chanel backpack looking for the paper that Nina had written the doctor's name and address on. "Forget this." She pulled out her flip phone. I'm about to be late. I'll just call Nina. Where is that girl? she wondered, snapping the phone closed. "Dang."

She found the building's roster located near the elevators, and ran a sepia-painted nail over the names of the cosmetic surgeons, looking for the doctor's name. Fischmann . . . that's it, she remembered as her eyes fell on the name Gradney. Gradney?

"Gradney, Germain M.D." she read aloud, unable to believe what she saw. It couldn't be him. Not living in Los Angeles. He's in Sweden . . .

She found Dr. Fischmann's office and flipped through a copy of *Essence* while she waited to see the doctor, but she couldn't concentrate on anything. She stuck the magazine in her bag and got up to leave. I have to find out if it's Germain. She had just opened the office door to walk out when the receptionist called her for her appointment.

"The doctor will see you now."

"It's a fairly simple procedure," the doctor explained.

"All right," Topaz agreed, although she hadn't really been listening. "I'll call you in a few days to set everything up."

"We can do that now, Ms. Black," he prodded.

"I don't have my schedule," she lied. "And I really have to go. I'll be in touch," she promised, taking one of his business cards as she practically ran out the door. It's him . . . I know it is.

She rushed down the hall and found the number of the suite for Dr. Gradney's office and walked in. It was a bright, bustling office with half a dozen examining rooms and a tastefully decorated waiting room where several women were waiting.

"I want to see Dr. Gradney," Topaz commanded the receptionist, a young attractive black girl with dukey braids.

"Put your name on our sign-in sheet and the doctor will see you as soon as possible." The girl smiled.

"No, darling. I'm afraid you don't understand." Topaz spoke smoothly and softly. "Just tell Dr. Gradney that Topaz is here."

"Ms. Black, I'm sorry. I didn't recognize you. I'll let the doctor know you're here." The young woman got up to go find him. Before she got to the corridor of examining rooms, Germain zipped down the hall.

"I knew it was him. I can't believe he's here with a business set up and everything and he hasn't even bothered to try and get in touch with me," Topaz mumbled to herself.

"The doctor will see you now," the receptionist informed her forty minutes later.

She was as mad as a snake when she was finally ushered into Germain's office. He was sitting behind a huge antique desk on which manila folders and medical journals were haphazardly stacked. Several Varnette Honeywood paintings were on the walls and Toni Braxton was playing softly in the background. He's a big-time doctor now, she thought proudly, and he still looks good. Dang . . .

Germain had definitely improved with age, like a bottle of fine wine. Through the silhouette of his crisp white doctor's jacket, she could see he was still slim. There was a fresh sprinkling of freckles on his nose, and his skin was tanned a permanent honey-bronze from the California sun. Topaz felt her stomach turn flip-flops and she couldn't think of a thing to say.

Why doesn't he just take me into his arms? she wondered. He knows he wants it as bad as I do.

I'm not going to allow her to weave her way back into my heart again. I knew when I moved here I would run the risk of seeing her. Now I have to be strong. "Hello, Topaz." He finally spoke, coolly. He scribbled notes in a file. "What can I do for you?" he asked, tossing the file aside.

Kiss me, hug me, love me, she wanted to shout. "I . . ." she began, but suddenly her mouth was dry. She swallowed and took a deep breath. "I didn't know you were living in Los Angeles, Germain." Her eyes fell on a photo of Chris. Look at my baby. He looks so handsome. He's seven now.

"I had no intention of ever letting you know I was here," he informed her coolly. "You never cared about us." His pretty eyes were mean and cold.

"That's not true—" she began softly.

"Topaz, what do you want?" he demanded rudely, cutting her off.

He's never spoken to me like this, she realized, wanting to cry. Even when we used to have fights, his eyes were always sweet.

"If you think you're going to see Chris, you can forget it. I'm not ever going to let you cause my son pain again."

What can I say? Topaz wondered, looking at the floor. I have done nothing but cause both of them pain. "I'm sorry, Germain," she whispered, no longer able to hold back the tears. "I'm sorry."

Don't give in, he kept telling himself. She's no good and she hasn't changed one bit. "Sorry? What are you sorry for, Topaz? Which thing? Are you sorry for running off and leaving your child when he was barely six months old? Or maybe you're sorry because you've never been any kind of a mother to him. Never watched him take his first step, never dried his tears, never helped him with his homework. And we won't even discuss how you treated me. You are so selfish . . . You didn't even have the courtesy to tell me you didn't want to get back with me or that you were getting married. I had to hear about it on *Entertainment Tonight*."

"That's because that marriage was a mistake, Germain. Do you know I was thinking about you when I said my wedding vows?" She fished in her bag for a tissue. "I didn't tell you because I never really intended to marry Gunther, and now he's dead."

"Look, Topaz," he continued icily. "I'm sorry about Gunther, but I've got clients to see. I have a son to pick up from school and a date to get ready for. Have a nice life." He walked out of his office and into the nearest examining room. "I did it," he whispered. "I was actually strong."

Topaz found the strength to pick herself up and walk out of the office and down the hall to the elevator. He doesn't want me anymore . . . I never thought Germain would stop wanting me. She stumbled down the street to her car and fell inside. "I don't care what Nina says," she cried, pulling a bottle of cocaine out of her bag. "I don't care if it does kill me. I want to die."

She felt herself hyperventilating as she drove north on San Vicente. By the time she reached Stone Canyon near UCLA she was crying so hard she couldn't see. She pulled over on the side of the road and sat there moaning and sobbing.

"It hurts, it hurts so bad," she wailed. "Oh, Germain, my sweet Germain, you finally stopped loving me." She cried until there were no tears left and then she drove herself home. When she walked into the house, Nina was in the kitchen dishing up some Chinese food that Niko had prepared.

"What's wrong?" Nina demanded as soon as she saw her face.

"Nothing," Topaz whispered, heading towards her room.

"What's wrong?" Nina followed her up the stairs.

When she got to her suite, Topaz walked straight to the mini bar in the suite where she kept an assortment of wine coolers. "Go away, Nina," she commanded with very little strength. She opened the wine cooler and drained half of it in a matter of seconds.

"What's wrong?" Nina demanded a third time. "You didn't see Reno or anything, did you?" Although Pete had paid Reno back his ten million, Topaz was still concerned that he might try to do something crazy.

"No, I saw Germain."

"Germain?"

"Yes."

"Where?"

"He has a private practice here in Los Angeles."

"What?" Nina screamed in shock.

"Yes."

Nina said nothing when Topaz spilled white powder on the back of a magazine and took several hits.

"So what happened?"

"He told me to have a nice life."

"What? What about Chris?"

"He told me he was not going to allow me to cause his son any further pain," she cried through a deluge of fresh tears.

"I'm so sorry, baby," Nina cried, rocking her. "But you have caused him a lot of pain."

"I know. That's what makes it so bad," Topaz sobbed. "He's right."

She sat in her bed for weeks, refusing to eat, unable to sleep. She even lost all interest in Pete. She refused to comb her hair and she spoke to no one on the phone. She just lay around in an old T-shirt doing coke and drinking wine coolers.

"All right, girl." Nina burst into her room early one morning. "Get yourself out of that bed. We're going out tonight. Just us girls. I made us a hair appointment with Janet. We're having facials and getting our nails and toes done. Then we're going shopping in Beverly Hills for something new to wear. Your old boyfriend, Sylk Ross, is having some sort of party. Anyone who's anyone in Hollywood is going or trying to go. Of course, you have an invitation. I already RSVP'd. It's some sort of opening for an art gallery . . . so get out of the bed, girl, and let's go party."

THIRTY-FIVE

SEAN'S BEEN acting so different lately, Jade noticed. He's a lot more distant. She watched him enter their bedroom and get some papers he had been reading and return to his office without saying a word.

"What's up with my baby?" she whispered out loud. She brushed away a tear as she went downstairs into the kitchen where Dora was making breakfast. "Good morning, Dora."

Jade picked up a plate of scrambled eggs with peppers, crispy bacon, and juice and went outside to sit on the deck, which overlooked the electric blue Pacific. It was a beautiful hot morning in June. The marine layer had burned off and the day was sparkling. It's my birthday and he hasn't said one word . . . I suggested that we go away to Cozumel for a week and he said no.

"I have a bunch of players coming in for consultations that weekend, and Eric might fly in, too. We can always go later," he had replied with a peck on the cheek.

She took a bite of the spicy eggs and washed it down with some juice.

"Good morning, sweetheart." Sean had snuck out on the deck and was standing behind her. "I have something to show you."

"What is it?" She beamed.

"Here." He handed her a fluffy white Maltese with a pink bow for a collar. "Happy birthday, baby."

"Sean, oh, baby, she's so cute." Jade cuddled the tiny puppy in her arms and kissed her on the head.

"Hey, don't be giving away my sugar."

"Never." She grinned, kissing him on the cheek.

"So what are you going to name her?"

"Satin. Now I have Sylk and Satin." She smiled.

"I thought we'd go into Los Angeles for dinner tonight. Eric and Keisha are coming, and I made reservations at Georgia's."

"That sounds like fun, baby." Maybe I was just tripping, but he has been a little distant. "Sean, is everything okay?"

"Yes, why?" He was puzzled by her question.

"You've just been a little distant," she replied softly, fixing her almond eyes on his.

"I'm sorry, baby, I've just had so much going on with the business. I didn't mean to neglect my favorite girl." I guess I have been a little distant, he realized. I want to tell you so bad, Jade, but I can't, not yet.

"That dress is to die for," Nina informed Topaz. "If you don't buy it, I will."

They were in Fred Hayman on Rodeo Drive and Topaz was modeling a shimmering silver mini. I wonder how Sylk would like me in this. Topaz smiled at her reflection in the mirror, twisting and turning, trying to view herself from all sides in the mirror.

"Okay, I'll get it," she finally decided. I can't wait to see the look on Sylk's face when he sees me in this. Heck, we might even be an item again. The press will be there and they can take lots of pictures of us together. Topaz flashed a dazzling smile at Nina. "This was such a good idea, cuz."

They had already gotten their hair done at Umbertos and gone to Elizabeth Arden for facials. Now they were on their way back to Bel Air, where the limo would pick them up for the party at seven.

"You look so beautiful, Jade," Sean told her as they got into the limo. "I didn't think we were going to make it to dinner after you put on that dress." He looked her up and down as though she were good enough to eat. Jade was stunning in an emerald beaded evening gown that flowed around her lithe body like rippling water. She wore long emerald gloves and silver jewelry set with crystals that sparkled around her throat, on her wrists, and at her ears.

"Thanks, baby. I felt like doing something special tonight since it was my birthday."

"Well, you look incredible," he stated proudly, admiring her.

"So do you, baby." He was wearing one of his favorite Armani suits with a crisp white shirt. The jacket was tossed across one of the adjoining seats in the limo. "And you smell good, too." Jade sniffed behind his ear so she could get a better whiff of his Escape colonge.

"Jade, stop." He laughed.

She smiled as she watched him pick up his jacket, feel around in the pocket, and produce a blue velvet ring box. "What's that?" She pointed to the velvet case.

"More surprises for my baby for her birthday."

She gasped when she opened the ring box and saw a huge diamond set in a cluster of smaller emeralds and diamonds. "Sean, it's beautiful, baby." He smiled and took the ring out of its case and placed it on her right hand.

"I'll never take it off," she vowed, looking into his eyes.

He noticed there were tears sparkling like little diamonds in her black, almond-shaped eyes. "I love you because I see love in your eyes," he whispered, brushing away a tear. They held hands and rode in silence for the rest of the way into the city.

"Topaz, hurry up," Nina demanded, walking into her bedroom. "The car is here."

"You look fabulous." Topaz smiled, admiring the orange silk party dress Nina was wearing. Her black silky hair nearly reached her tiny waist and the burnt-orange lipstick she was wearing gave her an exotic look, like a high-fashion model on a Paris runway.

"Thanks, Fresh Princess. I'm glad to see you looking like yourself again," Nina commented, admiring the silver mesh dress and silver pumps Topaz was wearing. Her freshly trimmed hair, blown silky straight, framed her exquisite face perfectly.

"Thanks, babe. Now let's go turn this party out." Topaz was excited for the first time in months.

"Why are we stopping here?" Jade looked out of the window of the car. "We're not at Georgia's."

"I know." Sean got out and opened the car door. "We're running a little early so I thought we'd walk up Rodeo Drive and look in the store windows. It's such a beautiful night."

"All right," Jade agreed as Sean helped her out of the car.

Sean tucked her arm under his and strolled up Rodeo Drive, where they gazed into the windows of store after store, oblivious to anyone staring at them: the pretty boy with a basketball player's physique and his gorgeous wife, looking like she had just stepped out of a fashion magazine, the epitome of the celebrated Bev Hills couple.

It was a warm night for June and the street lined with designer boutiques and other specialty shops was alive with activity.

"Look, Sean." Jade pointed to a brightly lit art gallery where a small crowd of people were gathering outside. "A new art gallery. Let's go take a look. Something's going on over there. Look at all those people."

"It does look like something's going on. Are you sure you want to go over there?" Sean questioned, trying not to smile. "I don't want to be around all of those people on your birthday."

"Come on, baby," she prodded, taking his hand. "We can mingle for a little while. You know I have to take a peek." She pulled him across the street to the gallery where a crowd of people, laughing and talking, was standing out front waiting for something to begin.

"Look, Sean. It's an opening for a brand-new gallery. See the ribbon across the door?" She caught a quick glance of a painting through the gallery window and tugged on Sean's sleeve excitedly. "I think I saw one of my paintings, an original, hanging on a wall in there. I don't remember selling my work to any dealers in Beverly Hills," she commented, wrinkling her forehead. "Look, baby, isn't that Eddie and Nicole Murphy?" Jade directed his attention to a couple getting out of a limousine.

"Sure is," Sean replied calmly. "And that's Keisha and Eric Johnson and their daughter, Kendra. And here we have Mommy and Daddy Ross, and Mommy and Daddy Kimura, the twins . . ."

"Sean, what's going on here?"

"Happy birthday, baby," he declared softly with a kiss. He handed her an extra large pair of scissors, decorated with emerald ribbon.

"What's this?" she asked as Sean led her over to the jade ribbon tied across the door of the gallery. Lightbulbs flashed in her eyes, but she could still see dozens of recognizable faces crowding around her.

"The grand opening of the Jade Kimura Gallery—"

"What? The Jade Kimura Gallery . . . my gallery?"

"Happy birthday, Jade. It's your very own gallery." Sean turned to face his guests. "My wife doesn't know what's going on here. I'm afraid she's in shock. But as soon as my father says the dedicatory prayer, we'll cut the ribbon and get this party started."

Tears of joy spilled from Jade's eyes as she stood silently staring at Sean. He smiled and took her in his arms and held her close while his father spoke into a cordless mike. His rich speaking voice resonated through the warm night air, turning prestigious Rodeo Drive into an alfresco house of prayer.

The crowd thundered with applause as Jade snipped the jade velvet ribbon in two.

"All right," Sean declared. "It's time to party."

Her fabulous paintings were displayed throughout the gallery on easels or hung on gleaming white walls. The jade ceiling with its gilded trim and the jade marble floors flecked with gold made the room palatial.

Hollywood's chocolate stars—the rich and famous of black Hollywood who sing, act, dribble, produce, and direct their way to the top were all in attendance. The paparazzi haunted the star-studded crowd, pacing up and down invisible boundary lines that separated them from the guests and snapping pictures like crazy.

Classical music played softly in the background. Tommy Tangs catered the event. There was a wonderful Asian buffet of crispy fried won tons and egg rolls, chicken and beef satay, various types of sushi and California rolls, chicken wings stuffed with glass noodles, Thai barbecued chicken, naked shrimp, pad thai noodles, chicken and mint leaves, seafood fried rice, sauteed eggplant, and spicy mushrooms. Tuxedoed waiters kept the sparkling waters and fresh-squeezed juices flowing, and there was a splendid birthday cake with whipped-cream icing and candles.

"When did you do all this?" Jade asked Sean through her tears. She looked every bit the woman of the hour in her fabulous gown. Her silky black hair was up in a French twist, and her black almond eyes crinkled and disappeared into her face every time she smiled.

"That's why I was so distant," he explained. "I wanted to tell you so bad, so I had to stay away from you. I almost slipped a couple of times. I'm sorry if I seemed to be shutting you out."

"I can't get over this. How did you manage to get my paintings in here, all framed? You're too much, baby." She continued shaking her head.

"Doesn't the party look great, Nina?" Topaz exclaimed when she peered through the windows of the gallery.

"There are all kinds of people here," Nina declared excitedly when she caught a glimpse of Magic and Cookie Johnson, Norm Nixon and Debbie Allen, and Babyface and Tracy Edmonds through the windows. As soon as Topaz stepped out of the limousine, the photographers snapped away.

" 'The much-sought-after millionairess, Widow Lawrence, steps out for a night on the town,' the copy will read," Nina informed her.

Topaz smiled for the cameras as she and Nina walked into the gallery. "I've got your widow Lawrence," she said through gritted teeth to Nina.

The girls greeted Robin Givens, Halle Berry, and Blair Underwood as they passed through the crowd to take a look at the paintings.

"This Jade Kimura person does fabulous work," Nina finally commented. "I'm going to get something for my room and a matching piece for my baby's house. That way when we get married, we can put them together."

"Okay," Topaz agreed, not really listening to Nina. Who's this Jade person? And why is Sean giving her this party? She must be one of his clients, she finally decided. I remember Nina telling me something about him managing athletes now that he's retired. He always did have a fascination for art, so I can see him handling a couple of artists. She is good, Topaz decided, admiring one of her paintings.

She turned around to take a glass of champagne from a passing tray and saw Keisha sitting in a chair on the side of the room and feeding a little girl. That must be her daughter. "Keisha," she exclaimed softly, frozen in her tracks. She looks great, too, she realized, admiring Keisha's hair, which had been cut slightly above her shoulders, and the simple gold dress she was wearing with gold jewelry. Keisha screams money, Topaz noticed, remembering the way her friend always looked so elegant with very little effort. She should, her parents always had money and she married Eric, Topaz concluded jealously. Just like everybody else in that stupid John-and-Jane. Now I have more money than all of them . . . She watched Eric bend down in front of the little girl and hold a glass of juice to her lips. They look happy. I'm glad things worked out for them. Keisha must have felt Topaz watching her because she lifted her head and looked around until her eyes met Topaz's.

Topaz smiled and walked towards Keisha. "Hi, Keisha." Topaz greeted her coolly but with a warm smile. "How are you?"

"I'm fine." Keisha was overly polite.

"I love your hair like that," Topaz offered sincerely. "It makes you look so grown-up and sophisticated."

"Thanks. Baby, look who's here." She tapped Eric on the arm.

"Topaz, how are you, lady?" Eric kissed her lightly on the cheek. "This is my daughter, Kendra." He proudly introduced the pretty four-year-old who looked a lot like Keisha.

"Hi, pretty girl." Topaz smiled warmly. She ran her fingers with metallic silver nails gently across her cheek. "I'm Topaz. Your mommy and I used to be very good friends."

"I know who you are." Kendra smiled. "Mommy, Mommy, it's Topaz. We see your videos all the time."

"You do?" Topaz smiled at the child, admiring Keisha's apparent happiness but feeling sadness for the years she had missed of her friend's life.

"I was sorry to hear about the death of your husband." Keisha's regrets were sincere.

"Yeah," Eric agreed. "I can't believe you're a widow."

"I know. When you think of widows you usually think of someone old and gray, not someone like me." Topaz laughed.

"Have you seen Sylk?" Eric questioned.

"No," Topaz replied softly.

"Go say hi," Eric suggested. "He'll be glad to see you."

"All right. I'll do that."

She took another glass of champagne from the waitress's tray and downed half of it before she realized she was drinking sparkling apple juice. Don't they have anything stronger in this place? She ignored the beautiful woman in the jade evening gown standing near Sean. I'll get him away from her somehow. She took a deep breath and walked over to him.

"Hi, Sean. Long time, no see." Topaz flashed a brilliant smile. He looks even better than I remembered, she decided, noticing the joy that just seemed to radiate from his handsome face.

"Hi, Topaz. I'm so glad you came." He kissed her gently on the cheek. "I was so sorry to hear about the death of your husband. It's good to see you out."

He knows about Gunther, she realized. This is good . . .

"I thought it was time for me to get back out and about. Are you still living in Santa Barbara?" she asked coyly. It might be nice to hang out at the beach with him and just chill. I hope he still lives there.

"I'm still in Santa Barbara."

"Great." She flashed her best smile. "Maybe we can get together and do something sometime."

"Topaz, have you met my wife, Jade?" he asked coolly.

Wife . . . She could feel herself turning a bright shade of red. "No," she barely managed to whisper, wishing the floor would open and swallow her alive as she felt herself begin to struggle for air.

"Jade." He reached out and took the beauty in the fabulous evening gown gently by the hand. She was standing behind him, talking to his mother.

"Yes, baby?" she replied softly, standing by his side.

"I want you to meet Topaz. Topaz, this is my wife, Jade."

"Hi, Topaz. It's a pleasure to meet you." Jade smiled with the utmost confidence and sincerity.

Topaz looked her over quickly. The girl from the gallery . . . I don't remember her being this beautiful. She was absolutely gorgeous, and it was obvious that the two of them were very much in love as they stood there beaming at each other like two glow worms. That's why he gave her this wonderful party. She's his wife . . .

"It's a pleasure to meet you, too," Topaz heard herself say. I've got to get out of here. I feel like such a fool. "I really must go now," Topaz apologized, fighting back the tears. "I have a baby daughter and I promised my nanny I wouldn't stay out long. Good night."

She found Nina chatting with Brandy. "I'm going home," she whispered. "I'll send the car back for you."

"What's wrong?" Nina searched her cousin's unhappy face.

"Nina, did you know Sean was married?" Topaz whispered in her ear.

"No." Nina's face registered the shock.

"Jade Kimura is his wife."

She cried all the way home. I've been such a fool, she realized sadly. Why did I ever leave Germain? Sean's married now. Everyone has someone special but me. I was too stupid to see that I was never in love with any of those guys . . . only Germain. Why did it take me so long to realize he was the one? And now it's too late . . .

Her tears had dissipated by the time she reached the house. She looked at the big empty mansion and regretted that she had not made Nina come home with her. I may as well get used to this, she convinced herself as she got out of the limousine, because one of these days Nina will be gone, too, and I'll be here all by myself.

The tap, tap, tap of her high heels clicking on the hardwood floors echoed throughout the silent house. I feel like I'm in a museum, she realized, not a home. I remember Sean said my home was like a museum when he came to visit once.

She tiptoed through the rooms on the first floor in the west wing, surveying all her worldly possessions. Expensive furniture, expensive artwork, expensive this, expensive that—expensive, expensive, expensive. But there's no one to share any of these expensive things with me, she concluded sadly. She walked into Turquoise's room. Her baby was almost a year old and sleeping soundly in her bed.

"Topaz children." She could hear Nina joking now. "Your daughter has no father and your son has no mother . . ."

Only it's not funny, she realized. It's sad. I'm always letting someone else raise my children. She stroked a lock of her daughter's copper hair. "It's not too late for us, Turquoise. You're all I have now. And I'm going to spend every moment I can loving you and being a mother."

Turquoise slept while her mother's mind drifted to Chris. That Thanksgiving I spent with Chris and Germain was the most wonderful time in my life. Why didn't I realize it then? she asked herself as the tears begin to flow. "Why am I such a fool?" she whispered to the darkened room.

When she entered her bedroom she caught a whiff of Gunther's favorite Boucheron fragrance and felt the tears swell out of her eyes again. "Why did you have to go and leave me all alone in this big old empty house, Gunther Lawrence?" She walked into her pink bathroom. It was much finer than the one she and Germain had made love in at his parents' house, but it had never been as much fun.

"I'll build you a house bigger and finer than this old thing with the most wonderful bathroom for us to play in," Germain had promised her.

She shut her eyes tightly. The memories were much too painful. She clicked on the television for company but she couldn't focus on anything, not even her favorite late night show, *The Jeffersons*.

She stared at the sunken marble Roman tub, intending to run herself a bath, but she couldn't move. A single drop of water squeezed itself out of the golden faucet. It seemed to symbolize her loneliness.

"Will this pain ever go away?" she whispered sadly.

She rifled through a drawer in her dressing table until she found what she was looking for, a framed photo of her and Germain from her debutante ball. This is where it all began, she remembered sadly, looking at their glowing faces. We were so young, so innocent, and so in love . . . She kissed Germain's face with her full, pouty lips, leaving traces of her Russian Red lipstick on the frame.

"I'll win you back, Germain Gradney," she solemnly vowed, gently wiping the lipstick from the glass with a slender butterscotch finger. "Because I know you still love me, and because Chris needs his mother and Turquoise needs a daddy. And because I need you and you need me," she whispered to his pretty smiling eyes.

"I love you, Germain," she managed to whisper as the tears flowed out of her eyes onto the Waterford crystal picture frame. "I always have and I always will."